A Star Called Henry

Roddy Doyle

A Star Called Henry

Volume One of
THE LAST ROUNDUP

Alfred A. Knopf Canada

PUBLISHED BY ALFRED A. KNOPF CANADA

Copyright © 1999 by Roddy Doyle

All rights reserved under International and Pan-American Copyright
Conventions. Published in Canada by Alfred A. Knopf Canada, a division
of Random House of Canada Ltd., Toronto, in 1999, and simultaneously
in Great Britain by Jonathan Cape Ltd., London. Distributed by
Random House of Canada Ltd., Toronto.

Grateful acknowledgement is made to the following
for permission to reprint previously published material:

'Cheek To Cheek' Words and Music by Irving Berlin
© 1935 Irving Berlin Music Corp., USA
Warner/Chappell Music Ltd, London, W6 8BS
Reproduced by permission of IMP Ltd.

Canadian Cataloguing in Publication Data

Doyle, Roddy, 1958-
A star called Henry

ISBN 0-676-97235-7

I. Title.

PR6054.O95S72 1999   823'.914   C99-931134-4

First Canadian Edition

Printed and bound in the United States of America

10 9 8 7 6 5 4 3 2 1

This book is dedicated to
Kate

Heaven—
I'm in heaven—
And my heart beats so
That I can hardly
Speak.

Irving Berlin

PART ONE

1

My mother looked up at the stars. There were plenty of them up there. She lifted her hand. It swayed as she chose one. Her finger pointed.

—There's my little Henry up there. Look it.

I looked, her other little Henry sitting beside her on the step. I looked up and hated him. She held me but she looked up at her twinkling boy. Poor me beside her, pale and red-eyed, held together by rashes and sores. A stomach crying to be filled, bare feet aching like an old, old man's. Me, a shocking substitute for the little Henry who'd been too good for this world, the Henry God had wanted for himself. Poor me.

And poor Mother. She sat on that step and other crumbling steps and watched her other babies joining Henry. Little Gracie, Lil, Victor, another little Victor. The ones I remember. There were others, and early others sent to Limbo; they came and went before they could be named. God took them all. He needed them all up there to light the night. He left her plenty, though. The ugly ones, the noisy ones, the ones He didn't want – the ones that would never stay fed.

Poor Mother. She wasn't much more than twenty when she gazed up at little twinkling Henry but she was already old, already decomposing, ruined beyond repair, good for some more babies, then finished.

Poor Mammy. Her own mother was a leathery old witch, but was probably less than forty. She poked me, as if to prove that I was there.

—You're big, she said.

She was accusing me, weighing me, planning to take some of

1

me back. Always wrapped in her black shawl, she always smelt of rotten meat and herrings – it was a sweat on her. Always with a book under the shawl, the complete works of Shakespeare or something by Tolstoy. Nash was her name but I don't know what she called herself before she married her dead husband. She'd no Christian name that I ever heard. Granny Nash was all she ever was. I don't know where she came from; I don't remember an accent. Wrapped in her sweating black shawl, she could have crept out of any century. She might have walked from Roscommon or Clare, pushed on by the stench of the blight, walked across the country till she saw the stone-eating smoke that lay over the piled, sagging fever-nests that made our beautiful city, walked in along the river, deeper and deeper, into the filth and shit, the noise and the money. A young country girl, never kissed, never touched, she was scared, she was thrilled. She turned around and back around and saw the four corners of hell. Her heart cried for Leitrim but her tits sang for Dublin. She got down on her back and yelled at the sailors to form a queue. Frenchmen, Danes, Chinamen, the Yanks. I don't know. A young country girl, a waif, just a child, aching for food. She'd left her family dead in a ditch, their chops green with grass juice, their bellies set to explode in the noonday sun. I don't know any of this. She might have been Dublin-bred. Or she might have been foreign. A workhouse orphan, a nun gone wrong. Transported from Australia, too ugly and bad for Van Diemen's Land. I don't know. She'd become a witch by the time I saw her. Always with her head in a book, looking for spells. She shoved her face forward with ancient certainty, knew every thought behind my eyes. She knew how far evil could drop. She stared at me with her cannibal's eyes and I had to dash down to the privy. Her eyes slammed the door after me.

And what do I know about poor Mother? Precious little. I know that she was Melody Nash. A beautiful name, promising so much. I know that she was born in Dublin and that she lived on Bolton Street. She worked in Mitchell's rosary bead factory on Marlborough Street. They made the beads out of cows' horns. All day, six days a week, sweating, going blind for God and Mitchell. Putting the holes in the beads for Jesus. Hands bleeding, eyes itching. Before she walked into my father.

Melody Nash. I think of the name and I don't see my mother. Melody melody. She skips, she laughs, her black eyes shine happy. Her blue-black hair dances, her feet lick the cobbles. Her teacher is fond of her, she's a fast learner. She's quick at the adding, her letters curl beautifully. She has a great future, she'll marry a big noise. She'll have good meat each day and a house with a jacks. Out of the way, here comes melody Melody, out of the way, here comes melody Melody.

What age was she when she learnt the truth, when she found out that her life would have no music? The name was a lie, a spell the witch put on her. She was twelve when she walked into Mitchell's bead factory and she was sixteen when she walked into my father. Four years in between, squinting, counting, shredding her hands, in a black hole making beads. Melody melody rosary beads. They sang as they worked. *Beautiful dreamer, awake unto me.* Mitchell wanted them to pray. *Starlight and dewdrops are waiting for thee.* Was she gorgeous? Did her white teeth gleam as she lifted her head with the other girls? *Beautiful dreamer, queen of my song.* The woman on the step had no teeth, nothing gleamed. Like me, she was never a child. There were no children in Dublin. Promises weren't kept in the slums. She was never beautiful.

She walked into my father. Melody Nash met Henry Smart. She walked right into him, and he fell. She was half his weight, half his height, six years younger but he fell straight over like a cut tree. Love at first sight? Felled by her beauty? No. He was maggoty drunk and missing his leg. He was holding himself up with a number seven shovel he'd found inside an open door somewhere back the way he'd come when Melody Nash walked into him and dropped him onto Dorset Street. It was a Sunday. She was coming from half-eight mass, he was struggling out of Saturday. Missing a leg and his sense of direction, he hit the street with his forehead and lay still. Melody dropped the beads she'd made herself and stared down at the man. She couldn't see his face; it was kissing the street. She saw a huge back, a back as big as a bed, inside a coat as old and crusted as the cobbles around it. Shovel-sized

3

hands at the end of his outstretched arms, and one leg. Just the one. She actually lifted the coat to check.

—Where's your leg gone, mister? said Melody.

She lifted the coat a bit more.

—Are you dead, mister? she said.

The man groaned. Melody dropped the coat and stepped back. She looked around for help but the street was quiet. The man groaned again. He drew his arms in and braced himself. Then he crawled one-kneed off the road, over the gutter. Melody picked up the shovel. He groaned again and vomited. A day and a half's drinking poured out of him like black pump water. Melody got out of its way. The stream stopped. He wiped his mouth with the filthiest sleeve that Melody had ever seen. He put his hand out. Melody understood immediately that he wanted the shovel. She held it out to him. She could study his face now. It hadn't been washed in ages and the specks and lines of blood gave him the look of something freshly slaughtered. But he wasn't bad looking, she decided. The situation – the coat, the puked porter, the absent leg – wouldn't let her take the plunge and call him good looking, but he definitely wasn't bad looking. He clung to the shovel and hauled himself up. Melody stepped back again to get out of his shadow. He stared at her but she wasn't frightened.

—Sorry, mister, said Melody.

He shook his head.

—Did you see a leg on your travels? he said.

—No.

—A wooden one.

—No.

He seemed disappointed.

—It's gone, so, he said. —I had it yesterday.

Then Melody said something that started them on the road to marriage and me.

—You're a grand-looking man without it, she said.

Now he looked at Melody properly. She'd only said it to comfort him but one-legged men will grab at anything.

—What's your name, girlie? he said.

—Melody Nash, she said.

And Henry Smart fell in love. He fell in love with the name.

4

With a name like that beside him he'd find his leg, a new one would grow out of the stump, he'd stride through open doors for the rest of his life. He'd find money on the street, three-legged chickens. He'd never have to sweat again. Henry Smart, my father, looked at Melody Nash. He saw what he wanted to see.

I know what Henry Smart looked like. She told me, sitting on the step, looking down the street, and up, waiting for him. And later on when he'd gone for ever but she still looked and waited. Her descriptions, her words, stayed the same. She never let her loneliness, hunger, her misery change her story. Her mind wandered and then rotted but she always knew her story, how she walked into Henry Smart. It was fixed. I knew what he looked like. But what about her? What did Melody Nash look like? She was sixteen. That's all I know. I see her later, only five, six years further on. An eternity. An old woman. Big, lumpy, sad. Melody Smart. I see that woman sitting on the step and I try to bring her back six years, I try to make the age and pain drop off her. I try to make her stand up and walk back, to see her as she had been. I take three stone off her, I lift her mouth, I try to put fun into her eyes. I give her hair some spring, I change her clothes. I can create a good-looking sixteen-year-old. I can make her a stunner. I can make her plainer then, widen her, spoil her complexion. I can play this game for what's left of my life but I'll never see Melody Nash, my sixteen-year-old mother.

She worked in the dark and damp all day. She squinted to fight back the light. Her hands were ripped and solid. She was a child of the Dublin slums, no proper child at all. Her parents, grandparents, had never known good food. Bad food, bad drink, bad air. Bad bones, bad eyes, bad skin; thin, stooped, mangled. Henry Smart looked at Melody Nash and saw what he wanted to see.

—What's your name, girlie?
—Melody Nash, she said. —How did you lose it?
—I haven't a bull's clue, said Henry.

He looked down at the ground where his foot should have been, and hopped away out of the porter he'd just thrown up. He wanted nothing to do with it; he was already a new man.

He was thinking quickly, planning. She'd seen him falling on his face and then getting sick, one of his legs was missing – he knew he hadn't been impressing her. But there were other ways to catch fish. He looked at Melody, and back down at the ground.

—It was my good one too, he said.

—Your good one?

—Me Sunday leg.

—Oh, said Melody. —It'll turn up, mister, don't worry. Maybe you left it at home.

Henry thought about this.

—I doubt it, he said. —I lost that as well.

She felt sorry for him. No leg, no home – the only thing holding him up was his vulnerability. She saw honesty. The men Melody knew showed off or snapped at her. Mitchell the rosary beads, her father, all men – they were all angry and mean. This man here was different. She'd knocked the poor cripple onto the street, his face was bleeding, he'd no home to hop home to – and he didn't blame her. She saw now: he was smiling. A nice smile, he was offering it, half a smile. He didn't look like a cripple. She liked the space where the leg should have been.

—Will we go for a stroll, so? he said.

—Yes, she said.

—Right.

He wiped the blade of the shovel on his sleeve.

—Let's get this gleaming for the lady.

He let the spade hop gently on the path. Melody heard music.

—Now we're right, said Henry Smart.

He held out his arm, offered it to Melody.

—Hang on, said Melody.

She took off her shawl and wiped his face with it. She dabbed and petted, removed the blood and left the dirt – that was his own, none of her business. It didn't bother her. Dirt and grime were the glues that held Dublin together. She spat politely on a corner of the shawl and washed away the last dried, cranky specks of blood. Then she put the shawl back on.

—Now, she said.

They were already a couple.

He leaned on the shovel and offered her his free arm. She leaned on him and off they went, on the ramble that would still deliver her smile when she recalled it many moons later, when she told us all about it on the steps of all the tenements we were thrown into and out of. A Sunday in June, 1897, when the Famine Queen, Victoria, was still our one and only. A glorious summer's morning. It took getting used to, the rhythm of their stroll. He'd lean out over the abyss that was his missing leg. She, clinging to his sleeve, would follow him out there. Then he'd haul himself in and forward on the handle of the shovel. She'd be pulled after him, then out again and forward. There wasn't much room for talking. The cobbles were tricky, corners were impossible. So they went straight ahead, out to Drumcondra and the countryside.

Who was he and where did he come from? The family trees of the poor don't grow to any height. I know nothing real about my father; I don't even know if his name was real. There was never a Granda Smart, or a Grandma, no brothers or cousins. He made his life up as he went along. Where was his leg? South Africa, Glasnevin, under the sea. She heard enough stories to bury ten legs. War, an infection, the fairies, a train. He invented himself, and reinvented. He left a trail of Henry Smarts before he finally disappeared. A soldier, a sailor, a butler – the first one-legged butler to serve the Queen. He'd killed sixteen Zulus with the freshly severed limb.

Was he just a liar? No, I don't think so. He was a survivor; his stories kept him going. Stories were the only things the poor owned. A poor man, he gave himself a life. He filled the hole with many lives. He was the son of a Sligo peasant who'd been eaten by his neighbours; they'd started on my father before he got away. He hopped down the boreen, the life gushing out of his stump, hurling rocks back at the hungry neighbours, and kept hopping till he reached Dublin. He was a pedlar, a gambler, a hoor's bully. He sat on the ditch beside my mother and invented himself.

—You didn't tell me your name yet, she said.

—Henry Smart, he said. —At your service.

Was it a name to compensate for the missing leg, a name to match hers? He fell in love with her name – Melody melody Melody Nash – and she fell in love with his.

They held hands.

Years later, looking into the night sky, counting her children. Poor ruined mother. She sat in the rain, the hail, the heat. She turned her back on the houses behind us and stared up at the soothing night. Behind her, the damp, scabbed walls, the rotten wood, the wet air, the leaking, bursting ceilings. Decomposing wallpaper, pools of stagnant water, rats on the scent of baby milk. Colonies of flies in the wet, crumbling walls. Typhoid and other death in every breath, on every surface. Banisters that shook when held, floors that creaked and groaned, timber that cried for sparks. There was no rest, nowhere she could lie down and forget. Shouts and fights, rage and coughing, coughing – death creeping nearer. And the rooms behind the steps got smaller and darker and more and more evil. We fell further and further. The walls crumbled and closed in on us. Her children died and joined the stars. Rooms with no windows, floors that bred cockroaches. We cried at the smell of other people's lousy food. We cried at the pain that burned through our sores. We cried for arms to gather and hold us. We cried for heat and for socks, for milk, and light, for an end to the itches that stopped us from sleeping. We cried at the lice that shone and curled and mocked us. We cried for our mother to come and save us. Poor Mother. Finally, finally, we crept down to our last room, a basement, as low as we could go, a hole that yawned and swallowed us. We lay down and slept in the ground water of the River Liffey, we slept piled together with the sewer slugs and worms. Mother sat on the crumbling steps, she turned her back on the sweating, appalling facts of her life and looked up through the acid smoke at the stars that twinkled over Dublin.

They got married in a side chapel, in the Jesuits' church on

Gardiner Street. Her father gave her away (and died the year after). The best man was Henry's colleague, a bouncer called Brannigan. The bridesmaid was a scrawny girl called Faye Cantrell who scratched so much and so loudly that the priest told her to stop it or he wouldn't let her friend get married. So she put her hands to her sides and concentrated so hard on keeping them there that she wet herself.

Melody was three weeks shy of her seventeenth birthday. She sailed out of the church, lifted by the smells of burning candles, the newly varnished pews and Faye's piss. There were kids outside, a scabby-headed mob, waiting for the grushie. Henry took a handful of farthings and ha'pences out of his trouser pocket and flicked it so that, for a second, the coins covered the sky. The children watched, enthralled, then woke up, ran and beat and mauled each other to get at the money. The losers turned for more. They stood there, the snot running out of them in ropes and waited for more of Henry's magic. But there was none.

There was a party in her parents' room on Bolton Street. Nothing swanky, a few bottles and some music. The neighbour women queued up to hand over the wisdom to Melody.

—Remember now, love, said old Missis Doody from the back parlour. —Give the babby half a bottle of stout every night and that'll kill the maggots.

—I'm not having a baby, said Melody Smart.

—Of course you'll be having a babby, said Missis Doody, a woman as old and as dirty as the house. —We all had babbies. I had five or six.

—I'm not having a baby *now*, said Melody. —And I don't know who told you any different.

—Ah now, said old Missis Doody. —One-legged babbies you'll be having. One after the other. They'll out-hop the hoppers.

And Missis Dempsey from the step next door told her all about syphilis.

—It'll rot the brain out of you, love, she said. —You won't get it, of course, but he might. And then he'll pass it on to you, so you'd want to be careful. Rots the brain till you fall over in the street because your legs don't know what they're supposed to be doing. You die screaming and roaring, there's no cure at all for it. If you're lucky they'll bring you to the Locke Hospital and smother you with a pillow. That's what they do to the unfortunate girls that catch it off the sailors. Just make sure he comes home every night and you'll be alright. Or rub a bit of whitewash from the wall of a church on him. When he has his dander up, if you can follow me; you'll learn, don't worry, love.

Melody was mystified; she was numb. Woman after woman sat beside her, one on each side, and whispered the deadly secrets into her maiden ears. *Now, if you smell a fancy woman off his coat you should boil it in water with the head of a Malahide mackerel.* She'd gone up the little side aisle in a state of sexual innocence, kissed only by one man and no further. She knew that sex happened, like she knew that God was up there behind the clouds. She knew that women went inside to their houses for a while and came out with babies. *Two good pulls like that now and he'll leave you alone for the rest of the night.* She'd heard noises under the dark stairs. *He'll never be off you, you mark my words. With the leg made of wood there the blood needs somewhere else to go.* She was impossibly innocent. Her mother had told her that she'd have to stay in her new home for three whole days after the wedding night. She was ready for the lock-in but she didn't know why. *A nice leaf of cabbage will do the trick.* She lived bang in the middle of a place that survived on the buying and selling of sex. It was in the air; its stains and howls were everywhere around her, the cries, whoops and gasps, babies and brats crawling over every square foot, brassers and sailors holding up every corner for miles around and, God love her, she'd never noticed. And now, she was being bombarded. *If he makes you do it the way the dogs do you'll end up with twins or even triplets or more. Unless the straw in your mattress came from under a priest's horse.* She looked around for her husband, to see if she'd see the monster she was being told about by these calm and bitter women. She couldn't see him. She couldn't hear him, his laugh or his leg. She couldn't breathe. *I got this jar of stuff from a Jewman and that got rid of it before I had the lid back on it.* She thought she was going to die, just a few more whispered words would kill her; her tongue was beginning to swell.

She was saved by the fight that broke out when a couple of

moochers that nobody knew were caught helping themselves to the bottles of stout.

—Yeh dirty lousers!

Granny Nash jumped onto one of them and bit him on the cheek. His screams saved Melody. She got away from the women. But the sight of her mother hanging on to the poor man's face filled her with fresh terror. Was this part of the wedding? Would she have to do it? The man was trying to save his face but his arms were stiffened by all the bottles and sandwiches stuffed up his sleeves. His friend was being pounded by Melody's father, using her new husband's leg. And her Henry sat on the table guarding the rest of the bottles. The neighbours queued up to have a go at the moochers but Granny Nash wasn't ready to give up and hand over. She was growling and chomping like a scorched bitch from hell; her dirty old thumbs were crawling across the man's face, looking for eyes to gouge. Faye was bawling and scratching herself under the table. Old Missis Doody was clapping her hands.

—Seven, EIGHT, open the GATE!

Melody had had enough.

—You're ruining my day! she screamed.

Granda Nash dropped the leg.

—Sure Jaysis, love, he said. —The day would've been ruined altogether if they'd got away with the rest of the bottles.

But the fight was over. The moochers tumbled out the door and down the stairs, whimpering and crying, and they left a trail of blood that the dogs of the district followed and lapped. They also left the bottles, none broken, and most of the sandwiches, some of which could be straightened and eaten. Henry strapped his leg back on and went over to Melody. He had a face on him that was bashful and brave.

—Ready?

—Yes, said Melody.

It was time to go. They said their goodbyes. Melody wouldn't kiss her mother; the moocher's blood was still on her chin, her eyes were tiny and mad. They strolled the short walk to their new home. Melody held on to Henry's arm and began to feel happy again. The air was cool and nice, she was married and walking home. Around a few corners, down a few dark lanes.

To No. 57, Silver Alley.

To a room in 57, Silver Alley. Up two flights of stairs, in the door, the top front room. A room of their own. A room with a window, a good working window that could be opened and closed. It had once been some child's nursery. A hundred years later, the newly married Smarts felt lucky to have it. They had it to themselves; all this space and peace, they'd never had so much before. They stood at the doorway, getting their breath back, and looked in at their home. They had so much. They had good thick walls and a window. They had a mattress, fresh straw, a chair and a stool. They had a tea chest for the coal and another for a table. They had a window box waiting for flowers. They had a mantelpiece and a blue statue of Mary already up there. They had two cups not too cracked and two plates not cracked at all. They had knives, forks and one spoon. A water bucket, a basin, a good big kettle and a slop bucket. A paraffin lamp and a brand new bar of Sunlight soap. An old biscuit tin for keeping the food and a piece of gauze for over the milk. They had clothes on their backs and some to spare. They had a man who'd call for the rent for the landlord, a policeman called Costello, every Friday at six o'clock and it didn't frighten them at all; they'd have the money stacked and ready on the mantelpiece. The floorboards were clean, their window was gleaming. Henry's everyday leg was parked in a corner. They had a sheet made from flour bags, and sugar sacks for blankets. They'd a bit of bread and cheese in the tin, and a dollop of butter staying fresh in the water bucket. They had everything they needed; they owned it all.

He sat on the chair, she took the stool.

A room of their own. They could close the door and keep out the rest of the house. They could forget the darkness they'd climbed through, the unseen filth that made each step an adventure. They could joke about the banister that wasn't there when they'd reached for it. They could ignore their drenched sleeves where they'd rubbed along the stairwell and the stench that had risen with them as they'd climbed the stairs. They could comment or not on the bloodied coughs they'd heard coming from the room below them as they'd passed, and could still hear now if they wanted to. They could hear claws in the attic, beyond the sagging ceiling, and claws behind their walls. They sat side by side like they were on a tram and, beautifully shy now that they were married and alone, they looked at the walls and at their window.

The walls were alive, looking back out at them. Crawlers and biters, cities under the layers. If they put their hands to the paper they could feel creeping and shuffling. Melody and Henry thought all walls were like that. They weren't solid; they were never reliable. There was cow hair in the paste, invented to keep the room warm. It smelt to high heaven and back down to hell.

They looked at the cracked pane of their very own window. They saw the yellowed, blackened newspaper, filling the hole under the sill. The front top room, a room with a view. They could look out and see the world. They could see the smoke floating by, smuts the size of kittens, grey, stinking rain. They could go to their window and see other windows just a few feet in front of them, a big man's reach over the alley. Houses bending towards each other, hooding the alley below, and ready to topple. Flaking brick and rotten wood; a good wind or a push would bring them down. Sneering replicas of their own room, leaning out towards them, they could see the houses dying. To the right of their window they could see the alley's missing teeth, three houses that had fallen into fire five years before. Three houses and eighty-seven people, the flames licking Melody and Henry's window. They could open the window and look down at the alley, at the stray dogs and children, bare feet and rickets, the beatings and evictions, the running dirt and pain. They could look out at their future. *Ah sure, God be with the days*. They could close the window and keep out the dead and the living, the screams and the heartache. Inside, they were happily married. Outside, they were doomed.

Henry and Melody sat on the chair and the stool. They were excited and frightened, frightened and excited. She was sixteen, he was twenty-two. My parents. My mammy and daddy.

13

I'm just around the corner, gathering steam. I was born in that room, or in a room just like it. I was born into that alley, that city, that small corner of the Empire. I'm looking for the door, trying to find my way in. It's dark, but I'm nearly there.

They paid the rent every Friday night. Melody handed it over to Costello the rozzer, a big, fat Dublin Metropolitan policeman who first saw Dublin the day before he started work. He hated the place, the people, their accents and their dirt. They deserved their streets and their slums. Collecting the rent was a nixer. He loved it, especially when there was no rent when he knocked. He had a huge moustache that matched his gut and feet that spanned three parishes.

He counted Melody's shillings and pennies. He weighed them on his palm, hoped they'd be a little too light.

—Grand so, he said after he'd waited long enough to make Melody worried.

He pocketed the money, dropped it down on top of more money. He wet the top of his pencil.

—Where's himself the night? he asked as he pretended to write in the notebook he held gently in his mitt.

—He's at his work, Mister Costello, said Melody.

—His work, said Costello. —He calls it work, does he?

Costello cracked Dublin heads for a living. So did my father. He stood in front of the door of Dolly Oblong's, the biggest brothel on Faithful Place, bang in the middle of Monto. In her dark room deep inside the house Dolly Oblong, a woman few people had seen, scoured the papers for news of troop movements, stock prices, football results. She knew what boats were on their way, the big race meetings, the date that Ash Wednesday fell on, years in advance. She saw business everywhere; she knew everything. It was said that, in her day, and still a child, she'd brought spunk to the eyes of the Prince of Wales; he'd been brought to her through secret passages that had been dug especially for him. And immediately after that, she'd serviced an unemployed navvy, the Prince's arse hardly back inside the passage. She'd fucked all classes, colours and creeds and her girls would do the same. She ran a house for all men. All men with the money and the manners.

And that was where my father came in. He stood on the steps all night and kept the peace. There was privacy inside for those who needed it and licence for those who wanted to whoop. The rozzers and clergymen could come and leave under cover of night. The sailors could come at any time they wanted. But they all had to get past my father. He stood there from six till six, all night long. The letter-in and chucker-out. Soldiers, butchers, politicians – they all had to pass his test. He glared at them as they came up the steps. He looked for something in their faces: crankiness, aggro, badness. If he saw it, they didn't get past him. He was a great big man but there was more to him than that. Compensation for the missing leg, his body had a sharpness that was quickly understood. Sailors with no English turned back when they read the tilt of his shoulders. Rat-arsed aldermen stopped boasting when they saw Henry's eyebrow lift. Bankers stared at his chest and knew that he was incorruptible. Others just knew him; they knew about him. In one neat hop he'd have the leg off and their heads open and the leg back on before they hit the ground. He was a good bouncer, the king of the bullies. He often went a full week without having to take off the leg. He was polite and agile. He stepped aside and let the men in, the ones with clear faces, decent men looking for a ride or a bit of after-hours singing. They often tipped him. The girls liked him too. They paid him to buy them their cigarettes and sweets. Dolly Oblong would never let them out; she wanted them white-skinned and captured. She called them all Maria; the clients liked it. She hated the coarseness of the girls who stood on the steps all down the street and the snootiness of the flash houses, like the one she'd worked in for years.

He made a living. He walked home at six in the morning, dying for his bed and the weightlessness that arrived when the leg came off. He was reliable, steady, a father crying out for children.

—He calls it work, does he? said Costello.

Every Friday night.

—Yes, Mister Costello, said Melody.

—Looking after hoors is work, is it?

—I don't know, Mister Costello, said Melody.

He did other things too, my father. He was reliable, he was steady. A man created from his own secrets, he was well able to keep other people's. He did things for people. Sometimes Henry wasn't on the steps of Dolly Oblong's. He was somewhere else. He gave messages, he delivered lessons. He gave lessons that were never forgotten.

Costello gave his money a fat jangle.

—What about you, Missis Smarty? said Costello. —Are you one of his hoors?

—No, I'm not, Mister Costello.

—No, he said. —Sure, who'd want you?

—I'm off, said Henry to Brannigan.

—Fair enough, said Brannigan.

Brannigan watched Henry hop down the steps. He watched, then listened to the leg as Henry disappeared across the street, into the dark. He pushed out his chest to fill the gap left by Henry.

Melody closed the door. Peace at last. For another week. She wished her Henry could stay at home on Fridays, at least until after Mister Costello had gone. It always took her hours to recover. She cleaned the floor. She dusted the statue.

Henry waited. He waited for the message to come to him. There was no such thing as a quiet wooden leg. Sometimes, the tap tap of the approaching leg was message enough; he walked under a window – tap tap – and back, knowing that the money, the promise would be delivered first thing the day after, or quicker. Tonight, though, Henry needed silence. His was the best-known leg in all of Dublin – tap tap. He needed silence. He stood back in the dark. He listened. He heard the shouts and howls from the streets behind him. A baby crying from a window above, a bottle breaking, a batch of cats singing for sex. He was listening for a wheeze. Any minute now. Any second. He knew his man. He knew his week. It was Friday night. Any second now.

He heard it. The wheeze, and good leather on cobbles. The message. Henry opened his coat; he unstrapped his leg. The

16

wheezing was louder, louder. Any second now. Henry held his leg. Louder, louder, louder. Henry lifted the leg.

Costello never knew what hit him. The weight of the rents pulled him quickly to the ground. He was already half dead. Henry had the leg back on. He stood over Costello, one foot on each side of him. He had to stretch; it was like straddling a sealion. Costello was face down. There was some of him alive. Henry leaned down to his right ear.

—Alfie Gandon says Hello.

Then he sat on Costello, hauled back his head and sawed deep into his throat. With a leather knife he'd sharpened that afternoon. Back and across the man's neck, like a bow over a fiddle. Henry even hummed. Costello's death rattle was a feeble thing; there was no fight or spunk in him. He quacked and properly died.

Henry stood up. He wiped the sides of the knife on the sleeve of his coat, the same sleeve my mother had leaned on on their first walk into the country. The dirtiest sleeve in the world.

Back home, pregnant Melody said her prayers before she climbed under the sugar sacks and tried to sleep.

2

No, it wasn't me in Melody's tummy. I'm getting there. I'm getting there.

Henry rushed, he skipped all the way, but he dreaded the quick trip home and what he'd find there. Melody was about to give birth. Again. Two children had come into the room over Silver Alley but neither of them had stayed. Henry, and Lil. Their final coughs still roamed through Henry's ears. Neither got past the first year. There'd been other losses, miscarriages. They'd moved to another room, in another house across Silver Alley. Melody looked over at her old window and saw her children's faces pressing against the cracked glass. They moved again, to a house on Summerhill. The room was smaller, the house meaner. And moving was easy. Henry borrowed a hand-cart, and up went the mattress, and the chair and stool. Everything else went into the tea chests – the blue statue of Our Lady, the sheets and blanket, the extra leg. They still had the knives and forks but the spoon had gone missing. There was nothing new to put into the tea chests. Henry pushed his failure through the streets to Summerhill. He passed carts, met others, some overflowing with bed-frames, rags, children and grandparents, others next to empty – families on the move. Henry longed for a child to park on top of the hand-cart. Up darker, damper stairs, through a door that promised nothing. There was a window that let them look out at the yards behind the house. The window box still waited for flowers.

This was the room that Henry was rushing home to. This

was their last chance, he was sure of it. He was panting when he turned onto Summerhill. He was getting old; he was twenty-six. His hair was greying, although he hadn't seen it. He was stooped, carrying the heavy ghosts of his children. He could still feel them in his arms. He could smell them. Little Henry, little Lil. His love for them was an unending fight in his chest. He was always on the verge of seeing them. He didn't sleep any more.

Henry was terrified.

Granny Nash was putting sheets of newspaper on the mattress, pages of the *Evening Mail* and the *Freeman's Journal*.

—The baba will have plenty to read anyway, said Missis Drake.

Missis Drake was the local midwife, the handywoman. She was a huge woman, a mass of muscle and slopes that looked like babies' heads bursting to get out. Melody wondered was there one in there for her, hoped and hoped there was. She sat on the chair and watched her mother laying the pages of paper on the bed. The buckets were full, one with hot, the other with cold water. The kettle was steaming.

—They say if there's news of a war on any of the pages then it'll be a girl, said Granny Nash.

She couldn't read the headlines she was spreading on the mattress. She was finished now. The papers were flat and orderly and her hands were black. Missis Drake was over at the window.

—Don't open it, said Granny Nash as she gave the papers a last pat, —till we've herself down on the paper. 'Else they'll all blow away on me. Now, my lady, she said to my mother, her daughter. —Up you get now.

Melody stood up out of the chair. Melody melody elephant Melody. It was cruel, all over again; it was only eleven months since the last time she'd had to lie down on newspaper. She struggled the few feet to the mattress.

—Good girl yourself, said Missis Drake. —Off you go.

Melody lay back on the newspapers – they cracked and rustled under her – and Missis Drake lifted the window.

—That's a grand lookin' day out there, she said. —A smashing day for bringing a baba into the world.

19

The steam dashed to the open window. And the pain dashed through Melody.

—Stop whingein', said Granny Nash. —You'll give the child a hare-lip.

—None of that shitery now, said Missis Drake to Granny Nash as she rolled over to Melody. —You're in charge of the water. Any more guff out of you and I'll fling you out the window. And then we'll hear some whingein'.

And Melody started laughing. More pain thumped her back right off the mattress. But she was still laughing when she landed.

Henry waited out on the street. He didn't want to be too near. He paced back and forth, watched at windows by hundreds of people who knew and feared his tap tap. Henry saw none of them. There was no window of his own to look up at; he was on the wrong side of the house. He went through the house to the yard and looked up at his window. It was open. He listened – nothing. He couldn't stay there – he felt trapped. His coat felt like armour. He'd be to blame if it went wrong again, if the baby didn't live. It was an idea that had become a rock-solid conviction in the time it had taken him to get from Dolly Oblong's to the house. It would be all his fault. He listened as he went to the back door – and heard Melody laughing.

She pushed.

—Good girl; there's no rush. Give yourself a rest.

Missis Drake gathered the sweat from Melody's brow with a cloth that was gorgeously cold. Granny Nash peered between Melody's legs; she didn't have to bend.

—Get away from there, you, said Missis Drake. —You'll frighten the baba.

Melody laughed and pushed again.

Henry, back out on the street, wore half an inch off his leg as he stomped back and back again. He tried leaning on the railings, sitting on the steps, but he couldn't stay still. He had to move. He thought about going for a pint or something smaller and stronger; his nerves were in dire need of settling, but he didn't want to leave his post. She'd laughed. It was years since he'd heard her laughing. He was so frightened, he

20

was terrified that that laugh would be the last thing he'd ever know of Melody. And it would be his fault, because of what he was. He hadn't noticed it getting dark. It was suddenly night. A bad sign, a bad sign – poor Henry tried to ignore it. Night followed day – he ignored it, he ignored it.

Melody pushed.

Henry's leg got shorter and shorter. He listened to the fading echo of his wife's laughter.

Melody pushed.

He tried to hear, tried to remember it. He didn't notice that he was listing dangerously, dangling over the basement steps.

Melody heaved; her back was turning to screaming stone.

—It's a hairy head.

—Get out of my light!

Miss Drake cupped the head in her magical mitts.

—The warmth of it, she said and sighed. —There's power there, I'll tell you. Welcome home, my treasure.

Melody Melody pushed again.

Henry toppled into the well of the basement.

Melody pushed and I —

me —

Henry Smart the Second or Third came charging into the world on a river of water and blood that washed the news off the papers. Melody fell back on the mattress. Missis Drake held me up by the legs. She dangled me for all to see, like an almighty salmon she couldn't believe she'd caught.

—It's a lad, Missis Melody, she said. —He must be more than a stone. A lad and a feckin' half, he is. His cord is as wide as me wrist.

She slapped my arse and the air around us sang. Granny Nash blessed herself, then high-tailed it out the door to tell my father.

Henry, my dad, looked up from where he'd landed on his back on the rubbish and waste blown down from the street. A shooting star went scooting across the black sky over Dublin. Henry forgot his pain and whooped. He saw Granny Nash squinting through the railings, trying to find him in the gloom and rubbish.

—I know, said Henry. —I know.

21

Where were the three wise men? Where were the sheep and the shepherds? They missed it, the fuckin' eejits. They were following the wrong star. They missed the birth of Henry Smart, Henry S. Smart, the one and only me. On the 8th of October, 1901, at twenty-two minutes past seven. They all missed it. Missis Drake was there. Her hands that cupped my head tingled for the rest of her great, long life. Granny Nash was there. She picked up the *Freeman's Journal* and discovered that she could read. And my parents? They were happy. For a tiny moment in their hard, hard lives my mammy and daddy were happy.

I was a broth of an infant, the wonder of Summerhill and beyond. I was the big news, a local legend within hours of landing on the newspapers.

—They say that he was born with the teeth already in his head.

—She has to use the blanket off the bed for his nappy.

—A woman seen him said he has enough meat on him to make triplets.

The local oul' ones all queued up, across the landing, down the stairs, out onto the street, to have a dekko at me. The stairs groaned and threatened to cave in but the prospect of falling into the black well and the waiting rats below wouldn't budge the oul' ones. They had to see the famous baby. It wasn't the weight of me they wanted to see – big brats were ten a penny, and cheaper – it was the glow. I was the Glowing Baby. I lay in a crib that was really an old zinc basin nicely stuffed and padded and I beamed out good health and vitality. I was pink and cream; every little movement of my adorable fists or face seemed to predict a bright future. The visiting women all looked at me, the great big bonny lad, and smiled. They said little, nothing that wasn't pleasant. Lots of soft oohs and aahs and sighs that joined the sunlight. They nodded to my mother and to Missis Drake who was still looking after her until after she'd been churched, and all walked home happy. The women who'd seen me went through the rest of the day feeling special. Ailing, fading women found long-forgotten spring in their

22

steps. Unhappy women caught themselves smiling. Grieving women tried to sing and found that they could. The Glowing Baby had entered their lives and tickled their misery with his pudgy wee fingers.

But that was all I was, a healthy, good-sized baby. The women had never seen one before. They looked at me and saw a fine lad who was going to live; there was no doubt about it at all, not a shadow. That was my miracle: I glowed guaranteed life. No fever would ever topple me; no cough would ever steal my last breath.

Only a week in the world and already there were stories spinning up and down the streets and alleys, through the open windows of the slums. There was the one about the rat family sitting on the rim of the basin looking in at me, mammy rat, daddy, the rat children and all the relations, tamed by my brightness when my mother woke up and saw them. She sat up and screamed, and they left calmly, out through a hole in the skirting board. The last one looked back and winked.

—Seen them with her own eyes, she did. They all marched off, like they were on their way to mass.

There was the one about Lady Gregory's head gardener knocking on the door wanting to buy whatever fell into my nappy to spread around Lady Gregory's rose-bushes; there'd be a man with a carriage and a bucket to carry my shite west to Coole every evening. Henry Smart the Second or Third – Henry, but not yet named – was famous.

Henry Smart the First, my father, was already famous. Still a bigger legend than his newly arrived son, the tap tap of his famous leg was a sound more feared than the banshee's wail. (The banshee wasn't folklore. The banshee was a fact, an evil old hag, perched on the roofs of the houses, combing her matted, rat-tailed hair, announcing the coming of death. She was a busy woman. Everyone had seen and heard her. My mother saw her many times. I saw her every time Granny Nash walked in the door.) After my birth, my father was also born. A new man – again – every time he picked me up and felt the life bounding through me he felt newer still. He held me gently, made an armchair of his colossal hands for me. He sat on his chair and I sat in him. He inhaled with me, and exhaled. And he sang to me. *Oh, the bridge is broke down and they all tumbled in.* This baby hadn't been snatched away, never would be snatched away from him. *We'll go home be the water, says Brian O'Linn.* My father adored me.

—Aren't they the picture? said Missis Drake.

—Yes, said my mother.

—A fine pair of men, said Missis Drake.

—Yes, said Melody.

The room was full of food, offerings left behind by the visiting women. There was a sheep's head, pigs' feet, a big bag of winkles; there were bananas, apples, an orange; there was fancy bread and two buns fecked from Bewley's. Missis Drake was skinning a rabbit.

—This boyo was out running this morning, she said. —The wind is still in his fur. Can you smell it?

—No, said Melody.

—I can, said Henry, but he was smelling me.

My mother was still in bed, seven days after my birth. Missis Drake wouldn't let her get up yet. Anyway, my father had the chair and the stool was somewhere under Missis Drake – there was nowhere else for Melody to sit. She wasn't to do any cooking until after she'd gone to the church and kneeled in front of the priest; she wasn't to cut bread, peel a spud, anything. She'd contaminate the food and poison the lot of us if she laid a finger on it before the priest's blessing had cleansed her. Melody was enjoying the luxury. For the first time in her life she was doing nothing.

Missis Drake was lowering the gutted bunny into the pot. My father stood and brought me over to my mother, holding me like a present he'd saved all his life to buy her. I left his confident hands and landed in my mother's.

—In you go now, said Missis Drake to the disappearing rabbit. —And mind you don't eat all the carrots.

My father sat on the bed. The air around him smelt of cleanliness and hope, soon to be joined by the stew. He felt good, strong. In the months coming up to my birth, an idea had taken hold and attached itself to the lining of his gut: he was to blame. It had clung, fed on him. It had grown and shoved its way through his body: he was to blame for the deaths

24

of all his children. It had slithered into every cell. His children had been taken from him and Melody because of all the things he had done. All the messages he'd delivered. All the people he'd scared, just by walking, tap tap, all the money he'd squeezed out of people with no money. All the skulls his leg had dented, all the men he'd murdered, and women. His children had been the price for all that bullying and killing, all that badness. And all the bodies he'd disposed of, let slide into the waters that crawled their way through Dublin, let slide in or just threw. There'd been one man called Traynor, fed into the Tolka in four neat pieces. There was a man called Farrell who'd been caught taking money from three of Dolly's girls. There were men whose names and crimes he never knew. Into the Liffey and the Tolka they went, and the other hidden rivers that ran under the city nibbling away at its floor or, overland, against high forgotten walls, through places that led nowhere and where no one ever looked. They were Dublin's secret rivers and my father knew them all. The Poddle and the Hangman's Stream, the Bradoge and the Cemetery Drain. He knew them all; his leg divined them. They took his offerings and kept them. And there were other bodies, vanished without the help of water. There was Costello, the fat rozzer. Costello, the greedy rozzer. *Alfie Gandon says Hello.* Costello had been fed to pigs in a farm beyond Tallaght, a farm with a beautiful view of the city. There were other men who'd ended up in the pigs and then on the morning plates of the city's merchants and chancers, on the plates of their wives and brats. Eating Henry's messages. There'd been a man called Lynch and another called O'Grady. There'd been a man with a huge purple birthmark pouring out of the neck of his shirt and another so handsome that Henry had almost let him go. And the women. There'd been two. Two of the girls. Got rid of for reasons he knew nothing about and never asked. One of them already dead, wrapped in bloody sheets, a parcel waiting on the bed. The other he'd killed, brought her for a walk. She'd told him about the town in Galway she'd come from, the last town before Boston, and about her family and her sister the nun and her brother the fisherman and about how none of them knew where she was or what she did, and that was when he'd killed her. Susie, and the other one was Antoinette, and both of them renamed Maria. They'd both gone into the water. He'd had nothing against any of them, the women or the men. He'd just done what he'd been told to do. He did a good, professional job, never got involved. He did what hundreds of others in the city were doing or waiting to do. *Alfie Gandon says Hello.* Once, just once, for some reason he didn't understand, for a change, he whispered a different message. *Alfie Gandon says Goodbye.*

Melody's eyes were closed. Missis Drake was humming. The stew was bubbling cheerfully; the rabbit was bobbing, sinking, falling apart into strings and chunks that Henry was looking forward to. He inhaled the fresh luxury, the certain knowledge that he was going to be fed. There was more than enough in the pot, enough for two days. There was nothing to worry about, more grub in the room than there'd ever been. The baby was asleep, under Melody's breast. *I* was asleep, under Melody's breast. Henry sat on the mattress. He would put his leg on in a minute but now he just wanted to rest in his happiness. For a while longer. Just a little while longer.

I gurgled. He looked at me. He wanted to hold me again but that would have meant disturbing Melody and he didn't want to do that. She needed her rest; she looked young and unharmed snoozing there. Henry smiled and gurgled back at me. My memory soup is full of my father's gurgles. I see a satisfied shape at the end of the bed. I feel my mother's breast pressing on my skull. I can smell her milk. I can taste it. Its bubbles are on my lips.

My father was a happy man.

—I'll soon be out of your way, said Missis Drake.

—No hurry, said Henry.

He liked Missis Drake. He felt grateful to her. She'd delivered me with the hands he now watched picking lint off her shawl, the hands that still tingled seven days after my birth. And Granny Nash was afraid of her; it was days since he'd seen the oul' witch. He watched Missis Drake moving around the room, graceful and huge, patting things as if ordering them to stay put till the morning, reassuring them that she'd be back. She'd rule the room for another two days. Henry watched her bringing the plates over to the pot. He would soon put on his leg. He had a new one, a beautiful, proud piece of mahogany. The old walked-away leg was up on the mantelpiece, beside the Blessed Virgin. He would put on his new leg. They'd chat for a few minutes, then he'd kiss Melody and his unnamed son goodbye and go off to his work.

I saw the shape at the end of the bed, and another moving shape behind it, Missis Drake, a massive, light-warm shadow. My mother's tit rested on my head. I could hear and feel her heart; my ear was right on top of it – a velvet pounding that gave life to the shapes before me. I was ready to nod off. The shapes and noises loved me. There was a burp crawling its way up towards the milk left in my mouth. It was making good, tickling progress. I was enjoying it, looking forward to it.

I delivered the burp.

—Thar she blows, said Missis Drake. —The little creature.

My father leaned across and wiped my mouth with his coat sleeve. *That* coat sleeve. My mother opened her eyes to the sight of Henry running his finger along the wee fat canyon that divided my chins. He felt the soft love of her eyes on him and he leaned down the few more inches and kissed her breast. She pushed his head away but she was thrilled; a push that was really a pull. They were in love like they'd never been. It was their new life. And me in the middle of it, the little one who'd started it.

—I'll be off, so, said Missis Drake.

—Thanks very much, Missis Drake, said Melody.

—Yeah, said Henry, and he nodded at the full plates now waiting for them on the tea chest.

—Ah sure, said Missis Drake. —It's only a drop of water with a rabbit floatin' around in it.

—It smells lovely, said Melody.

—It was a handsome rabbit, said Missis Drake.

I gurgled for Missis Drake. Twin dribbles ran over my chins, especially for her.

She was gone. Bye bye, Missis Drake. Melody rubbed my back and lowered me into my zinc crib. I missed her heart. I looked up at a face, then the big grey space that was the ceiling. My parents sat at the tea chest and ate the stew.

—Jaysis, Melody, my father gasped, —the woman's a genius.

27

—She is, my mother agreed.

They sucked the soup off carrots, swallowed chunks of the bunny. They coughed and filled their mouths with bits of spud that melted to wonderful slush on their tongues. There was no room for talk. I listened to the music of the forks on plates and to the ferocious, happy groans and gulps as they shoved Missis Drake's grub down pipes that had never known anything like it. My mother's breasts hummed to me. My lips searched for her.

The groans and forks slowed and stopped. A screech – the chair scraping the floor. My father was on his way. I squirmed, I gulped. My lips nibbled the air – it was my turn now. My father strapped on his new leg.

—There's a lovely shine off it, said Melody.

—Only the best, said my father.

She watched him, admired the speed and confidence. Then she spoke again.

—What'll we call him, Henry?

I was the Baby with No Name. I'd been baptised quickly, on the spot; water had hit my head before milk had gone near the back of my throat. God waited for no baby in the slums. He took them back as soon as He'd given them, but He threw them away if their souls were still stained. He delivered them soiled but expected them back spotless. It was a race. Each day of life was a fight and a triumph, an endless race to stay a few inches in front of the greedy hand of God. God's gift, Original Sin, had to be washed away in case God sent another of his gifts – fever, typhoid or whooping cough, smallpox, pneumonia or rats. So I'd been baptised. I was without sin. But I didn't have a name either.

—Baba Smart, Missis Drake had said.

—That's not a name, said the priest.

—I know that, Father, said Missis Drake.

—I cannot give the sacrament to a nameless child, said the priest.

—Of course you can, Father, said Missis Drake. —Sure, it'll only be temporary. They're not in a fit state to come up with a little name right now. Look at them, sure.

The priest looked. An hour after I'd been born. My mother

was asleep and giggling. My father was one-legged, bleeding and hanging onto the mantelpiece, trying to get his leg to stand up beside the Virgin; happiness was pouring out of him in snot and tears. Granny Nash was reading the small ads in the *Freeman's Journal*, gasping as each word opened its meaning – there were bespoke suits going for 35s and a parrot with talking warranty for only 12s 6d. She wondered how much the parrot would cost without the warranty.

—What's your own name, Father? said Missis Drake.

—Cecil, said the priest.

—I'll let them know, said Missis Drake.

Cecil the priest looked at me in Missis Drake's arms. He saw a magnificent baby, a baby with a glow and heft that offered immortality. He saw Cecil the Immortal Baby. He saw the story of his name being passed from neighbour to daughter and on, the story of Father Cecil and the baby. So he gave in and baptised me with water from one of the cups and I became Temporary Smart, Baba Smart, the boy without stain. He mumbled his mumbo-voodoo and dabbed a trickle on my angry head. The Immortal Boy was now ready for his death.

A week later I was still alive and un-Cecilled. I was still the Baba. Missis Drake had never mentioned the priesteen's name to my mother or father. She'd had a cousin called Cecil, a wee pus-filled gurrier who'd made her young life a constant misery until he'd run under a tram. Even dead, he'd terrified her. Cecil was no name for her baba. (Cecil Smart? Thank you, thank you, Missis Drake.) Missis Drake had told a lie to Cecil the priest; she was never going to recommend his ugly name to my parents. She'd taken the sin and swallowed it.

My father let his trousers drop over the new leg. Then my mother spoke.

—What'll we call him, Henry? she said.

My father looked at my mother and smiled. This was his moment.

—Henry, he said.

If I'd been in her arms she would have dropped me.

—No!

My father was surprised, and very quickly annoyed. He held back his anger, felt it battering his chest.

29

—Why not?

My mother was trying not to get sick. She couldn't talk yet. Not yet. There was nothing in front of her; movement meant falling. But she was still ready to believe: she'd imagined it. There'd been some sort of mistake, a distortion made by the wind. She waited to be saved.

—Well? said my father. —Did the cat get your tongue, or what?

He was angry but he didn't want to be; there was no enjoyment in it, no triumph. It was a fight he didn't want. He wished now that he'd never said the name. He'd have taken back the last minutes and started again, differently, if he could have. There were other names. But he'd been thinking about it all week. He'd imagined the moment, a gift to Melody, handing it over to her. Henry. He'd been sure she'd love the idea. He'd been positive about it. Henry. The name would float between them. Just the two of them. A perfect moment.

Just the two of them? And what about me? I was annoyed, I was hopping. I was struggling, squirming. There were two growing things, two smothering throbs, crawling over each other inside me, two sensations that I was going to have to get used to – hunger and neglect. Now though, I was going to let go of a stream of roars and yaps in the sure knowledge that results would immediately follow, hands would come and pick me up.

—Well? said my father. —Melody?

There was silence out there, beyond the crib. Not for long, though. The Nameless Baby would be heard. I was squirming, fretting, working myself up into a fit state for making noise.

—Melody?

—Yes.

—Are you alright?

—Yes.

—D'you not think it's a good idea?

I heard a sob. My mother had got there just before me. I was furious now, robbed and ignored.

—Well?

She sobbed again. Then silence.

—Well?

30

—No.

—No what?

—No, I don't think it's —

Sobs, a string of them, and silence.

I sent out a string of my own, linked sausages full of protest and slobber, the strangled outcries of an angry wee man.

—Why not?

What about me?

I heard her breathing, measuring her breath.

—We already have a Henry.

I sent out more exploding sausages. The zinc walls were closing in on me.

—But he's dead, said my father.

I heard a gasp. My mother shook her head and hid behind her hair.

—He's dead, love, said my father.

He wasn't being callous, he wasn't being cruel. The last sounds of his dead children were in his ears; he could measure their weight in his arms. But they were dead. Gone from him and Melody. My father didn't believe in heaven or after-life reunions. His children were gone. Naming me Henry would take the pain and weight away; it would let them start again. It would let them include the dead in their new life. A gift to my mother.

I was crying now, full blast; everything was in my wail.

—He's not, said my mother.

—He *is*, said my father. —For God's sake, love. Where is he? He's dead. And the other little one. They're dead.

What about me? What about *me*?

I was a pink-cheeked howl in need of arms and milk. I was alone.

My mother shook her head. She looked up at the ceiling, at her children beyond it, waiting for her. She looked up at her first Henry. Her one and only Henry.

What about *me*!

My father looked up and saw the ceiling, just the ceiling. Nothing but the grey, sagging, cracked, stained ceiling.

—Stars are only stars, he said. —Melody?

My mother looked through the ceiling.

31

What about *meeeee*!

—Don't pretend you can see anything up there, love, said my father. —Look at me; d'yeh hear me?

My father was angry and not interested in stopping.

—It's the fuckin' ceiling! he shouted.

He had to shout. I was making noise to drown anything less. I was becoming noise. Adding to his anger. I was choking, screaming. Disappearing.

—It's a fuckin' ceiling and the stars are only stars and his name's Henry, d'you hear me.

I was named.

—His name's Henry! Henry! So you might as well get used to it.

He got up, the chair fell back. He came over to the crib. I heard the charging tap tap. He looked down at me. I saw an angry blur, shimmering fury.

—Listen, he said to my mother. —Are you listening now?

He bent down – I felt his heat – and roared into my purple face.

—Henry! Henry! Shut up! Shut up, Henry! Shut up, Henry!

My mother kept shaking her head, hitting the name back with her damp curls.

—Shut up, Henry!

Was I obedient? Did I obey my daddy? I did like fuck. I screamed back up at him, my purple turned to black. I shoved my terror up into his face. And he stopped. He stopped shouting at me. He saw that I'd die before I'd stop, I'd scream my life away before I'd let him better me. What about *meeee*? So he stopped. He stood up straight and looked back down at me from a safe distance. He searched me, looking for some way past my screeches. His hands slowly surrounded me, gradually grew more solid. He picked me up. I left the crib behind.

—There, there.

He put me on his shoulder.

—Now, now.

I looked for a nipple in his coat. My lips met dust and blood. I tasted awful secrets. I kicked and shook. I fought his care and hands. He brought me quickly to my mother. Tap tap tap. I went from hands to smaller hands – shaking, frightened hands.

Frightened faces watched me as I found a nipple, drank and fell asleep.

I was the other Henry. The shadow. The impostor. She still fed me, held me, doted on me. But when her husband was in the room she began to feel sharp cuckoo lips on her breast. She stopped eating. There was no Missis Drake to coax food into her and Granny Nash was too busy with her head in *Knocknagow* and *Bleak House* to be bothered with feeding herself, let alone her half-wit of a daughter. My father saw the food left on the plate, saw her fading. He cursed the vanity and sentimentality that had suckered him into giving me his old name. And he hated the sky over Dublin for not being thick and dirty enough to hide the stars; he hated the wind for making open curtains of the night-time clouds. And he looked at me and saw a different child. He began to see the baby who was eating his wife away. He wanted to hold me but sometimes, even as he bent over me, he couldn't lift his arms to do it.

I was Henry but they never called me that. She wouldn't; he couldn't. But I was still Henry, too late for any other name. So they called me nothing. I was the boy. The lad. Himself. He. The child. I grew out of the zinc basin; my knees and elbows crushed its sides. I screamed as I stretched. My glow became a crust, my skin dry and furious. My mother swayed between fat and skeletal. She was a different woman every week. I went from breast to solids, straight to spuds and chunks of gristle; I bit with teeth that were robbed from a graveyard. I crunched and swallowed everything that was put in front of me. I gnawed at my father's leg until he had to leave it on the landing before he came in. I struggled and walked and threw myself around the room. The ceiling shed its grey skin; it snowed all day on top of us. There were no more visitors, no more aahs and sighs, no food left behind. I claimed the mattress, marked my boundaries with my muck. I stopped their sleep; I muscled in on their sex, their messy efforts at saving their love. I crawled all over legs and arses and bit whatever seemed soft. They picked me up, patted me, smacked my arse, fed me, loved me,

33

cleaned me – but they never called me Henry. I flooded the room with my stinks and waxes. I roared and screamed my right to be named.

I drove my mother out onto the step. She had to get away from walls. Already big and pregnant with the next one, she fumbled her way down the black stairs, trying to hold me on her suffering hip. She sat on the cold step and sweated. She waited for twilight and night. I beat her. I climbed onto her hair. I pressed into the breasts that were no longer mine. I scratched my sores and bled for her. She rocked me and soothed me, waited for her stars. It got colder and darker. I scratched her face. I puked white loads on her shoulders and lap. She rocked me, rocked me. She looked up at the sky and waited for the grey to turn black. She wrapped me in her shawl. She trapped my hands and legs. The North Star appeared. I fought against her arms. More stars lit up and twinkled. She held me tight. She gazed up at all the stars. She wandered from one to the next. She wrapped me tight in her shawl and lifted her free hand. I struggled to escape; I puffed and shook and spat. She lifted her hand and chose a star. Her index finger swayed, then stiffened.

—There he is, she said.

I bucked and tossed. I screeched blue murder.

—There's my little Henry.

The star grew and shimmered. Blood ran from my nose, in a rush that failed to shock her. She put her shawl to my nostrils and continued to gaze at her star. She wasn't being vindictive. There was no cruelty in her pointing. She wanted me to see him, and him, far away, to see me. Henry met Henry. She hoped we could be friends, that we could love each other. She smiled as I screamed. That was what my father saw the moment I was born; the shooting star was big brother Henry charging across the sky in a fit of celestial jealousy. If my father had listened too, if Granny Nash hadn't distracted him, he'd have heard the star's wail slicing the heavens —

—Maaa-*meee*!

She turned my head to the star and held it firm.

—See? See?

Years later, when I lay under my blanket on the lonesome

prairee, full of beans and disgruntlement, or I sat on a rock in the Utah Desert and shivered, I'd gaze up at the huge, cold, black-blue sky and I'd find the star – I always knew its sly twinkle and fade, it could never hide from me. I'd stare at it, fix my eyes on it and refuse to let them stray to any of the other millions of its still and shooting siblings. I'd stare at my star till I knew I had it. I'd make a copper rope of my gaze and I'd lasso the twinkling bollocks. Then I'd yell.

—My name is Henry Smart!

I'd watch it shimmer and fuss. My voice was hard and sure and triumphant, hard as the rock I was sitting on, cold as the air that was lying on top of me. There was no one else to hear me. My nearest neighbours were as distant as the stars above me.

—My name is Henry Smart! The one and only Henry Smart!

I'd watch its gases splutter and die.

—My name is Henry Smart!

I'd yell until I could no longer see its shadow against the blueness of the night, until there was nothing out there. I killed my brother every night.

3

He went to work every evening. He kissed my mother. He kissed me. He patted his coat, then left us. He sat on the landing floor outside and put on his leg. Then he was gone.

Off to his work.

Henry Smart, the tap tap man. He stood outside Dolly Oblong's kip house. Henry the Leg. In the week after my birth, he went at his work with new enthusiasm and vim. My birth had freed him. There'd be no more punishments; there never had been any. The earlier deaths had been bad luck. Just that. Dead children, thrown on top of all the city's dead children. Henry looked at the certainty barrelling through my arms and legs and decided that he could do whatever he wanted. He stood on the steps of Dolly Oblong's, a new man yet again. A new man with a new leg. The ships spat out ruffians and bowsies from far-flung, savage corners of the world, hard men tired of riding each other. They scoured the city with pockets full of itchy cash and found my father on the step of the brothel, between them and the women they dribbled for. They pointed at his leg and laughed and said things in languages that my father had never heard. They started up the steps, these nut-tough bastards, and suddenly the leg was gone and, even more suddenly, they were on their backs and bawling. They looked at my father rejoining his leg. They saw the warm gleam of the streetlamp purring in the wood, and the same warmth in my father's face. They went away, and carried the legend of the leg back to the creaking, tinder-built outposts they'd sailed from. Bollixes from Stoneybatter got the same treatment. Men who had never been to sea in their lives, who'd never even gone

36

down to the docks to look at it, men whose only language was a few dozen words of nose-propelled English, crawled away from the steps of Dolly Oblong's with cracked skulls and wilting langers. Only the meekest and the mildest and, of course, the wealthy regulars got past my father in that first week of my life. He swung his new leg with a conscience as clear as my blue, blue eyes.

And after that, after he'd named me Henry, he still cracked heads, and more and more heads. He brought the leg down and took chunks out of it. He battered and hammered. One small thing, a name; one tiny mistake, a moment of sentimentality, and that beautiful week became a mocking memory. Melody cried and closed her face to him; she buried herself in her shawl. She started grieving a week after the birth of the healthiest child anyone had ever seen. My father found her at dawn on the steps outside the house looking up through the fog to where there were no stars. She was shivering, soaking, me inside the shawl fighting her. He took me and looked. My glow was now a flake-skinned crust, scratched raw, cracked by the cold. My baby blues were a fierce black, throwing outrage, revenge at him. I was the baby with the bloodshot eyes. He kissed my hard cheeks and tried to call me Henry. He brought us up to our room. He pretended that his wife saw him, pretended that his son's rage was an infant's fun.

—There there, there there.

He put us to bed and sat on the chair. He took off his leg. I screamed and he threw the leg at the fireplace. It bounced back out like a skittle and rolled along the floor and stopped at his foot, like a dog wanting to be petted. He put the leg back on, picked me up and tried to sing to me. *Oh the bridge it broke down.* I heard the gulps that broke the song's back. He stopped and dropped big tears onto my head.

He put me back into the bed beside my mother. He moved gently around the room while we slept. He waited for things to get back to normal, the return of that wonderful week. He waited for it all to come back. Every day. He never slept. He guarded us all day and waited. And he went to work every evening, at ten to six. He kissed my mother. He kissed me. He

37

patted his coat, then left us. He sat on the landing floor outside and put on his leg. Then he was gone.

Off to his work.

And then the violence and hurt poured out of him. He raged and whacked. He roared and blew. The few who still braved the steps walked into the shadow of my father's towering anger. He defended the steps so efficiently that there was one night when no one at all got past him. No one even tried to. And one of the girls opened the door a chink and called him in.

—Herself wants you.

And he went inside. Into the smells and hints that men paid for. The darkness and promises. He went up the stairs to Dolly Oblong's room. Up the carpeted stairs, where his tap tap carried no threat. It was quiet. No grunts or laughter, braces snapping, beds protesting. Only the piano downstairs, some tune that Henry didn't know or like, some plonky-plonky thing that you had to be drunk to feel. He hadn't been drunk in years, since the day he met Melody. He was nervous now. He made his way down the dark red corridor; behind each shut door a lonely girl.

He was there. He knocked on Dolly Oblong's door. It was a good, thick door; his knock was a small thing on it.

—Come in.

He opened the door.

—Come in.

He stepped into Dolly Oblong's room for the first time. It was dark. He saw a line of light where the closed curtains didn't quite meet and the strict shapes of furniture.

—Shut the door.

He heard the door's canvas cover settling back into place. He stood there in the dark and waited. He could hear no breathing. A sideboard, a chair. He began to know the room. There were no colours yet. He was standing on a rug that rubbed his ankle.

Now he heard a neat cough.

—What is the weather like?

—Grand, said Henry. —Not too bad.

—And how is your family?

—Grand, said Henry.

38

He could see more chairs now, big armchairs, and there was a large, high bed right in front of him but he couldn't find the woman who was talking to him.

—The baby?

—Grand, he said. —Gameball.

The bed creaked.

—The baby has both the legs?

—Yes.

—Good. And a brain?

—Yes.

—Good. But you must not be the father. A fool like you could not produce such a baby.

The bed groaned again and a black mountain grew in front of Henry. A head took shape, and shoulders. A head that was made huge by hair that would have been plenty for five women. It was a wig, Henry knew. It was one of the things he knew about his employer: she was bald. One of the very few things he knew.

—What kind of a nincompoop are you? she said.

He took the question seriously. He stayed quiet. He began to see her, not just her outline. She was sitting up now. The wig was massive and brown. She was wearing a red gown, or something. She shifted, and powder quickly reached Henry's nose.

—Well? she said.

Another thing he knew about her: she was twenty-five. She looked and moved like a monument but she was younger than he was. It had been her brothel since he'd been the bouncer; she couldn't have been far past fifteen when she became the madam.

—Has your tongue gone the same way as your leg?

—No.

—Good.

She sighed, and peppermint joined her powder.

—I am a businesswoman, she said.

There was a hint of the foreigner in her words, just now and again. Nothing as strong as an accent, just a bend or a tiny fracture in a phrase. Or each word precisely delivered where the locals took shortcuts.

—A businesswoman, she said. —Yes. And, Mister – tell me
your name.

—Henry.

—Henry and?

—Smart.

—And, Mister Smart, what is my business?

—Em —

—Men come into my house, they fuck my girls and then
they leave with less money. That is my business. Yes?

—Yes, said my father.

—They drink some gin and listen to the piano player
murdering my piano but, essentially, they fuck my girls. Is that
right?

—Yes.

—Yes, she said. —Prostitution. That is my business.

She stopped. He was sure that she expected something from
him.

—Yeah, he said.

—Yeah. Yeah yeah yeah. The men are happy, my girls are
happy, I am happy. Say Yeah.

—Yeah.

—No. I am not happy. Why not?

—Em —

—Because there is no business taking place in my house.
Because you will not let it take place. You will not let the men
in to fuck my girls. There is not one man in my house at this
moment. Except you. And you do not count, Mister Smart.

—Sorry, said Henry.

—Your apology I accept, she said. —But, still, I must
dispose of you.

How? he wondered. He considered telling her about his
dead children, his son's name, his fight with God. But he
couldn't.

—I pay you how much?

—Fifteen shillings a week, said Henry.

—I will pay you fifteen shillings and fifteen shillings more
and you will go. You are not good for business.

He was getting the sack. He wasn't going to be flung into the
Liffey or fed to the pigs beyond Tallaght. It was only the sack.

40

There'd be other jobs. There was always work for bullies, or other work.

—However, said Dolly Oblong.

Henry waited. He felt stronger now. He knew: she wasn't even going to sack him.

—However, she said again. —However, Mister Smart, I have other business ventures. You know this. I have partnerships.

She was a grand chunk of a woman, Henry decided. Red suited her. Especially in the dark.

—Mister Gandon speaks highly of you, she said. —You are efficient. You are cautious enough not to ask questions, stupid enough not to care. He likes this.

—Good, said Henry.

He was being insolent, he knew. But not too insolent. Fresh peppermint arrived at his nose. He liked it.

—Yes, said Dolly Oblong. —I am glad that you say Good. Mister Gandon tells me that you do a very professional job. This makes me happy.

He decided against more insolence. Stupid first, now he was being cautious. Mister Gandon knew his man.

—Yes, said Dolly Oblong. —There are two Mister Smarts. One makes me unhappy, the other makes me very happy. Which Mister Smart am I addressing? Well?

—I've always admired Mister Gandon, said Henry.

Never met the man, he said to himself. Then, again to himself: *She's* Alfie Gandon. It made him smile. It was brilliant; it thrilled him. He liked her even more.

—Good, she said. —Good.

He wanted to serve her.

She clapped her hands. Powder and sin danced around his face. He decided to shave. And brush his coat.

—Very well, she said.

And varnish his leg.

—I will not dispose of you.

He waited for more.

—I am going to give you a second chance, said Dolly Oblong.

—Thank you, said Henry.

41

—But you must allow the men to come into my house and spend their money.

—Yes, said Henry.

—That is how society works. Money. Making it, taking it, spending it. Without money we are nothing, not even animals. We are not efficient enough to be animals, Mister Smart, so we make money instead. So. You must give the men the opportunity to spend their money. This makes more money. It is good for society. It is good for the city, the country and the Empire. Everybody. Food, clothes, roofs over our heads. Because men like to fuck nice girls. You may go.

What a woman, all the same. He found the door. A leader, a genius and a floozy. He was close to swooning, falling over. Dolly Gandon, Alfie Oblong. And dozens of other mixtures, more than likely. And, maybe, his name in the mixing bowl. The open door brought some light.

—Mister Smart?

—Eh —

He turned to face her.

—Yeah. Yes?

There was more of her to see now. A shoulder he wanted to kiss, hair he wanted to drown in, or just touch. A wig – he didn't care, no one knew for sure. It looked real enough, better than real. Teeth – Jesus, her teeth. He wanted to kneel at the bed and whimper. And offer himself. Give her his leg to beat him with.

—Yes? he said, hanging on to the door.

—You never fuck my girls.

—No.

—Why not?

—I'm married, he said.

She smiled. He saw teeth, and more teeth. False, like the hair? It didn't matter. The lips were real and impossible, red, huge and open.

—How lovely, she said. —You are a breath of fresh air, Mister Smart. You may go. But also.

He waited.

—From now on I will pay you twelve shillings a week.

My father closed the door. A new man. Again, yet again. A

slave this time. What a woman. He was floating. She had force to match God's. She *was* God. She was her own invention – like him, but successful – her hair, teeth, her name, everything about her and around her. She'd created her own world and made it happen. She pulled strings from her bed – Henry almost fainted at the thought – and all of Dublin shook. People died, people lived while she sucked peppermints. She was the Queen of the city, and nobody knew. Except herself and, now, my father. My father was in love.

Side by side, they'd take on God and win. They'd rule the world. He'd never let a name destroy his life again. They'd invent and change names as it suited them – Dolly Gandon, Alfie Oblong, Dolly Smart. He'd be the puppet at the end of Dolly Oblong's strings. Pinocchio Smart. He already had the wooden leg. He'd be a good boy for her and it would become flesh.

There was a man at the bottom of the steps. Henry stood aside, and the man came up and ducked past him.

—They're inside waiting on you, said Henry.

He knew that Dolly Oblong had heard the door opening, would now hear it closing. She would hear another door inside opening, money being spent. She'd be pleased. She'd think of him. She was already thinking of him. There were more men, coming up the street. More money for Dolly Oblong. There was no anger left in my father, none at all, no bitterness, no past. He really was a new man.

I grew.

I grew and stretched and raged around the room, filled the place with my fists and feet. I got my knees off the floor and walked. I hit the walls and clawed them. I broke through the clothes that were put on me. I wailed and cursed, hard words that came through the open window to me. I only stopped to swallow snot and any food that got in my way. My mother grew fat on the air that I left her. I slept where I fell.

More newspapers were put on the mattress, carefully and slowly as Granny Nash read down through the columns and tut-tutted and sniggered. She tore off corners, left neat holes in the middle of pages and hid the pieces under her shawl. My mother's groans came out of the clouds of steam. I charged right in and ripped the pages from the bed. I tried to knock over the buckets. I screamed and kicked as the tingling hands that had brought me into the world picked me up and dumped me gently on the landing outside.

—Stay out here for a while, little manny.

A rope was tied around my waist and to the stair-rail. I pulled and pulled and scraped at the hempen veins of the rope until my blood had drenched them. But it was too late. A new cry filled the room on the other side of the door. Alexander came first and, before I'd got used to that invasion, Susie joined Alexander and I was the oldest. The little man of the house. I smelt milk that should have been mine, and went mad.

Alexander this, Susie that, name-dropping all day long, the only thing my mother and father had left in common, the odd time he remembered who he was and came home. They patted me when they could catch me, but would they drop my name? One word, two syllables, so easy to remember. *What about meeee!* Then there were no names at all. She was closing down, packing up to join the stars. He was off, away knocking heads for Dolly Oblong, wearing his big thick heart on the sleeve of his bloodstained coat. He wasn't with us any more. There was no tap tap outside on the street when Alexander and Susie were being born. He was on important business, delivering love letters from Dolly to Alfie. He'd come home now and again, wherever the latest home was. He never took the leg off; he didn't have the time and he knew I'd have my teeth into it the second he put it down. So he got up on the bed with the leg, made his noises, filled my mother, and went. To his new life. And, sometimes, he'd look my way and recognise me. He'd smile, and go.

I broke free of the room, pulled the door from its hinges, and attacked the house. I dug my heels into the stairs, smashed the banisters. I rolled down the stairs and steps, out onto the street. I screamed at the sky.

—Where are you off to, Sonny Jim?

—UCK OFF! I roared.

And I invaded Dublin. Out under the horses and the wheels

I went, through the puddles and hawkers, dung and carters, the noise and the soot, in bare feet that became as hard as the stone under them.

—Seven plums a penny! Seven for a penny!

I hit the bad streets of Dublin, a three-year-old earthquake, a bomb going off, a complete and utter brat.

—Cheaper the apples! Even cheaper the apples!

Infested, hungry and unloved, I fell in with the crowd. I wandered up and down outside the house, a wolf in a rusting cage. I slid under big legs and climbed along the railings. I looked up at women's faces, passing women and women on the other steps. Remember me? The Glowing Baby. The baby who made you smile. They looked at me and saw the screaming get from the top back in No. 7, the little get who made his poor mammy's life a red hot purgatory long before her due. Or else they didn't look at all. They'd enough on their plates, screaming gets of their own.

But I loved the street, from the second I landed on it. The action, the noise and smells – I gobbled them all up, I was starving for more. I was looking at misery that matched my own. I was at home in the rags and scarcity, dirt and weakness. And there were new things too, colour, laughter, chaos and escape. It was glorious. It was my world and it could be as big and as small as I wanted it to be. There was a corner and, beyond that, more corners. There were doorways, and more doors inside. There were carts and cabs and the music of tram bells coming from beyond the packed houses, somewhere I couldn't yet see, but near, around more corners and off. There were hawkers' shouts and foreign accents, and new smells spilling over the old ones. I heard a foghorn and it told me that there were places far away.

—Where's your mammy, little man?

—UCK OFF.

—Holy God. What's your name?

—HEN'Y.

I was there, at home, an instant street arab, welcome and ignored. I fought my corner. I looked and learned. A police whistle, an ice-cream seller's bugle, wheels going over stone, women shouting for their children, a woman fighting the price of a brush —

—D'you call them things bristles?

—Good bristles, yes. Feel, please.

—I can see them from here, sure. It's hardly a brush at all. It's only a piece of oul' wood that needs a shave. If I gave you a penny for it, it would be only to give it a home.

—Is good brush. I use it myself.

—I can see that. Sure, the poor thing's nearly worn away.

A milkman filled a jug from a churn on the back of his cart. He tilted the ladle again and let more milk fall onto the milk already in the jug.

—And a drop more for the cat.

He handed the jug down to a woman and the jug and milk went under her shawl. He led the horse to the next door where the house's women were waiting for their milk. Already, there was sex. I watched all the women. I followed them, I rubbed against them. I breathed them in and waited for them to arrive. I fell in love fifteen times a minute. I followed them to their doors. I heard their noise and bustle; I heard them crying. A woman crying – and there were plenty – made me furious and thrilled. You need *meeee*. Pick me up; I'll take your tears. And I went weak when they were together, laughing or complaining or fighting; I needed the railings to keep me standing. Women together. The sounds they made, the way they walked, the shawls that wrapped and hid them. Oh God, those shawls. I wanted to climb in under and die for the rest of my life. I saw them looking at men. I watched their eyes following as they tightened their shawls and stood still. I wanted to feel their eyes. I wanted to get up to their eyes. I sat down on the street and ached.

I stayed out until I was falling, and when I got back to No. 7 my mother was on the steps. I'd climb into her lap and stare into faces angry like mine. I'd spit and I'd gouge. I'd fight for the lap, for my rightful place under her shawl. We'd stay out there till Daddy's tap tap set us howling. And often, always, it was the wrong tap tap, the tap tap of another leg. Some old veteran of some old war staggering home after a night of boasting and bawling. Dublin was suddenly full of one-legged

46

men, their limbs left behind on the Empire's battlefields or under the screeching levers and wheels that powered Dublin's feeble industry. And they all walked past our door. I knew my father's tap from theirs, the distance between his taps, their power and majesty, but the sound of any wood on the footpath or cobbles filled me with cruel hope.

We moved to another house. I was put into the cart with Alexander, Susie, another new baby and Granny Nash. We were there to give it weight, to stop the straw from escaping out of the mattress. We were moving from Summerhill, to somewhere nearer the river. My mother pushed the cart and Granny Nash navigated as she turned the pages of Rousseau's *Confessions*. I clutched my father's leg, the one he'd worn to the butt the night I'd been born. I was afraid that he wouldn't be able to find us. I spat on the ground at every corner and hoped that he would come looking before it rained and washed my marks away. Granny Nash lifted her bony hand, pointed right and we turned off Summerhill. My mother had to hold on tight to the cart as we sailed down towards the Liffey, down into a lightless hollow where the fogs met and fucked.

Into a smaller, darker room. The walls were wet. The smell of earth and death came up through the floorboards. The window was a hole that offered nothing.

Home.

But we were back in the cart and on to Standfast Lane, a short stump of a street, a place made for lurking or dashing through, too narrow for carts, too poor for trade; even daylight stayed away. Into another crumbling house, down steps this time instead of up, down to a basement. The smell was waiting for us, daring us to keep going. My mother was behind me, wheezing, trying to manage her cough. I heard water settling and the house above us groaning like a ship fighting a rope, objecting to our presence.

Home.

My father must have found us because another baby arrived, after two funerals. Two Victors. They stayed only for a day or two – I saw neither of them – then went up to the stars, and hung on either side of twinkling Henry. My mother swayed as she tried to pick them.

47

—There. See?

She held our hair and made us look.

And the new baby was called Victor too. No objection from my mother. No sobbing or hiding behind her hair. There were four children, countless ghosts and my growing, dying mother packed into the only corner of the room that wasn't flooded, all fighting for space on the poor old mattress. We had nothing to burn and there was no mantelpiece for Daddy's leg and the Blessed Virgin. We packed in together, too furious for cuddling and comfort. No light from the window, Standfast Lane wasn't worth a streetlamp of its own. We crouched in the dark and all the one-legged men in the world tapped past, above us.

I got out of there. I climbed over the family and paddled out of that kip. I took my time going up the steps. It was pitch, pitch dark, like climbing out of deep water. I felt something at my side. It was Victor. He'd followed me, climbed the steps all by himself; not bad for a nine-month-old whose only nourishment was whatever memories of milk he could suck out of our mother's empty breast. I picked him up.

—Come on, I said. —Let's go lookin'.

I was five.

4

He was Dolly Oblong's faithful delivery boy. *Alfie Gandon says Hello.* He carried the message all over Dublin. And he slept in a hole under a back stairs. He put his ear to the floor and fell asleep listening to the house. He guarded it while he slept. He gave his life to Dolly Oblong. He went back to her room only twice in those years and, once, he stepped aside as she left the house and went down the steps to a waiting cab. He was so overpowered by her magnificence, by the eyes made huge by belladonna, by the smell of peppermint that strayed from her mouth to his, he didn't think of dashing down to open the cab door until the cab was a dying sound beyond the light of the streetlamp. And he cursed his stupidity. The chance to be of help, to touch her sleeve, and he'd let it go right past him. The fading horse's hooves drove nails into his stupid, saturated heart.

The visits to her room were short. Once, she gave him two pounds and the name of a man.

—Mister Gandon does not like this man, she said. —He is not good for business.

The second time she gave him five pounds and two names, on a piece of paper. He didn't look at the names; he knew that this, his first look at her handwriting, would make him weak.

—These men do not like each other, Henry, she said. — Mister Gandon thinks that this is what they would want.

Henry. Her voice held up his name in front of his eyes. It caressed and slapped it. He took the fiver and fell out of the room. He stood outside and, again, cursed himself and his numb, useless tongue. It was too late to go back in, to start

49

again. He had the money, he had the names. Two names on a small piece of paper. The perfect grease stain left by her fingers – it was heart-shaped; he could see it – where she'd held the corner of the paper, there for him to see and keep. And her writing – she was in the lines and dips, the ink was from inside her. He remembered the names, folded the paper and gently lowered it to the bottom of the pocket inside his coat, as near to his heart as he could estimate.

Two names. Two unmarried brothers in one house. An easy job. The Brennans. Desmond and Cecil. A very easy job. In the kitchen window, not a squeak or objection. Up the stairs. No secret creak or hidden toy. Into the bedrooms. He tied them fast to facing chairs, to let them watch each other bleed. He sawed one throat, and then the other. He wiped the blade on his sleeve and left the room so the brothers could enjoy their last moments together. He went downstairs and found some biscuits.

It took him three nights to get rid of the bodies. He dropped parcels into water all over Dublin. A heart went into Scribbles-town Stream, a torso into the Little Dargle. He climbed down drains and into granite caves. He went further and used new rivers. Naniken River and the Creosote Stream. He was careful and fair. No river got too much. If an arm went north, another went south. It was a job of work, and he was tired. He felt like a man who'd walked all over Dublin.

He was on his way back, to the hole under Dolly Oblong's stairs, when he turned a corner, into a huge crowd. Flags and bunting flapped above him, lots of red, white and blue, some green and gold, and there was a band off somewhere ploughing through *The Minstrel Boy*. The crowd stretched all along the road, through Ballsbridge, over the canal, on into town. There was a roar that was getting louder, as if coming nearer.

—They're coming! They're coming!

He saw hats being waved, hats thrown into the air. The flags became frantic. *The Minstrel Boy* was getting nearer, beginning to sound like well-played music. Henry didn't venture into the crowd; tight crowds made him feel like a one-legged man. He stayed at the back. *God Bless Our King*: the banner across the road explained it all to him. Edward VII was in town. Henry had forgotten: it was a holiday. He'd be busy later, on the steps. He'd need some sleep.

He couldn't see, but he could tell by the agitation running along the crowd that the King and Queen were on their way past. People got up on their toes, leaned on strangers' backs for a second's glimpse of the approaching carriage. There were children on their fathers' shoulders. Servants hung from upstairs windows. There were more kids clinging to lampposts. There was clapping and cheering. The girls would be on their backs all night, raking it in for Dolly Oblong. Some of the older girls still talked about Victoria's last visit; they still said God save the Queen every time they scratched themselves. He could see the plumes of horsemen. He watched the crowd as shoulders and heads turned with the passing carriage.

—Fuck off!

There were gasps. He saw people looking for the owner of the treacherous roar.

—Fuck off!

And he saw men grabbing at the legs of a small lad clinging to a lamppost, a small lad with an even smaller lad parked on his shoulders.

Who was the angry little man hanging on for his life?

—Fuck off with your hat!

It was me up there, ankles scratched, the trousers being yanked off me. It was five-year-old me – July, 1907. I kicked at grabbing hands and tried to bury my fingers in the green-painted iron of the lamppost. Victor kicked and spat; he was doing his best to save us. But, inch by inch, we were slipping into the crowd. The King's loyal Irish subjects admired our guts but they still wanted to box the ears off us. We were sliding down into their hands.

—UCK, said Victor, and I loved him so much just then I let go of the lamppost to hug his legs. And we fell into the angry crowd.

Why had I done it?

We were under the feet of the crowd but I was far from ready to surrender. Victor already had his teeth, three tiny sharp needles, in a leg. I heard screaming above us. The socked leg went up and Victor went with it.

Why had I told the King of Great Britain and Ireland to fuck off? Was I a tiny Fenian? A Sinn Feiner? Not at all. I didn't even know I was Irish. I saw the procession from my perch on the lamppost and I saw the fat man at the centre of it. I saw the wealth and colour, the shining red face, the moustache and beard that were better groomed than the horses, and I knew that he didn't come from Dublin. I didn't know that he was the King or that the floozy beside him was the Queen. I didn't even know what a king was; no one had ever read me a fairy tale. He looked like an eejit, yet thousands and thousands of people were cheering and waving for him. I was angry. He didn't belong. I looked at his carriage and thought of the cart that had carried us from house to house to basement. And they climbed over one another to get half a goo at him. And I remembered women, face after face, looking down at me in my zinc crib, smiling faces, all the smiles and love, and my mammy and daddy safely behind them. This picture lit up for a second, less than a second, then was gone. And they were still cheering and smiling for the fat foreigner. So I told him to fuck off.

And now I was paying for it. I protected my head with my arms and searched for Victor through the adult legs. I couldn't see him but I could hear him far away. A metal-tipped foot scraped the back of my leg. Hands grabbed me. I was being hauled up by the scruff. Then I heard wood hitting the pavement, wood *tapping* the pavement. The tapping stopped and, suddenly, my scruff was my own again as the hands let go and I heard the one-note song of a mahogany leg slicing the air.

A thud and a yelp and I was standing on my own and looking at my father. He balanced without needing to hop and brought the leg down on the cap of a man who was standing next to me. I heard bone breaking and screams and a police whistle. My father's leg went under his coat. He had it back on in a blink and me in his arms before he'd taken two steps. More police whistles.

—Where did you learn language like that? he said.

—Don't know.

I held on to his neck. I knew the smell of his coat and I never wanted to walk again.

—You're a shocker, he said. —Off we go.

52

—Victor, I said.

—Who's Victor?

—Me brother.

Then I saw him and pointed. He'd been left behind on the road. He was lying on his back, holding a black shoe to his chest and a grey sock in his mouth.

There was little of the crowd left. I saw the rozzers coming at us, saw them over my father's shoulder. I'd never seen so many in one place. They had their batons out and swinging. They pushed and charged through the stragglers. They were gasping to get at us, red and angry.

—See what you've started now, said my father as he picked up Victor. —You can't be saying things like that to the King. He's a visitor.

Victor let go of the shoe and put his arms around my neck, the way mine were around my father's. I saw a baton rising up above my father's head. And we were gone. I felt the baton's shadow as it passed over my cheek. Then I felt the air get out of our way as my father made our escape. He took a crazy route through the gathering rozzers. The wooden leg sent him in mad circles and swoops, everywhere except straight ahead. Batons slammed the air and even other rozzers. I started to laugh.

—Good lad, said my father. —There's nothing as slow as a fat D.M.P. man when he's feeling hard done by.

And Victor started laughing.

—Good lad, said our father. —Good and loud. Let them have it.

We were through the last of the batons. He was still running, first back towards the rozzers, then away, down Elgin Road. But they were coming after us. And my father was slowing. There was a raw wheeze in his breath. His chest was aching; I could feel it through his coat.

—It's the oul' mahogany, he said. —It's no good over long distances. Hang on.

He threw us onto one shoulder, and freed his right arm. He worked it like a piston as he ran and got back some of his speed. The free arm also gave him direction; he could now go straightish, away from the rozzers. We kept laughing back at them but they were gaining on us. We bounced on my father's shoulder, and I hung on to his collar as he turned onto Clyde Road. He nearly tripped as he brought us off the path, under the shade of a tree and across the road. I looked around me. There was no crowd to get lost in, nowhere to hide. I was suddenly scared. Where was the life, all the people and carts? Where was the noise? These houses should have been packed; people should have been spilling out of them. The great steps to the front doors were crying out for women's arses and chatter. But there was no one, except us and the rozzers. All I could hear was the leather and wood of my father's feet, his fighting breath and the laughter that Victor was still spitting out as he bounced on the shoulder beside me. And the rozzers' boots – I could hear them as well, louder and flatter.

We were going down a lane now, over uneven ground. There was no speed under us. I was slipping from my father's shoulder.

—Hold on to the top, said my father, and, before I knew what he meant, we were off his shoulder and he threw us at a high wall. He took a trouser-arse in each hand and lobbed us together. I rose, sailed, hit the wall and hung on. My chin was grazed. I could taste blood and I felt Victor's hands on my neck. A rozzer's whistle came from right beneath us. Terror found grips for my feet. My fingers, then elbows dug into the wall as I raced to the top. The wall shook as my father hit it. I nearly fell back but his fingers grabbed a chunk of me and I was yanked up just as other fat fingers were closing around my ankles. I was pulled headfirst over the wall and we landed on top of the famous coat and my father who was in it.

—Jesus, lads. You're like two bags o' spuds. Get off me there till I get up.

We were in a garden. There was the house to the right, a palace of redbrick and glass. There was a slick lawn and what looked like a miniature bandstand. We'd landed behind a willow tree.

—Come on.

We could hear the rozzers on the other side trying to get over the wall.

54

—Try knockin' it down, my da shouted. —Yeh fat bastards from hell.

He knew where he was going. We followed him out onto the lawn. I'd never felt anything as soft; I was in my bare feet, remember. I looked at the opposite wall. I dreaded having to climb it, and more walls after it. There was blood still flowing over my tongue. But I followed my father and he led us towards the wall. I saw faces at the windows of the house, staring out at us, indignant, frightened faces and one huge grin on a well-fed pup of my age in the clothes of a little important man. Victor saw them too and sent them the old Smart greeting.

—UCK OFF.

—Stop that this minute, said my father. —We're trespassing.

He turned away from the wall, to the left, off the lawn, onto a patch that had been left deliberately wild. We went behind some bushes and trees and I couldn't see the house anymore.

—Come here, he said.

The ground shook: rozzers were falling over the wall.

He lifted me and Victor. We sat in an arm each and hung on to his collar. More rozzers hit the ground. We were trapped.

—Laugh, he said.

And we did.

—Good lads.

He walked behind a big bush. He prodded the ground under with his peg.

—Grand, he said.

He gave the bush a good shove with his fleshed leg, pushed it back with his knee.

—Hang on now, boys, he said, and stepped into the bush.

And we fell.

We fell into darkness and nothing. The only things that existed were my father's neck and coat. There was no other proof that I existed, nothing else to see or feel. We were falling out of our lives.

But we landed. There was the shock of stopping and I heard splashing. My father grunted. My feet were near freezing water; I could feel it under them. I scrambled up to his neck. I could hear other noises, but nothing that I could recognise. I was lying against my father's head but I couldn't see him. My face was pressed to his neck but my eyes still gave me nothing. I heard breathing, and hoped it was ours. My father's sweat warmed my face. I felt his head moving.

—Perfect, he said.

He was looking up; I felt his neck driving his head upwards. I copied him. I had to tell myself to lift my head; there was nothing for me to look up at, nothing to help my eyes climb. I looked up, and saw nothing.

—They'll never find the opening, he said. —They won't even be looking. They'll be trying to climb the wall. Slipping on their own lard.

I could hear the water.

—Welcome to the Swan River, lads, he said.

Victor was starting to cry, a wet blubber like an engine starting.

—Shush shush, said my father. —You're grand.

There was still nothing except the noise that was running water. I was surprised at how big my voice was. I enjoyed it.

—Is it deep? I said.

—Are your feet wet?

—No.

—That answers your question.

He stepped forward – I thought it was forward. He went on the wooden leg first because it was the second flat step that thumped the water.

—Mind you, he said. —Mine are wet enough. Let's get going.

We moved through the freezing, dripping darkness. He felt us shivering, and stopped. He opened his coat, then tucked us inside it; I liked the smell of animals and blood that crept from the fabric that now cuddled me – I didn't know that I was inhaling years of violence and murder. Then he started moving again. He hummed bits of songs. *We'll go home be the water.* And he chatted to us all the way.

—That's the great thing about having one of your legs made of wood, he said. —I'm only freezing half the time.

He splashed on.

—Where are we? I asked.

—Under Dublin, he said.

He took us out of Ballsbridge, along Pembroke Road, under Northumberland Road, under Shelbourne Road and Havelock Square. But he was carrying us through unbroken blackness. He crouched, and slowed down, straightened, rested. By his movements and stops, I could tell how close the walls were to my face, how low the ceiling. I felt wet, slick stone against my legs. I heard the river just below me, fast and slow. I heard other faint noises that could have been anything – claws on stone, wet fur parting the water, dry wings being shaken over my head. I could smell the water, as hard and cold on my nose as a clout from a dead man. And, when the roof was near my head and the walls were almost meeting, when it felt as if my father was burrowing into the earth, I was hit by the whiff of the rubbish that had come from the west with the river, the shit and rot from Kimmage and Terenure, Rathmines and Rane-lagh.

—I'll tell yis something for nothing, boys, said my father. — Wherever you find water you'll find people queueing up to piss in it. If I could swap me leg for a wooden nose I'd be a very happy man.

Water dripping and climbing, the splash of his real foot, our coughs and snorts, his heart when I buried my head in his chest. No sounds from above, no carts, shouts or seagulls. No roaring rozzers. Dublin had disappeared, and so had every-thing else. There was just us and the water. Nothing else. Me and my father and Victor.

And he talked all the way. As he plodded and crept, he filled the black emptiness with words. He led us across Dublin, told us all that we couldn't see.

—That's Beggars Bush above us now, boys. There isn't much to see up there, so we're as well off where we are.

He invented the world above us.

—The house on top of us belongs to a doctor that can make babies disappear.

—How?

—Money, he said. —He can do it with money. It's a sad house, boys. Full of ghosts and tears. And his wife's in the madhouse.

—Why?

—Because she's mad, he said. —She ate her dinner without blessing herself and a big bit of spud got caught in her gullet. She coughed and coughed for days and weeks till her common sense dropped onto the plate in front of her. She has a beard and a tail that swishes every time she coughs. And that's so often, by the way, that the rough hairs of the tail have scrubbed the arse clean off her.

The three of us laughed and we became dozens, hundreds of laughing boys and men as the ground over us trapped our noise and multiplied it.

—And here now —

He stopped.

—We're right under the house of a man who made his money by making the pips for oranges. Listen.

We did.

—What can yis hear?

—Nothing.

—Exactly. And do you know why?

—No, I said. —Why?

—He's dead.

—How did he die?

—He just got fed up and stopped, said my father. —That happens sometimes. We're nearly there now. We'll have to go back up now or we'll be washed into the Dodder and that's not a river you can just walk through like this one.

We saw the striped light above us.

—Here we are, said my da. —Bath Avenue. Hang on tight, boys.

He stopped holding me and began to climb what I could see was a wall of slick blocks. Victor and me could see each other, side by side inside his coat. Victor began to laugh.

—Hang on, said my father. —Not yet. Quiet a sec till we see if the coast is clear.

The side of his face was pushed into the rusting slats of the shore. He pushed the shore up till he could straighten his head and see the world. He looked left and right.

—Right, he said. —You first, mister.

And he shoved me up onto the street. I rolled and then

Victor was beside me, the two of us lying in the gutter. I turned to watch my father climbing out. But he wasn't there. And I knew immediately that he wouldn't be. And I knew, as the terror and rage raced out from my stomach, before I had words to give to them, I knew that I would never see him again.

I knew it even as I heard him talk to us and his voice came out of the ground.

—Bye bye now, boys. Be good for your mammy.

His words burst and disappeared in front of me as I crawled over and peered through the slats and tried to see him. But there was nothing. The memory of his voice was still down there; it drifted just under my face, and then I could hear splashing as he marched away from us.

I dropped my head to the street. I lifted it, and dropped it again.

I wished now that he'd never seen me. Only an hour, maybe two hours before. The royal procession, my perch on the lamppost – I tried to knock them all out of my head. His hands as he lifted me, the crazy escape, his laugh, his hands as he lifted me, his hands as he lifted me – I dropped my head onto the cobbles again, and again and again. I made darkness to match what we'd had down below but nothing came back with it. I was absolutely alone.

But then Victor was crying, pining for something he'd never had. I could hear him now but I didn't want to. I tried and tried to forget the last hours and minutes. I moved and hit the shore with my forehead and tried to kill my father's face and his hands and voice. I hit and hit until I could see nothing and all I could hear was Victor bawling and my blood roaring to escape and I knew that it was dropping through the shore, although I couldn't see it, falling onto the stones and into the Swan River below and on to the Dodder and the bay and the sea. I could feel it hit the water. I could feel it sink and join.

And then I was dead for a while. There was nothing at all. I was dead and gone nowhere. Until something dragged me by the collar, pulled me so that I had to breathe, lifted my head and dropped it, and there was pain again. And did it again. It was Victor. I could hear him before I saw him.

—ENY, he cried. —ENY.

59

And I loved him so much. I was able to stand up through the pain and blindness. I shook my head – lights and flakes flew into my skull. I roared. I shook my head again against the pain. I let the blood fly away. But I could see again. I took off my ruined shirt and pushed it into my forehead, pushed until I could feel the blood retreating.

Victor was beside me.

—Come on, I said. —Let's go.

—SO-DOR, he said.

He wanted to get up on my shoulders.

—ENY, SO-DOR.

—Fuck off, I said.

We went home. Home to the stinking, smoke-choked hollow and the wet basement and our share of our poor mother's lap. I led the way, staring through the dried blood and the agony and the heartache that made a little death of every step away from the rusty shore and the river under it. And Victor held on to my trousers.

My father was a gobshite.

He went back to Dolly Oblong's and slept soundly for a few hours, with his leg at the ready beside him. He woke up, and stretched, then put his ear to the ground and listened to the singing of the floorboards. The house was already busy. There were beds rocking, drifting away from the walls. He strapped on his leg and stood up. Duty called.

He walked down the hall. He listened to the piano and to the noise right over his head, the strangled groan of a man emptying and the bored encouragement from one of the girls. One of the girls from the country. Mary from the dairy, the other girls called her.

—Good man yourself; one more for the pot.

He stopped and picked a dead cigarette from the mat inside the door. Then he opened the door. In time to stop a huge crowd from charging in. A crowd made entirely of rozzers. And the rozzers went mad when they saw Henry. Before he'd a chance to retreat, before he had time to think about it, they were around him and on him, clubbing him into the granite of

60

the steps. Their anger was wordless. Only when he began to sink below the chests and guts of the blue uniforms did Henry remember the morning's fun.

—Now, lads, he said.

But a baton hit him straight on the face and he knew two things: words were useless and he wanted to live. He screamed and shoved his shoulders and massive head into the bodies and pulled away from those who had gone behind him. His face was nearly on the ground but he kept shoving. He ignored the boots, fists and truncheons. He saw steps right below his eyes, his chest was on the ground. He broke away from hands and slid down the steps, under rozzers, and he was on the street. He had the leg off now. Wood hit bone, and he had room. He could see individual uniforms. He had a piece of railing to hold him up. And he held back the rozzers with the promise of his leg. He made it whistle through the air in front of him.

—Come on. Come on!

But they were surrounding him again. He saw a quick shape, and a rock hit the side of his head. He had to get away, didn't let himself realise that he could never come back, could never serve Dolly Oblong again. Escape was all he knew. He looked at the faces on the rozzers as they slowly closed in on him, testing his reach, testing themselves. They were going to kill him. Another rock slapped him and bounced down into the basement well behind him. One last vicious swing – he lit the air – and, as bodies fell back, he skipped and had his leg back on. And he charged.

He was through. Nearly there. Batons hit his head and back but they were nothing. There was fresh air in front of him. He elbowed and shouldered through the last ranks, tearing with his nails, gouging. His shoulders worked and fell. He was through. Just the weight of the ones behind, holding on to him; he lifted and dropped his broken shoulders and fell out of his coat. His palms met the street and lifted him back up. He was weightless without the coat, and gone. Nothing could stop him. He ran out into the dark and the ones who ran after him soon gave up. His hurried tap taps echoed off the walls and back out from the alleys and sent them in every direction. He was gone.

61

They had the coat. Four of them held it. Held it up as if Henry was still in it, or at least a dangerous part of him. Some more of the rozzers looked into it. They held their breath as they peered down the sleeves, tapped the collar with a baton. A rozzer who held one of the shoulders felt the dirt and ooze and let go. The coat dropped like a solid thing and another rozzer kicked it.

—God, it stinks.

—Like its owner.

They all wanted to kick the coat. One of them lit a match and bent down to light it. Another one kicked it away, and something inside it clinked.

—Hold your horses.

A rozzer with gloves picked up the coat and shook it. He found the clink and took Henry's knife from a pocket. He held it up. He passed the knife to another rozzer and gave the coat another shake. Nothing. His glove went into another pocket and came out empty. He laid the coat down on the street and looked for more pockets. He saw one, and put his hand in. It came out empty. He took off the glove and sent his hand back in. It came out holding a piece of paper.

They followed him over to the streetlamp. They crowded around him.

He unfolded the paper. Names.

—Brennan.

—Is that all?

—Desmond, Cecil.

—Jesus.

The love letter from Dolly Oblong. They queued up and read it. They knew the names. They knew the story. The empty house. The blood. Warm kettle and crumbs. The chairs and blood-soaked ropes on the floor. They looked into the darkness my father had gone into. They huddled and named other names. And other empty houses. People who had disappeared. One of them thought of another name, a name from way back.

—Constable Costello.

I never saw my father again.

5

—Tell me again, he'd say.

We huddled in any corner, under any box or bin that we could claim and I made us warm by telling him about the times before the bad times. I told him about Missis Drake, the visiting women, about our father's hands and how he could make a cradle of them.

—Was I alive? he asked me once.

I thought, and decided.

—Yeah, I said. —You were just a baby.

I shared everything with Victor, even the stories that were only mine. He went into the crib beside me. There was never me; it was always us. We slept where we fell and ate whatever we could find and rob. We survived.

The streets were ours. No one could touch us. We knew every sound and warning, every escape route. We grabbed what we needed and ran. No looking back, no need to look left or right, we knew and expected everything. And we could escape without moving. Our dirt merged with the streets. We were made of Dublin muck.

We made a living. We robbed and helped, invented and begged. We were small, so hard to grab. We were pathetic – our mournful, crusted eyes hauled farthings and ha'pennies from purses and pockets. There were thousands of street arabs just like us; we were impossible to find. We were little princes of the streets, little packs of enterprise and cunning. We were often cold, always hungry but we kept on going going going.

We helped the tuggers. We pushed their basket cars for them when they were tired, the stooped men in dungereens and women in blue and pink smocks, the colours fading into sameness, uniforms provided by Mister Lipman, the Russian Jewman. They sang in the mornings when they set out from the yard, pushing the empty baskets. *My hat is frozen to my head. My body's like a lump of lead.* They walked all day, out to where the rich lived, out further to the country towns, Lucan and Dundrum, Sutton and Man o' War, to collect the unwanted clothes and delph, pans and bottles, jars and anything. *My shoes are frozen to my feet from standing at your window.* They tumbled everything into the baskets, made them heavy, and me and Victor were waiting for them for their last stretch home, the last mile to Mister Lipman's scrap yard. They liked Lipman. He was fair. A decent man. And they liked us too. Our timing was always perfect. At the end of the day, when the cold was beginning to remind them that spring could be as cruel a bastard as winter, we'd come up from behind a wall at the bottom of one of the canal bridges and offer to push the rest of the way, or at the corner of Hill Street and Great Britain Street or the last stretch of the North Circular. The bridges and hills of the city paid our wages. We heaved a side of the cart each; we couldn't see where we were going but that didn't matter – we knew every cobble and rut of every street. We knew when to heave or hang on. And when the streets were tarred for the motor cars we knew where we were by the black blisters and stones under our feet.

—You're grand lads altogether. My chin was nearly hopping off the road, only for yis.

They paid us with food they got given out the back doors of the rich houses or with little bits of money after they'd been paid by Mister Lipman.

We blew the ice-cream seller's bugle after his own lips rotted on him; we brought him his customers but we never tasted ice-cream. We caught rats for the dog fighters. We sold bones to Keefe's, the knackers. I was a beggar's assistant and Victor was my own assistant. Rafferty was the beggar's name.

—Call me Mister Rafferty. D'you hear me? I'm down but I'm not out.

He sat outside the Coffee Palace and we gathered the coins

that were thrown at him because he had to hide his legs under his coat.

—Help an old soldier and his childer, missis.

But Dublin was a small city – you couldn't be legless and still walk home without getting caught. He left for bigger cities and we were on our own again. We sold newspapers we'd stolen. We stole back flowers we'd sold. We ate while we ran; we slept standing up. I was learning to swing my daddy's leg, the spare one he'd left behind. I had a blade sewn into the peak of my cap, and I did my own sewing. There was nothing I wouldn't do.

I had charm and invention. Women saw the future Henry under my crust and they melted; they saw a future they wanted now and badly and knew they'd never get. They wanted to touch me but couldn't, so they patted little Victor instead.

—Isn't he gorgeous?

—God love him, he's a dote.

But I knew who they were talking about and what they really wanted. I was never a child. I could read their eyes. I could smell their longing and pain. I'd stand right up against them, confuse them, harass them. Guilt would open their purses. And shame threw the spondulix at us. We were the beggars who never asked for money.

I sometimes crept by the house to see that my mother was still alive. I left food when I had any, even a bottle of gin. There was always a bottle now under the pile of children. She'd suck on it as if her only life was deep inside. I'd seen her crying when a wasted drop slipped down into her chins or shawl; her fingers poked and scratched for the drop and she mourned the loss in little, killing whimpers. If she was on the steps I'd go over and say hello. She knew me; she'd smile. She'd open her arms and I'd crawl in, with Victor, over the other children, just for a minute. She'd cry, and sometimes I would too.

—You're. Get. Ting big.

I'd watch her mouth fighting, remembering shapes. I had to look at every word.

—Are. You. Being good?

—Yes, Mammy.

—Good. Boy. What. Have you. Brought me?

65

I'd stay on her lap for a few minutes but I'd never let myself rest there. I'd grab Victor and go. If it was early enough she'd have the attention for a few last words.

—Stay out. Of troub. Trouble now.

—Yes, Mammy. Bye bye.

—Bye. Bye. Tell. Tell your father. His tea's read. Y.

We fended and coped, we survived and grew, side by side or with Victor on my shoulders. We survived but never prospered. We were never going to prosper. We were allowed the freedom of the streets – no one gave a fuck – but we'd never, ever be allowed up the bright steps and into the comfort and warmth behind the doors and windows. I knew that. I knew it every time I jumped out of the way of a passing coach or car, every time I filled my weeping mouth with rotten food, every time I saw shoes on a child my age. I knew it every time a strange man would offer us money or food to come with him. I knew it, and the knowledge fed my brain. I was the brightest spark in a city full of bright and desperate sparks.

I reinvented rat-catching. We didn't go after the rats; they came to us. We found their nests and took the babies, boiled them and rubbed the soup onto our arms and hands. (We never ate it. You can laugh or gag, but you've never been hungry.) The scent – Jesus, the scent – it drove their parents wild. We dangled our hands in front of their holes and they came at us as if, in their dreams, they'd just seen the dogs that were going to destroy them. They'd scream for the children they could smell on our hands as we dropped them into the sack. We carried the screeching, pounding sack to the betting men around the pit. They loved our rats. They paid me extra to put my hands into the sack. I always did it but I wouldn't let Victor risk his fingers. I loved watching the faces of the men around the pit; I read their contempt, pity and admiration. I stared at the rich ones, the ones I knew already felt guilty about being there, with the worst of the scum of the slums; I'd stare at them as I sank my hand into the sack and felt the fury in the rats' backs and the men would look away. I'd let them see the little boy being asked to maim himself for their entertainment. I'd leave my hand in there until I was ready to faint, I could feel my heart waiting for death; I'd feel the maddened rats sniffing for their children on my wrist and fingers, and I'd hang on just a few seconds longer – before the rats knew that they were licking the hand of the killer. They were all looking at me, the men and boys around the pit; I was more important now than the dogs that were howling and digging into the ground. I loved the silence that I could make with my eyes. It was power. Even the dogs noticed and stopped still. Then I'd grab at the heat and pull out my fist with its screaming rat. I'd hold it over the pit, the rat breaking its back to get its teeth into my veins. Then they'd cheer. I'd hold it a while, looking around, letting them all know that I was the one who was giving them their night out. Then I'd drop the rat. I didn't care what happened after that. I had no interest in the dogs or the betting or kills. I never watched. The dog men paid me, the bookies paid me, the winners paid me. The rich men held out closed hands and let me take money from them. We walked back into the city through the dark, me and Victor. We remembered to wash the rats off our hands and arms before we went looking for a place to sleep. We lay together and I warmed us with my stories. I never slept until I knew that Victor was asleep. Then I joined him. We were in each other's dreams.

We went out to Kingstown to see the *Lusitania*. We got into the crowd and looked out for bulging pockets. Pockets were Victor's speciality. He could empty an inside pocket without touching it. We emptied pockets while their owners stared up at Halley's Comet. I heard one man tell another that it was heading for Earth. I looked at it, the comet, to see if it was getting bigger, but it didn't frighten me. It was just a big star, someone's dead brother.

And we helped the drovers. We met them at Lucan, the muddy men with their sticks and cigarettes, driving the cattle from the Midlands to the sea. We threw small stones at the cows, ambushed them and sent them running into Dublin. And the drovers liked that. They'd see the city in the valley waiting for them and the fit ones would start running too, alongside us, in their cracked boots. They'd get excited; they were spending their money already. They'd laugh when a well flicked stone sent a cow's back legs up and skidding. They thought we were great, the gutties from Dublin. We'd run

67

ahead to make the cattle turn their corners. There'd be twenty and more children, sometimes more than cattle. All forming walls to send the cattle to the yards of Cowtown or down as far as the docks if they'd already been sold. It was a stampede of cattle and children and countrymen, across the river at Kingsbridge, past the Royal Barracks, charging through the big and back streets, careening off the walls of corner houses, sending women and men up the steps to safety, throwing shit and more dust into the air. I'd feel the ground jumping under me. We rustled the cattle when the drovers were slow. If we had the room and time, we could send a bullock down one of the alleys behind the Four Courts and get him lost.

—D'you want to buy a cow, mister?

No butcher in Dublin could resist that offer.

Or we butchered them ourselves. We'd hound the cows into one of our corners and beat their heads with sticks and bits of brick; we'd climb onto a wall to get at their heads. They were stupid but they eventually died. I took the stitches from my cap and took out the blade. The other kids would gawk and giggle and one or two would cry. But they were all hungry and they knew where meat came from. And I was giving it to them. I slit one bullock's throat when it was still running and me running under it. I felt its scorching blood on my head before I got away and I heard the life charge out of it and felt the weight of its death as it fell. I made lines of the blood down my cheeks with my fingers and Victor copied me. And the other children did it. We built a fire with wood that the other kids collected, and dragged the carcass on top of it. We leaned into it and drank the smoke.

And then the drovers weren't so happy to see us when we came out of the bushes at Lucan. Their sticks and anger were no good against us, so they paid us to make sure that none of the cattle or sheep got lost. And butchers with back doors and deeper pockets paid us to make sure that a few of the beasts went astray. There was money in cattle. The police started to join us. The gombeen men from down the country paid them, their younger brothers, to escort the cattle, to make sure that they got to the yards and onto the boats to England. But there was no stopping us. We heard the horses of the mounted rozzers stumbling on the wet, slippery cobbles and we laughed. Eventually, the drovers stopped coming through Lucan. They headed north and south and tried to get the cattle and sheep into the city by backways and along different rivers. But they were wasting their time. It was our city. The destinations were always the same and we didn't mind waiting. There were other ports in Ireland but they were all full of starving children and cute butchers. They had to come our way.

And then there was another source of income from the cattle. Men came to us when we were eating a bullock off a fire. They had beards and hard eyes, two of them, big men made bigger by their greatcoats. We were ready to run or fight – I grabbed a hold of Victor – but they made soothing noises and one of them showed us money in his hand. We were used to strange men offering us money; they were usually uncomfortable and worried, a doddle to confuse and rob. These men were different. They were serious-looking men. They looked straight at us; they weren't interested in what was behind their backs. I stood my ground and the others stood with me.

—Do you love Ireland, lads? said one of them.

They got no answer.

We didn't understand the question. Ireland was something in songs that drunken old men wept about as they held on to the railings at three in the morning and we homed in to rob them; that was all. I loved Victor and my memories of some other people. That was all I understood about love.

I waited for more.

The other man spoke.

—Do you want to earn a few shillings for yourselves?

He wasn't from Dublin. Or from the country. The voice was English but the head on the shoulders was definitely Irish.

One of the bigger kids answered him.

—We might.

He'd taken the words out of my mouth. So I stayed quiet.

—Easy money, said the second one.

—And noble, said the first.

—What do you want us to do?

—Strike a blow for the smallholder.

—What?

69

They wanted us to join the fight against the ranchers, the absentee bastards who were pushing the small men off the land, to help them win back the land that had been stolen from us. They wanted us to go into the yards and maim the cattle. With tar and feathers, and they'd pay us by the tail. They gave us a leg up and we slid into the pens, in among the cattle. We listened for the muttering of watchmen, climbed on gates and poured buckets of the black stuff over the backs and heads of the eejit cows. (I've always loved the smell of tar. It's the smell of life.) They were slow to react but, once they started howling, there was no end. It was Cowtown falling apart. They bucked and slammed into each other. It was no place for children. I got Victor onto the wall and tied the tails around my waist. I slipped among the hoofs and shit, and cut, and draped more tails over my shoulder. For the smallholder. For Ireland. For me and Victor.

I watched and listened, sniffed the air, grew up. Things were happening. I made my own vending licence, hammered out a piece of metal from a biscuit tin one of the tuggers let me have, and I sold old newspapers, week-old news. I listened to the men and women reading the headlines as they walked away, before they realised that they'd read them before. A thing called Sinn Féin was mentioned. The name Carson was followed by curses or spitting. And Home Rule. It meant nothing to us who had no homes, but I listened and tried to understand. King Edward died and I didn't see anyone weeping as the news got carried around Dublin. They'd wanted to kill me when I'd insulted the King but, now that he was dead, they just shrugged and kept walking.

I was eight and surviving. I'd lived three years in the streets and under boxes, in hallways and on wasteland. I'd slept in the weeds and under snow. I had Victor, my father's leg and nothing else. I was bright but illiterate, strapping but always sick. I was handsome and filthy and bursting out of my rags. And I was surviving.

But it wasn't enough. I was itching for more.

—Come on, Victor, I said. —We need to better ourselves.

I washed myself and Victor from a bucket at the back of Granny Nash's house and then we went down to the national school behind the big railings. It was late morning; the yard was empty. We went into a huge hall. I stopped at the first door. We could hear children reciting something on the other side. I knocked and waited. I held Victor's hand.

—Yes, said a voice that belonged to a woman.

I didn't look yet. By not looking, I could hope that the face would be smiling and lovely. I could even expect it. I could keep talking.

—We've come for our education, I said.

—Have you, indeed? said the voice.

—Yeah.

I looked at brown boots that had a woman's toes neatly packed into their points.

—What age are you?

—Nearly nine, I said.

—You are not, said the voice.

—Yes, I am, I said.

—You're certainly a fine lad, she said. —But, you know, you're four years late.

—I was busy, I said.

—And what about the little man beside you?

—He's me brother, I said. —He wants his education too. Where I go he goes.

—Is that so, now?

—Yeah, I said. —Once you know that, you'll have no trouble from either of us. We've come here to learn.

She started laughing. I looked. She was looking down at me, a big-sized mess of a lad, with eyes made khaki by ancient scabs and hair that stood up to get away from the nits. But I had a smile that made women wonder and I used it now. I smiled up at her and watched the results.

She blinked, and coughed. She reached out, then stopped herself. But she had to touch me; I could see that. And she reached out again; she braved the filth and rested her hand on my hair. I looked straight back at her.

—What's your name, so? she asked.

I saw brown eyes and some slivers of hair that had escaped

71

from a bun that shone like a lamp behind her head. There were little brown buttons, in pairs, running the length of her brown dress, like the heads of little brown animals climbing quietly to her neck.

—Henry Smart, I said.

—And the little lad?

—Victor Smart, I said.

—Where do you live, Henry?

—Over there, I said, but I didn't point. —What's your name?

—Miss O'Shea, she said. —Do you have any friends in my class?

—No, I said.

I held up my father's leg for her to notice. It was my birth cert. She looked straight at it. Her eyes seemed younger than the rest of her face. She looked at the leg; I could see shock and amusement.

—What's that? she said.

—A leg that's made out of wood, said Victor.

—It used to belong to our daddy, I told her. —But he's gone now.

And Victor started crying.

I put my arm around Victor's shoulder as his crying turned to coughing and I smiled at her again, although I could feel Victor's coughs through my arm and they were real. She smiled back and we were elected.

I liked her.

—Come on in, she said. —*Tar istigh*. That means Come in, the pair of you.

—*Tar istigh*, I said.

—Very good, she said. —You're quick.

—I know, I said. —I've never been caught.

By the end of the first day I could struggle through the first four pages of a book about a happy woman washing her doorstep and Miss O'Shea had fallen in love with me. In a room that was warmer than anything I'd ever known, full of snuffling and learning off by heart, holy songs and dust that was bright and clean. Victor fell asleep beside me. He coughed but didn't wake. And she was beside me too. She was fighting the urge to pat me again. I could hear her joints crying, pleading to let her go.

—Two and two? she said.

—Don't know, I said. —Two and two what?

—Cows, she said.

—Four, I said.

—That's too easy, a kid behind me complained.

I looked back and he shrivelled.

—Twenty-seven and twenty-seven, she said.

—What?

—Bottles.

—What's in them?

—Porter.

—Fifty-four.

I heard her elbow give up the fight, then felt her fingers on my shoulder.

—Are you a genius, maybe? she asked.

—What's a genius? I asked.

—A boy with a big brain, she said.

—More than likely, I said.

I learnt that the best toilets came from Stoke-on-Trent and that God was our father in heaven, creator of heaven and earth. Then someone outside walked past jangling a bell and all the other children stood up. I nudged Victor and held him up as I stood with the rest. The desk came part of the way with me; my legs were squashed into it. I straightened and it fell back to the floor. There was some laughing behind me but it stopped when I lifted a shoulder. They said a prayer I didn't know – I didn't know any. Then they trooped out, line by line.

—Will your mammy be waiting for you? Miss O'Shea asked as we passed her at the door.

—Yes, I said. —Can we come back tomorrow?

—Yes, of course. This is where you should be.

—It's nice, said Victor.

We slept near the school. The memory of the warmth kept us going for the night. Victor's coughing slowed and levelled and I joined the rhythm of his breathing and rode it to sleep. He woke me up.

—She was nice, wasn't she? said Victor.

—Yeah, I said.

—Are you going to marry her?

—Don't know, I said. —I might.

We stood up for the new day. I was hoping for more. Less prayers, more information. That was what I was there for. And reading. I wanted that power.

We were two hours early. We were hungry but I didn't want to stray. We stayed out of the yard, on the street side of the railings, until we saw her arriving. She carried a basket with books poking out of it. Her coat was open and she was wearing the same brown dress. She went to the door and we followed her. She turned when my foot stopped the door.

—Wait for the bell, she said. —You're keen, aren't you?

—Yes, I said.

—Are you married, missis? said Victor.

Anger glanced across her face but didn't stay.

—No, she said. —Would I be here if I was?

She brought the door over before Victor could answer.

—The bell, she said. —It won't be long.

And she shut the door.

—Never ask questions, Victor, I said as we turned back to see what was going on in the yard.

—Why not? he said.

—If you just watch and listen, I said, —you'll get better answers. I could have told you she wasn't married meself.

—How?

—No rings, son. No rings on her fingers.

—Oh yeah.

—Oh yeah is right. Watch and listen and the answers will come strolling up to you. What do you do?

—Watch and listen.

—Good man.

So we watched the playacting in the school yard. Kids playing. Running and tumbling, hanging on to each other. It didn't make much sense to us. But there were others there like us, at the sides of the yard, looking at or ignoring the chasing and skipping. There was money changing hands in one corner. I noted the faces, the bare feet, the readiness to run. We weren't alone in the yard.

Holy God, we praise Thy name. Lord of all, we bow before Thee.
We sang for most of the morning. It annoyed me but Victor
liked it. He caught on to the words quickly and yelled them at
the ceiling. But it wasn't what I'd come for. I could sing
whenever I wanted to – I'd sung for money outside the Antient
Concert Rooms. I didn't need a school or a teacher to show me
how. And the songs – hymns, she called them. *Angels, saints
and nations sing. Praised be Jesus Christ our King.* I knew I'd earn
no shillings singing that shite on the streets. But it was warm
and I sang to the skies whenever Miss O'Shea walked up my
aisle, which was a lot more often than she walked up any of the
others.

But, eventually, she tapped her tuning fork twice on her desk
and we all sat down.

—Now, she said, up at the blackboard. —Sums. Henry?

It took me a while to realise: she was talking to me.

—Yeah?

—Yes, Miss O'Shea.

I didn't understand. I waited.

—Say Yes, Miss O'Shea, she said.

—Yes, Miss O'Shea.

—Very good. Stand up, please.

—I'm only after sitting down.

More laughing at the back.

—Stand up, Henry.

She said it kindly, so I got out of the desk, tried to hold it
down as I rose. Victor's weight beside me helped.

She picked up a long piece of chalk and wrote $6 + 6 + 14 - 7 =$
on the blackboard. She did it without looking at the numbers;
her eyes roved the classroom. Then, tapping the board under
each number, she spoke.

—Now, Henry. Tell us all. If a man has six very valuable
male dogs and six very valuable bitches and they have fourteen
puppies but he has to sell seven of them because he's been a bit
slow with the rent and the landlord is threatening to evict him,
how many dogs will he have left?

—Nineteen, I said.

—Yes, she said. —Six plus six plus the fourteen puppies
minus the seven for the rent equals nineteen. See? It's easy,

75

isn't it? Thank you, Henry. Now, I want you all to use your heads like Henry.

Victor slapped my leg. He was delighted. And so was I. My first compliment.

—You can sit down again now, Henry.

I slid easily into the desk.

A hand went up in front of me.

—Yes, Cecil?

—Who did he sell the pups to, miss?

—Different people, Cecil. Now.

She cleaned the board.

—Hey, miss. My uncle buyed one of them pups.

We spent the rest of the morning buying and selling pups and dividing bits of cakes. I was several slices ahead of the rest and Victor was no slowcoach either; I could almost see the jam on his chin. I was learning nothing new. But I was happy. I knew that I'd be able for anything.

But it couldn't last.

I was writing my first sentence, MY NAME IS HENRY SMART, on a slate with my own piece of chalk, and Victor was busy beside me, MY NAME IS VICTOR SMART, his letters straight and evenly white. The room was quiet, just the noises of fifty-seven concentrating children and the scraping of fifty-seven pieces of chalk, when the door opened and, before I looked up to see who was coming or going, a voice announced the end of our education.

—Two strange boys.

Victor's chalk skidded across his slate. I couldn't move. I was too big for my desk again. I was stuck, trapped.

The nun at the door wasn't even looking at us. She was looking at Miss O'Shea who was standing beside her desk, straight and twitching, like a cornered rabbit. So the first thing I saw of the nun was her profile. A nose shaped like a sail and just as white. The rest of her face hid behind her habit. The nose was aimed at Miss O'Shea.

—We've a couple of strangers with us today, said the nun.

—Yes, Mother, said Miss O'Shea.

76

—You've taken over enrolment duty now, have you, *Miss* O'Shea?

—No, Mother.

Miss O'Shea sounded like a child; it was me and Victor against the nun.

—Good, said the nun. —It's an onerous, thankless task. Better suited to an old crow like me.

She moved and turned like a boat in water. She was facing us. Glaring at us. Two black eyes divided by the white beak. Coming at us.

—Let me see the strange boys.

And she was in front of us, and over us.

—Do you have a name, the bigger boy?

—Yeah.

—Yes, Mother.

—You're not my mother.

—You think I'm going to get angry, don't you? You think I'm going to lose my temper. Don't you?

—No.

—No, Mother.

—You're not my mother.

Victor coughed.

—Cover your mouth when you're coughing, the smaller boy, said the nun who called herself Mother. —We're all marching towards our eternal rest without needing help from the likes of you. Your name, the bigger boy?

—Henry Smart, I said.

—Are you English, with a name like that?

—No.

—As far as you are aware. Do you know your father, Henry Smart?

My father's leg was under the desk.

—Yeah, I said.

She sniffed. Her nose and eyes went on Victor.

—And the smaller boy. What do they call you?

—They don't call me anything, said Victor. —Henry would kill them if they did.

—Yes, she said. —I am sure that he would. Who sent you here?

—Our parents, I said.

—Who are they when they're at home?

—They're our mother and father.

—You're being cheeky again, aren't you? I don't think you'll be staying here. No, I don't. You were let in by mistake. This is not the place for you. You must be twelve, she said.

—I'm eight, I said.

—He's nearly nine, said Victor.

—No, he is not, she said. —No, no. I don't think you'll be staying with us.

I didn't care any more. There was no point. I felt stiff and huge and too old for my desk – maybe she was right about my age – so I stayed put. I decided to say nothing until I was angry. I trusted my anger. And answering her without it had only made me feel stupid.

—Have you heard of Our Lord?

She was talking to Victor.

—What?

—Our Lord. Do you know Jesus?

—I do, yeah, said Victor. —That's him there, your man hanging over the blackboard.

She grabbed his arm.

—Pagans. The pair of them. It's Saint Brigid's you should be in, she hissed. —I knew it!

Saint Brigid's was the orphanage up on Eccles Street. I knew all about Saint Brigid's.

I was up out of the desk and I grabbed Daddy's leg on the way. The desk fell apart and Victor fell with it but she held on to him.

—Give him back! I shouted.

I didn't wait for an answer. I just lifted the leg and whacked at the nose. She rose and flew and skidded across three desks and landed in a black heap on top of half a dozen screaming boys. She'd left Victor behind.

—Come on, Victor.

We ran to the door. I held his hand. He was coughing again. Miss O'Shea let us past. I turned at the open door and shouted into the room.

—MY NAME IS HENRY SMART!

I nudged Victor.

—MY NAME IS —

He coughed. It came from somewhere dark inside him. I watched the colour drop from his face as he waited for the air to turn and let him breathe.

—VICTOR —

He grabbed more air.

—SMART.

—Remember those names, all of you, I said.

I looked at Miss O'Shea.

—And you remember. That you were the woman who taught Henry Smart how to write his name.

She was blushing and her mouth was wobbling. I wanted to stay. But the nun was back on her feet. She was swaying a bit, but getting her head back. She came at us.

—Let her have it, Victor, I said.

Victor filled the room with his roar.

—FUCK OFFFFF!

And we were gone. Out onto the street and away. We ran until we were safe, just two snot-nosed, homeless kids among thousands. We ran to the other side of town.

Far away from Saint Brigid's.

I'd had two days of schooling. But it was enough. I knew it was in me. I could learn anything I wanted. I was probably a genius. Victor started crying and I knew why. It was the warmth, the singing, making words, the chalk working across his slate, the woman who'd made him feel wanted. I missed it too, already, but there were no tears. We sat under the wall at Baggot Street Bridge and hid from the world.

We were well out of it. Miss O'Shea had just been a bit of good fortune. A lucky knock on the door. The nun had been the normal one. Mother, she'd wanted to be called. Never. Not even Sister. Fuck her. And religion. I already hated it. *Holy God we praise Thy name.* Fuck Him. And your man on the cross up over the blackboard. Fuck Him too. That was one good thing that came out of all the neglect: we'd no religion. We were free. We were blessed.

—Hey, Victor, I said. —Come here till I tell you. We haven't had a thing to eat in three days. Are you hungry?

79

—Yeah.

I got him onto his feet.

—Come on, so. What d'you fancy?

—Bread.

—Fair enough. Is that all?

—Yeah.

—You're easily pleased. What does V.I.C.T.O.R. spell?

—Victor, said Victor.

—Good man.

We went off looking for a shop with bread in it, with a good wide door for escape and some short-sighted old josser behind the counter. Dublin was full of them.

And then Victor died.

On the same day as the new king was crowned. I woke up but Victor didn't. But, actually, he did. He woke me. His coughing. I was awake. Terrified, like I'd never slept. Like I'd just been born; empty. It was so dark. I felt something over me, and lifted my hand. I touched something and I remembered where I was. We were under a tarpaulin, behind the Grand Canal Dock. We'd crawled under it, out of the rain, the night before. Victor coughed again and I remembered the noise that had pulled me from sleep. I'd never heard it as bad. It was a cough that broke bone, an unbelievable hack that would destroy anything in its way.

—Victor?

I couldn't see him, although I knew that he was right against me, where he always was when we slept. I could feel him. I touched him, waited for another cough.

—Victor. Stop. Sit up.

I tried to wake him, to get him sitting. But I couldn't. I couldn't get a proper grip. I found his cheeks and rubbed them. All I wanted was to hear another cough. I still couldn't see him. I searched for the edge of the covering, to give him air. To see him. I rolled along under the low tarpaulin and kept rolling until I was out from under it. I stood up and lifted it and peered back in.

I could see him now. I let morning light in by lifting the

tarpaulin roof with my back. I knew he was dead, even as I rushed back in. His mouth was open, and his eyes, staring into the darkness. There was a mark, where a line of watery blood had run from his mouth past his ear. I rubbed it away with my sleeve. There was nothing in his eyes now, just what I thought was the memory of his last agony and terror – the last cough and the utter darkness on top of him. I'd been right beside him. He was white and glazed. His mouth was stretched, the cracked, bursting lips were losing colour as I looked. He was changing there under me, hardening, gone. I thumped his chest, and got nothing back. He was dead. I thumped again. I felt his face. He was warm. I put my cheek to his mouth, waited to feel a breath, hoped, any tiny tickle. There was nothing. I pressed my cheek to his mouth, tried to go deeper for signs of my brother's life. I pushed; I tried to climb into him. I felt wetness on my cheek. My own tears. Victor was dead.

I held his hand. I waited for his fingers to curl around mine. To prove me wrong. I dragged him out from under the tarpaulin, hauled him across to a cinder path. I was a shadow across him. I got out of the way of the sun's early rays. I still hoped. The heat would loosen him, send a shiver of life through him. His fingers would stretch, curl and squeeze mine. He'd sit up and grin. And cough.

The sun made a wet skin of the frost on the path and weeds but it did nothing to Victor. His neck was crooked, as if he'd been hanged.

I left him there.

He was dead. I wouldn't let myself be fooled into thinking anything softer. I wasn't going to see him up there with the other stars, with the first Henry – burning gas, a celestial fart – and all his brothers and sisters, twinkling up there in a happier place. He was dead. I wasn't even going to look at the sky.

The city was quiet. None of the morning charging and madness that usually had us on our feet and ready before we'd time to remember where exactly we were. Us. We. I'd no more use for those words.

I walked.

There were some people out. I could hear a car off somewhere and a man shouting at a dog or child. I passed a

81

woman who was waiting for a shop to open. She wanted to be the first, to have the shopkeeper to herself for a minute, to plead with him to extend her credit. I could tell by the way she hid in her shawl and by the aggression in her eyes as she looked out at me. I went on. I put my hands in the holes which had once been pockets. Could she tell that I'd just walked away from my dead brother? I took my hands back out.

The flags were out and flapping and there was brand new bunting hanging over Grafton Street. I remembered now: the new king was being crowned, over in London. It was a holiday. That was why the day hadn't taken off yet. We were going to walk out to Kingstown, to work the crowds around the bandstand on the east pier; that had been the plan – Victor's idea; he loved the boats and the music.

I walked all over the city. Away from the main streets and bridges there were no flags, no banners. George V's coronation. And Dublin didn't care. And my brother was dead on a cinder path behind the Grand Canal Dock and nobody cared about that either. Another dead child. We'd found dozens of them on our travels, me and Victor. There wasn't even a reward for them.

I walked all day. The city filled. People came out and strolled. It was a warm day, with a nice breeze that made the flags snap. What had killed Victor? Consumption, probably; I didn't know – I was only nine. It was the cough. I knew that now. It had got darker and deeper; it had brought blood with it in the last months. But we'd never said anything about it. It was just a cough. In the dead of night, when we walked alone through the streets, when the horses were stabled and the hawkers were at home, that was what we heard – the city coughing. That was all we heard at four in the morning, before the seagulls got up on the air and started their squawking, bullying the city into waking up. Dead, dead silence except for the thousands coughing, a steady, terrible beat coming from the rooms above us and the basement areas, children and adults being choked to death by poverty. They were too late; we could hear the pain in the noise, we could feel life desperately clinging. It was how night-time was measured in the slums, in blood coughs and death rattles. And Victor had been coughing along with them and I had refused to hear it. I was only nine. There was only me and Victor. We were all that mattered. He would never leave my side. His cough had been different. Just a cough. It was what you did when you breathed Dublin air. When you slept on the ground. When you didn't have shoes. (Just a few years later, when I smashed the window in the G.P.O. and started shooting, it was at shoes that I was aiming, in the window display across the street in Tyler's.) You coughed when you ate bad food or none. When you'd never worn a coat. When everyone else around you coughed. When you'd no mother to fix you and no father to run for the doctor. And no doctor who'd come, anyway. When you'd nothing except your big brother. Who was only nine. And scared.

The city killed Victor. And, today, the King was being crowned. In another city. In London. Did they cough till they died in London? Did kings and queens cough up blood? Did their children die under tarpaulins? I imagined myself on a street in London, and Victor was trotting beside me, chatting away and keeping the eye on everything. But someone knocked against me and I was back in Dublin and alone.

There was something happening. A crowd had gathered and others were running to join it. I was on College Green, beside the statue of King Billy. Some in the crowd cheered and I could see the shape of a fight push its way to the edge. I went over, out of the shadow of the Bank, and burrowed my way to the front.

Two men and a woman, their backs to the railings of Trinity College, watched by a tight crowd of maybe a hundred men and some women, riddled with creeping, quiet urchins like myself. The woman was holding a burning torch; the flames were black and raging, climbing over each other. The men held up a Union Jack.

—It's a disgrace, said someone.
—On today of all days.
—It's an absolute disgrace.

One red-faced man came out of the crowd with a walking stick raised but other men grabbed him and pulled him back in. And now the woman touched the flag with the torch. The flames caught the cloth and devoured it. Some of the crowd cheered, some booed, and by the time the two men dropped the flag there was very little of it left. The woman stood still and unimpressed. I heard police whistles but the woman didn't budge. Others ran; still others cheered.

—You're in right trouble now, yeh Fenian bastards.

The men and woman didn't move as the rozzers filled the street and scattered the crowd. I stayed and watched. The wind picked up tiny flakes of charred cloth and scattered them over us. I grabbed a piece and expected to be burnt. But I felt no pain. I wondered had I missed it and I opened my fist. It was there. My fragment was red; a tiny island of red left in the middle of a burnt-black triangle.

The rozzers had arrived but there wasn't much left for them.

—It's the fuckin' Countess again, said one of them.

—God, she's a terrible woman. And Griffith, the hoor.

The rozzers surrounded the two men and the woman they'd called the Countess and led them away. They held her arms and pushed her forward but she said nothing and didn't look back. And they were all gone. It was over. I was alone again.

I wanted my mother's lap. Just for a little while. I wanted to feel her shawl against my neck. For a while, an hour or two – a minute. But she was gone, and all the children too. She wasn't on the step and she wasn't in the basement. There was no one down there, and nothing at all left. They'd been evicted again. I hoped; still in the city, still alive. I sat on the step for a while. For hours, perhaps; I didn't know. I ignored the night above me; I never looked at it. Then I stood up and went looking for my mother.

PART TWO

6

I held my left arm across my eyes and smashed the window. I heard the glass breaking into smaller pieces on the pavement outside. Glass was breaking all around me and more glass from the two floors above was falling past the window, glass crashing onto glass. I hacked away at the remaining shards with the butt of my rifle. There was nothing outside, beyond the broken windows and the pillars, except the street and the usual noises that came with it – whining trams, the yells of children, shoe nails on cobbles and pavement, the women at the Pillar Stall shouting the prices and varieties of their flowers. Only the shock and curses of people dodging the falling glass outside stamped significance on the morning.

Inside, behind us, it was different. Commandant Connolly's voice drove through the rest of the noise.

—Barricade the windows with mailbags, typewriters, anything that's handy.

The main hall was being transformed. Men in the uniforms of the Volunteers and Citizen Army, and most in bits and pieces or no uniform at all, were carrying bags of sand on their shoulders, and tables, chairs, ledgers, mailbags, sacks of coal and piling them into defensive walls at the main and side doors and all the windows. The women of Cumann na mBan carried urns and cauldrons, trestle tables and baskets to the stairs and down to the basement. Other men humped provisions and guns, sledgehammers and laundry hampers in from the courtyard. Others had been sent down to the Metropole Hotel and across to the Imperial for bedding, supplies and anything else that might come in handy. Orders were barked, barked again and obeyed. There were younger ones running back and forth between the officers, delivering and bringing back messages. They moved frantically, riddled with excitement, while the older ones, the men and nearly men, were slowed by the knowledge that they were witnessing their own most important moments.

A shot sent us to the floor. Bits of the stuccoed ceiling fell on us; I felt a chunk of it hopping off my back.

—Who fired that shot?

—Me, said someone at the other side of the hall. —I only dropped my gun and it went off.

—Will yis all be careful. We don't want to kill someone.

A huge man with an axe was demolishing one of the counters; he cut through the red teak like it was cake. He needed the wood for the big kettle that sat on the tiles near his feet; Commandant Clarke had called for tea. Another man, without a uniform, ran a coil of copper wire around table and chair legs and a pile of typewriters, strengthening his barricade. Post office workers were running to the main door and I could hear the thundering feet of the last of them coming down the stairs, escaping before it was locked and barricaded.

—You're welcome to stay now, comrades, Paddy Swanzy told them as he knocked the white dust off his Citizen Army uniform. —Jesus, look it. I'm already filthy and we haven't even started yet. My mother would kill me if she saw me.

—If you knew your mother, said Seán Knowles.

—Ah now, Paddy shouted after him. —If I die today at least I can say that I once knew *your* mother.

—Keep the voices down, boys, said an officer I didn't know, a Volunteer. —And no mocking the mammies, for God's sake. If Commandant Pearse hears you, you'll be out on your ears before the fighting starts. And there's few enough of us as it is.

Few enough of us.

Easter Monday, 1916.

One of the runners came up to the officer. He wiped his nose on his sleeve and reported.

—There's tills full of money over behind the counter, sir.

—Good man, O'Toole. Good man. We'd better find a safe place for them.

Good man, O'Toole. The fuckin' eejit. I looked at his trousers as he went off with the officer and there wasn't the bulge of a wad or a pull on a leg that would have come from the weight of half-crowns or florins. The eejit. I could tell from the back of his head, he was one of the Christian Brothers' boys, here to die for Ireland, dying to please his betters. With a little rifle that had once belonged to an American Boy Scout, tied to his back with a bit of string. I was ready to die myself – I was banking on it – but I'd still been hoping to get a few quid into my pocket in case the worst came to the worst and I lived. We were locked into the biggest post office in the country and, even though it was now the centre of the new republic, it was still a post office, a land of opportunity, a great big building full of money. And I wanted some of it. My conscience wouldn't let me ignore it. I watched O'Toole carrying a pile of till drawers out to the stairs, the self-importance running out of him in his snot. His mammy had combed his hair that morning, before he'd gone off on his manoeuvres for Ireland. He was seventeen. Three years older than me. And lifetimes younger.

—Barricade those bloody windows. Quick!

—Less of that language!

—And someone go out and spread that broken glass over the street. It'll stop the cavalry.

I was fourteen. None of the others knew, or would have believed it. I was six foot, two inches tall and had the shoulders of a boy built to carry the weight of the world. I was probably the best-looking man in the G.P.O. but there was nothing beautiful about me. My eyes were astonishing, blue daggers that warned the world to keep its distance. I was one of the few real soldiers there; I had nothing to fear and nothing to go home to.

Paddy Swanzy and some other men jumped over the counter and came back with books and more ledgers, everything and anything that could be built into barricades – a filing cabinet, half-filled mailbags, stools, empty tills, pads of money orders, more ledgers, desks and telegram pads.

—These things'll be useless after we take over, said Charlie Murtagh. —We'll put harps on everything.

—The starry plough on everything, you mean, said Paddy Swanzy. —Including the arses of newborn babbies.

I kept watch while the barricade began to climb up the window, and I pocketed some of the money order pads and a rubber date stamp.

Felix Harte was at the window next to me.

—How long will we last, Henry?

—They don't even know we're here, I said.

We waited for the Empire to wake up.

It was Monday, the 24th of April. Just after noon. A beautiful, windless holiday. And Henry Smart, stark and magnificent in the uniform of the Irish Citizen Army, was ready for war. In a uniform he'd bought bit by bit with money he'd robbed and squeezed. In the uniform of the workers' army. I had the whole works – the bandolier with pockets full of bullets, a snake belt that rested nicely on my hips, riding britches that had never touched a horse. They were strictly for the officers but nobody had complained when I'd turned up in mine.

—That's a grand pair of britches on a bugler, Michael Mallin, the second in command, had said.

—I'm not a bugler any more, I'd told him.

I'd played *The Last Post* at the grave of O'Donovan Rossa the year before. The history books will tell you that it was William Oman but don't believe them: he was tucked up at home with the flu.

The left side of my slouch hat was held up by the Red Hand badge of the Irish Transport and General Workers Union. I was a member of the union, although I'd never had a job. I was walking dynamite in that uniform.

Sackville Street was emptying. The city was beginning to notice. There was a crowd still clinging to the area in front of Nelson's Pillar and out in front of the G.P.O., waiting to see what happened.

—Remember now. Shoot anything in a uniform.

—Wha'? said Paddy Swanzy. —Even the postmen?

—No lip.

The street and the whole city had been packed; strolling crowds on their way to the races in Fairyhouse and even to the

90

beaches at Sandymount and Malahide, and the Spring Show at the R.D.S. Off-duty soldiers held up the corners. I saw people across the street, on the corner of North Earl Street, looking up at the men on the roof, the old boys from St Enda's, Pearse's school. I wished that I was up there with them. They could see everything, and when night came, if we were still here, they could point their rifles at the stars and shoot. And they'd know before the rest of us when the war had started. Better yet, I could have been outside, on top of Nelson's Pillar. With the old one-armed bollocks protecting my head, I could have commanded the city; I could have watched the whole place topple.

Few enough of us.

I liked it that way. *We Serve Neither King Nor Kaiser*. So said the message on the banner that had hung across the front of Liberty Hall, headquarters of the Irish Transport and General Workers Union. If I'd had my way, *Or Anyone Else* would have been added, instead of *But Ireland*. I didn't give a shite about Ireland.

I could hear gunfire now. Probably from Boland's Bakery, or the Four Courts. And a soft thud that might have been an explosion; the Magazine Fort up in the Park. Or maybe the Citizen Army lads had taken the Castle. It was hard to tell where exactly the firing was coming from. The revolution had started. But outside, it was still a holiday.

Connolly and Pearse, and Clarke with them, were about to go back outside.

Only four or five hours earlier I'd been sitting on the steps of Liberty Hall, letting the sun send me to sleep. The Hall had been my home for the last three years. I'd been up all night. The sun was warm and tolerant; its heat was already in the stone – I could feel it rising around me. I'd been sitting there since just after dawn. I'd seen Commandant Pearse arrive in full uniform, pistol, provisions, sword, the lot, all under his greatcoat, cycling over Butt Bridge, the Commander-in-Chief of the Army of the Irish Republic and President-Elect, struggling across the bridge and sweating like a bastard. And his little brother and faithful hound, Willie, pedalling away behind him. The other officers had arrived after him. Some of them had gone straight off to the other battalion meeting points around the city, bringing some of the waiting men with them, and the rest were still inside the Hall. We'd be moving off soon. But now, the excitement of the day and days ahead was far away from me. My slouch hat seemed to be pressing my head to my chest. The gulls above were floating and silent and there was the hot-day smell of old drink coming off the river. I closed my eyes, and everything was gone.

Cheers woke me and the first shock was the numbers of men around me. They were suddenly there, right beside me, sitting, starting to stand, dozens of them, most of them Citizen Army, but strangers too I'd never seen before. I had wondered if anyone at all would turn up after Eoin MacNeill's cancellation the day before – *no parades, marches, or other movements of the Irish Volunteers will take place. Each individual Volunteer will obey this order strictly in every particular* – but there was a fair gang now outside the Hall; not the thousands we needed to win but enough to be starting with. The thousands, the whole country would follow. That was the plan. The hope. The men were cheering the arrival of a car, a sparkling De Dion Bouton. I recognised the driver. It was The O'Rahilly, in the uniform of a Volunteer officer; the story had been doing the rounds that he wasn't going to turn up. The back of his car and the front seat beside him were packed with guns. He climbed out of the car and saluted. His waxed moustache couldn't hide his grin.

A crowd had gathered, across at the quay wall and in the shadow of the Loop Line bridge. They had no idea of what was about to happen, despite our guns and uniforms. And many of the men in uniform didn't know, either; they thought they were going out on manoeuvres. There were more onlookers now than rebels. And the rebels, the new Irish Republican Army, made up of the Volunteers and Citizen Army – and, again, few were aware yet of its existence – were a sorry-looking gang. Some of them had just the hat. Others made do with a bandolier. Some had the trousers or a jacket but, except for the officers and commandants, Henry Smart was the only one with the lot. The most common gun was the single-shot Mauser, from the pile that had come off the *Asgard*, a good rifle when it was made fifty years before, but much too slow in a fight

92

against an empire, and inclined to overheat. There were plenty who didn't have guns at all.

A voice got us moving.

—Form fours!

We assembled in front of the Hall, the main noise now our feet finding position, until Willie Oman started his bugling. There was no stopping the little fucker once he'd started; he must have died with blisters on his lips. I was given two sledgehammers to carry.

—Can you manage the two?

—Of course he can, the buck.

Connolly was on the steps now, and Pearse beside him, and other officers coming out of the Hall. A fine body of men: Clarke was there, as old and as frail as Ireland; MacDiarmada, left lopsided by polio, was leaning on his stick; Plunkett had his neck wrapped in bandages and looked like death congealing.

A woman ran up the steps and shouted at Pearse.

—Come home!

Pearse turned from her. He spoke to Mick Collins, behind him.

—Who's your woman? I asked Paddy Swanzy who was standing to my left.

—Can't say that I know, said Paddy. —She's put the colour into Pearse's cheeks though, look it.

—She's his sister, said Seán Knowles.

—Ooops, said Paddy. —Watch it, lads. Jimmy's hopping.

He was talking about Connolly and he was right. Connolly was furious. He barked something over his shoulder. Collins barked at somebody else. Then we heard the order.

—By the left. Quick march!

And Pearse's sister was left alone on the steps as the generals ran down before we'd marched off without them. They went to the front. The crowd cheered and jeered as we went past.

—Here come the toy soldiers!

—Bang bang.

—Do your mammies know you're out?

There weren't many of us – there couldn't have been more than two hundred after the others had followed their officers to the other posts throughout the city – but the thump of our feet in unison, like strange echoes that preceded bullets or the knocking off of seconds before something momentous, shuddered through me and shut up the crowd. Two hundred marching men, and Winnie Carney, Connolly's secretary, with her huge typewriter in a case and a Webley revolver, almost as long as her leg, in her holster. We looked odd but we sounded like business.

At the corner of Abbey Street and Marlborough Street Paddy Swanzy tried to sink into his jacket.

—The missus, he said. —I'm not here.

—Paddy! Paddy! I see yeh!

He gave up.

—What?

—Will you be home for your tea?

—No talking in the ranks!

—I doubt it, love, Paddy shouted back to his wife. —But don't give away the rasher, just in case.

—Did you not tell her? Walt Delaney asked him.

—No talking in the ranks!

—Not at all, said Paddy. —She's a fuckin' Unionist, God love her.

We marched out across Sackville Street. Behind me, the horses pulled two lorries, full of our pickaxes, crowbars, sledges – weapons for the working men's war: Connolly's idea of urban warfare was tunnelling and more tunnelling, knocking down walls, advance and retreat without having to go out into the rain – our few extra rifles and pistols, boxes of cartridges, bayonets, hatchets, cleavers. We marched straight across the wide street and felt the power as we stopped the trams and cars and the people gaped and wondered. There were British officers outside the Metropole Hotel. They were used to marching Paddys. They laughed and one or two of them waved.

—Laugh away, you gobshites.

Then we turned smartly to the right and our target was in front of us.

—Company halt. Left turn.

We were outside the G.P.O., the General Post Office, right under the portico. It was colossal, block on top of granite block, held up by white pillars that would stay put for ever. I could see Victor swinging behind a pillar, and a man going in to buy stamps with money no longer in his pocket.

Then I heard Connolly's voice.

—The G.P.O. Charge!

And I ran. The hammers jumped on my shoulder, the rifle smacked my back. A few of the men fired into the air. I ran past Plunkett who was being held up by Collins and another officer, his arms around their necks, two enormous rings on his fingers. For a second, I thought he'd been shot – there was blood seeping through the bandage on his neck – and I ducked, half expecting to be knocked back by a bullet. But I looked back and I saw the signs; I'd seen them on Victor and thousands of others: the man had T.B. I ran into the main hall and my boots joined the chaos, in time to see the remaining shock on the faces of staff and customers.

Again, Connolly was in charge.

—Everyone out!

Some of the staff, men who hadn't exerted themselves in years, hopped and skidded over the counter.

—Jesus, will you look at them, said Paddy Swanzy. —Men, women and children first.

And now, only a few minutes later, Pearse and Connolly were about to go back outside, and Clarke with them. We heard cheering: the crowd across the street was watching the green, white and orange flag of the Republic being hoisted to the top of the flagpole above us. They clapped and cheered. I pictured the flag being caught by the wind and opened, colour by colour. And Countess Markievicz's bedspread was flying up there as well, with its gold and mustard lettering – *Irish Republic*. I cheered too; I couldn't help it.

Connolly, Pearse and Clarke went out. I couldn't see them now but I soon heard Pearse.

—He's reading it, I whispered.

—Reading what?

—The *Sacred Heart Messenger*, said Paddy Swanzy.

—Shush in the ranks!

We declare the right of the people of Ireland to the ownership of Ireland, and to the unfettered control of Irish destinies, to be sovereign and indefeasible. There was jeering and laughter, small spells of applause, but at times as he read there wasn't a noise. And his voice was soft; it drifted in the heat, barely there. The men with me were hearing the Proclamation for the first time. I watched their faces as the words rolled up to them. I watched the pride and excitement. I saw eyes shine and moisten...*We hereby proclaim the Irish Republic as a Sovereign Independent State, and we pledge our lives and the lives of our comrades-in-arms to the cause of its freedom.*

Paddy Swanzy hadn't said a word in at least a minute.

—Them's fighting words, he said.

The Republic guarantees religious and civil liberty

—Go home!

—Go home yourself. Let the man speak.

and declares its resolve to pursue the happiness and prosperity of the whole nation and all its parts, cherishing all the children of the nation equally —

My part. My contribution. My present to Victor.

Only the night before.

Connolly had put the sheets of paper under my nose. We were in Liberty Hall. I'd been sitting on a bench outside his office, waiting to bring the finished Proclamation down to the *Worker's Republic* printers in the basement. The sleeping bodies of Citizen Army men, and their bikes and haversacks, were all over the place. I could see that Connolly was excited; he was lifting himself onto his toes.

—Here, son. Have a read of that and tell me what you think.

I read it, the first man after Connolly and Pearse to do so. The Proclamation of Independence. (It was Connolly who'd finally taught me how to read. He'd slapped me, three years before, during the Lockout, when he'd heard me telling the women in the soup kitchen that I'd no use for reading or writing. He'd pushed me into a room and forced my face down to the pages of a book.

—It's gibberish now, wee Henry, he'd said. —But by the time I'm finished with you it'll be as precious as bread and water.

And he'd relaxed his grip on my head before I drowned in the words.) Three years later, I felt my heart in my fingers as I turned to the second page. I knew that Connolly was watching me carefully. He knew exactly when I'd reached the final full stop.

—What do you think? he asked.

—It's the stuff, I said.

—Is it perfect?

—Well, I said.

—Go on, said Connolly.

—There should be something in there about the rights of children.

He looked at me. He saw my pain, and the pain of millions of others. And his own.

—You're right, he said. —Where, though?

—Here, I said. —Between that there and the bit about the alien government. That's where it would fit.

—Good, he said. —I'll suggest that, so.

He looked straight at me again.

—I'll insist on it. Anything else?

—I'd take out all that stuff about God.

—Can't do that, son. We need Him on our side. And all His followers.

I nodded at the Proclamation in his hand.

—Can I sign it? I asked.

—No, he said. —No. You're too young. You'll be needed for other things.

He turned to go back into his room, and stopped.

—Thanks, son. All set for tomorrow?

—Yes, sir.

—I know you are.

We place the cause of the Irish Republic under the protection of the Most High God, Whose blessing we invoke upon our arms, and we pray that no one who serves that cause will dishonour it by cowardice, inhumanity or rapine.

—What's rapine when it's at home? said Paddy Swanzy.

—Messing around with the women, said Charlie Murtagh. —With a bit of robbery thrown in.

Pearse read off the names of the men who'd signed the Proclamation. We cheered when we heard Connolly's name. Then he was finished, and the crowd dashed forward to have the first look at the Proclamation which was now being pasted to one of the pillars.

—Welcome to the Republic of Ireland, lads, said Charlie.

—That's all fine and dandy, said Paddy Swanzy. —But I heard nothing in all that about the workers' state.

—That comes after, comrade. Hold on to your rifle.

—Jaysis, said Paddy. —I definitely won't be home in time for me tea.

Pearse and Connolly came back in and the big doors were shut with a resounding thump that left us still for a few seconds. Then men started to tear down the recruitment posters – *The Irishmen in the Trenches are calling for YOU* – and put Proclamations up in their place. The building and waiting continued. And Kitchener and George V were put propping up one of the barricades; someone had fecked them from the Waxworks around the corner on Henry Street. The far-off gunfire was still sprinkling the city.

Connolly did the rounds. He terrified all of us. He walloped one of the window barricades. Wood and paper fell to the floor.

—What use is that to us? he shouted. —Will that thing stop bullets? Some of us aren't playing here, you know. I want barricades!

He sent men running, grown men scampering. They loved and feared him. He was sharp, always on the prowl, never ever happy. But everything he did and said, everything he slammed, lambasted, everything he was, was for us. And the men knew it. He came growling over to my barricade and tapped it with his foot. It stayed put, except for a loose page that fluttered out the window. He winked at me and moved on.

—Here come the military!

The call came from outside and it ricocheted from walls to ceiling of the main hall and upstairs to the other men and sent feet punching the boards and tiles, and officers shouting across each other. I climbed onto the bench we'd put against the barricade and watched for the arrival of the enemy. My rifle roamed the street, followed the retreating onlookers, searched for creeping men in khaki. A few people stayed behind, under the Pillar, including a family with a dog on a string. And there were some perched up on the lampposts. There were priests out there too, in black stovepipe hats, moving in a row, trying to disperse the crowd. They were wasting their time. The crowd let them through and immediately re-gathered.

The soldiers could have been coming from any or all directions, from North Earl Street right in front of us – the parked trams were blocking my view. Or Sackville Place or Abbey Street further down. From the streets behind us, or from Rutland Square, to the north. Or over the river, from the south. The city was full of military barracks; we were well and truly surrounded. I searched for khaki, horses, the glint or clink of metal, hooves, engines – anything that would allow me to declare war.

We listened for noise from upstairs, any confirmation or excitement. I leaned over, stretched out across the dusty ledgers and sand sacks as far as I could go, and aimed at Tyler's window, far across the street. The safety was off. My rifle was a composite weapon, a bastard of many makes, from America and Germany, Lee-Enfield, Mauser – *Waffenfabrik Mauser* – and an evil old bayonet all the way from Russia. I was aiming at Tyler's, the shoe shop, with its windows full of single shoes, its special corner for children's boots. I knew where my first bullet was going. I waited for the order, the first shot, the sighting of a creeping Tommy or an officer with sword drawn and waving.

But there was nothing out there.

Just the heat and the silence – not even distant shots now – and the hidden enemy crawling nearer and nearer.

—Come on.

—They're acting the maggot, said Paddy Swanzy.

—Come on. Come on.

I had to blink; the sweat stung my eyes. My trigger finger was aching, my calves, the elbow that anchored the arm propping up my rifle; every muscle and sinew I owned was hardening, screaming. A hint, the slightest thing or sound would save them and release all the anger and rage I'd been storing for today. I wanted to demolish every bit of glass and brick in front of me. The creak of stretched leather, a boot on a kerb, the sun on a badge, any tiny thing would let me go.

But the world out there was absolutely still. Absolutely nothing. And in here, around me. Nothing at all. From upstairs or anywhere. We hadn't a hope. We were waiting for the world to drop on us.

Then we heard laughter, and more joining it. From outside. Over at the pillar.

—I was only havin' yis on!

I kept my gun on Tyler's but I looked at the gobshite who'd stepped onto the street in front of us. With his butties coming after him. A thick-looking eejit with a cap jammed down on his head.

There were explosions of breath throughout the building, shouts of fury and disappointment.

—Let me up there till I shoot the fucker!

It was very, very tempting. He was standing right in front of us, with the grin dripping off him.

—Yis didn't panic, anyway, he shouted. —Fair play to yis.

—Permission to kill him, sir.

—Denied, said Connolly as he got down from the barricade after gawking out at the gobshite who'd set the Republic wobbling. —We can't spare the bullet.

Then something hit the street. A grenade. One of our home-made ones. One of the lads on the roof had dropped it. A can full of metal chunks and a generous knob of gelignite. It landed with a dull, threatening thunk, in front of the gobshite and his pals. They saw the fuse sticking out of it and they scattered and disappeared behind Nelson. The unlit fuse. And we heard Ned Mannix's voice from upstairs.

—Yis didn't panic, anyway!

Connolly was furious. His face raced beyond purple. He spat and stamped his foot. He roared at the ceiling.

—Mannix!

He roared at us all.

—You thicks! You bloody eejits! They might be out there to distract us!

I looked out again. Connolly was right; I expected to see tight rows of advancing troops, covering, swallowing the street, already scaling the barricades, in on top of us. What I saw was the gobshite.

—You're in right trouble now! he roared.

He stood well away from the grenade.

—There's worse than the military coming now! he roared.

Connolly had calmed down.

—Retrieve that grenade, someone, before one of those gutties outside decides to throw it back at us.

The main door was opened – the gobshite ran again – and Frank Lawless dashed out and grabbed the grenade. He was on his way back when the women arrived. He legged it back into the hall and the doors were slammed fast on the faces of the women.

—Here!

They started pounding on the doors; twenty, thirty, more angry fists chopped at the wood.

And the gobshite was back.

—I told yis! Yis'll have to surrender now!

The women weren't giving up. I could see some of them, climbing over their friends to get at the door. A bunch of shawlies they were, all shapes and ages under their black hoods; they'd come down from Summerhill, and I knew why. They were here to collect their allowances. Their men were over in France, or dead under the muck. And the shawlies wanted their money.

The door was shaking.

—Let's in there!

Pearse spoke.

—Tell them to go home.

—Is he serious? said Paddy Swanzy.

Seán Knowles was at the window nearest the women. He climbed onto his barricade, so they'd be able to see him.

—You're all to go home, he shouted.

The hammering stopped and, for a few seconds, those who didn't know any better – some of the country lads, the poets and O'Toole – thought that the women had obeyed Seán and gone home.

Seán fell off the barricade and a barrage of spit and broken glass came after him. I felt a chunk of glass bite into my skull as I landed on the tiles behind the barricade.

The words followed the glass.

101

—Give us our money, yeh bastards!

The glass was falling all around us, its dust like sugar on our clothes and skin.

—Fuckin' wasters! Playing at being soldiers.

—And our husbands off doing the real fighting.

—Bastards!

The officers came and hauled and kicked us off the floor.

—The Tommies'll tan your arses for yis!

I felt my jacket tighten as I was picked up. It was Collins. He dropped me on my feet.

—They're only women! Get up.

The shawlies had run out of glass. We saw one of their heads above the barricade; they were climbing in on top of us. Collins got his Browning automatic from his holster and jumped onto the bench. He put the gun in front of the woman's face.

—Get down out of that now, missis. There's a war on.

—I know there's a fuckin' war on, said the woman back at Collins. —Over in France, with my Eddie.

—This is a fuckin' post office, said another one who was climbing up beside her.

—You can't come in, said Collins.

—Who'll stop us?

—The Army of the Irish Republic.

—The Irish wha'?

—Republic.

—We don't want a republic.

—That's right. God save the fuckin' King.

—Call yourselves men? You're only molly men.

—Wait till the real Army catches yis.

—Yis'll taste steel then, I'm tellin' yis.

—You'll have to go away, ladies, said Collins.

—It'd take more than a big-eared country boy to make us go away.

—What's under your hat, love?

Collins gave up.

—Shoot the first one that tries to get in, he told me. —Up you go now and defend your country.

I climbed back up to my perch and looked out.

—Ah now, *there's* a man.

102

—Howyis, girls, I said. —What seems to be the trouble?

—We only want our money, said one of them.

—Fair enough, I said. —Get down off the ledge there, so you don't go hurting yourselves.

—Can we have our money or wha'?

—I'll see what I can do, I said.

Collins was near.

—Permission to suggest something, sir.

—Go ahead, he said.

—Those women have children to feed, I said.

—And themselves, he said.

Jesus, I hated the Volunteers. The poets and the farm boys, the fuckin' shopkeepers. They detested the slummers – the accents and the dirt, the Dublinness of them. When was the last time Collins had been hungry? I knew the answer just by looking at the well-fed puss on him.

—There's plenty of money upstairs, sir, I said. —It was in the tills, beyond.

—So?

—So, seeing as there's no one outside to fight, why not let the first act of the Irish Republic be the paying out of these women's allowances?

—Because their husbands are in the British Army?

—A job's a job, sir, I said. —Some of the men here were in the Army. And most of the military garrisoned here in Dublin are Irish.

—It'll start a riot.

—A riot of support, I said.

I'd heard the stories about Collins.

—There's some good-looking women out there, sir.

—I'll talk to Commandant Pearse, he said.

And ten minutes later I was up on my barricade again with one of the till drawers, handing down neat piles of silver and copper to an orderly queue of grateful shawlies who went home happy and republican, with their money under their shawls – minus my 10 per cent – and their husbands far from their minds, buried beyond their eyebrows in the mud of Verdun and Ypres.

—What are you doing after the insurrection, young fella? said one of them.

She tightened her hold on my hand so I couldn't drop the money onto her palm.

—I seen him first, said another.

—He's fit for all of us.

—Where will I find you? I asked.

—Go up to Summerhill and ask for Annie, she said. —They all know me.

—Piano Annie, said another one behind her. —She'll play a jig on your spine, sonny.

Annie pulled my hand.

—What about a kiss to keep me going?

—Hang on to my feet, Paddy, I said over my shoulder to Swanzy, and I was sliding over the end of the barricade, past the last few shards of broken glass, sliding down to Annie, to see what was under the shawl; she was only young, not much older than myself, and gorgeous now that her mouth was shut and hiding the butts of her teeth. Her eyes were starving, greedy and dark, and darker as I got nearer to them. I hung on to my hat and Paddy's hold on my ankles tightened; I felt other hands grabbing my legs and feet. I was being held by three men – maybe they thought I was deserting, and maybe I was – by the time I had my face down to Annie's and I gave her my eyes –

—Holy Jesus, where did you get them?

and I touched her cracked but lovely lips with mine – and I heard something. I definitely heard something.

Brasses.

And nails on stone. And I looked and saw hoofs knocking sparks out of the tramlines.

—Get me up! I shouted.

—Aaah, said Annie as my face rose over her and she was left with nothing but her allowance in her fist.

—I'll come looking for you, Annie, I said. —Don't worry.

I kept looking at her until I was hauled over the top of my barricade and I was back inside.

—They're coming, I said.

—We know, said Charlie. —The Lancers.

—A horse is a grand big target, said Paddy.

104

I was ready.

At last.

I aimed at Tyler's window.

I heard the first shot crack brick. And then I fired. I heard, then saw the shop glass break and disappear as the trigger threw my finger forward. I pulled back the bolt, the empty cartridge flew over my shoulder. I grabbed the trigger back and fired at the exposed boots and slippers. Then I fired at Noblett's window, and the cakes and cream jumped out of their stands. O'Farrell's. The glass fell onto the tobacco and cigars. The cartridges hopped around me, the recoil was taking the shoulder off me but I kept at it. My aim was true and careful; every bullet mattered. Two for Lewer's & Co. and their little boys' blazers, suits and knickerbockers. I felt my fingers burning; the barrel was overheating. But I kept on shooting. A bullet for Dunne & Co., and their hats danced in the glass. One for the All-Ireland Servants Registry Office – there'd be none of that shite in the new republic. And Cable and Co., and more and more shoes. And back over to the Pillar Café – I'd been thrown out of there before I was properly in the door, me and Victor; I could still smell the manageress's breath – and I took out all the café windows with timing and precision that impressed but didn't surprise me. I shot and killed all that I had been denied, all the commerce and snobbery that had been mocking me and other hundreds of thousands behind glass and locks, all the injustice, unfairness and shoes – while the lads took chunks out of the military.

They drove their bullets into the dragoons – the Sixth Reserve Cavalry Regiment, from Marlborough Barracks, I found out a few years later when I was comforting one of the widows – and their fat, gleaming steeds. By the time I was finished with the shop windows, there were horses, dead or twitching, lying all over Upper Sackville Street and their riders were under them or hobbling and crawling away, back up towards Cavendish Row. The bullets still pinged and skipped and the street-sides tossed back the echoes. I aimed at a chap who'd lost his helmet, whose face was cut in half by a moustache with ends standing up like black candles. He looked stranded out there, trying to control his horse and hold on to his lance; the horse was spinning on its hind legs, propelled by its terror. I waited till horse and rider gave me their side view again. Then I let go of a bullet that went through the rider's leg and the horse dropped flat onto the street.

They were beaten. A mess of flesh and shit on the street. We cheered and gave hard slaps to the nearest backs. I'd never been so close to people before. There'd only ever been Victor. I was sharing the world with these men. I trusted them; their nearness lit me.

It had been so easy. We had occupied a solid block of Wicklow granite and they'd sent a few toy soldiers on horses to get us out. The knowledge made us giddy; they were eejits. The Empire was collapsing in front of us. I had the last of the till money in my pocket, so I didn't join in in the victory dance; I didn't want it to jangle. Paddy and Felix swung each other till it got dangerous and Connolly let go of a roar. He was furious again. He shook himself at us.

—Why didn't you wait until we had them all in our sights? he said. —That wasn't even the start of it.

—God, said Paddy, —there's no pleasing that man.

We got back to our posts and waited. A gang of Volunteers arrived on a commandeered tram. The Kimmage men, they all slept in a barn out on Count Plunkett's farm, having come back from England to avoid conscription. They'd spent their days helping on the farm and making home-made bombs.

—Sorry we're late, said one of them as he climbed in the window.

—Did you pay your fare? I asked him.

—We did in our arses, he said.

It was the last tram to run that week. De Valera's men had got into Ringsend power station and taken away some of its vital parts. The trams sat dead around the Pillar. Some of them ended up in barricades; they were easy things to topple.

Some of our men, led by a Volunteer officer, ran across the street and occupied the Imperial Hotel. We watched as our own flag, the Starry Plough, the flag of the Citizen Army, flew over the hotel, property of William Martin Murphy, the bollocks who'd locked us out in 1913.

—Hope the fucker can see it.

—If he can't, he'll hear about it.

I watched the flag being played by the wind that was bringing in the evening over Dublin. And night followed that and we still waited.

I slept that night. On the floor in the basement of the G.P.O. Sandwiched between Paddy and Felix, the three of us wrapped in a roll of carpet we'd liberated from an office upstairs. I was asleep before I lay down properly. Cuddled by two bowls of Cumann na mBan stew, tucked in and utterly gone. I dreamt of nothing and woke up new and wondering who and where I was. It was still dark.

—Cock-a-doodle-doo, said Paddy Swanzy, beside me.

I listened for gunshots or shouting but there was nothing, no loud or hurrying noises from above. I searched the dark for my boots and shook blood into my legs; they'd gone numb in the britches. There was light coming from the big room to the left, and a smell with it.

—Porridge, said Paddy. —That'll stop the bullets. There's murder going on over at City Hall. They say. The Devil's Half-Acre is submerged in blood and liver.

I listened again but could still hear nothing.

—Whose blood? Theirs or ours?

—Most of it's imported, said Paddy.

He was joking. He knew as well as I did: most of the British soldiers were Irish. Irishmen who'd needed the work. And anyway, we'd nothing against Englishmen either, or Scots or Welshmen. We were fighting a class war. We weren't in the same battle at all as the rest of the rebels. And they'd find that out soon enough.

I stood up, strapped on my bandolier and joined the queue of men still numb and crooked from the night. The porridge in the air set my stomach yapping. I grabbed a bowl from a card table and held it out to be filled.

—Two and two?

I was looking at two brown boots that had a woman's toes neatly packed into their points.

—Don't know. Two and two what?

—Bottles.

—What's in them?

—Porter.

I looked at her.

—Four.

—I knew it was you, said Miss O'Shea.

—It's me alright. It always has been.

—You're still a great one for the answers.

Brown-black eyes and floating slivers of hair that had escaped from a bun behind her head. It had been five years since I'd last seen her, since Mother the Nun had come into the classroom and ended my education. She hadn't changed a bit; the five years had done no damage. But I'd changed, of course. I was up over her now and, as I stood there, I could remember what I'd been like when I'd knocked on her door, with Victor. I could feel Victor beside me; I could feel his sweat in my hand. Henry, the small, filthy boy who'd been a whopper for his age was now a man, and big for any age. He was tall and broad with the skin and hair born of sound blood and clean living. The sores and crusts had fallen off me. I was a sparkling young man; I fought every day for my cleanliness. My eyes were blue and fascinating whirlpools; they could suck in women while warning them to stay well away, a fighting combination that had them running at me. And I knew exactly what my eyes could do.

And Miss O'Shea hadn't even got to them yet. She was still feeding on my britches. I stood at ease and let her. She was mesmerised. I looked down at the bun that had been above me the last time I'd seen it. It was a mass of the finest brown hair, endless hair that was dying for fingers to comb it. And, under it, her neck, and my eyes slid down to the start of her Cumann na mBan uniform. And the badge on her breast, the rifle held by the slender curling letters. *C na mB*. She saw me and blushed and I remembered that too.

—You still have your leg, she said.

It was in my holster, my da's leg, varnished and ready to knock heads for Ireland.

—I do, I said. —I'll be seeing you.

And I left her there, dangling. I went into a corner and

downed my porridge. It was early days. There'd be more porridge and, with a bit of luck, wounds to swab and bandage. We'd be seeing each other again. Miss O'Shea wasn't going anywhere, and neither was I.

Another day of waiting. Day Two of the Revolution and I was already bored. Staring out at the empty street and the rain. Listening to the far gunfire, waiting for it to come closer. Waiting to be surprised. Wanting it. Badly. Wanting to shoot and wreck and kill and ruin. But Dublin, that part of it outside my window, didn't really wake up at all. No trams now, four empty tramlines outside, no hawkers, hardly any people, or acknowledgement that we were ready and wanting a fight. Only the odd group or individual coming up to the window. Most were bored and some were angry, kept from their work. They remembered the hunger of the Lockout, and they were blaming us now.

—You're a shower of irresponsibles.

—Is Mick Malone in there with yis? He has the keys to the print-shop and we can't get in.

—Nothing but a shower of irresponsibles.

—Tell him we'll have to break the door down or lose a day's pay and the foreman says the door'll come out of his wages if he still has the job when he comes back.

—Where's Mick Malone? I shouted.

—With de Valera, said Felix Harte.

—He's over in Boland's Bakery, I told the young fella outside, under my barricade.

—What's he doin' there?

—Eating all the fig rolls, said Paddy Swanzy.

The Cumann na mBan women were cycling all over the city and coming back with news. The stories were flying, facts and rumours and little bits of extra we made up ourselves to get us through the day. There was full-scale war going on out at Ashbourne; Thomas Ashe and Dick Mulcahy were up to their thighs in Saxon gore and cow shite. Michael Mallin and Countess Markievicz had taken Stephen's Green; the Countess was training the ducks in the finer points of urban warfare.

There were boatloads of guns and machine-guns being run onto the beaches of Kerry, and other huge killing machines, already on their way to us. German boats full of weapons for us; they'd got through the British blockade. The British had been off their guard after the *Aud* was sunk in Queenstown harbour, down in Cork. They thought they'd dealt with the crisis but the *Aud* had been just the first of many, the nose of a long convoy. There were even German troops coming off the boats, squads and squads of them, big twins and triplets; they'd marched through Tralee. They were marching up the Naas Road. And the Irish Brigade with them, homesick Irishmen from the German prisoner-of-war camps, marching towards us. And boats of Irish-Yanks already on the Atlantic, heading our way, with new guns and muscle; Jim Larkin had landed at Sligo with an advance party. The whole country was up, Wexford, the West, Kerry. The Irish regiments were defecting and the Orangemen had marched through Balbriggan the night before, on their way to flush us out; they were going to join up at Ballybough with the cadets from the School of Musketry in Dollymount. But we weren't worried. De Valera and the Third Battalion were holding back all the armies to the south and Ned Daly and Éamonn Ceannt were doing the same to the west. They'd taken over the South Dublin Union and armed the sick and mad. Dublin's nuts were holding back the armies of the Empire. And they were doing a good job of it; we didn't see a hint of a soldier or hear an angry shot all day. Or even a fat rozzer to have a crack at. All we fought was the boredom and abuse.

I kept a tight watch on all the street corners and let Miss O'Shea make up my dreams for me. She was down there waiting for me, with a bowl of stew, slices of thick, warm brownbread or maybe even a couple of chops. She was down there, dreaming of me. As my eyes searched the broken shop windows across the street, I licked Miss O'Shea's ear. And she felt it, downstairs in the basement, I knew she did, as she drove her wooden spoon and watched the potatoes breaking off the wall of the cauldron. Her ear had never been licked, not even by a pup or a sister. I could feel her skin shivering under my tongue, felt the slight heat of her blush as I crawled up the little

110

creases behind her ear, three little rivers, towards her bun – I was going to free that hair and lie down in it. I knew exactly what I wanted. I was no ordinary boy. I was practised and cool, an out and out pleasure machine, my hands oiled and scented with the stuff that made my rifle sing. I moved another half-inch and her hair melted on my tongue. I pressed myself into the barricade.

—Will you look at those gobshites.

It was Paddy and his timing was perfect; I'd very nearly shoved the barricade out the window. There was an extra leg in my britches, fighting for space and purpose. Baying for a republic.

—What gobshites? I said.

I kept my eyes on the street and my bollix on the sandbag.

—Those gobshites, he said.

I didn't have to look now; I heard them. Some of the Volunteers had their beads out and were down on their knees, humming the rosary.

—The revolutionaries, said Felix. —Will you look at them?

Plunkett was in there with them. He could hardly stand; he spent most of his time on a mattress. The man was dying, a waste of a bullet, but he had the energy to beat his breast and drive his knees into the tiles.

—The first sorrowful mystery, said Paddy. —How we ever ended up with those gobshites.

Like a come-all-ye, the prayer was taken up by other men and others up and downstairs; some of our lads too, down on their socialist knees. I took my eyes from the street for a few seconds and watched Connolly across the hall, grinding his teeth; I could almost hear them crumbling above the rosary drone. Pearse was in a corner, on a high stool, his head in a notebook; he was mumbling as well. Collins, to be fair to him, looked ready to go in among them and kick them back to earth.

I looked out. The shadow of the G.P.O. had stretched right across to the other side of the street, up the walls of the Imperial, to the barricades at the windows and our men behind them. Higher up, on the roof, the Starry Plough was still in the sun's white gaze. The last of the day's heat was in the sweat at the corners of my eyes, and the blackness now in front of me –

I couldn't trust what I was seeing. There was nothing out there but I couldn't be certain of it. There were shadows moving but they were nothing. Around corners, over the river, down on the quays the city was moving; it was the usual racket and whine but it could have been the Army coming at us. There was a spark behind a window that could have been a rifle barrel. There was a sharp, lonely crack that might have been a Vickers gun accepting its magazine. All was quiet but maybe appalling. And, behind me, my colleagues and comrades, my fellow revolutionaries, were on their knees – and they'd been on them and off them all day – with their eyes clamped shut, their heads bowed and their cowering backs to the barricades. What sort of a country were we going to create? If we were attacked now, we were fucked. I didn't want to die in a monastery. I'd made up my mind to jump.

But I thought I saw something – the hint of fire behind glass across the street, beyond the Abbey Street corner. I was looking at it, waiting for it to become something definite, when the fireworks started. Real fireworks – whizz-bangs and cart-wheels – tame, crackling, happy holiday sounds and then the whiff of powder, like a burning box of matches just beyond my nose. The sparks and whizzes were coming from way down the street, near the river, so they lit up the edge of my vision – I couldn't see causes, anyone running or lighting fuses – until the bangs came from above our heads. Rockets zipped into what was now the night and exploded, and dropped their colours and I watched them melt and disappear and waited for the next explosion.

Most of the men ran to their stations but some of the rosary boys seemed to think that the Chinese crackers were a sign that their prayers were being spurned. They started shouting the responses; their foreheads were virtually on the ground, rubbing the flags to a new smoothness.

—Up off your knees!

—There's a war on, lads!

They jumped or were kicked upright; they clung to their beads like their mammies' fingers. Collins was in there with his boots swinging.

—Get rid of the beads and pick up your rifles!

And the firework sparks fell and died over Sackville Street. The streetlights were smashed and it was darker than ever before out there. Except for the odd flame and rush of a rocket, there was nothing to see. Were they finally coming at us, crawling in under the rockets and whizzers, taking us out with bangers instead of shells and bullets? Were the roman candles the measure of their contempt? They were already celebrating the easy certainty of victory. Crawling closer and closer, in fancy dress and drunk. They were going to push us over.

But I knew what was actually happening just after the fires started and lit the street and started to consume it. The flames lit the figures and they became people – boys and men, women, girls and strange shapes stooped under piles of furniture and clothes.

I heard the shock in the Volunteer voices.

—They're looting over there, sir!

The kids had broken into Lawrence's toy and sports bazaar, and had released all the fireworks. Now that it was night and safe and the rozzers had hidden themselves away, the citizens of Dublin were lifting everything they could get their hands on. And, once again, I felt that I was on the wrong side of the barricade. I leaned out and watched the show.

A small army of street arabs struggled past with a rocking horse held over their heads. They turned at North Earl Street and climbed over the barricade; they struggled up, dragging the horse, and the horse's head disappeared as they slid down the other side. They were followed by another gang hauling a piano, with a young fella on top of it; he glowed in the dark, covered in iodine to kill his ringworm. Another kid, dressed in the threads of a golfer five times his size, dashed by with his back parallel to the street, held down by the weight of a full golf bag. An oul' lad, already drunk from the promise of the unopened jars of whiskey he was lugging, staggered up towards Cavendish Row, his neck kept cosy by a feather boa that trailed for yards behind him. And there were ordinary sights too, people getting away with all the things they could carry. Dipping in and out of the shop displays, over my broken glass, and deeper into the departments and vaults behind them. Climbing into the gift horse's mouth. Voting with their feet and backs; welcoming the new Republic. Prams and hand-carts full of fur coats and stoles, bloomers and stockings. And the sucking and gasping going by; I knew that the kids had liberated Lemon's sweet shop.

The fireworks were gone or made lifeless by the real fires that had joined to destroy the far side of the street. I heard the approaching bells of the fire brigade and my heart let go of a whoop as Tyler's in front of me ignited and joined the blaze. Almost immediately, my nose welcomed the bracing tang of burning leather.

An outraged voice beside us cried out.

—They're Irish shops they're robbing!

—Good for them, said Paddy Swanzy back at the Volunteer.

—It's all Irish property!

—It'll still be Irish after it's taken.

Without saying anything, without even looking at one another, we – the Citizen Army men – suddenly knew that we would have to protect the people outside. My barrel still faced the street but I was ready to turn it in on the Volunteers who were itching to save Irish property.

One of the Volunteer officers, a red-faced chap called Smith, came storming towards our section. He was unbuckling his holster as he went but his fury made his fingers hopeless.

—We'll have to make an example of them, he shouted. —Or we'll be hanging our heads in shame among the nations of the world.

I turned from the window and pointed my rifle at Smith and waited for him and the others following him to see it. Paddy Swanzy and Felix had done the same thing.

—If it's examples you're looking for, said Paddy, —just keep doing what you're doing and see what happens.

—And fuck the nations of the world, I said.

The Volunteers saw our barrels smiling at them and, before they could respond or do anything at all, the floor between us was awash with generals, commandants and poets, most of the Provisional Government of the Republic. Five seconds that very nearly shook the world – the revolution, the counter-revolution and the Civil War were all waiting to happen in that five-second spell in the G.P.O., as Dublin outside burned. I put my rifle on Pearse. I didn't know what was happening upstairs and on the roof or downstairs with Miss O'Shea – she was still dancing to my tongue, even as I got ready to shoot Commandant Pearse – but, where we were, not one barricade was manned, not even one pair of eyes faced the street. For the duration of those five, crawling seconds Britain stopped being the enemy. Pearse saw my rifle and saw my eyes and my intentions in them, and he turned slightly, giving me his profile, hiding his squint; he was ready for an elegant death.

Then Connolly spoke.

—There'll be no Irishman shot by an Irishman tonight, he said.

—How will we deal with them then? said Smith.

—You won't, I said, still aiming at Pearse.

—We'll send out a squad now to get them off the streets, said Connolly.

It was over. We looked across and stored away the faces for another day. I met the hard stares of country boys and shopkeepers, met and matched them. But, for now, it was over. I could hear the fire engines behind me and sniper fire from Trinity College. And over their heads, at the door to the stairs, I saw Miss O'Shea. How long had she been there? We looked at each other. She rubbed her neck, right behind her ear where she hid her little creases from the world. And she frowned at me.

—We'll do it nice and politely, said Connolly. —Those fires will be getting dangerous.

—I'll go, I said.

—No, you won't, said Connolly. —I want you here.

The barriers were pushed away from the front door and Paddy Swanzy and other men slipped out. I looked over to the stairs door. Miss O'Shea had gone.

—You wouldn't have come back.

Connolly was beside me, his moustache almost in my mouth.

—I resent that remark, sir, I said.

—Good man. We're surrounded by gobshites, Henry.

—I know, sir.

—Catholic and capitalist, Henry. It's an appalling combination.

—Yes, sir.

—I want you near me, Henry.

—You can count on me, sir.

And I meant it.

—Back to your post now, he said. —But keep your hand on your father's leg.

—I will, sir.

I could hear the vicious hiss as the rain and the fire brigade hoses smothered the flames, and people ran from the flats above the shops. And I watched as the steady trail of people went by, adding to their height and bulk with bits and lumps of Irish property. Two men rolled by with a cooper of stout. About twenty people marched past with a long roll of carpet over their heads; it must have come from one of the hotels and, against the fires, the procession looked like the march of a huge, headless centipede. Straw and wrapping paper tumbled down the street, some of the straw on fire and spilling tiny lights. A gang of women wore pots as head-dresses. They clanged their new hats with wooden spoons and spatulas – *Oh thunder and lightning is no lark* – and they sang into the flames – *when Dubellin City is in the dark*. A kid skidded past with four tiers of a wedding cake. *If you have any money go up to the park.* Four more women went by with a bed on their backs. *And view the zoological gardens.* A man was trying to stop them; he was pointing back down the street with his umbrella, obviously asking them to take their stuff back to where it had come from. One woman started fencing with him, ladle versus umbrella. I'd seen him before.

—Who's your man?

—Sheehy-Skeffington, said Charlie Murtagh. —Skeffy. He's a pacifist, so the smart money's on the brasser with the big spoon.

I couldn't tell where the bullet had come from but, across the street, right in front of me, I saw a man being shot. He stiffened; he dropped slowly to his knees, grabbed a pillar, and stayed there, kneeling. For two days. Further up the street, two drunks were getting sick at the stony feet of Father Mathew and a woman made an armchair for herself out of one of the dead horses; she wrapped herself from the wind and rain in velvet curtains and cuddled up between the horse's legs. There was serious madness going on out there. And, in the middle of it all, Pearse gave us a speech. *Dublin, by rising in arms, has redeemed its honour forfeited in 1813 when it failed to support the rebellion of Robert Emmet.* I looked out at Dublin rising. And there she came, through it all, out of the darkest of the flames, the loveless old hoor herself, Granny Nash. She was carrying a wall made of books; she had two of them open on top of the pile, reading them already, one eye for each, as she strolled up Sackville Street. She looked singed and half-destroyed but she moved like a dreaming child on her way to school. And I cheered her on. I shouted with all I had but she never looked up from her books. *The country is rising to Dublin's call.* And we waited. We waited for the advance or attack. We wondered what was happening behind the cracks of distant bullets. We didn't know that we'd been cut off, that the military now controlled the line along the river and the land to the north. Or that there were dead men scattered all over the city, soldiers and rebels and people who'd been in the way. *Irish regiments have refused to act against their fellow countrymen. Such looting as has occurred has been done by hangers-on of the British Army.* We didn't know that there were eighteen-pounders coming in from Athlone, blasting everything in the way. Or that they were taking back everything, the train stations, Stephen's Green, the bits and plots of Ireland we'd freed the day before. We were alone and stuck and we didn't know it.

Someone came back from outside with news of a charge; they'd be coming over the river any minute.

—This is it, men, said Connolly.

We waited.

—Fix bayonets.

And we waited for the attack. Old Clarke came over to my window and stared out.

—Our time has come, he said.

I'd never seen a man look so happy.

The rosary was whipped back into life. We waited all night. All the time searching, listening. Listening.

117

* ★ ★

—What the fuck was that? said Paddy.

It was different. The firing had intensified since before daybreak; we'd been pulled awake by noise that was sudden and near. The walls and street were being shredded by machine-gun and sniper fire and we'd heard the first awful booms of an eighteen-pounder from somewhere across the river, opposite the Custom House, somewhere. The story whizzed around the building that it was the German guns nearing but the same story died as we felt the streets rock, heard the first walls and roofs collapsing, not far away any more, and we knew that these shells weren't being sent to support anyone. There were marksmen and machine-guns on the roofs of Trinity, the Burgh Quay Music Hall, Jervis Street Hospital, all around us, the tower down at Amiens Street station, the roof of McBirney's – a vicious bastard who even shot a blind man with a very white stick and the St John's Ambulance man who ran to help him – the roof of the Rotunda, all raking us and our other positions nearer the bridge, Kelly's tackle shop on the corner of Bachelor's Walk and Hopkins & Hopkins, the jewellers; we'd a few men in each of those buildings, pretending they were whole squadrons. We were surrounded and we all knew that the end was coming up the street; the bombardment was a yawning sky above us, waiting to fall. The rosary had broken into a sprint and there was a queue upstairs for the priest. The bullets and silences were getting nearer and nearer and the air was a soup of brick dust.

But this was different. A huge clang. Like the world's gong toppling over. The end, and its echo. Like nothing we could ever have been ready for. A new, appalling weapon. Rage roaring up from the earth's core.

—What the fuck was that? said Paddy.

He was the only one who could speak. The rest of them waited for the next roar and its result, and hoped they'd understand it.

Word came down from the roof. A shell had hit the Loop Line bridge. They were bombarding Liberty Hall from a gunboat on the river and the iron bridge had got in the way; it

118

was really a fishery protection vessel but *gunboat* made us feel better. They were dropping hot bombs and incendiary shells on the Hall, to flush out all the rebels. They didn't know that Peter Ennis, the caretaker, was the only man in the building. The headquarters of the I.T.G.W.U., my home and the birthplace of our revolution, was being battered into the ground.

And Connolly was delighted. He clapped his hands and thumped his chest.

—Now they're taking us seriously! he shouted at the dome. —They're rattled!

—They're not the only ones, said Paddy.

What did I say back to Paddy? Nothing at all. Too scared? Too busy? No. I just wasn't there when he said it. I was downstairs, in the basement, in a hot little room with much more dust than air. Did I hear the shell hitting the Loop Line? Did I hear the clang? I did, but I thought the noise was coming from me. I was falling onto my back when it happened. I'd been pushed on top of a high bed made of blocks of stamps, sheets and sheets of the things, columns of them, sticky side up. I was stuck there with my britches nuzzling my ankles as Miss O'Shea grabbed my knees and climbed on top of me.

—This skirt, she said. —Wait.

I heard a rip that set my balls butting each other.

—Now, she said. —That's better.

Her fingers landed perfectly on my hips.

—What'll you say about the skirt? I asked her.

I couldn't cope with silence.

—I'll say I tore it for Ireland, said Miss O'Shea. —And it's no lie.

Her hair washed over me. I was in her mouth so quickly – Jesus, the heat! And her teeth and tongue! – and out again, before I'd the time to know it. And again, for longer and out, and she climbed up my jacket. I tried to grab hair, cloth, anything – it was pitch black in there, just heat and fingers – but she slapped my hands away, and harder when I slapped her back.

—I'm still your teacher, Henry Smart, she said.

—Yes, Miss, I said.

Her hands were on my neck; she prodded and glided,

119

looking for ways to kill me. I hadn't a clue what was happening. My slouch hat hit a wall.

—We won't be needing that.

And she was right over my face now. She kissed the top of my head, then filled her mouth with hair and pulled. She let go and lifted herself. I heard tugging, a ping and there was warm flesh on my face, velvet skin swaying over me then pressing down on me. A nipple closed my eye as a hand grabbed my wee fighting rebel and he skipped from her fingers and she grabbed again. And she was gone from on top of me and my eye clung to the memory of her nipple. And her weight was gone. I was ready to let go of a shout, a howl – I'd never been so furious, so exposed – but I was in her, just like that – the scorch, the heat! – and she was on me again. And now she let me hold and find her.

—Keep your legs down, Henry, she said.

She tickled my balls and I went towards the ceiling, and she slapped the side of my leg.

—Do what you're told, she said.

I dropped my legs again and she rode me slowly, with a rhythm that was cruel and wonderful and could never have held on to music. It surprised and taunted, dragged and built me and made me feel like the king of the world and a complete and utter fuckin' eejit.

Henry Smart, the freedom fighter, had gone down to the basement with conquest on his mind. There were new territories to explore, uncharted rivers behind little ears. I was coming off the bottom step when she saw me. She looked around, saw a clear coast and pulled me by the bandolier into the store room.

And now she was shoving my shoulders down into the stamp sheets and lifting and dropping and there were wet slaps now banging out a beat and gumming my arse to the stamps. She'd break the rhythm now, again, dip herself to my face, to remind me that she was there, the inventor, and torturer if she wanted to be.

Her mouth was on my ear.

—What if they came in now, Henry?

—*Who?* I said. —The other women?

120

She grunted.

—Pearse and Plunkett?

She licked my ear.

—The *British*?

—Oh God.

—The Dublin Fusiliers?

—Oh *God*.

—The Royal Norfolks?

—Yes.

—The Royal Irish Rifles?

—Ye*sss*.

I was running out of soldiers. She pulled my ear with her teeth. She growled.

—The Scottish – oh fuck – the Scottish Border*ers*?

—*Maithú*, Henry!

—The Sherwood Fah-fah-foresters?

—*Maithúúúú* – oh – *maithú* —

—The Bengal fuckin' Lancers!

And we came together – although I didn't know it – in a froth that cemented the pair of us to the stamps and nearly frightened the shite out of me because nothing like this had ever happened to a woman before and I didn't know if she was dying or laughing on top of me. She hammered me into the gum. (My forehead still carries two nipple-made pockmarks.) She pounded my chest. She cut my neck. She gave me a hiding I never recovered from. She growled and hummed while I guffed and heaved, my teeth were chattering, I'd spurted everything and she dumped herself beside me. We were freezing, gasping and soaked in sweat, spunk and post office glue.

—God, she said. —The mess.

They'd never seen walls shake before, and the gunboat's shells, and now the shells from two nine-pounders across the river at Trinity, reminded them that they weren't just up against superior numbers; they had no shells of their own to send back. The Vickers guns and snipers were closing in and impossible to find. They were playing hide-and-seek with the men on the roof, using and vacating all the vantage points around. The spray of lead coming from the Anzacs on the roof of Trinity and other shifting points was constant now and nearing all the time.

The G.P.O. had no electricity, no radio or telephone link-up. The only outside contact was a line of twine running across the street, over the tram wires, to the Imperial, and messages carried in a can that had already been hit by a sniper. The ceilings were crumbling and falling, pipes had been pierced. The smell of escaping gas made the men feel trapped, and Connolly had them strengthening the barricades, locking themselves in.

—They're busy upstairs, I said when I thought I could trust my voice again and my spine had stopped yelping.

—Are you surprised, Henry? she said.

—Surprised at what?

—Me. Are you surprised at me?

—No, I said. —Not really.

The biggest lie of my entire life. I was still so surprised, I was almost unconscious.

—I didn't come here to make stew, Henry, she said.

She sighed. She sounded angry.

—I never asked you for stew, I said.

She sighed again.

—I'm here for my freedom. Just like you and the men upstairs.

—Yeah, I said.

—I want my freedom too, she said.

—Yeah.

—To do what I want.

At Mount Street Bridge, the Sherwood Foresters, fresh off the boat from England, thinking at first that they'd landed in France or even Russia, were being sliced by the bullets of thirteen hidden Volunteers guarding the bridge. It was the only bridge in the city being held by the rebels, and their officers, armed with maps they'd ripped from hotel guidebooks, kept sending them forward. They marched through blood and entrails and the cries of dying teenagers calling for their mammies and the vapour coming from the guts of the ones already dead. The *Helga* and the eighteen-pounders were smashing Sackville Street and the streets off it, trying for a straight route to the G.P.O. Wynn's Hotel was falling in on itself and, above the *Freeman's Journal* building, the flames played with charred flakes from the burning bales of newsprint. Connolly had men tunnelling into the buildings beside and behind us and, across the river, de Valera released the strays and runts from the Cats' and Dogs' Home.

—Do you know what I'm talking about, Henry?

—Yeah, I said. —You want to behave like a man.

—Yes, she said. —I think you understand.

—But they'll never let you, I said.

—Who?

—The shower upstairs.

—I know, she said. —I knew it the minute they started shouting for their tea.

—I hate the stuff, I told her.

She didn't seem to hear me.

—But at least, she said, —I'm not wasting my time completely.

Our heads clashed as we rushed at each other and it was dark on the other side of the door by the time we fell apart and I pulled up my britches. The bombardment had stopped but the burning street was a roar that allowed no sleep or rest. Collapsing walls nearer the river were huge, furious footsteps, and barricades were mended against the coming end. There were men crying now; the vicious smell of burning varnish bit into eyes and the smell of cordite made fingers slip on triggers. The rosaries were difficult to resist as the gas from the mangled pipes dragged coughs from clogged lungs and the ceiling plaster fell in nasty, quick slices. Even the rebel songs were being sung like hymns – *whether on the scaffold high or on the battlefield I die* – a whisper from a dark corner.

—It's just as well it's dark out there, she said. —We must look a state.

—Lesson One on your road to freedom, I said. —Always care about how you look but never, ever care what other people think about it. Unless it suits you to. Is my hat on straight?

—You care.

—It suits me.

—So does your hat.

123

—I know.

—Where did you learn to think like that?

—I stopped caring. You can ride whoever you want as often as you want. If you don't care what people think about it. Including whoever you're riding. Now, I'm going upstairs to die.

She'd made a man of me. We kissed till we bled.

Pearse tried to hoist himself. He was fat and his arms had no more muscle than his poetry. He managed to get his head over the barricade, and looked out. He stared at the flames outside.

—Would you ever mind ducking, sir? said Felix.

—Of course, he said.

He dropped back to the ground and walked away.

—Well, Henry, said Paddy. —Back from the war. You survived the bombardment.

—I had help, I said.

—Good man, said Paddy. —D'you know how to use a pick?

We bit chunks out of the wall with seven-pound hammers and picks. We were at the back of the building, upstairs, burrowing into Henry Street. Solid masonry, the best of Wicklow granite flew back at us. The bombardment had stopped with the night but that made our work even more urgent. There was no one sleeping out there. Snipers at every height. Men with grenades crawling under our window. And armoured lorries now too, free to go where they wanted, carrying men and sandbags for barricades, towing field guns to kill us, right under our noses. They'd been made in Inchicore, in the railway works; locomotive boilers with sniper holes in the sides and phoney painted holes to trick us. The boilers were lowered onto Guinness lorries. We dug and sweated and baked in skins of dust and mortar; we broke through the party wall into an abandoned flat behind the G.P.O.

—Keep away from the windows!

There were troops out there, behind their own barricade across Moore Street. I was dodging the fizz of their bullets but I hadn't seen a soldier yet. The sky behind the roofs, over towards Bolton Street, was red, like the sun going down three streets away; the Linenhall Barracks was on fire.

—We could win this one yet, boys. The British have no experience of this class of warfare. They're used to fields. And castles.

We dug on, to the next flat. My arms ached, my back; my eyes were clogged and desperately sore. But the agony kept me awake; there'd be no more sleep. We took over Henry Street from the inside.

We hammered and burrowed, through plaster into solid rock. We forgot why; there was just the wall in front of us, and the pain. And the heat on our backs. And the endless squeal of the city's roof timbers bursting into flame.

—The Germans are on the way, boys. There are submarines in Belfast Lough.

—And the Yanks.

—And the Eskee-fuckin'-moes.

And we were back downstairs, at the barricades. There was nothing like fresh air any more; the fires outside had eaten it. The cordite, breweries and dead horses fought the battle of the smells. In pockets of calm behind us, men swapped cigarettes and rosaries and the cake kept coming up from downstairs. Somewhere in there, in the digging and eating, Wednesday rolled into Thursday: there was no night. The fires lit the sky and the air right up to our windows was red. Flames were licking the clouds; more walls growled and fell. The Lewis, Vickers and Maxim guns kept going at us, from the Gresham, from the Rotunda, over the river, above, everywhere. And we fired where we saw the flame of their guns and expected to die every time we lifted ourselves to the window. There were streams of melted glass creeping onto the street, the sparks fucked above us and the heat whipped slices off my face. The fires were running across the streets, along our barricades. There were no fire engines out there; the British were firing at everything. And so was I – my hands were raw and scorched but I kept shooting, shooting. Only a few hours before I'd been lassoing Miss O'Shea with my tongue; it was dead in my mouth now, choking me as it broke to ash. I leaned into the barricade.

—Jesus!

It was burning, smouldering, the bags of coal, the ledgers, and everything else, ready to burst on me. I jumped away and roared at Paddy and Felix.

—Back off! A hose over here! Quick!

They came on their knees, for fear of bullets, hauling a hose that was rotten, and leaking where the bullets and broken glass had dug in. More hoses arrived, and buckets. Everything was hosed and drenched. And old man Clarke was suddenly everywhere, shouting on the work. The ceiling groaned, black water ran down the walls.

New orders, from The O'Rahilly: we were to get the bombs and ammo down to the cellar; the sparks were becoming too friendly. More work, more aching muscles, humping cases and boxes – the lift was dangerous, a cone of sparks and whirlwinds – while we ducked the bullets and tried not to slide in the water. Plunkett climbed off his bed as we were passing him.

—This is the first time a capital city has been burned since Moscow, he said.

—Fascinating, said Paddy, as Plunkett dropped back onto the bed.

I looked for Miss O'Shea as I went up and down but I didn't see her. The injuries were mounting, men lying everywhere and dead men in a corner. And we were upstairs again, breaking through the walls. Through two shops, over a short roof, up a ladder. Through another wall. Burrowing. All the way to the country. And there were men in the basement, trying to dig under Henry Street and other men had been sent into the sewers. The word came up: Connolly had been shot. It stunned us.

—No.

Stopped our work.

—Out on Prince's Street. A ricochet.

—He's not dead, is he?

—No, he's not, but he'll lose the leg.

—Is his tongue still working?

—Yeah.

—He'll be grand, so.

It scared us, though. We had to force ourselves to work and

get back our rhythm; it seemed like a waste of time. The idea of Connolly even bleeding rattled us badly. He wasn't just a man; he was all of us. We all needed him. He'd made us all believe in ourselves.

—Is there anyone better than you, Henry?

—No, Mister Connolly.

—That's right. No one at all. Do you ever look into your eyes, Henry?

—No, Mister Connolly.

—You should, son. There's intelligence in there, I can see it sparkling. And creativity and anything else you want. They're all in there. And my daughter tells me you're a good-looking lad. Look into your eyes every morning, son. It'll do you good.

And I did. Every morning. And I saw what he'd seen, smouldering away, knocking to get out. He'd fed me, given me clothes, he let me sleep in the Hall. He made me read. He let me know that he liked me. He explained why we were poor and why we didn't have to be. He told me that I was right to be angry. He was always busy and distant but there was always a wink or a quick grin as he looked up from his work or passed me. He wanted me there.

Paddy and Felix were the same, and the rest of the Citizen Army men. They'd all been made by Connolly and Larkin. They'd been told that they mattered, that things could be different. And should and would be different. That it was in our hands. We could change the world. That all we had to do was do it. We had time on our side, and the numbers, and God if we wanted Him and, most of all, ourselves. It was up to us.

And now we were scared.

—I always said two legs were wasted on Jimmy, said Paddy.

He drove the hammer with force made of terror and fury. It went into the wall with a killing thud and, outside, as if ignited by Paddy's rage, an explosion shook the city and changed the colour of the air. It was suddenly white, I felt my eyes blister. A scorching heat ran over us; my skin shrank and cracked. We heard more glass break and beams crashing through boards and plaster. Then we heard a metal whop, and another. We braved the windows and saw flaming oil drums, dozens of them, falling from the night onto the street. And escaped oil fell with them. And splashed sparks and ropes of fire everywhere.

—They're after hitting Hoyte's.

The oil-works up the street had been hit by an incendiary shell and we watched as the drums continued to drop. One of them fell and spilt its oil onto one of the armoured lorries. It swerved and turned, like a cat with its back on fire. And it looked to us like the raining oil was on our side. But the light was scalding and the window frame ignited around us. The oil was landing on everything, trying to climb in; its stink was catching us. My hat was on fire. I grabbed it off my head and threw it at the window. I beat at my head, to kill thoughts of flame. The flames had driven Paddy's hair back. His eyebrows were gone.

—Look at that old prick out there.

We followed his eyes and saw Nelson, at the end of the street, on his perch high above the smoke and untouched by the war.

—Where's me weapon till I fix him.

He went back to the window and, while bullets zipped past him, buried themselves in the window and hopped off the granite sill, he shot Nelson.

—Got him in the other eye, the hoor. Now, lads. Back to work.

We crawled to our hole in the wall, away from windows and snipers.

—A bit of peace and quiet.

And we burrowed again. Became a machine again. Through the wall, we had a hole we could climb through. We looked in first, carefully, expecting to find hard, killing faces staring back at us.

We saw mirrors, velvet, bottles.

—It's the Coliseum, said Felix. —The theatre. I know it. It's the bar.

—Last orders, gentlemen, said Paddy.

I had my arse through the hole when I heard a voice behind me.

—Commandant Connolly wants Private Smart.

It was O'Toole, the honest Boy Scout.

128

—Buy yourselves a drink, lads, I shouted into the bar, and I threw some of the change from my pocket in after them.

—Thanks a million, big fella, said Paddy.

I pushed past O'Toole, jangling what was left of my change.

Four men had gone out next door to the Metropole. As the first shell hit the roof of the hotel, they brought back a brass bed on good, true castors, so Connolly could continue to run the show. I took one bed knob, his bodyguard, Harry Walpole, grabbed the other and, together, we shoved the bed all over the post office. Beside Connolly as he moved, his adjutant, Winnie Carney, took down his thoughts and orders and shouted at people to get out of the way. She ran back to her typewriter, in a corner behind one of the counters; the rat-tat of her typing sent men diving for the ground. *Courage, boys, we are winning, and in the hour of our victory let us not forget the splendid women who have everywhere stood by us and cheered us on.* He was mad, I think, in the last hours. The burning building was dripping all around us. His face was yellow and drenched. He must have been in agony. I could see where bone had come through the skin above the ankle; the bandages and brace couldn't hide the bloody points. And he'd been shot in the left arm.

I pushed him away from the huddled officers.

—Over to Clarke now, son, he said.

I could just hear him above the gunfire and other explosions. We heard, then felt stone toppling above us. A shell had hit the balustrade, the first direct hit. I kept pushing as more shells shaved us and hit the Metropole and Eason's beyond it. There was an eighteen-pounder at the Parnell Monument, pointed straight at us and, behind it, a pair of howitzers, testing the range, playing with us.

—They have us in their sights, he said.

—They took their time.

—True.

Another shell hit the roof. I waited for the toppling to continue down on top of us, horrible seconds, and still the bullets bit at the walls around our heads. Men, on ladders being nibbled by the bullets, knocked holes through the plaster and floorboards, to get the hoses up to the roof.

—We'll never be forgotten, Henry, said Connolly as I rolled the bed up onto Clarke's foot.

Outside, the people inside the military cordon were beginning to starve. There was no one to bake bread or milk a cow. Even the pubs were shut. The bullets were constant. Anything moving was shot; anyone at a window was a sniper. Our last outposts were alone and falling. There were now twelve thousand soldiers in the city, and another four thousand on the way, and a huge pit had been dug in Arbour Hill for the rebel dead, with a hill of quicklime beside it: there'd be no republican funerals.

The shells were dropping on us now in a steady, reliable stream. The machine-guns never stopped. And dinner was served.

—I won't eat that.

I watched a Volunteer turn his back on the tin plate offered to him by one of the Cumann na mBan women, crouching under the bullets in a nurse's uniform.

—Why not? she said.

—I won't eat meat on a Friday.

It was Friday. What had happened to Thursday?

—I'll have it, I told her.

I stood up straight in the main hall and ate the Volunteer's dinner, the best bit of chicken I'd ever tasted. I felt the hot draught of passing bullets, a slice of shrapnel flew into one of my spuds and fizzled, but I ate it all up, every last mouthful. They watched me, waited for God's bullet to send me down to hell. But, as two of the gawking Volunteers were hit by machine-gun spray and fell screaming onto the wet tiles, I lifted my head up, brought the empty plate up to my face and licked it clean. Then I handed it back to the woman.

—Thanks very much, I said. —That hit the spot.

—You're very welcome, she said.

She was trying to control a grin.

—Compliments to the chef, I said.

—She'll be dizzy, she said.

—Good.

We were trapped and cooking. The lift shaft was on fire, rushing flames to the basement. And, while the Provisional Government pow-wowed around Connolly's bed, The O'Rahilly sent me up to the roof, to help keep the flames away from the ventilation shaft.

I crawled below the choking smoke with a hose tied around my waist. There were other men there but I couldn't see them. Shells were falling behind me; I held on every time. I crept. Across the frame that had once held the glass of the dome, onto the safety of slates. In a gap in the smoke I saw a statue, one of the three stone women that topped the post office. Fidelity, I think. I cuddled up behind her skirt. I was right on the edge of the roof. Sackville Street was gone, buried in flame and black smoke. There was a short gap in the smoke, and I saw Clery's: it had a front but no back, sides or roof; the flames tore out of its centre and steel girders hung black and useless. The Waverly Hotel had collapsed and there was nothing now where the D.B.C. building had been. The rubble was scattered in piles across the street. I unwrapped the hose. If the ventilation shaft wasn't drenched quickly the G.P.O. would burn from the centre, clean down to the basement, the explosives and ammo and Miss O'Shea. I aimed.

No water. Not a trickle or cough. We'd lost the supply. Bits of stone nicked my skin, chipped from Fidelity by the bullets. I was down on my belly again. I slid through black water that was starting to boil. I couldn't lift my face. I rolled down over slates that were cracking and melting as my weight flew over them. I stopped on hot concrete and the door was right beside me. It was slammed as I got to it. I butted and thumped it.

And I saw Collins.

—You're not locking me out, bub, I said.

I pushed past him, down the narrow stairs. The O'Rahilly was there too. They put sand in the gap below the door and wet it with water from a bucket.

—Yis might as well piss on the flames, I shouted, but they didn't hear me. I didn't hear myself. The fire was eating every sound. There was a wind scooping up flames and a locked, raging roar from the lift. I heard a slow groaning, building into something huge; the pillars outside were about to give up. I tumbled down the stairs.

The women were being led to a side door, out to Henry Street. Some were scared, but most were angry. And I saw Miss O'Shea. She was being brought along by two other women and shouting back over her shoulder.

—I can fire a gun as well as any man!

One of the women in front had a Red Cross flag and they were all being led by a priest in a stovepipe hat.

—Jesus Christ! They'll be killed out there!

But no one heard me and the door was cleared and open and the women were out. Miss O'Shea didn't look back. She didn't see me. The last thing I saw was the back of her neck, and she was gone. I gripped the banister. It was seconds before I realised that it was burning; I was trying to hear if the shooting outside had stopped.

Most of the men were now in the sorting rooms at the back and in the covered courtyard where glass fell in drops on top of them. I found Paddy and Felix there.

—What's the plan? I said.

—We're going to break through their barricade at the top of Moore Street and then go on into Williams and Woods.

The sweet factory. I'd often put my mouth under a pipe and swallowed the waste that poured out of Williams and Woods; it had been my dinner and tea.

—Then we're going to break through again and head north to the country.

—Just like that?

—Just like that.

We got out from under from the dripping glass. In the main hall, on the last table in the G.P.O., was a pile of food. Sugar, tea, hairy bacon, more cake.

—Fill your knapsacks!

I could see the ham curling, roasting in the heat. Pearse was up on the last chair, delivering a speech I couldn't hear. Kitchener and George V were melting, slithering to the floor. Then The O'Rahilly and Collins were among us and there was action. The whole place was about to cave in.

We were in the first group, about thirty of us.

132

—Fix bayonets! Connolly shouted, from the bed.

Some of the men cheered.

—Henry, said Connolly. —Get out your father's leg.

—Yes, sir, I said.

I took my daddy's leg from its holster and lifted it into the air. The Citizen Army had seen it before, and seen what it could do; it had broken heads and rozzers' fingers during the Lockout. They cheered and laughed.

—Up the Republic! I shouted.

The O'Rahilly was at the front.

—This is it, lads.

He looked back at Connolly.

—Cheerio, he said.

—Now!

The gate was open and we were out. Across Henry Street. In single file. A man fell in front of me. I jumped. His body was riddled with bullets meant for my legs. I landed awkwardly but terror gave me back my stride and now Paddy was in front of me. The men ahead of us threw aside sections of our barricade and we ran through the gap onto Moore Street. And at last I saw the enemy. At the top of the street. At last, the khaki uniforms. We broke into two lines, to the left and the right, and kept running at them and it suddenly seemed very quiet and then the noise was deafening and trapped by the walls of the street, and I heard nothing extra but Paddy fell in front of me and he was dead and his brain and hair were on my jacket and hands and I kept running, and The O'Rahilly had been hit but he kept going, he ran in a zigzag that brought the bullets to him, and Felix fell and I left him behind me, and I was the first, the only man left upright on the street and I could see the bullets, the air was packed with them and, for a fragment of a second, I could think and I jumped at a doorway and hid.

Four or five men were crawling and diving, trying to get out of the hail of bullets. The rest were on the ground; their blood was already like an oilcloth on the street. Paddy's scalp was on my hand, as if I'd beaten his head with the wooden leg. I couldn't cry. I couldn't see him properly back there but I could see that Felix was dead as well; the bullets were still going into him but he didn't know it.

133

The bullets chipped at the doorway, eating away my hiding place. I abandoned my rifle, put the leg in its holster and slithered out. I hugged the house wall and crept back towards Moore Lane. Every bullet ever made flew up that street, at me, at my feet, at my head. They gouged paths in the wall an inch above me. They fractured, made powder of the pavement right beside me. But I kept going, inch on inch, my face to the wall, inch inch inch, and I could see the corner and I was round it. And up. I ran at a door and it broke in front of me. I fell into the hall and heard screams from upstairs. I got away from the door, in to the parlour window in time to see the second wave of men running onto the lane. And there was Plunkett, held up by two men, trying to hold his sword up, one spur hanging crookedly and alone from one of his boots. He saw me. He stopped and made the two men stop in the sea of bullets, and shouted.

—Come out and fight, you cowardly cur!

And he was gone. Connolly was brought past on a blanket, carried by four kids. I ran to the door, back out to the street. I could see men in the alleys and doorways but there were many more men on the ground. I ran to Cogan's, the grocer's on the corner. And through it – the smell of boiling ham – with the other survivors. To a cottage in the yard behind. And there was crying, wailing and a dead girl in the hall, face up on the earth floor, shot in the head – by one of us, there were no other bullets here. Men lay on the ground. I could hear nothing. But I could think. I was catching up. I sat against the cottage wall. Paddy was dead. Felix was dead. I waited to feel something.

—Let's have a look at the animals.

A lit match was pushed into my face.

—You one of the leaders?

I said nothing.

—One of the ringleaders?

I said nothing and stared past the flame into faces I couldn't see.

—You used dum-dum bullets, you cunt.

I said nothing.

134

—Didn't you?

It was Saturday night and we'd surrendered. After hours of moving back and forth with white flags from our last outpost, Hanlon's fish shop on Moore Street, to the army barricade at the Great Britain Street end. Elizabeth O'Farrell's steps on the street outside were the first thing I'd heard since the day before, when I'd seen Paddy, Felix and The O'Rahilly falling. She walked past the window towards the barricade with her white flag held steady as the last of the gunfire died and her fading steps were replaced by the groans of our wounded and the tearing cough of a man upstairs with a bullet in his lung. And somebody's whispered prayer from behind a wall outside. *Jesus, Mary and Joseph assist me in my last agony.* We waited for a shot or a warning cry. The silence hurt my ears; it was forcing me to remember. I heard Elizabeth's returning steps and, this time, Pearse went with her.

—Shall we go? he said, and he held his sword back so that Elizabeth didn't have to climb over it. He followed Elizabeth onto the street. We never saw him again.

More hours. Mumbling and groans; the smell of new blood and old fish. The coughing upstairs had stopped. She came back alone, with a note. *In order to prevent further slaughter of Dublin citizens, and in the hope of saving the lives of our followers now surrounded and hopelessly outnumbered, the members of the Provisional Government present at H.Q. have agreed to an unconditional surrender —.* Signed by Pearse.

We marched, four abreast and steady, down Moore Street. Eyes ahead, arms sloped. Past the silent Tommies; they looked as wasted as us, red-eyed, faces blacked by gunpowder. Another bright, glorious day. Great rebellion weather. We marched onto Henry Street, past the dead and the burning, the bullet-riddled walls and shutters, through the brick dust and heat, into the stink of the horses and smoke, onto Sackville Street, what was left of it. And, for the first time in days – a lifetime – I felt alive again. I felt the blood running through me: I'd wrecked the place, brought it to its knees. I wanted Miss O'Shea. Now. On the street. I wanted to celebrate and cry. Felix and Paddy. We'd really wrecked the place.

We swung around the Pillar, to the left. The flag of the

Republic was still up there, scorched and smoking, on the remains of the roof, swinging from a pole that was hanging over the street.

We stopped outside the Gresham. The military were waiting for us, up at the Parnell Monument.

—Step five paces forward and deposit your arms!

We laid down our guns on the street.

—What's that in your holster, Paddy?

—My father's leg, I said.

—Out with it. With the rest of the weapons.

—No.

The rifle butt went into my back.

—Drop it.

—No.

The butt again, and others. They struck and lashed till I was numb. I wouldn't fall. But the leg was gone, flung onto one of the fires. I was pushed and carried with the rest, up the street to the Rotunda lawn. And there all night without food or drink or permission to piss. The coldest night. I was a statue. Surrounded by soldiers who waited till dark before they got close in and robbed us. My date stamp and money orders, my shawlie commissions.

—Any German marks in your pockets?

I didn't object or budge; I stood absolutely still. My snake belt and holster, the bandolier. Men cried, awake and in their sleep, continued to die in their dreams, cried out for their mammies and God. They shat themselves and stayed put in their shit, afraid of the drunken officers who kept Mooney's open all night. Every streetlight broken and out, it was a darkness that only the farmers' sons had ever known. And the soldiers were all around and among us. Beating and touching, strange accents in our ears. Promising revenge. All night. I stood still and straight, in a ring of bayonets and machine-guns.

Daylight came and the G-men with it, and other slinking bastards who walked around us and looked over the shoulders of the Tommies minding us. Clarke was pulled out and hauled away. And Daly. Two more men we never saw again. And, one by one, the rest of us were taken out.

136

—Name? said a fat rozzer.

He never wore a uniform but I'd seen him many times, hanging around the railings outside Liberty Hall and against the quay wall. A fat rozzer trying to look like a citizen.

—Name? he said again.

—Brian O'Linn, I said.

He looked at me.

I'd walked past him dozens of times, in and out of the Hall, but he'd never seen me before.

—Address? he said.

—None, I said.

—Are you being smart now?

—No.

—Britches but no home.

—I couldn't afford both, I said.

He smiled, and saved himself a slow and painful death.

—Jesus, he said. —What were yis up to?

—It was a holiday, I said. —You have to do something special on a holiday.

—True for you, he said. —Go on.

We were marched across the city, to Richmond Barracks. No drink or food, still no permission to go to the jacks. Brian O'Linn was bursting and gasping. But he walked head-up through the rubbish and abuse, the sticks and smouldering masonry that were thrown at us as we crossed Dublin. The kids and shawlies, beggars and workers came out and lined the streets. They spat and cursed, followed us down through the Cornmarket and James's Street, all the way. We marched right through it. Rotten meat, loosened cobbles, the contents of their chamber pots.

—Bastards.

—Hangin's too good for yis!

They hated us. They absolutely hated us. I could feel it, a heat coming off them. The British were protecting us. I didn't blame the women. It was the first anniversary of the first Battle of Ypres; many of them were in mourning for their husbands. And I didn't blame the others. They were starving, some of them homeless, and a slum was better than no home at all.

They wanted to tear us with their own nails and teeth. There were men around me sobbing.

—We did it for them. Don't they know that?

And other men sang. *She's the most distressful country that ever yet was seen.* I marched. *For they're hanging men and women for the wearing of the green.* Stones hopped off me. A gob of poor man's spit landed on my cheek. I could smell the furious breath of the city. I marched right through it. I saw other men hanging back, and women, faces behind the angry ones. Sad faces, looking out at us. Standing there to let us know: they didn't all hate us. I saw them.

Into Richmond Barracks. We were stopped on the parade ground. More cursing and kicking. More G-men and rozzers. Roll-calls. Searches, robbing and pushing.

—O'Linn, Brian.

No one laughed.

—*Anseo.*

—Step forward.

There was a face in my face, daring me to flinch or twitch.

—In English, you bastard.

—Here, I said.

And de Valera marched into the barracks, the Spaniard himself, led by two Foresters on bikes, surrounded by other soldiers who looked thrilled to be off the streets. A man near me cheered and was butted to the ground. De Valera walked straight up to us. He had the staring, empty eyes of someone who hadn't slept in years and knew he'd never sleep again.

—Solitary for that one, said an English voice to my right.

—Photograph first, sir. The last of the Shinners.

The famous photo. The last man to surrender. Hands behind his back, a Tommy on each side of him, another behind. I was there, to the left of de Valera (I never called him Dev). The photographer was a bollocks called Hanratty. A slithery little get with premises on Capel Street and connections in the Castle. I was beside the great man but Hanratty wouldn't see me. I'd just put my life into the hands of the Empire by answering back with one of the few Irish words I knew – *Anseo* – still defiant, still proud and unrepentant. But I wasn't important. The first time I saw the photo my elbow was in it, but even that went in later versions. No room for Henry's elbow. Just all of de Valera and his guards, three English kids barely bigger than their rifles. If Hanratty had moved his camera just a bit to the right, just a fraction of a bit, I'd have been in. You'd know my face, you'd know who I was.

—Big smile now, said Hanratty before he disappeared under the focusing cloth. I was smiling. I hadn't eaten in a week, I was manky and sore, I'd watched my friends die, but I still smiled for him. And he missed me. It became the photograph of Éamon de Valera. It became proof, part of the legend. There he is, the soldier, the father of the state. A foot taller than his guards. Serious and brave, undaunted and straight. I was there. He was wearing red socks and he smelt of shite. They marched him away.

We were put into cells and taken out. More roll-calls. The G-men strolled and took their pick. Hoey, the biggest bastard of the lot, pointed his finger. And MacDiarmada went. Never seen again. There were still snipers out there, refusing to surrender. Every distant shot brought khaki down on top of us. But something was happening to me; I was beginning to shake. I could feel my blood racing, starting to pull. I was being dragged away from the parade ground. By something I couldn't see or hear. Something inside me.

—Name?

—O'Linn.

The G-man, a new one, stared at me. He knew me, but I didn't care. There was something more urgent; I could feel it – water. Under me. Running under the barracks. And it was dragging me. Every bone I owned was bending towards it, quivering, promising to snap if I didn't move.

—Smart, said the G-man.

And my blood was steaming now too, roaring, refusing to wait. I yelled; it was agony.

The G-man mistook my cry.

—Caught, he said.

—My hole, I said.

And I didn't have to search for the manhole. I knew exactly where I ran. Across the parade ground, I was there without moving and I had my fingers in under the cover. A loose part of me remembered that there were other men and I forced myself to stop – my bones; I'd never known such pain – and I shouted.

—Come on, lads!

The cover came up for me like paper and I held it up, a shield against the bullets that were coming for me, and I walked backwards into the hole. I sent the cover spinning at the G-man.

And fell.

Into darkness and nothing. I fell and the pain left me and, just before I hit the water, in the second it took to fall, I caught the sweet smell of my father's coat and I could feel his neck against my face as he held me to him, and I could hear Victor's excited and terrified breath from the other side of my father.

Into the Camac River. I came up out of the water. *The bridge it broke down and they all tumbled in.* My legs could feel the bottom and my hands found a wall. *We'll go home be the water.* I pushed myself, fell away from under the opening and the light that came through it. I fell into the water and let it take me away from the bullets that were churning the river. I could see nothing. *Says Brian O'Linn.* I went under – I had air enough to take me anywhere – and up. I used my legs and the current. I saw nothing and I could smell nothing except the water, sewer that it was. Right under Inchicore. And Goldenbridge. I knew exactly what was over me, where I was being brought. I saw light and the river rushed out into the day, but I knew that I was safe; weeds and overhanging branches hid me from harm. Past the Metropolitan Laundry. Suds and the washed-out shit of the filthy rich tore at my eyes but a hand I knew I could feel lifted my head, then lowered it into clean water and I was under again, in darkness. Light again, behind Kilmainham Gaol, tucked under the wall, and away. Back under the city. Bow Bridge and the Royal Hospital, under St John's Road and I was in a sewer again and I felt fingers under my chin – safe safe safe – holding my mouth over the goo. Kingsbridge Station, right under the buffers, I could feel the locomotives, under all the rail-lines and ballast stones, and I was dropped into the Liffey. Opposite the munitions factory: I felt its burning sludge in my eyes as I swam back up to the surface.

I was on my own again. I could feel it through me; it was up to me and me only. Safe as long as I worked at it. I hugged the quay wall, in under any shadow or ledge that could hide me. Under Bloody Bridge, I created no foam, never kicked my legs. I let the retreating tide carry me. Victoria Quay, Usher's Island. No faces looking down. Whitworth Bridge. No wheels or footsteps. Martial law all over the country; the half-seven curfew was approaching. Merchant's Quay, Wood Quay, under a barred-up hole in the wall of the quay, and the River Poddle dropped its load of shit down on top of me. I crossed the river under Grattan Bridge, and heard the last shouts of a paperboy.

—Castle official hit be a manhole cover!

Getting dark now, he was going home, off the streets. Selling all the way.

—Official hit be manhole!

Now that it was dark enough, I climbed out of the river at the Metal Bridge. I ran across to Liffey Street and went looking for Piano Annie. The river had dyed me. I took off the jacket and dropped it as I went. There was no uniform now. I was just a big wet boy in a pair of brown britches, caught out in the street after the curfew.

On Wednesday morning, the 3rd of May, in Kilmainham Gaol, Pearse, Clarke and MacDonagh were taken out to the Stonebreakers' Yard and shot. At dawn. And across the city, in Summerhill, Henry Smart couldn't get out of his britches.

—They're welded to you.

Annie grabbed my waistband.

—Come here to me. One. Two. Terr-eee!

Together, we pushed and pulled my britches down to my thighs. Then Annie grabbed my arse before it had had a chance to draw breath.

—Jesus, what's that?

It was a sheet of twopenny stamps, still stuck to my cheeks a week after Miss O'Shea had thrown me down onto them.

—Stamps, I said.

—What are they doing there?

141

—It was the only way I could smuggle them out. You can write to your husband now, Annie, I said.

—The dead can't read, said Annie. —And he couldn't read, anyway, when he wasn't dead.

—Oh, I said.

—Oh is right.

They brought the bodies across the river to Arbour Hill and threw them into the pit and covered them up in quicklime. *Huns, huns, huns.* There were cheers in the House of Commons when the news was announced.

Annie threw my britches out the window, down onto Langrish Place.

—Don't do that, I pleaded, too late. —Ah, Annie.

—They stink.

—Could you not have washed them?

—Fuck off. Come here.

The britches would have been gone by now, wrecked and all as they were, already covering someone else's arse, so I took my shirt off on the way over to the mattress.

Annie placed her fingers on the knuckles of my spine. She blew into my belly button, as if clearing it.

—You stink too, she said. —But I like it. And your bruises.

Her fingers tapped my spine.

—Now, she said. —What'll I play for you?

—Do you know *The Boys of Wexford*?

—Every fuckin' one of them, she said.

And we fucked each other into the curfew, and slept and fucked again. We hung on to each other and whimpered and laughed and tickled and bit and cried.

—Four more exee-cutions! Four more exee-cutions!

Ned Daly, Plunkett – he'd married Grace Gifford the night before, in the prison chapel – Michael O'Hanrahan and Willie Pearse. Into the pit with the other three, another blanket of quicklime.

—Why do you want it? said Annie.

She was looking up at the wooden leg. I'd put it on the mantelpiece. It was burnt black but still a leg. I'd spent the night, before arriving on Annie's step, roaming the rubble of Upper Sackville Street, searching for it. Looking in the pitch

142

dark, over still smouldering walls and plaster. Dodging the scared eyes of Tommies and rozzers. I lay on hot brick and let it dry the river off me.

—Old times' sake, I said. —It's been good to me.

—Did the real one grow back?

—I hope so, I said.

—One more exee-cution! One more exee-cution!

John MacBride. *It is hoped,* said General Maxwell, *that these examples will be sufficient to act as a deterrent against intrigues, and to bring home to them that the murder of His Majesty's liege subjects, or other acts calculated to imperil the safety of the Realm will not be tolerated.*

Paddy's head broke apart in front of me. It kept happening, there was no let-up; his brains and dry shards of his skull flew back at me, into my nostrils and mouth and eyes. There was an eyeball in my mouth, growing, sliding, I couldn't get rid of it. Dying, drowning, the shout that would save me couldn't get to my mouth. My mouth was open, stretched, trying to reach the noise. But I was drowning.

Annie hauled me up. She fought me, slapped back my flaying arms and feet; she pulled me, held me tight with her arms and legs, tighter.

—There there.

I knew her. It was Annie. Paddy was gone. I searched her room, looked for him in the dark. He was gone. I was sure he'd gone. He was dead, buried by now. I could move my mouth.

—There there, she said. —That's right.

She cried too. I could feel her tears on my face; they were warmer than mine.

—Poor little Henry. Poor poor poor poor, poor little Henry.

And she felt the other little Henry pressing against her.

—Feeling better?

—Yes, thank you, Annie.

In the merry month of May. Her fingers were on my back again – *from my home I started* – lifting and dropping – *left the girls of Tuam* – brushing and pinching the rhythm – *nearly broken-hearted* – as she whispered right up to my ear. *Saluted father dear, kissed me darlin' mother.* I was wide awake now; I'd never slept. *Drank a pint of beer my grief and tears to smother.* I was on top of Annie now, ready for the chorus, dying for it, bringing her to it, and through to the rest and black sleep that would follow. *On the rocky road to Dubellin, one two three four five.*

—Four more exee-cutions!

Heuston, Mallin, Con Colbert, Éamonn Ceannt. Annie was out foraging. I pushed away the sacks she used for curtains and looked down from her window at the top of the house. The trams were running again; I could hear them climbing past the bottom of the street, on Summerhill. The kids were in the school yard at the other end. My old school. I wondered was Miss O'Shea out there, looking after them, or was she in jail? Or hidden, or dead? I put my tongue to the window and licked her little rivers. But all I tasted was grey air and dirt on the glass that became black as my breath steamed the window. It was just the same old place out there. The same old buying and robbing, stray dogs and children, bare feet and sores, matchstick legs and rickets. Flaking brick and rotten wood, running filth, and dying coughs from open windows. But there was a young chap down there at the corner. I leaned out to hear him. He was selling something.

—Last of the rebel pictures! Last of the exee-cuted rebels!

And there was a small queue, made of the same people who'd thrown stones and shit at me a week before. And now they were buying prints of Pearse and Clarke and Plunkett that they could never afford. And Annie brought me home the stories. Gunshots at dawn. The slaughter on North King Street. Sheehy-Skeffington's murder. The last words and letters of the dead men. *My darling wife, pulse of my heart, this is the end of all things earthly.* Locks of beloved hair, buttons from jackets and shirts. *I kiss this paper that goes to you. . . I and my fellow signatories believe we have struck the first successful blow for Freedom.* A wedding at night in a prison chapel lit by a single candle. *My darling little boy, remember me kindly. . . Ireland has shown she is a Nation. . . Slán leat. Do not fret.*

And I ventured out in a pair of dead man's trousers, with a dead man's wife on my arm.

—He wasn't very big, was he, Annie?

The wind was whipping away at my ankles.

—He was big enough, said Annie.

Every woman we met, every black shawl, had me itching to run; they'd all seen me hanging from the post office window, kissing Annie, on Easter Monday. Annie felt it in me, the way I held back. She squeezed my arm.

—You've nothing to worry about, she said.

—Are they on our side now?

—I'm not on your side, darling, and you're perfectly safe with me. They'd like to tan your arse but they'll never hand you over to that shower of murderers. And I'll tell you another thing.

—What?

—They're wondering what sort of a love letter you'd write to me if you were going to be executed.

—A great one, I said. —Anyway, they could find out if they informed on me.

—God almighty, said Annie. —You're all the same. You can fire your bang-bangs and march till your arses meet the ground, but you'll never understand romance.

We crossed Gloucester Diamond.

—They'll never turn you in, she said. —And what's more, they'll make their husbands join the rebels if they ever come back from the war.

—Even though they don't believe in it?

—That's right, said Annie.

We crossed Tyrone Street and on. It was early morning but there was no room for the sun in Faithful Place. The bullies were already on the steps of the kip houses; the city was full of soldiers, far from home, angry and victorious. I'd spent hours and nights down here, with Victor, waiting for our father to come back. I'd felt all the boots and eyes; we'd crouched in every shadow. It was the only place I knew that could frighten me.

Annie stopped us outside Dolly Oblong's.

—That's where I'll be going when the war's over. If I'm not too old by then.

—Why, Annie?

—There'll be no place else for me. There'll be no more allowances once it's over and won. Or lost. Whatever way it

145

ends up. The Germans won't pay us and you republicans won't be handing out money to the widows of His Majesty's forces, sure yis won't?

—We did already. Remember?

—*You* did, Henry. But they'll never let you do it again.

—I'll be with you, Annie.

—I don't want you to start lying on me, Henry, she said.

—I'm not —

—Shut up.

We were moving again, out of Faithful Place, past the corn- and sawmills. Their mixed dusts whirred all around us.

—I don't know much, Henry, said Annie. —But I do know this: the times never get better for the likes of us.

She pulled my arm.

—Still and all, she said. —There's a short while as well when they get no worse.

We strolled on down to Amiens Street, around piles of rubble, to Beresford Place. I looked at the Hall from behind one of the pillars of the broken Loop Line. There were soldiers and rozzers on the other side. I didn't know what they were doing over there. It was just a shell now; there was no one in there and no one coming back.

I heard feet. Lots of them. Marching.

Annie nudged me before I could start looking for ghosts.

—Here's all your butties now, she said.

And here they were. Marching over Butt Bridge. Several hundred Volunteers and Citizen Army men, familiar faces, not ghosts either although still masked by powder and dirt, and fiercely thin. They were marching between lines of armed troops and other soldiers on bikes, led by a nervous officer on top of a white horse. They turned right, under the bridge, and I was right beside them. I winked at Charlie Murtagh. He saw me and grinned and stopped himself. He leaned and nudged the man beside him, Seán Knowles. Still alive, still alive. And Collins was in there too, in among the Volunteers, half a head over them, out for a stroll.

The crowd that had been following them sensed that their time was nearly up; the men were about to be loaded onto a boat, so the shawlies and scuts ran to catch up and surround them. The parade came out from under the bridge, past the Custom House, towards the North Wall and the waiting cattle boat. There were supporters there too, and people newly converted by the executions, and fighting broke out in the crowd. I let go of Annie and went after them. I picked up a good stone as I ran. The soldiers ducked to avoid stones meant for rebels. I ran ahead of Collins, turned and skimmed the stone on the air. It whacked him neatly and dropped off his shoulder. He grabbed his ear and glared at – and saw me and stopped. Men marched right into his back.

—Will you feed the cat till I get home? he yelled.

He was pushed towards the gangway.

I nodded, and he went on. I dropped back, in case there were government eyes in the crowd. More stones hit him but he didn't acknowledge them. I watched him walk up into the boat. Annie was gone when I got back to the railway bridge.

On Friday morning, the 12th of May, James Connolly, a dying man in brand-new pyjamas, was brought from the hospital in Dublin Castle to the Stonebreakers' Yard in Kilmainham Gaol. He was tied to a chair and shot. MacDiarmada had been shot minutes before him, the last two bodies thrown into the pit.

Annie tied her legs around me. She grabbed my hair, to pull me away from the window and the newsboy's roars. She dragged me back to her side of the bed, dragged, and let go when she realised that I wasn't resisting. Her legs stayed around me.

—Did you know him? she said.

—No, I said. —Not really. He was dying anyway.

—Poor Henry, she said.

She rubbed the backs of my legs.

—There'll be no stopping you now, said Annie. —The country'll be needing new heroes now that the English are after shooting all the old ones. They'll need new men to shoot and love.

She tightened her leg-hold on me.

—You'll write that letter to me, won't you?

—I'll do it now if you want, I said.

—No, you won't, she said. —You'll be too busy.

147

She lifted herself and climbed onto my chest.
—Now, she said. —Lie back and think of Ireland.

PART THREE

7

Three years on a stolen bike. Through wind, rain and bullets. Henry Smart struck strange, hard blows for Ireland and disappeared.

I did nothing at first, after the last of the executions. I stayed with Annie. I even got work. Annie went out foraging and came back with bread under her shawl and a job for me. Down on the docks.

—Just go up to the stevedore and tell him Piano Annie sent you.

—What's his name?

—Don't know. But he has lovely eyes.

I looked for a man with lovely eyes on Custom House Quay and found a fat dwarf standing on a chair and shouting out names over the heads of the dockers who waited at the quay wall.

—Piano Annie sent me.

—Fair enough, said the dwarf. —What's your name?

—Fergus Nash.

He scratched my new name on the end of his list. We were the same height, with the help of his chair. His eyes didn't look that lovely to me. They were well hidden behind hair and lids. I wondered what Annie had done to make him show them to her.

—Right, said the stevedore. —O'Malley, he shouted.

The voice was a lot bigger than the rest of him. The ships and boats seemed to creak more as it pushed against them, and

151

it sent the seagulls flapping back out to sea. It lassoed a man walking away from us, down towards George's Dock. He stopped dead, and turned.

—We won't be needing you after all, the stevedore shouted. —Go home and have a rest and come back tomorrow. Now, mister, he said to me. —The Inner Dock. Off you go. The good ship *Aristotle*. Ask for Kavanagh and he'll give you a nice shovel.

I walked past O'Malley. He looked old, ready to lie down, but there was enough of the stuff left in him to spit at the ground I was about to walk on.

—Scab.

I kept going.

—Scab.

I was angry, ready to go after him and lock my jaws to his back but, really, I didn't blame him. I'd robbed his job. But I'd done it fairly. Every morning for the best part of a year I'd go down to the Custom House and stand with the hundreds of other men, and wait for the stevedore to remember my name. There was no job for life, or even a week. Every day was a fresh start, a terrible wait until the stevedore remembered or forgot you. I saw O'Malley every morning and more often than not, and more and more often during the winter of 1916 and '17, he went straight back home, wherever that was. He was already an old man at thirty-eight or nine, and me and the other young lads were the ones who were making him old. And one day, in February, a freezing morning that was never going to get any less vicious, there was no O'Malley. That was the end of him. His days as a man were over.

The older men hated the young ones, even when they were their own sons. They saw a new young lad strolling up and perching his arse on a bollard, waiting to be spotted by the stevedore, and they knew that their working days were almost done. The dockers were the toughest men in Dublin, but old ex-dockers were just old, nothing more, old men, like all the other old, broken men crawling around the city. They watched the young lads arriving, shy but big, bursting out of kids' clothes, raring to burn energy, and they knew it: they were dead. And they hated me more than the other young lads

152

because I could do the work of three of them; I couldn't help it. They could see it in my shoulders, before I even picked up a shovel; they could see it in my walk and eyes, in the way my cap loved my head. I was the first name off the stevedore's lips every morning that year. I often wished he'd do the decent thing and ignore me, but he never did.

The *Aristotle* was a crumbling bucket full of coal from Lancashire and I was sent down into its rusting centre with ten other men. All day, on a diet of coal dust and cold tea from a bottle, we filled the tubs that came down to us, dangled over us, blocked out what small light we could grab. I swallowed clouds of dust; I virtually smuggled it off the boat, enough to get any decent fire going. I could taste it, feel it settling in my belly, tumbling towards my lungs. But after four or five hours, I found that I could still talk as I shovelled, small bursts that didn't leave my mouth hanging open for too long.

—The stevedore, I said.

—What about him?

—How come?

—He's the stevedore?

—Yeah.

—He shrank, said the man beside me, a chap somewhere in his twenties who still swung his shovel like a show-off.

—Shrank?

—True as God.

—How?

—Don't know.

We stepped back onto the coal as the full tub was hoisted up out of the boat's gut. The light lit the dust and the coughing around me intensified; it was easier to breathe in the dark.

—You hear stories, said my new friend.

—Go on.

—Too much of the gee, he said.

—Go on.

—Took all the sap out of him.

I was fourteen, remember: it made sense, although the idea of there ever being too much of anything, especially sex, was out there in the dark, way beyond my experience or imagination.

153

The new tub was dangling over us, dropping our way.

—Used up all his marrow, he told me. —And serves him right. He's been up on every man's wife that's working here today. Except mine.

—And mine, I said.

—Fair enough, he said. —That makes the two of us. We're a very small club, pal.

He let his voice drop under the noise of the approaching tub and all the other noise that constantly shook the dockland.

—It's how they all got the start here, he told me.

We filled the new tub together.

—And the bloody young fellas, he said. —Half of them are his. More.

—I'm not, I told him.

—Oh, I know, he said. —I can see that. Think about it, though.

He left me thinking while I heard his shovel bite under the coal and he lifted the load and dropped it into the tub.

—The whole of Dublin and most of bloody Ireland is getting its coal and everything else from the sweat of that dwarf's bastards. That's no way to run a bloody country, is it?

—How did it go? Annie asked me when I got home that night.

—Grand, I said. —What colour are his eyes, anyway?

—A colour that has no name, she said. —The state of you.

Dried sweat and coal dust were a shell on my face, neck and hands. And I liked it.

Annie tapped my cheek.

—Jesus, she said. —Are you in there at all?

—I am, Annie, I told her. —Bursting to get out.

The *Aristotle* was gone the next morning, replaced by another coal bucket, and we climbed in and emptied it. I was digging coal for Tedcastle one day, filling my lungs with dust, and it was a boat full of pitch another day, and the eyes were burnt out of my head; dropping the lids over them was an agony at every blink. But grain was worse. Coal dust came with every breath but grain dust soaked up the air, robbed it as it hinted itself at your mouth. There was nothing at all left to breathe. I stood, surrounded by loose, high hills of wheat from

154

Alberta or Dakota, in the dark of a wreck that should never have made it across the Atlantic, and willed everything to stop and stay absolutely still, just for a few seconds, the other men's shovelling, the noise, the bobbing of the boat against the pier, and the other boats along the dock and the tugs making waves, the gulls landing on the water, everything, the chaff whirling around my face, for a second, just for half a second stop, so I wouldn't faint and die. I suffocated all day long, fought back death with my shovel.

And then there was phosphorite. The phosphorite left your eyes more or less alone, or did no more damage than the pitch, but it went straight for your teeth instead. A day in the bowels of a boat full of phosphorite was a message from hell and the stevedore. A quick mouthful of the stuff was a lesson you never forgot. Digging away, as if to escape but actually burrowing deeper into it, while I felt my gums being eaten, a growing itch and pain, teeth wandering if I clenched them. It was said that Guinness's porter was breakfast, dinner and tea to the dockers and it was literally true of the ones who'd been banished to the phosphorite boats once and twice too often. The gummy ones. The men with collapsed faces. They couldn't eat, they hadn't even the gums for porridge; the porter alone kept them alive. I saw these men and could easily believe that the stevedore's whole body had collapsed. They were huge men with tiny, crumpled heads. Hardchaws and trouble-makers who'd been sent to melt in hell.

I got into a fight. With the only other man on the docks whose wife hadn't been fucked by the stevedore. We stood at each other with bale-hooks. I'd bumped into him while hauling a stray crate of German ball bearings out of the path of a cart. He shoved me back, and there we were.

—Come on! he said.

I let him bluster.

—Come on, yeh dwarf's bastard!

He swung at me. It was a careless, furious lunge. I grabbed his arm on its way back and pulled him to me, and gave him the butt of the hook to the side of his head. I held him by the hair that came out the back of his cap and got ready to smack him again, to knock him right into the ground. His hook went

155

around my leg. I let go of a thump that took years and inches off him. He fell back and the hook followed him, with some of Annie's husband's trousers and a chunk of my leg. I fell onto him and decided to kill him. I kneed and bit whatever was under me, and searched for some meat to park the bale hook. And, suddenly, there was a foreign roar – there was a third party in the ruck. The stevedore. He was in between us. I didn't know how long he'd been in there or how much of a hiding I'd given him. His fingers were in my nose and eyes. His face was in my face and Annie was right: there was no word for the colour of his eyes. And I understood something else: he was gorgeous.

I jumped away off him. Two of the other dockers broke my flight over the quay and into the water; I didn't care where I was going.

The stevedore stood up. Then he got down off the only man's stomach and let him stand up.

—Go home, he said. —The pair of yis.

There wasn't a sign of exertion on him, not a wheeze or a smudge.

—He started it, said the only man.

His fury was still hopping around inside him.

—Go home, said the stevedore. —Come back in the morning.

We did just that, home and back the next day, and the only man was sent home again to cool off for another day and I was sent to shovel phosphorite, and the next day and the next. It was my last fight on the dock; I learnt my lesson very quickly. Working inside a cloud of phosphorite was the hardest money I ever earned. By the end of a phosphorite day, I didn't know how much cash was being put into my hand. I couldn't really see, my mouth was a loose, angry mess, my hands red and screaming, barely capable of holding onto the readies. We were paid in the pub, every night; and a pint out of the wage for the stevedore, every night. A phosphorite veteran helped me to get my glass to my mouth. He held my wrist and guided the glass to my bottom lip.

—'hanks, I said, afraid to let my tongue touch my teeth.

I was being eaten alive by phosphorite, losing substance by

the shovel-load. But on the sixth day the stevedore hesitated after shouting out my name, then sent me off to the Old Dock, to hump bananas. Annie must have worked hard on him; she must have gazed long and hard into those eyes.

And I loved it. The work. Every minute of it. I loved the dirt that settled on me. I loved the racket and the danger, the smell and feel of foreign things, even when it was only coal or even the phosphorite. I loved the mystery of the chests and crates, the origins stamped on their sides – Kashmir, Dresden, Lille, Bogotá. I saw them, I smelt them. Coffee, hair oil, jute, tobacco. Rubber, pencils, copper, sugar cane and the oil that nursed machinery parts, the invisible dust of packed marble and the wild aroma of mahogany. And all the stuff we could feck – top hats, cuckoo clocks, all the finished goods and fruits. And the weight and importance of steel and iron ore. I was in the heart of the world. And I loved the escape in the evenings, the tiredness and the end of it, the first drink and then home to Annie. I was alive all day and night. The screech of unwilling metal, the weight of a load on my shoulder and back, biting through the sack and jacket that covered me, the unmerciful, slow progress of weighed-down cart-wheels. Cattle and sheep sliding on the ice, the thumps of their hoofs on the gangplank, the shouts and accents of the drovers. Running kids, making balls of the slack, to bring home or sell, from coal that had been crushed under wheels, doing what me and Victor used to do, escaping from under horses' feet and the stevedore's boot.

—Yeh dwarfy fucker! Yeh dwarfy fucker!

All of it.

The smell of the water, the way it lapped against the lock that kept the high tide of the river out of the docks. And the foreign lads on the boats, men from everywhere; they shouted to one another and it killed me that I couldn't understand them. Chinese and Nordic, and black men of all the shades. Scots and Spaniards and travelled Irishmen. And the working girls waiting for the foreign men on the North Wall Quay, on the other side of the suspension bridge, exposed to the wind and daylight, the gulls squawking over them. All that life and hardness, misery and possibility. The Custom House Docks became my favourite place in the world. I belonged there.

And I liked bringing things home to Annie. Annie knew more about living than anyone I ever knew. There was never enough – good, bad, pain, pleasure, too little and much – Annie took the lot and fucked the consequences all and every day.

I held up a pineapple. I was proud of this one; it had taken more sneaking than the bananas I'd smuggled the day before. She was sitting on my chest.

—What's this yoke here? I said. —I'll give you three guesses.

—It's a pineapple, said Annie.

—You knew, I said, disappointed. I'd been sure it would be new to her; it was the weirdest looking thing I'd ever held in my hand.

—Listen, buster, she said. —I was bringing home pine-apples, and better ones than that one, a long time before I ever laid eyes or hands on you. But, sure, sling it over anyway.

She threw the pineapple over her shoulders and licked the tiny pockmarks Miss O'Shea's nipples had left on my forehead.

—Someone got here before me, she said.

Ball bearings, big nuggets of coal, oranges, a box of needles for a gramophone —

—All we need now is a gramophone.

Lisle stockings, tea, a gramophone – smuggled out in instalments over the best part of a month. I hid the remaining parts in a corner of the Tobacco Store, a warehouse alongside the Old Dock with enough in it to feed, clothe and make the world. I hid the parts in a high corner, in under the eaves, beside all the other items that the dockers hid there.

Annie and I listened and, with the window open all that summer and autumn, all of Summerhill listened to John McCormack singing the same song – *The little toy dog is covered with dust but sturdy and staunch he stands* – until there were no needles left in the box.

Annie ran her fingers up and down my back.

—What's it this morning? she asked.

—John McCormack, please, Annie.

She plucked at the knuckles of my spine. *The little toy soldier is red with rust* – her ankles gave my arse an encouraging shove it didn't need – *and his musket moulds in his hand.*

The wire mesh for a meat safe, the tassels off the border of a Persian rug, anything I could get under her dead husband's jacket, at once or in instalments, they all came home to Annie. One chest in every hundred we'd break open with our bale-hooks and divvy out the contents. We'd fill our pockets with tea and on days when it was raining, combined with the sweat of our labour, the tea stained our jackets a shade near purple and we wore the sacks low on our shoulders until we were safe past the stevedore and his lickspittles. Home to Annie and her gramophone. When I eventually got home.

The dockers were the hardest men in the world. Their guts were lined with coal dust and pitch. They came to work armed with blades, iron bars, bale-hooks, their own knuckledusters. They drank to wake up in the early houses before work. And they drank during work, washed down the world's dirt and grit and fed the headaches. And after work when they went to collect their wages, in Paddy Clare's or Jack Maher's, the dockers' pubs, they drank what was left in their hands after the stevedore had finished doing his sums. While their children starved – and their wives too, on top of being fucked by the stevedore after he'd drunk his cut of the wages or sold them back to Paddy Clare – the dockers drank themselves into fighting form and looked around for some poor goat to take the place of the stevedore. Glasses of whiskey went into the pints of porter. And God help any poor eejit who walked in on top of a roaring docker swinging his belt. Harmless men ended up in the river and some of them never climbed out; they went under the lock and fed the mullet. The dockers were beyond the law. They knew no rules except their own and the stevedore's. They were heady company for a young man who'd been left all alone by the dead. And I started to keep up with them.

So it went for the best part of a year. Work and drink and Annie. I knew that there were things happening, that the match we'd lit in Easter Week was becoming a bit of a fire. There were by-elections down the country, victories for Count Plunkett and Joe McGuinness, Joe the jailbird.

—Put him in to get him out, said Annie when she saw me coming at her.

And there was the return of some of the Easter Week men

159

from the camps and prisons in England and Wales. I knew that they were back in town but I saw no one and I didn't go looking. I had Annie and food and my memories of Miss O'Shea; I had my strength and sweat and the company of the hard men. The dockers didn't have much time for republicanism; they lived too close to the water, I supposed, and spent most of their days with their backs to the country. Collins was back and the other big fellas but I saw and heard nothing of them. Liberty Hall was a pile of rubble that I walked past twice a day. I wasn't part of anything now. It was the only year of my life that crawled and the pace suited me beautifully. Annie, work and drink. I walked home after a couple of drinks, home to dinner and John McCormack.

But then I wasn't interested in dinner because of the drink inside me. I roamed the city and roared at the stars, whenever I saw them. I fell into Annie's room at the end of my wanderings because even I had to sleep somewhere and lying on the ground outside reminded me too much of Victor. Sometimes she let me in and, when she didn't, I fell asleep against her door whispering into her room.

—He had a wooden leg, Annie. Did I ever tell you that?

—It's on my fuckin' mantelpiece.

She locked me out but she never left me all alone.

Until, once, there was a chair against the handle inside. I kicked and fell and kicked again with the flat of my boot and shouted at Annie to let me in, it was too cold for the landing and I'd pulverise the door and the rest of the room and whole fuckin' house if she didn't let me in.

Her dead husband opened the door and stood over me as I turned over on the floor where I'd dropped.

—Who the fuck are you? he said.

He was in his khaki uniform, a Dublin Fusilier. There was nothing tin or rusty about him, although the poker in his hand had seen better days.

—Who the fuck are you, yourself? I said.

He had the poker hanging over my head and I was wearing his trousers and jacket. I was sober now and hoping to Christ he didn't remember them.

—I'm Annie's husband, he said. —Who the fuck are you?

160

—Who the fuck is Annie? I said.

My arm saved my face from the poker. He had a fierce swipe, for a dead man.

—That's Annie, he yelled, and pointed at her with the poker. She was sitting on the mattress. She didn't look worried or scared. She knew me: I wasn't going to let her down. I looked at the mantelpiece but my father's leg was missing.

—Where's Nellie? I said.

—She's up in her room behind the wallpaper, he yelled, and he got ready to let me have it again.

He'd been away for three years; back from France, back from the dead, he needed to be in charge. And here was me, proof of his wife's infidelity, of the waste of those years and mud, wriggling on the floor under him, caught and stupid, a big, strapping lad, in a jacket that delivered a familiar smell when he whacked it with the poker, while he'd been away, spitting away his life for every country in the world except Ireland.

I could have killed him. I was armed for it. But I stayed on the ground and gave him the chance to reject the proof between his feet. I did the decent thing; I acted the eejit. I saved Annie and her husband.

I looked around me.

—This isn't Nellie's room, I said.

—Who's Nellie?

The voice was softer, clinging to the chance.

—I'd show her to you, I said. —If she was here. I'm in the wrong house.

—Which house should you be in? he said.

—I'll never drink again, I said. —That's the problem. I'm no good with houses when I've drink on me.

He stood away, to let me up. I let myself stagger, although I'd never been more sober.

—Sorry about this, I said. —Am I after getting yis out of bed?

And I noticed that the hand not holding the poker wasn't there, and I knew that he was home for good: I was homeless again.

—What colour's your front door? I asked.

—Black, said Annie. —When it's anything.

—Ah, there, I said. —So is Nellie's.

—Most of the doors in Dublin are black, said her husband; we were friends now. —You've your work cut out for you, pal. Finding your Nellie.

—Ah sure, I said. —She'll know where I am. Everywhere except where I should be. I'll wait till I've my head back and I know what's what.

—Not here, you won't, he said.

—No no, I said. —I'm off. Sorry for disturbing yis. If it happens again you'll know it's only me.

—Cheerio, said Annie.

—Cheerio, I said back, and I hoped she'd hidden my da's leg in a very good place, in a place where a one-handed man would never find it.

I wandered.

I walked the city until it was time to walk to work. I walked in circles and bigger circles, over the Easter Week rubble that hadn't been shifted yet, over the hidden rivers that turned my blood to running steel, through Cowtown, along the canals. That night and the nights after, I walked every square inch of Dublin and looked on every step for my mother. I hadn't seen her in years. I'd run out of basements to search. One day she was where she always was, face pressed to the black sky, the next day she'd vanished, not a hint or child left behind. I couldn't fool myself into thinking that my father had come back for her. I still looked, sometimes in the weird hours before day when I was numb and unable to think properly. I'd turn corners, expecting to see her, a lump on the steps smothered in children. I looked for her shadow in the windows of the South Dublin Union. I climbed into Glasnevin Cemetery and tried to feel her as I crawled among the paupers' graves. And, on the nights when I had to lie down, I even visited Granny Nash.

—Where's Mammy, Granny?

—God knows; the eejit.

Head in the book. Nose sliding down the valley between the pages. *Don Quixote de la Mancha. Confessions of an English Opium Eater.* Looking for spells.

—Have you seen her?

—Not at all.

She didn't see me lying down on the floor.

—She should never have married the fella with the leg.

She had to lift her head while she turned the page. I heard the paper scraping across the tip of her nose.

—Him and his Alfie Gandon, she said.

—Who's Alfie Gandon? I said.

—The cause of all their troubles, she said. —And they never even knew it, the eejits.

And that was all. She was in the book again and, by the time she got to page-turning time again, she'd forgotten I was there.

I started bringing her books. I'd take them off the stalls outside the bookshops and run. I'd dangle them in front of her and try to get her going. She'd read the title on the spine. Then she'd put the book on top of the others beside her or fling it over her shoulder.

—Read it already, she said.

Ivanhoe hit the wall above the stove.

—What about this one?

I put it in front of her. *Mountain Charley, or the Adventures of Mrs E.J. Guerin, Who Was Thirteen Years in Male Attire.*

—This'll do, she said, and she put it on top of her pile.

—Who's Alfie Gandon, Granny? I said.

—He thought he was a woman, she said.

—Who did?

—The Smart eejit, she said. —The wooden fella.

—Who did he think was a woman?

—Gandon.

—What woman?

—Oblong.

—Dolly Oblong?

—There's only one.

The hoor, the madam, owner of the biggest and best brothel in Dublin. Her son-in-law's former employer.

—Did Gandon dress like Dolly Oblong?

—Not when I saw him, she said. —The wooden fella was an eejit. Gandon walked past him every night of the week and he never saw him.

I was lost, but I knew that I was close. Close to what, I didn't

163

know. I took away what clues she gave me and let them fall apart and reassemble while I roamed the streets and alleys and waited to go to work. And before I turned for the docks, when the noises of the city waking up told me that I could go, I often stood at the railings of the big school and waited to see if Miss O'Shea would arrive early. It was a year since I'd seen her, since she'd walked out the Henry Street door of the G.P.O. But I didn't see her. And on days when the stevedore didn't want me I went back to the railings and watched the children and other teachers, nuns, priests and mothers. But I saw no brown dress or buttons, no boots or bun or basket full of books. She was gone. She was dead. Or working somewhere else. I started looking for her in the nights when I walked the city. I went further. Rathmines, Clontarf. Rathfarmham, Killester. Places where a rebel teacher might live.

Now that Annie was confined to barracks, the stevedore's eye skipped over my name every four or five days. He had wives to ride, sons to employ. So I wandered the city in the daytime and waited. And every night, without fail or decision, I ended up in front of Dolly Oblong's. I watched the sailors and locals coming and going, the fighters being thrown out, the guilty scurrying back into the dark, the shadows at the windows.

I saw the huge, glorious woman, Missis Oblong herself. I saw her glide down the steps, into a waiting car.

—*A Vindication of the Rights of Women*, read Granny Nash. —I'll hang on to this one, she said. —The wooden fella loved the Oblong item.

I didn't have to ask her any more: a clue for a book, that was the deal. I handed over a book; she handed over the information. I broke into a house on Merrion Square and walked out the front door at five in the morning with two matching suitcases full of books, all of them written by women.

Missis Oblong slid into the waiting car. There was a man with her and this man was, I found out from the bouncer of the kip across the street, the famous Mister Gandon. (My father, as usual, had been wrong. Dolly Oblong and Alfie Gandon were never the same person. —Mister Gandon speaks highly of you, she'd told him. —You are efficient. You are cautious enough not to ask questions, stupid enough not to care. He likes this.

—*She's* Alfie Gandon, he'd decided.

Just there. It had thrilled him. He'd been overpowered by her and the bedroom when he'd been called up to her from his place on the steps outside; the carpet, the bed, that mountain of a gorgeous woman in front of him, the hair that was plenty for five or six women, the hint of the foreigner in her words, the peppermint that sailed from her mouth to him. She'd moved in the bed like a monument. She couldn't have been that sensational without being equally brilliant and devious. He'd become devoted to a woman of his own making, as false as her teeth and hair. He'd fallen in love with my mother's name, a woman that was never my mother; then he fell in love with another of his own creations, the Dolly Oblong that was also Alfie Gandon, a woman that never existed. —I am a business-woman, she'd told him. And she was. She ran a kip house, a good one, and she made a packet. But she wasn't Alfie Gandon. Alfie Gandon was Alfie Gandon. She'd passed Gandon's messages on to her one-legged bouncer but she'd never composed them. She knew how to make money but she was just a big old tart who was too lazy to get out of bed more than once or twice a week.

My father was a gobshite.)

But who was Alfie Gandon?

Mister Gandon was a businessman, and one of our own, the bouncer from across the street told me. He was a Home Ruler and a Catholic, not like most of the tail-coated fuckers who robbed the people blind and called it business.

—He's a landlord and a killer, said Granny Nash. —Now give it here to me.

I'd let her see the spine: *The History of Mary Prince, a West Indian Slave, Related by Herself*. I'd noticed something: she got excited when the books were by women. That was why I'd spent hours in the library in Merrion Square while the owners slept above and their servants slept below me, filling the suitcases with only the works of women. She was repaying me now with better and more information.

Mister Gandon had his first bootstraps on a ribbon around

165

his neck, the bouncer across the street told me, to remind himself of where he'd come from. Mister Gandon had joined up with the Sinn Féin crowd and, now that they had him, we wouldn't be long in getting the English to pack up and go home.

He was elegant, I could see, small but properly shaped, still managing to dominate the solid men who hopped out of his way when he left and arrived. He was much smaller than Missis Oblong but fitted perfectly beside her as he slipped into the car after her.

—Alfie Gandon says Hello, said Granny Nash.

—What does that mean, Granny?

The Wonderful Adventures of Mrs Seacole, in Many Lands. I put it on the table in front of her.

—Alfie Gandon says Goodbye.

—And what does that bloody mean?

—Alfie Gandon says Hello, she said. —And you mind your mouth in front of your poor granny.

I was patient. I stored it up and waited for it to fall together. I'd enough stolen books hidden away in the Tobacco Store to keep the old witch fed and talkative for another couple of months.

I was down and homeless but there were days when I was welcome to warm my feet quickly at Piano Annie's fire. On mornings when the stevedore didn't want me I ran back up to Summerhill, past Annie's. If there was a wooden leg in her window it meant that she was waiting for me. She never had to wait for long. While she played on my back the new songs from America she was picking up off the gramophone, the stevedore was giving work to the only one-handed docker in the world.

—How does he manage? I asked.

—How do *I* manage? said Annie. —Don't bother taking your boots off. I'm expecting a little visitor.

And she showed me how to play the piano standing up. She was as enthusiastic as ever but necessity was forcing her to play by the one fast rule:

—More than three minutes is waste.

She was out from under me; she left me holding myself up

against the door with my forehead, gasping for the first indoor breath my lungs had had in days.

—More than three minutes is dangerous, she said. —Out you get now till I hide your oul' fella's leg.

—When can I come again?

—You'll know, she said.

Three days later the stevedore ignored me again and I saw Annie's dead husband marching off to the docks. Lugging bananas one-handed wasn't so hard and he'd never have to shovel phosphorite. I was happy for him and by the time he got to the Inner Dock, before he'd the sack on his back, Annie was fingering my back with one of her American songs – *Sooooo send me away* – good man, good maaaan – *with a smile*. You finished before me there, Henry, my lovely lad.

—I'm a fast learner, Annie.

—If you can get out of here as fast we'll be a very happy couple.

I didn't want to go yet.

—Is he good to you, Annie? I said.

—Which he?

—Your husband.

—He's grand, she said. —He's had a hard time these years. He finds it hard. Go now.

—What about a walk?

—Don't be stupid, Henry. Go on.

I knew I'd never be at home in Annie's house again. I missed her.

Letters of a Javanese Princess. I slid it under the old witch's eyes.

—How come you can tell me so much about Gandon but nothing about your own daughter? I said.

She shoved the book back at me.

—I seen that one already, she said. —Who d'you think you're codding?

—How come?

She might have noticed the anger; she didn't look up.

—Some things are worth knowing, she said. —And some aren't. She's dead.

—Where?

167

—Nowhere.

—Fergus Nash?

I turned away from Paddy Clare's counter but I brought my bottle with me, in case I needed a club. I had a chisel in my pocket but I didn't want to go for it.

—Your name is Fergus Nash?

—Yeah.

He was like the rest of us, in a coal-covered jacket and trousers. His cap was off and I could tell from his forehead that he'd washed himself quite recently. He had a half-gone pint in one hand and the other was in his jacket pocket. I'd never seen him before.

—I knew you when you were Henry Smart.

He spoke softly. The accent wasn't quite right. I studied his face again, looked behind the dirt. Nothing came back; I still didn't know him.

—You've got the wrong man, pal, I said.

—No, he said. —I don't think so.

He was nervous but sure of himself. He looked straight at me like someone who had other men to back him up. I looked past him, but I knew all the others, and none of them were with him. I fit there; he didn't. He was by himself, although Paddy Clare's could have been surrounded by uniformed rozzers and the more dangerous men from Dublin Castle, outside waiting for the signal to roar in and take me. I was in trouble. He was a G-man, I decided, a detective from the Castle, but the decision didn't bring recognition. He wasn't one of the bastards who'd stared at us over the shoulders and heads of the soldiers as they rounded us up and marched us off to Richmond Barracks the day after Pearse had surrendered. I'd never seen him at any of the roll-calls in the days after, when they'd taken away the leaders and shot them. And back before that, before the Rising, he wasn't one of the ones who'd hung around outside Liberty Hall, trying desperately to blend in with the railings. I didn't know him at all.

—Who are you? I said.

—Dalton.

I still didn't know him. But I was changing my mind about him. He edged a tiny bit closer to me. I stayed put.

—Jack Dalton, he said. —I was there the day you dived down the manhole. And that, man, is one day I'll never forget.

He held out his hand, and I took it. I felt the softness in his fingers under the blisters and cracks; real dockers' hands were always hard and smooth, like worked mahogany, from years of rubbing the shovel. I let go of his hand when I saw the pain slip across his eyes.

—I've been away for a while, he said. —A hotel across the water.

—And now you're back.

—That's right, he said. —Will we go somewhere else?

—Fair enough.

And that was how I found my way back in. Jack Dalton had been in the College of Surgeons in Easter Week, with Michael Mallin and the Countess. He'd spent the time since then in Frongoch and Lewes, until two weeks before I met him. He'd joined the Volunteers – F Company of the First Battalion – before he had a job or a roof over his head, two hours after he got off the boat from Liverpool.

—They're in a dreadful state, he said. —There's none of the old crowd. It's all students and kids.

The job on the docks came the next morning.

—He's one of us, he said, of the stevedore.

—Are you married? I asked him.

—No. Why?

—Just wondering.

He had a room in a house in Cranby Row by the end of the same day.

—The landlord is with us as well, said Jack.

—No rent then?

—You're joking, man, he said. —He's not that bloody committed.

By the end of the night we were old friends. We went on a crawl that left us holding each other up on the way back to Jack's room. I liked Jack; I knew him immediately. He was a great swinging mixture of passion and fun. His eye could pin you dead, then wink at you. He had both eyes for the women and a tenor voice that could open cans. He loved singing out of doors. *He fought like a lion with an Irishman's heart.* He was singing as we turned onto Rutland Square, trying to co-ordinate our march.

—You could be arrested for singing that, I told him.

—Quite right too, he said. —It's shite. But its heart's in the right place.

And he sang to the lit windows of the Rotunda. *The pride of all Gaels was young Henry Smart.*

That stopped me. I nearly fell onto the street. Jack laughed at my shock. He held me up by my collar.

—You didn't know they were singing about you, did you, Henry?

—No, I said. —I haven't heard that one.

—You haven't been listening. It's doing the rounds, man. I heard Dev himself singing it when he was in solitary. He hasn't a note in his head.

—Who wrote it? I asked him.

—Who knows? he said. —The people. That's where all the real songs come from. Come on now. I'm starving.

—Sing the rest of it, will yeh.

—Tomorrow, he said.

He had tea and bread and butter and thick slices of cooked ham and even a hunk of porter cake. I felt them all settle down inside me and the sugar in the tea told me that life was just great as I sat on the floor and listened to Jack. He wasn't a born docker; my reading of his hands had been right. He was an architect, but wasn't going back to it until after the revolution. He didn't have time for blueprints or building.

—What revolution? I said.

I'd had my fill of revolution; I thought I had.

—The one that's coming, he said. —It's on the way, man.

When the country was free, when the last Englishman was on a boat or in a box, then he'd start designing houses that were fit for people. He'd build halls and cathedrals. Dublin would be a jewel again. We'd go at every reminder of the Empire with a wrecking ball made from all the balls and chains that had fettered the people for centuries. There'd be no

170

evidence left of England by the time we stopped for a rest and our dinner.

—We'll have no use for granite, he said. —It's the stone of the empire builder.

—But it comes from Wicklow, I said.

—Along with most of the other traitors and Protestants who've made our country's history such a misery. Don't talk to me about Wicklow. Renegades and adulterers, the lot of them. We'll have our own architecture, man.

He could deliver sense and shite in the one sentence. And it struck me even then, although I didn't think much about it at the time, that his Ireland was a very small place. Vast chunks of it didn't fit his bill; he had grudges stored up against the inhabitants of most of the counties. His republic was going to be a few blameless pockets, connected to the capital by vast bridges of his own design. But I liked listening to him and loved the idea of knocking down Dublin and starting afresh. I'd roll my sleeves up for that particular job.

—So what'll you do when you've built the turf post office? I said.

—I'll build a bridge across the Liffey and name it after you, he told me.

And I believed him. *The pride of all Gaels was young Henry Smart.* The night before I'd been homeless and alone and now I was warm and full, in the wild and generous company of Jack Dalton, my new friend and old comrade in arms. The plans and dreams rolled out of him that night and other long nights.

—And when I'm finished with Dublin I'm going home to Limerick. I'll tell you, man, it'll be the Venice of the west by the time I put down my pencil.

And by the time he announced that he had the legs walked off his tongue and he needed some sleep for the next day, I was ready to die again for Ireland; me, who had never been further than Lucan, who less than a year before had jumped over the bodies of friends lying dead and destroyed, who would never have given a fuck what de Valera sang in his prison cell. I was ready to die for Ireland. I was ready to die for Limerick. Ready to fall dead for a version of Ireland that had little or nothing to do with the Ireland I'd gone out to die for the last time.

171

I lay on Jack's floor and slept well and dreamt of nothing at all. We walked down to work together the next morning and collected our wages together and by dark that night I was a Volunteer. And when we got back to Cranby Row there was a mattress waiting for me where the bare floor had been the night before.

—Where did this come from? I said as I fell back and let the mattress cuddle me.

—I told you already, said Jack. —The landlord's one of us.

—Good man, the landlord, I said. —Fresh straw as well.

—Fresh straw in every mattress, said Jack. —It's only a matter of time.

—That sounds like socialism.

—What it is, said Jack, —is a lot of straw in a country full of straw. It's an easy enough promise to keep. And don't be bothering yourself with socialism. That stuff's only old Jewish shite.

The next weeks and months were the best of the war, when none but a few – and I thought I was one of them – knew that there was a war. Long before a shot was fired, an ambush or an execution. It was the prelude, the build-up, and I was in at the beginning. Like Jack, I was in the First Battalion, F Company, the Company made up of recruits from the area north of the Liffey. And, like Jack, I caused a silent stir when I walked into the room. I was one of the legends, one of the survivors of Easter Week. I was Fergie Nash every morning on the Custom House Dock when I waited for the stevedore to shout that name – and he did, every morning when I was there, from then on – but every night I was Henry Smart again. They gawked at me like I was an apparition, one of the executed men come back. They were afraid to speak to me, scared even to meet my glance; their arses hovered over their chairs, in case I wanted to evict them. It was heady stuff; I was a walking saint. And there were women there too, secretly looking at me. I'd forgotten for a while what that was like. I'd hear their talk and whispers, the boys and girls, before I entered the room, and I quickly loved the silence and adoration that were coming my way.

We met at 25 Rutland Square, in rooms rented by the Gaelic League. We came and left through different doors, carried copybooks and pencil cases to prove to G-men and their lurkers that we were there for our Irish lessons. I'd seen death and handed it out, only a year before; I'd seen the G-men taking men away to be shot; they'd stared into my face looking for the excuse to do the same to me – but there was nothing like the excitement now of walking past a frozen G-man in a trenchcoat, in a Rutland Square doorway. The sheer fun of it: for the first time in my life I was behaving like a kid.

—That's a cold one, Sergeant.

We were laughing our way to the new Ireland. Robbing apples for Ireland. Crawling over roofs, spitting down on the G-men, dropping slates to their feet. Shouting down names at them.

—Hey there, Bollicky! Does your mammy know you hang around street corners?

—How much for a ride, Sergeant?

Bringing them out cups of tea.

—Enjoy that now, Sergeant, because one of these days, man, we're going to shoot you.

He laughed because he was afraid not to. He looked down the street, to the safety of another trenchcoat in another doorway.

—Would your friend like a cup or will yis share?

—I don't want it, said the G-man.

—You'll have the biscuits at least, said Jack. —They're Irish, like ourselves.

—No.

—We could have them delivered for you, said Jack. —We know where you live.

We walked back into the hall before the G-man could gather himself.

—Do we really know where he lives? I asked Jack.

—No, said Jack. —But we will.

For those first months, before Dublin Castle knew how to cope with us, we flaunted our secrecy, right up to their faces. Jack had done his spell in jail. We both knew the fizz of passing bullets. There wasn't much that could frighten us. We'd already won.

Annie noticed the change in me.

173

—Jesus Christ, she said.

She climbed down from where I'd ridden her, up on to my shoulders. In the last seconds, before I came – she'd got there a good minute before me – her fingers couldn't reach my back. They lost touch with my shoulders and she'd been singing *a cappella*. Her head was close to the ceiling.

—Who's been feeding you meat?

—No one, Annie, I said.

—You're up to something, anyway, she said. —Aren't you, mister?

—No, Annie, I said.

—Go 'way, yeh pup. The last time you rode me like that you were crying for all your dead friends. You're a soldier boy again. All ready to die for the dear little shamrock. Remember that letter you said you'd write to me before they shot you?

—I do, I said. —But don't worry. There's no reason for me to be writing last letters.

—Just don't forget it. Because you're up to something.

Back on the floor, she held on to my arm; she didn't trust her legs yet. She took a good deep breath and shook her head.

—What about another song? she said. —It's early yet.

—Sorry, Annie. I'm a busy man.

—I knew it, she said. —Dying for Ireland.

—I'm dying for no one, I told her. —Have you heard *The Bold Henry Smart* yet?

—I'm listening to him, she said. —Unless it's a song you're talking about.

—Keep an ear out for it, I said. —I'd love you to play it the next time.

—I only take my songs off the gramophone these days, said Annie.

—Maybe that's where you'll hear it, I said.

—Maybe, she said. —But I'm only listening to the ones from America. I've had enough of the Irish ones.

—Maybe the Yanks'll be singing it yet.

And I was gone.

Jack and I spent hours of the night in the lanes and back alleys of the north side, looking for sniping positions and escape routes. We'd been trapped in the G.P.O. and the few

174

other outposts the year before. It wasn't going to happen again. We were going to control the city.

—We won't be caught this time, man. They'll be the ones coming out with their hands up.

We mapped the city, planned our victory. And we ended up the nights in pubs, houses that were friendly to us, with other men who had seen action in Easter Week or had just missed it, men who had experience and, in the snugs or safe corners, we drank and laughed to the future. We were young and having a ball. The older men, the ones who were going to knock us into shape, they were still in the prison camps in England. Or they were dead: the ghosts of Easter Week followed us everywhere and we had to drink hard and quickly to be able to ignore them, and I had extra ghosts of my own to ignore. We were having our holidays before the real work started; we knew we'd deserve them. Those of us who had already killed, the old-young men of Easter Week, knew what all the nightly meetings and open furtiveness were leading us to. We were toasting our own deaths. *To give up my gun they'll need tear me apart.* And every night when we were walking home Jack Dalton sang sedition. *The heart of a Fenian had the bold Henry Smart.*

Sometimes, just to keep the G-men fit, we met up in the social hall of the American Rifles on North Frederick Street and, our noise disguised by the dancing classes that shook the building most nights of the week, we practised our drill.

—Are you out for the dancing, Sergeant?

With mop and broom handles on their shoulders and even shovels we took home from the docks, we put the youngsters through their paces. *Proud sight, left right, steady boys and step together.* We had them going at each other with wooden bayonets, up to their thighs in imaginary gore, all the evening while the dancing ladies and gents below hid us behind their wall of sound and the blood dripped onto their heads. The G-men must have noticed the parade of grazed knuckles and broken fingers that walked past them at the end of every evening.

—A waste of time, said Jack. —But it's good for morale.

He was right. The only useful tool for bayonet practice was a bayonet. The only way to teach a man how to kill with a gun

175

was to give him a gun and someone to kill. So we started collecting money every week, threepences and sixpences, all marked into the Quartermaster's green book, which I minded, the money and the book, until we got round to electing a quartermaster. And we started buying guns. Dublin was a garrison town; there were more barracks than houses. The Great War still had more than a year left to run. The city was crawling with Tommies and Irish-born squaddies, and lots of them were broke and desperate enough to sell their rifles to us. Officers, even Unionist officers, came looking for us once word got round that ready cash could be had from the Shinners in exchange for working weapons. We gave four quid each for Lee-Enfields. We upped it to a fiver when a colonel in the Munster Rifles threw in his Official Army Military Manual with the gun, as well as a box of bullets and a map of Dublin Castle. We carried the manual around inside the covers of a book, *Uncle Tom's Cabin*, one of the few that Granny Nash hadn't wanted.

—I had an Uncle Tom, she said. —I won't to waste my time reading about another one.

—What was there between Alfie Gandon and my father, Granny?

—Everything.

—What does that mean?

—Everything.

I could smell women again. And I could look up at the stars again and grin.

—Oh Henry Henry HenREEE!

I shouted at the black sky.

—Are you looking!?

—Oh mother! Who are you talking to?

—Relax, relax. Just my brother.

—Where where?

—He's dead.

—I want to go home now.

—No, you don't. Lean back against the wall there and I'll tell you how we charged the G.P.O.

Me and Jack just had to look in the door of a *céilí* or concert, a fund raiser for the dependants of the dead and jailed of

Easter Week, and the women of the Gaelic League and Cumann na mBan were queuing up for their own three minutes of immortality – longer, maybe, if they went with Jack, but Piano Annie had trained me well. I loved women again. All of them. And I wasn't looking for a new mother or a shoulder to cry on or hair to bawl into, a dinner, a bed for the night, someone to listen to me. I was just doing what came natural: I was fucking women who wanted to fuck me. I was a living, breathing hero – and the best-looking man in the room, owner of the eyes that brought tears to the fannies of every woman who ever as much as glanced at them. I scored at every *céilí*, sometimes two and three times before the night was over and we all had to stand for *The Soldier's Song*, and I never once had to dance. And I never paid in; I was my own dependant. I often didn't make it through the door. I'd go up and they'd be waiting for me. They shared me. I wasn't interested in conquest. But I didn't have to be. I ended up riding the unconquerable, the unimaginable.

I felt the floor hop under me – there were three hundred women and men next door doing The Walls of Limerick – as I pushed in from behind. She leaned her hands against the toilet door, keeping intruders out and helping me in. The choice of venue was mine, the position hers. This was something I did four and five times a week. I remember them all, every woman, but this one stands out: I was riding the arse off the mother of one of 1916's executed heroes. I won't name names. Her son's portrait was wobbling on the opposite side of the wall as the dancers cantered past him and his grieving mammy backed into me. But I won't name names. Her husband was taking the money at the door.

And another girl, another cold night, rummaged in her coat pocket after we'd gone for a walk and found a lane off Gardiner Place and a wall that would act as a bed.

—Will you do a favour for me, Mister Smart?

—Henry.

—I couldn't —

—Henry, I said.

—Ah, I can't.

—Ah, go on.

—Henry, so. Will you do me a favour?

—Sure, I said. —What?

She took her hand from her pocket.

—Will you bless my beads for me?

And I did.

I met them all and I never got tired. I loved arriving at the steaming door of a *céili* in full flight and waiting there; I'd close my eyes for the surprise of age, size, skin. But always, always, before closing my eyes, I looked first for Miss O'Shea. But she was never there. And when I opened them again, she still wasn't there.

We paraded with banned hurleys, we saluted in public. We nailed a flag and greased the pole and watched the rozzers climbing and sliding. We learnt our tricks from the Harold Lloyd and Charlie Chaplin films we watched all afternoon in the La Scala when the stevedore gave us the day off. We got in for nothing. The staff were sympathisers and came to all the *céilís* when they weren't working. We ambushed pigs on their way to Britain. Our own butchers slaughtered them in a yard beside Binns' Bridge and we delivered them to Donnelly's bacon factory in the Coombe – Irish pigs, Irish labour, Irish stomachs – in a procession across the city, dozens of carcasses on four drays, our men with Lee-Enfields guarding both sides of the bridge as we crossed the Liffey. And now, as we rattled through the narrow streets of the Coombe, the people who'd spat on us not long before applauded.

Somewhere in the excitement of ambush and convoy I remembered my time in Liberty Hall. I looked at the sharp, angry cheekbones of the women we passed and the skinny, meatless legs of the children who ran beside us.

—We should give this bacon out to the people, I said to Jack as I steered the cart onto Patrick Street.

—No, Henry, he said. —Not a good idea. We don't want to interfere with internal trade or anything like that. What we want to do is show everyone that we can run our own country. We have to show the factory owners and the rest of them that these things will go on without the English. And that they'll go on even better without them.

We turned off Patrick Street, onto Hanover Lane.

178

—These people know what all this means, he said.

He nodded back at the dead pigs behind us and the other drays following us.

—Jobs, he said —Making bacon and making the money to buy the bacon. That's what this is all about. Keeping our own money. We get rid of the English and everybody's happy, man. Everybody. The owners, the workers. Even the pigs because they died for Ireland.

He had everything figured.

—This is just the beginning, Henry. We're going to take over everything. Commerce, the post, the courts, tax collection. The works, man. We'll run the country like they're not even here. And all the time we'll be persuading them to go.

—And what happens after that?

—After what?

—After they go.

—What do you mean?

But we'd arrived at the front gate of Donnelly's and I never got an answer. I forgot all about the question.

—Are you going to arrest me, Sergeant?

I marched in front of the G-man with a hurley on my shoulder.

—I'm breaking the law, Sergeant, look.

I stopped right under him. He stood three steps above me, leaning into the door pillar, hoping it would turn to rubber and hide him.

—Under the Defence of the Realm Act, I said. —I'm breaking the law. You have to arrest me.

—That's what you'd like me to do, said the G-man.

—Of course it is. I'm breaking the law.

—Trying to make fools of us.

—It's your law, Sergeant. Not ours. So, arrest me.

I was provoking him. And I was breaking the law. Carrying a hurley for mock-military purposes was now illegal, probably more unlawful than walking around with a rifle on my shoulder. We wanted the Castle rozzer to arrest me. We wanted to expose the absurdity of the law, the stupidity and callousness of the regime we were stuck under. We wanted to provoke them into action. Once they started, then we could

179

really start. And once we started, they'd have to try and stop us. They had the uniforms, the numbers, the weaponry. And they'd push the people, and the rest of the world, into the choice: us or them. The war was already won; all we had to do was get them to react.

—I need the leg, Annie.

—Take it, she said. —No one's stopping you.

—I'll still call, though, I said.

—Maybe you will, she said. —And maybe you won't. And maybe you'll be welcome and maybe you won't. Remember that letter.

Frongoch and the other jails in England had been emptied of Irish rebels and Dublin was full of restless men, desperate to get back into action, still sweating and giddy after Easter Week. They'd learnt the mistakes and were set to go again. These were the rosary boys come home, the lads whose knees had polished the tiles of the G.P.O. while the incendiary shells and molten dome glass had rained on top of us. They were grim fuckers, most of them, and made even more saintly and self-important by their time in the cells across the water. We could feel their impatience drilling into our necks at meetings in the Gaelic League rooms and they held up the walls at the *céilís* and puddled the floor with their disapproval. Not for them dancing or sandwiches. There was no more riding in the jackses and, the odd time when I went in for a piss, I always remembered to wash my hands.

The fun was over.

I had to give back the green book and the gun money. (Minus my 10 per cent.) One of the saints was now the Quartermaster, a clerk in Hely's of Dame Street. I had to start handing up money myself every week. Then they wanted money for uniforms.

—No, I said.

The kids who'd been singing about me a few weeks before slumped in disappointment. They'd wanted uniforms even more than the rifles.

—We can't have an army without uniforms.

The speaker was Dinny Archer, a graduate of Frongoch – he

later became known as Dynamite Dinny – and he was looking straight at me.

—True for you, Dinny, said someone behind me.

—The uniform didn't do me much good.

Piano Annie's dead husband was the speaker and he was waving his stump. He'd joined up a couple of weeks before, a heart-stopping event when I looked up from the green book to take his name and gun money, until I was reasonably sure that he didn't recognise me.

Archer spoke again.

—A man with a gun is a criminal. A man with a gun and the uniform is a soldier.

—Hear hear.

—True for you.

—A man with a uniform is a target.

Ernie O'Malley was the speaker this time. He was several cuts above the other young lads. I liked him. There was an intelligence about him, a twist to the lines on his forehead that impressed me. He was a saint who hung up his halo now and again.

Archer spoke again. He'd stood up and walked to the top of the room, put himself in charge.

—There are men in this room, he said, —who wore the uniform of the Empire and they now feel qualified to give us advice on what we should wear.

—I wore no uniform, said O'Malley.

—You have a brother, said Archer.

—I have several brothers.

—Serving the King of England, said Archer.

—This is ridiculous, said O'Malley.

—I needed the work, said Annie's dead husband. —I couldn't get work anywhere in Dublin after the Lockout.

I looked at Annie's dead husband again. I tried to remember him, in a different place, four, nearly five years before, in the corridors or the soup kitchen in the basement of Liberty Hall, or up around Drumcondra at night, on the hunt for scabs. But I couldn't see him in that time. He'd have been a young man back then, not the man I was looking at now, nothing like him.

There was no support at all in the room for Annie's dead

husband, no sympathetic nods or True for yous. Dinny Archer filled the gap.

—You and the likes of you were put out of work by unions controlled from England, he said. —They set Irishman against Irishman. And then off you went and did exactly what they wanted. You joined the King's army, you and thousands like you too stupid to be called traitors, and you put back the real struggle by years.

—True for you, Dinny.

Annie's dead husband wasn't the only old soldier in the room. *The trenches are safer than the Dublin slums*, the recruitment poster had claimed, and it was true if it referred to the chances of your children getting a good meal. There were men in the room who'd gone to France to survive. Yet no one interrupted Archer. They were vulnerable, even frightened.

—The unions are there to deflect us, he said. —Larkin's an Englishman. We don't need or want their unions. Or Labour. If you want that, well, Russia's the place for you. This is a fight for all Irishmen, not just a couple of west Britons.

What was I doing there?

There was a portrait of Connolly, another west Briton, on the wall behind Archer.

What the fuck was I doing there? Now, according to Dinny Archer and the True-for-you men behind me, that was what Connolly and Larkin had been up to: setting Irishman against Irishman, colluding with the Empire, forcing young men to become fodder for the King. I'd lived in Liberty Hall during the Lockout; I'd been taught to read, write and stand up straight by James Connolly himself; I'd been one of the first and certainly the youngest to join the Citizen Army, and I'd watched my comrades – there was a word I hadn't used or thought of in a long time – I'd watched them being mown down on Moore Street as they ran at the barricades for Irish Labour. And now, I sat there and listened and left Annie's dead husband stranded. I watched him shrink deeper into his threadbare jacket. I was tempted to hand over mine – his – to him; it was in much better condition. I let Archer insult him and me and the only people and everything I'd ever believed in.

Why?

And why did I come back the evening after?

Jack Dalton.

—Let them have their uniforms.

—What about secrecy —

—Listen, man, he said. —The half of them are spies, anyway. Remember that every time you open your mouth. Say what you want them to hear. And the other half are eejits. Let them buy their uniforms and then let them march up and down every bloody street in Dublin all night and all day. The more of them the better. And while they're doing that and the peelers and their spies are following them, we'll be somewhere else doing the real work. There are wheels within wheels, Henry. Cells inside cells. Put your coat back on. It's time you met someone.

It was one o'clock in the morning when we went back out onto the street. We looked for the shadows of men hiding, we listened for scraping shoe leather before we moved off. And, as I always did in the real quiet of night, I listened for the tap tap of a wooden leg. We were alone on Cranby Row, as far as we could know.

We took a crazy route, across and back across Dorset Street three times before we headed north and east.

—Where are we heading?

—Someplace nice, said Jack. —*Oh he slipped through the night, did the bold Henry Smart.*

We slid over a back wall, onto empty barrels and crates of empty bottles. Jack gave four raps and another one to a black back door. It opened and we were in.

Phil Shanahan's pub. Not far from Dolly Oblong's. Shanahan's was one of the centres of the revolution. No pub ever did more for Irish freedom. There was no Phil or even a curate behind the counter but the place was full of men making smoke and quiet conversation. I followed Jack across the low-ceilinged room. There were faces I knew, that I'd last seen blackened and charred as the G.P.O. fell on us, and others I'd never seen before. Then Jack stood aside and I found myself looking at the broad, straight back of Michael Collins. The coat fit him well but it was ancient; his shoulderblades were coming through. There was a tear at the back of his trousers, below and behind the right knee.

He sensed us there and turned, a hefty lad with a face that was very pale, even in the half-dark of the room. He brushed back a lock of hair from his forehead.

—Well, mister, he said in that accent of his. —Are you ready for the next round of the fight?

—I am, I said.

He looked at Jack and back at me.

—The best of men, he said.

Before I went back to my bed that night I'd been sworn into the Irish Republican Brotherhood, the secret society at the centre of the centre of all things. I was a Fenian. I was special, one of the few. And before the end of the week, by late Saturday afternoon, I'd murdered my first rozzer.

8

A protest meeting, proscribed, as we'd hoped it would be. Beresford Place, in front of the ruins of Liberty Hall. We were demanding prisoner-of-war status for the remaining Easter Week prisoners in Lewes Gaol. Things got ugly – we made sure they did, although the police never needed much help. During the scuffling and shouting I took a running swing at a Castle rozzer with my father's leg. The papers the day after said it was a hurley. He hit the ground at the same time as the wooden smack came back at me, and the leg stung nicely in my hand. We were off the street and gone before the dead man, an inspector, was noticed. He was in plain-clothes, so the uniformed lads thought that he was one of us at first. They stepped over or on him in their efforts to get at more people and I was well away, making plenty of noise in a very public bar, whingeing about a horse out in Leopardstown that was chewing one of the fences instead of jumping it earlier in the day, before they noticed the elegant cut of the rozzer's jacket and turned him over. And they saw the dent in his forehead.

That was the plan: one dead man.

—A taste of things to come, said Jack. —A little prologue.

One dead man. I wasn't to shoot or knife him. Nothing too murderous; that was the order. The whack of a piece of wood, almost an accident.

—Only the lads in the Castle will be able to read the message properly, said Jack. —They'll see the intention in the hollow.

And the British would hit back; they'd over-react. They always did. Over the next four years, they never let us down. It wasn't that they made bad judgements, got the mood of the

185

country wrong: they never judged at all. They never considered the mood of the country worth judging. They made rebels of thousands of quiet people who'd never thought beyond their garden gates. They were always our greatest ally; we could never have done it without them.

Count Plunkett, the non-sitting Member of Parliament for Roscommon North and father of executed Joseph Mary of Easter Week, an old man with a broken heart, was grabbed and arrested at the Beresford Place meeting. The Defence of the Realm Act – Big DORA – was swung threateningly all over the country. There were to be deportations, court martials for illegal drillings and marching and for the making of speeches likely to excite the populace. Swinging a hurley became an act of rebellion; being Irish was becoming seditious. We were forcing the issue and nobody knew who we were. And by the time the one hundred and twenty-two released men of Lewes, with de Valera looking well and sane again after his rest in jail, by the time they sailed up the Liffey and disembarked in exactly the spot where they'd been shoved aboard the year before, they were ready-made heroes: they'd sailed home into a new country. They were greeted by thousands and carried on eager shoulders through the streets to Exchequer Hall, where they signed a linen scroll, designed by Jack Dalton, embroidered by two fast-fingered girls from Cumann na mBan, a message for President Wilson and the United States Congress.

—We're making history, said Jack. —Not just acting it out, man. We're writing it. D'you know why there were thousands down at the docks today?

—Because I whacked the rozzer.

—Yes. That's why, exactly. *We're* deciding what's going to happen next. Not them. If we do something, they'll do something. If we do something else, they'll do something else. It took us hundreds of years to figure it out but that's what we're doing now. Writing the history of our country. That's what. We're going to change the course of history, man. There's only one future. The Republic. All others are going to be impossible by the time we're finished. Fate, Henry, is my arse. We're the gods here, man.

I believed him. One swipe of the da's leg and the gobshites in the Castle had hopped. We had them on strings. *Now Henry Smart was a Dublin boy, a lad without equal or peer.*

—It was your daddy's leg decked the polis, wasn't it? said Annie.

—Ask no questions, Annie, I said.

—I'm being ridden by a killer, she said. —Help, help.

He was prince of the city streets, no other lad came near.

And Collins sent me back to work on the docks.

—We need strong men and true down there, boy, he said.

He was sitting up on the desk in his new office on Bachelor's Walk. The rip in his trousers had been nicely stitched. He nodded towards the window and the Liffey below it and the docks, and the world beyond them.

So back I went, past the nod of our little ally, the stevedore. I picked up a crate marked BIBLES – NO COMMERCIAL VALUE – Annie's dead husband led me to it and winked – and I carried it back past the stevedore, around the corner, past Store Street D.M.P. Station and the morgue beside it, to Coolevin Dairies, a café under the Loop Line Bridge on Amiens Street, through the empty café, past the owner and his sister, into a back room, another of Collins's offices. The man himself was there.

He looked at the crate in my hands. I was sweating.

—For me? said Collins. —Ah, Henry.

He yanked the lid off the crate without help from a crowbar or the skinny end of a hammer. He pulled back some straw and showed me the neat row of rifles, Smith and Wessons, new and beautiful, greased like things just born.

—We have friends all over the world, boy, he said.

From Sheerin's they'd be carried under Cumann na mBan coats and petticoats, on trams and bicycles, to Kingsbridge Station and on down to the country, and across the road to Amiens Street, on up to Belfast and the north. I never met or saw any of the couriers. Collins kept his friends and contacts well away from one another. I delivered bibles, machine parts and fancy goods to Sheerin's, the Bookshop on Dawson Street, even Harry Boland's tailoring business on Abbey Street, off boats coming from Liverpool and Boston and strange places where there was no branch of the Gaelic League: Lagos, Bombay, Nairobi. I did this two and three times a week, carried my death sentence through the spy-filled streets of the city, and no one ever as much as brushed against me.

—Some of the peelers are ours now, said Jack. —Mick's making friends everywhere.

—There'll be no one left to fight, I said.

—We're not home yet, man. A couple of crates of bang-bangs isn't going to win it. They've two million squaddies in France and that war isn't going to last for ever. And another thing.

He punched my arm.

—Only a few of those peelers are ours. Remember that the next time you're delivering a crate of bibles.

—I'll just leave this crate over here, Granny, alright?

—What did you steal this time? she said.

—I'll come back for it tomorrow.

—Suit yourself, she said.

She blew the dust off the cover and devoured the first page of my latest offering, *Behind the Scenes, or, Thirty Years a Slave and Four Years in the White House*, by Elizabeth Keckley.

—Is it any good? I asked.

—Remains to be seen.

She liked it.

—Tell me more about Gandon, Granny.

—Killing, she said.

—Killing?

—Killing. The hoppy fella did the killing for Gandon.

—What killing?

—All of it. There's not much reading in this. I want more. There's a Yank called Wharton. Get anything by her.

—I'll keep an eye out for her.

—You do that.

—Tell me about Alfie Gandon, Jack, I said.

We were in Shanahan's, way after midnight, when the pub became a headquarters.

—Gandon?

—Yeah.

—How did you find out? said Jack.

—What?

—That he's our landlord.

—You're joking, I said.

—He's one of us, man.

—Organisation?

—Not at all, said Jack. —He can't get his hands that dirty. Although he has been fitted for a Volunteer uniform. Harry Boland did the measuring himself. He's a giant in this city, man. Property, transport, banking, Corpo. He's in on them all. He's a powerful man, Henry. And a good one. There's more widows and orphans living off that fella's generosity than the nuns could ever handle. And he doesn't like to boast about it either. Chamber of Commerce, Gaelic League and a great sodality man. He's perfect. I'll tell you what Mister Gandon is. He's our respectable face. He'll declare for us when the time is right. We're keeping him on ice.

I said nothing more on the subject of Gandon. I had to think and watch. There were two versions of the man, Granny Nash's and Jack's. I walked past Dolly Oblong's at night and dawn and early evening but there were no Alfie Gandons at all to be seen.

Then Thomas Ashe died.

A veteran of 1916 – he and Dick Mulcahy had ambushed and beaten a gang of the rozzers in Ashbourne, our only victory that week – he'd been arrested for talking rebellion in a public place. He refused to recognise the court and was marched off to Mountjoy. There were already forty other DORA men in Mountjoy so, with Ashe in the lead, they went on hunger strike. They'd been tried by special court, so they wanted special status. Ashe was pulled out of his cell and force-fed. He was strapped to a chair and an eighteen-inch rubber tube was shoved down his throat; two eggs were beaten in a pint of milk and pushed down to his gut in twenty strokes of the stomach pump. Nausea, vomiting, internal bleeding. By the end of the day he was dead.

The funeral was huge. *Let me carry your Cross for Ireland, Lord. For Ireland is weak with tears.* The Volunteers took over the city. Wearing banned uniforms, carrying banned hurleys, we marshalled the crowd and walked behind the coffin with thousands of mourners from all over the country, de Valera in the lead in his new uniform and the Countess leading what was left of the Citizen Army. And, for just a second, shame burnt holes in my cheeks: I was in the wrong uniform. But I was busy. *For the aged man of the clouded brow, and the child of tender years.* I pushed through the crowd at the graveside. I passed my hurley to a weeping woman and took a Smith and Wesson from under her coat. There were two other men beside me now. Brigade Commander Dick McKee gave us our orders – three crisp shouts, like black birds in the silence – and we fired three volleys into the Glasnevin trees. Then Collins, every step a decision, walked in front of us and turned to the heaviest section of the crowd. His first words were Irish. I didn't understand him. *Anseo* – Here – and *Tar istigh* – Come in, the pair of you – learnt from Miss O'Shea, were as much as I knew of Irish and I'd spent every second of the march to the graveyard searching for her. Then Collins moved over to English.

—Nothing additional remains to be said. That volley which we have just heard is the only speech which it is proper to make above the grave of a dead Fenian.

That was all. He moved away and went off to mourn in privacy; Ashe had been one of his closest friends. There was work to be done. Jack and I wrote *The Last Poem of Thomas Ashe* in the back snug of the Gravediggers.

—What rhymes with *years*?

—*Tears*, I said.

—Oh, good man, said Jack. —Loads of them in a good lament.

By the end of the day Volunteers in mufti were selling sheets of our poem on the streets – *Let me carry your Cross for Ireland, Lord. My cares in this world are few* – and there were thousands more of the things going down and across the country to the markets and church gates – *Let me carry your Cross for Ireland, Lord. For the cause of Róisín Dhú.*

—You didn't know that Jesus was an Irishman, sure you didn't, Henry? He's one of us.

—Like our landlord.

—Exactly.

190

He defined propaganda for me.

—Getting your boot in first, man. And propaganda is the shine on your boot.

The funeral was filmed and the film developed in a window-blackened car on its way back into town; it was ready for viewing in the cinemas that night – another of Collins's strokes.

The suits were the work of a genius.

We were back in Collins's office, weeks after the funeral. He stood and twirled, to show off his new suit.

—What d'ye thinks, lads? he said. —The best of bull's wool.

—Very nice, I said.

There were two small, neat piles of cash side by side on the edge of his desk.

—Get your own, he said, pointing at the money.

—Why? I said. —I'm a docker.

—Not all the time you're not, boy. You're a rebel and there'll be a price on your head. And I've a friend in the Castle who tells me that you can evade arrest much more successfully if you're dressed like a company director. So buy a fuckin' suit and no more lip out of you.

So we went over the road to Clery's and I bought a grey suit like the ones I'd seen the Yanks wearing in the pictures and it became my real uniform.

They were the work of a genius. Not the cut of them – mine left me with red, merciless trenches under my shoulders – but the idea of them, the use of other people's snobbery and stupidity for our gain, that was class. Collins was full of plans and skits that dropped us there with admiration, obvious notions that no one ever worded but him. He slept in the beds of men who'd just been arrested – the rozzers would never search the same house twice in a night, especially when they'd found their man the first time. The safest bed in town, he said. He was a plastic man. Everyone knew him but no one could describe him. His hair was brown, fair and black. He was broad but not particularly tall; he was the tallest man in the room. He grew a moustache and the years grew with it; he filled out, became middle-aged. He shaved it and became a lad again, much too young to be Michael Collins. He smiled at the rozzers when he met them at the roadblocks; he helped them in

191

every detail; he joined them. He never hid in a coat, behind a collar.

—Michael Collins, he said once in answer to a young, fresh rozzer's enquiry.

I was with him.

He laughed. We laughed. They laughed.

—I'm just having you on, he said.

In a cap and muffler or less impressive in the overcoat, he'd have got the butt of a rifle in the chops. Not Mick, though. He was a company director, a man about town, a class above them and one of their own.

—Michael Collins, I said to the same question.

They laughed again. They let me away with it because I was with Michael Collins.

—Keep it up, lads, said Collins as we passed through the block. —You'll soon catch the bastard. And you can give him a root in the hole from me.

—Good-night, sir.

The British ruled the country through the police. They had their own spies and other spies and touts and stool pigeons; the country was covered in a close mesh of whispers, all sliding back to Dublin along voice-made wires, to G Division headquarters in the Castle. The man beside you on the tram, the barman washing the glasses, your brother helping you with the mowing – spies. The woman you were fucking, the man she was marrying, all of them, all whispering back to Dublin Castle, into big ears, big books, onto dusty shelves. All of them paid and looked after from G Division, the political crime unit of the Royal Irish Constabulary. Anyone suspected of disloyalty to the Crown, treachery alive or dormant, was put in a big black book and a large S, like a brand, was scratched beside the name – marked for life, and watched. At the ports and railway stations, in the picture houses and churches, from hedges and roofs. 'S' for what? Sedition, suspect, special? I never knew. With the S beside your name you were never lonely. Half the men at Volunteer meetings were spies, deliberate or accidental, married to spies or the real McCoy themselves.

So Collins invented the circle. An I.R.B. member knew nine other men, no more – his circle. I knew more than nine but

192

never at the same time. The dead and arrested were quickly replaced. I knew faces, winks, nods but not names. The worst torture, flames, even phosphorite, couldn't have produced more than ten names, including my own. The ignorance made us braver. And we knew who the spies were and we whispered our own messages into their ears, dropped home-made hints, filled them with shite.

The police ruled the country.

—And that's why we're going to kill them, said Jack. — Assassinate every bloody one of them.

I was on for it; I came from a line of cop killers. I'd been chased by them; I'd dived into underground rivers to get away from them. They were never people, the rozzers. And they were stupid too; seven hundred years of easy rule had made them lazy. Collins's own cousin, Nancy O'Brien, had a job in the Castle; her duties included filing the secret-coded messages of the Under-Secretary, Sir James MacMahon. Another cousin, Pearce Beaslai's, a woman called Lily Merin, worked behind the walls as a typist. A couple of times a week she got the tram from work to the top of Clonliffe Road. She walked to a house and entered. The house was unfurnished, except for a desk, a chair and a typewriter. She typed verbatim what she'd typed throughout the day, and left. And I gathered the pages and brought them to Collins or Jack. On other evenings she walked Grafton Street and Dame Street and, by flick of a finger or tap of her heel, she identified intelligence officers and other familiar faces to men like me, men she didn't know who were right beside her. We were getting ready. Gathering names, faces, addresses.

—They're the cement, said Jack. —The peelers. We get them and it all falls apart.

But not yet.

There were weddings and by-elections. Diarmuid Lynch, Sinn Féin's Director of Food, had commandeered another herd of England-bound pigs and slaughtered them for Irish commerce and consumption. But he'd been caught with the blood on his mitts and, because he was a returned Yank and a citizen of the U.S., he'd been sentenced to deportation. He wanted to get married in Dundalk Gaol, so his fiancée could

193

have a Yankee passport and get herself deported with him. But the men in charge were having none of it. They'd already seen one jail wedding, Plunkett's in 1916, turned into a republican legend. But Lynch got married anyway. The fiancée smuggled a priest in – under her coat, in her handbag? I never knew – and a couple of witnesses as well, and herself and himself were hitched in Lynch's cell.

Collins made sure that the new bride – a looker, by the way; I could see why Lynch had been keen on bringing her into exile with him – Collins made sure that she accompanied her husband and the screws on the train to Dublin and deportation. A huge crowd, Henry Smart among them, met the happy couple and their minders at Amiens Street Station and followed them on foot, up along the river, to the Bridewell. Collins and I, in our Sunday suits, hopped up the steps and in the front door of the station. No one stopped us; several big rozzers got out of our way. Collins, looking like a lawyer or the Castle official in charge of deporting Shinners, strolled straight up to Lynch. I stood at his back, my Widowmaker warm against my chest. He gave Lynch names, American contacts, men to keep Lynch in the fight. Then he shook hands with both Mister and Missis.

—The best of men and women, he said.

And we walked out, myself at the rear, back into the safety of the crowd on Chancery Street. Another lad in a brown suit walked up with a bike. Collins took it from him, mounted without bending a knee and cycled away.

They were our horses, the bikes. I'd been robbing and selling them since before I'd learnt how to ride one but I'd never had much use for them, other than as currency. Disappearing around a corner was always easier on foot, and Dublin was a city of sharp corners.

—Men on bicycles, said Collins. —That's what I need. Good men on bicycles.

—I don't have one, I told him.

—I'm only after buying you the suit, he said. —So you can manage the fuckin' *rothar* yourself.

So I found one left against the railings of Trinity College, a grand big Protestant bike, and I took it. The saddle fit me like a cuddle and I cycled up Dame Street. I passed the motor cars and hung off the backs of trucks. I kept going, past Guinness's and Kingsbridge, and didn't stop until I got to Granard, without a rest except when I fell off the bike. It was the first time I'd been further than Lucan and, over the next three years, the thin green dome on top of the Spa Hotel became my own lighthouse, the sign that I was heading home or, like now, far from home and further with every shove on the pedal.

Three years on a stolen bike. Through wind, rain and bullets. Me and the Arseless Horse. No lamp in front of me for fear that the fine fat men of the R.I.C., and later the Black and Tans, would be hiding behind a wall or a hedge waiting with guns for rebels on bicycles. I cycled into black darkness, across and up and down the whole of Ireland. The bottomless whirr of the bike chain swallowed up the next three years.

And on that first trip to Granard, with letters from Collins stitched into the lining of my coat and duplicates hidden in the tubing right under the saddle, with the Widowmaker tidily holstered to my back, a blade stitched into my cap and my da's leg in its holster under the coat, I met fresh air for the first time in my life and it nearly killed me. There was nothing in it, just the air itself and I was suddenly starving; stars and pebbles swam in front of my eyes. Air straight off the Atlantic, brand new and fierce. The sting and the bigness of it, the way it filled my head – I couldn't cope. Anything I'd ever inhaled before had always come at me through the Dublin soup or, on the wintry days when it blew from the north-east, it came over the smokestacks of northern England and Scotland. Now, the Arseless cut through the fresh stuff and I hung on and drowsed. While my legs did the work the rest of me slept.

There were no corners out there in the country, no names or measurable street lengths. I had sixty-odd miles to travel but I'd no idea what that meant in effort. I rode between the hedges, and later the hedges trapped the night and disappeared. I kept going through the black. There was nowhere to stop, nowhere to see. I looked ahead for light to aim at but, unless a cloud got shoved aside or a small town's light gathered above its roofs, there was nothing. I'd travelled through blackness before but I missed the help of river water, the solidity and closeness of the cave walls. The rivers out here were overland but hidden. I could hear them in the dark, running beside me, laughing. I could feel their draughts on my ankles. And the whip of bending branches. There were animals out there that should never have been in Ireland, their paws and teeth tearing at my tyres. I could hear it all but I couldn't see a thing.

—What are you fuckin' gawkin' at? I yelled at the clearest of the little stars that had just been freed by the shifting wind as I rooted around in thick ditch water for the bike I'd just cycled into it.

I was drenched and half-broken but I gave the Arseless a pat and a kick to shake the running filth off. The second my soaking arse hit the soaking saddle the clouds knit together again and took away the stars. I shut my eyes and pedalled into the wind. That was the direction for the next three years, always – straight into the wind. Even when I was cycling east, home to Dublin, even when I was passing under the Spa, my chin on the handlebars, the prevailing winds abandoned me and let the freezing stuff from Siberia push me back. It was a battle all the way.

I crossed a bridge somewhere early in the second day. I looked down at the river and hoped to Christ it wasn't the Shannon because, if it was, I'd ridden too far.

—Where am I?

—Mullingar.

—Am I on the right road for Granard?

—There's no right road for Granard, sonny.

—Will I get there if I go this way?

—You will, God help you.

I rode into Granard at noon, along the road from Castlepollard, a day and a chunk after robbing the bike. I climbed the last fuck of a hill and sailed into town on its steam, and left onto Main Street. I scooped the sweat and dirt out of my eyes and looked around.

—Where's the Greville Arms, pal? I asked a thick-looking kid who was holding up a pole. He had the hair and eyes of an old man but he wore short trousers that bit into his legs.

—Where it always is, he said.

196

He wasn't being snotty, I could see that. He was nodding down the street. I followed his forehead and there it was, the Greville Arms Hotel, my destination.

—Thanks.

—For what? he said.

—Thanks anyway, I said.

—For what? he said.

I thumped some of the dust and harder dirt off myself and the Arseless before I walked the rest of the way to the Greville Arms. Now that I was off the bike the wind had gone away and it was suddenly a very hot day. I wanted to take my coat off but it was the only thing hiding my gun so I put up with its heft and sweat for a while more.

Sinn Féin had won five by-elections since 1916: Plunkett's father in Roscommon, Joe McGuinness in Longford – Joe the Jailbird. *Put him in to get him out.* He hadn't wanted to run but Collins had ignored him – de Valera in East Clare, Cosgrave in Kilkenny and Arthur Griffith, another man in jail, in East Cavan. And now there was talk that the sitting M.P. for nearby Leitrim was on the way out, an oul' lad who'd been old even when Parnell was his boss; the gout was spreading from his feet, nibbling at the outskirts of his brain. Collins wanted to be ready for the by-election that would follow his funeral, and the general election that might come sooner, when the war in Europe ended. I was carrying orders direct from Collins for the men from the Midland and Connaught constituencies who were meeting in the Greville Arms to discuss strategy, tactics – and gun running, when the democrats among them had gone off to bed.

I lifted the pedal and parked the Arseless against the bottom step of the hotel and I took the cap off my dripping head for the first time since I'd put it on, a few hours before I'd robbed the bike.

—Is that sweat I see on your forehead?

It was Collins, on the top step.

It made no sense.

—How—?

—The train, Henry, he said. —It's quicker than the *rothar* but it's not nearly as good for you. You're looking well, boy.

I moved slightly to the right, to get the sun away from my eyes.

—Why—?

—You didn't think I could let these bucks have a meeting all on their ownio, did you?

—Why me?

—On the bike, d'you mean?

—Yeah.

—It was a bit of a test, Henry, said Collins. —You were fast, boy, I'll give you that. You didn't stop on the way, not once. Don't ask. I know. You even wee-weed off the side of the bike, fair play to you. And most important. Most important, you didn't mess with the stitches in your coat and you never once took your arse off the saddle to see what was in the envelope under it. I knew you wouldn't. I knew it all along; you'd come through for me. Will I tell you what was in the envelope now, will I?

—Nothing, I said.

—Right you are, boy.

Even now I didn't run up the steps to kill him. Because I knew that that was part of the test as well.

—Right you are, he said. —And you're not the bit annoyed with me.

He jumped the steps and thumped me onto the street. He followed me. Luckily, the traffic was scarce and slow, a few drays keeping up with the sun. Collins was playing. He loved his horseplay. As long as he was the horse. You had to be careful. He liked a bit of ear. He bit when he was winning and turned nastier if he was losing. I thumped him now, so that it wouldn't hurt too much. He laughed and grabbed my neck. I laughed and grabbed his. I'd never had much time for this kind of cod-acting, unless I actually intended strangling the neck's owner. But I was adaptable. The bossman liked a mill, so I gave him one, enough to let him think he was winning. I slapped the back of his neck. And laughed. He whacked both sides of my face with open palms. He laughed. I made to kick the side of his arse, then thumped him nicely just above his belt buckle. I'd let him play for a few more minutes. It gave me time to think. He drummed his fists into my coat and raised all the dust.

I really had been tested. I'd been watched all the way. In the pitch dark. When I'd cycled into the ditch. Right through Kildare and Westmeath. When I'd slowed down for directions. When I'd shouted into the sky at my twinkling brother.

I got out from under Collins. He grabbed from behind and lifted me.

I was rattled. I hadn't been trusted. Not enough. Until now. And where was Jack? Was I trusted now? And enough?

I filled myself with some of that fresh air, and Collins had to loosen his grip as my chest grew. I turned and grabbed him on my way back down. I wasn't angry. Or hurt. I searched for those feelings and anything like them as I turned on the street and brought him with me headfirst, and the speed and strength of my turn knocked him onto his knees.

I was delighted, that was what I was. Thrilled. I'd passed. The big test. A bit hysterical, to be honest. Not that far from angry. A real test, a true test of my loyalty and strength. I was in now.

I got behind Collins and pushed him the rest of the way to the street. I'd forgotten that I should have been losing. And I sat on his back.

—D'yeh give up?

He was a great man. I loved him. But I wanted to hurt him.

—I can't hear you. D'you give up?

He grunted.

I stood up and got out of his way. I took my coat off and draped it over the handlebars; I'd forgotten about the gun on my back. I didn't know when I'd accepted his grunt as surrender that he was being watched – or thought he was being watched – by Kitty Kiernan, from one of the hotel windows. I found out about her later. She ran the Greville Arms with her sisters and Collins was in love with her and probably one of the sisters. Big savage kid that he was, he thought that knocking the living shite out of me would impress her or, going back thirty seconds, the sight of a dusty messenger boy from Dublin sitting on his back would definitely not impress her. He got up slowly and shook himself. Then he stretched. He laughed.

—The best of men, he said.

Then he punched me.

I woke up in a bed in Roscommon.

In a dark, windowless room, with the immediate knowledge that one of my eyes was missing.

I sat up and shouted.

—Good, good, good.

There was someone else in the room.

—Who's there? I said.

—Good.

—Who are you?

—Ah, good.

A woman. It was in the voice. And her age was in the cracks between the words. She was very old.

—We were worried there, young fellow. We thought it might be one of those coma occurrences and not right sleep at all.

I heard a chair groaning as weight came off it.

—But then himself told us that you'd bicycled all the way from Dublin in the one sitting and we knew that it was only sleeping you were doing after all. Even with your eye the way it is. Your gun is under the pillow. With the leg.

—What about my eye?

—You'll be grand. It's just gone black. Is the black one as handsome as the good one?

—I've been told it is.

—They weren't lying who told you.

I could see her now. It wasn't so dark. There was an oil lamp on the floor; its light rose from somewhere in front of the bed. It was an attic. I could see and smell the thatch.

—It won't be the first shiner you've worn, I'd say now. Am I right, young fellow?

—You are, missis.

—There now. Good. I'm not going to ask you your name because then, when they ask me for it, I'll be able to say I don't know and it no lie.

—Who'll be asking for my name?

—Ah now, she said.

200

She was small and ancient, and partly hidden in a shawl that might have had more colours than black.

—But you'll be wanting to call me something, she said. —I have a name and it's no secret. I'm Missis O'Shea.

She dropped the shawl to her shoulders. Her grey hair was in a bun.

A bun.

Brown eyes and some slivers of hair that had escaped from a bun.

I leaned forward quickly; I felt my sore eye shift and protest but it didn't matter at all: I had to know.

—D'you have any daughters?

—Awake two minutes and he's already thinking of the girleens. The men, men, the men. They're desperate animals altogether. Good. Good. I've a power of daughters. And granddaughters as well coming along after them.

—Are any of them teachers?

I prayed to the thatch above me.

—Not a one, she said. —You'll have a dropeen of soup now. To put some colour into those sad Dublin cheeks of yours.

I heard her climbing down the steps as I lay back on the bed and waited for my cheeks and neck to stop burning and for my eye to stop hopping. She'd seen my blushes, she must have, even in this gloom; that was why she'd denied their colour. I inhaled deeply – I could smell turf smoke coming through the boards from below – I inhaled and hauled my soaking heart back to its proper place. I'd almost seen her, Miss O'Shea; I'd been so close. For a second or two I'd been looking at her mother. *Brown eyes and some slivers of hair that had escaped from a bun that shone like a lamp behind her head.* I'd been under her roof, on the bed she'd been born in. Where she'd sucked on her mother's tit, against this pillow, on her mother's tit, and grown. Her hair, skin, her neck. I'd felt them here, for just that second. They were still here. Fading, going.

There was nothing.

I heard feet on the ladder.

—I've two of them nuns with the Little Sisters of the Poor and one a housekeeper in Mullingar. I've another a nurse beyond in London, a big handful of farmers' wives and another one married to a man with a shop in Castlerea. And I've the youngest one that's loose in her head still here with me. And there's the granddaughters all around and scattered, married and not, up to everything.

I lifted myself in time to see a bowl of soup rising out of the floor, held high by two claws. Folding steam grabbed at the dust, followed by the rest of old Missis O'Shea. Her mother, but just for a cruel spit of a second.

—But none of them school teachering, said old Missis O'Shea. —Good. My poor knees crack on those steps. Two knees, seventeen steps. It isn't a fair fight. Sit up now, young fellow, till we feed you.

I sat up, slowly this time, aware now that my sore eye didn't want movement and that my erection was making a mountain of the blanket.

—But the men, the men, said old Missis O'Shea, looking only at the soup and the spoon and its journey to my mouth.

—I can do it myself, I said.

—Then what'll I do?

She pulled the spoon from my closed mouth and I'd never tasted anything like the soup she'd left behind. It was vile.

—Good, she said.

More joined it. A shattering mixture of the raw and the rotten, and scalding with it, and I had to swallow the lot. I'd grown up on bad food but nothing as fundamentally evil as old Missis O'Shea's soup and I ate it without a whimper because she'd nearly been my lover's mother.

The house was on a farm. The farm was forty-odd lumpy acres of cow fields and bog, divided by low stone walls. There was no sight of a hedge.

—What's all the yellow stuff? I asked.

—That'll be gorse, she said.

I stood at the half-door the morning after I woke up from Collins's thump and looked out at the rain running across the yard.

—Where am I?

—Rusg, she said. —The bog, it means. It's a nice name but not fair. It only describes the half of it. And the next parish is called Rusgeile. The man who gave out the names in this part of the county had only the one good eye and it was only the

202

bad he saw with it. Mind your own eye going over the bumps, young fellow.

—I will, I said. —Don't worry.

—Off with you, so, she said. —Himself says you'll be needing a safe bed now and again and you'll always be welcome here. It's not a big house but it's a friendly one. We're all for the Republic around here.

I hadn't seen anyone, only herself.

—And it's always nice to feed a handsome man. Off with you now, she said. —It's a long ride to Dublin and we're not getting any younger standing around here flirting.

—Thanks very much, I said.

—For what?

Poisoning me, I said to myself as I went through the rain in search of the Arseless, to a long barn that smelt of old oats and horse leather.

I caught up with Collins in Phil Shanahan's.

—Sorry about the eye, though, Henry boy. I'll let you win the next time.

But he didn't.

I wasn't angry now. My wounds always mended quickly. I grew fond of them as they faded and women were always fond of nice scars, and I was very fond of women. The black eye gave me the look of a lost pup. A big girl in a field behind Kinnegad had told me that as she licked it, and women were fond of pups as well. I'd taken my time cycling home from Rusg. I'd climbed off the Arseless several times, at Ballagh, Athlone, to look at the Shannon I'd crossed the first time in my sleep, and Kinnegad.

—We're nearly there, Henry, said Collins.

He gave me his full face and attention: there was no one else in the room while he talked. He had the startings of a moustache that already added years to him; he was a businessman, a family man on his way home.

—We've Dublin organised and the other towns are more or less sorted and soon, soon we'll have enough of the country ready for action. We have the men and the houses but not enough know-how or weapons. The bang-bangs are coming and you and some other good boys are going to supply the know-how. We're going to give the British what's what in the bogs, boy, and in the towns and all over the bloody place. No G.P.O. this time, Henry. To fuck with it. We won't be trapped this time. You're going back the way you just came from. First thing, tomorrow. To train the country lads. And to pick out the best ones for ourselves. We want our own boys holding the reins. We'll have a drink now for tomorrow's road and then you'll go home and get some sleep. You'll need all the energy you can muster, boy. And, by the way, Cathleen in Kinnegad says you're the best and the slowest ride she's had in weeks.

9

Three years on a stolen bike. Over mountains, rivers and provinces. But first I said goodbye to Annie.

—Does it make me look like a lost pup, Annie?

She grabbed my ears and stared at my black eye.

—It's just a shiner, she said. —Don't listen to anyone who says different. They're only taking advantage of you. Now.

I watched her bruised knees slip past my eyes.

—Will I sing? she said.

—Yes please, Annie. A slow one.

—The slow ones are sad.

—Fine.

—And they still last three minutes, no matter how slow.

—Fine, I said. —I'm going away, Annie. For a while.

—You were never here, she said.

—I was, I said.

—No, she said. —Not really.

She tapped my head with her knuckles, and then tapped my chest.

—Not really you weren't.

—I'm here now, Annie.

—You are at that, she said, and her fingers left my ears and I watched her rub her thighs as we began to push and pull and her hands drifted from her thighs to mine and up to my back, to my neck, and back down along the knuckles of my spine and she found the right notes and sang to me. *She lives in a mansion of aching hearts, she's one of the restless throng.* She hoisted herself against me and did the work as she sang and I stayed as stiff and as still as I could. And it was easy. She was old and young

205

at the same time, Annie. Young thighs, old neck. Young wrists, old hands. Young hair, old teeth. Young eyes – gorgeous, brave things drilling into me – and an old voice made filthy by a life of Dublin air, a thing made of smoke and sex. She blew on one of my nipples – oh Annie – and continued. *Though by the wayside she fell, she may yet mend her ways.* She slammed and sang and we came together that one last time. *Some poor mother is waiting for her* – we fought each other and won – *who has seen better days* – and lost, and lost. We fell apart just in time before we died.

I sat up.

—Are you crying, Annie?

—No, she said.

She was turned to the wall.

—Poor Annie.

—Poor nothing, she said. —There's nothing poor about me. Except for the lack of spondulix. Worry about yourself.

—I've no worries, Annie, I said. —Was that one of the American songs?

—It was, she said. —I want to go there. I could do things there.

She turned to face me.

—I want to own a piano, Henry.

And she turned away again.

—Why don't you go then?

—Because he wants to die for Ireland.

—He?

—I'm married, remember.

—I thought you were talking about me for a minute.

—I don't care whether you die or not.

—Ah, you do.

—No, I don't, she said.

And I believed her.

—Just remember that letter, she said.

—I will, I said. —Don't worry.

—I'm not worried.

—Anyway, Annie, I said. —I'll be back soon.

—No, you won't.

—I will, Annie.

She shrugged my hand off her hip.

—You won't.

—I will, I said. —I swear.

But she was right. I never did see Annie again, but I did write her the letter.

The Great War finally ended but not before the British did us another favour and tried to bring in conscription. The country was packed with able young men unwilling to die for the King and their mothers and lovers unwilling to let them go and by December 1918 and the general election, even though the threat of a forced holiday in France had gone, they all queued up, all men over twenty-one and women over thirty, the young and the poor, and they voted for Sinn Féin. De Valera, Griffith and most of the other leading lights had been arrested again. They'd decided that they were of more use to the cause in jail, so they'd made themselves easily caught. It worked out very nicely. Forty-seven of the candidates were in jail on polling day. *Release the Prisoners, Release Ireland.* Sinn Féin had very quickly become respectable, the party of the parish priests and those middle-class men cute enough to know when the wind was changing. It was the party of money and faith, and thrilling with it because of its links to the buried martyrs; it was outlawed by the British, but cosy. While I was under a wet bush teaching country boys how to stay still and keen until the approaching uniform was an unmissable target, many of my fellow revolutionaries, in their Sinn Féin guises, were adding letters to their names. There was Michael Collins M.P. There was Dinny – Denis on the posters – Archer M.P. There was Alfred Gandon M.P. And there was Jack Dalton M.P. *Give Him Your Vote and He'll Give You Your Freedom.* Jack was one of the candidates at liberty to campaign, but he spent most of the weeks in the run-up to the election dodging arrest in Dublin. Collins and Jack and other men like Harry Boland and Cathal Brugha who were busy on both the political and military fronts, and who knew that incarceration might get them elected but would leave the Volunteers and I.R.B. lost and nervous and in the sweaty hands of the moderates and johnny-come-latelys, had decided that it was wiser to stay out of jail. Sinn Féin and the Volunteers were controlled by the gunmen; the election was being controlled by men who had no belief in it. Collins made occasional appearances at public meetings around the country – *Come in your thousands* – but, to stay in control of the underground movement most Sinn Féin voters and members still knew nothing about, he and Jack stayed on the run. Collins's contacts kept him well up to date on raids and cordons and he and the others played hopscotch with the G-men all the way to Election Day and past it.

So Sinn Féin, just a few years before a little gang of cranky nuts and bad poets, swept to victory everywhere except the bitter parts of Ulster and Trinity College, the original home of my bicycle. On the day the votes were counted I was on the same bike heading south from Limerick to Kerry, cycling into a wet gale that blew for me and me only.

There was no Henry Smart M.P. I was four years short of the voting age, I was never a member of Sinn Féin; I wouldn't have stood for election if I'd been asked, but that was the point, and a point that didn't drill itself into my head until 1922: I hadn't been asked. I was bang in the middle of what was going to become big, big history, I was shaping the fate of my country, I was one of Collins's anointed but, actually, I was excluded from everything. I was on a bike in the rain, all alone on the road. I was never one of the boys. I wasn't a Christian Brothers boy, I'd been unlucky enough to miss Frongoch, I'd no farm in the family, no college, no priest, no past. Collins slept in the Greville Arms; I never made it up the steps. There was no Henry Smart M.P. There was no Annie's Dead Husband M.P. And none of the other men of the slums and hovels ever made it on to the list. We were nameless and expendable, every bit as dead as the squaddies in France. We carried guns and messages. We were decoys and patsies. We followed orders and murdered.

But as I cycled into the wind, as I swam across the Deel with the Arseless on my back because there were R.I.C. men standing on the bridge downriver at Mahoonagh, as I got back on the bike and pointed it at a place of stubborn roads and people, I was one self-important little rebel. I had no idea of my tininess and anonymity. I was the Henry Smart of song and legend. I was the inspiration for a generation, a giant on a bicycle, moving from county to county, leaving my mark on the foreheads of the gallant young men, a living example to them all, and a man with a secret mission beneath the one that was whispered into the ears of all the young men of the parish: I was one of the chosen. I was a gunman. I could hear Jack Dalton's song even in the loudest storms – *He was prince of the city streets, no other lad came near* – I could hear Collins talking only to me – *We're nearly there, Henry, we're nearly there.* I had no time for elections or voting, even as a screen to hide the real fight. I was no democrat, no more than Jack Dalton or Brugha or Ernie O'Malley were. The will of the people wasn't measured in votes. The vote meant choice, but there was no choice. There was only one right way. Some of us knew the way and it was up to us to lead, not to ask permission of a voting majority, but to lead, to really lead, to show, demonstrate, live, die. To inspire, provoke and terrify.

I was good at it, and getting better all the time.

Sinn Féin had fought the election on the promise that they would abstain from taking their seats at Westminster, so none of the newly elected members, those not in jail, went over to London. Instead, they met in the Mansion House on the 21st of January, 1919 and formed Dáil Éireann, the parliament of the Irish Republic. De Valera, still absent, was elected Taoiseach and President. Collins was Minister for Finance. He wasn't there either. He was called present but he was actually in England with Harry Boland, also called present, planning de Valera's breakout from Lincoln Gaol. Griffith became Minister for Home Affairs and Count Plunkett got Foreign Affairs. Brugha got Defence, the Countess got Labour and Mister Gandon got Commercial Affairs and the Sea.

Henry Smart got wet.

I was cycling with scouts in front and behind me; an R.I.C. lorry had been seen in the vicinity and I was a wanted man, although there was no face on the posters that were gummed to the barracks and post office walls and the details and even the name were elusive – *Henry Smart aka Fergus Nash aka Brian O'Linn aka Michael Collins. Is not to be confused with the other*

Michael Collins. Age: between 21 and 29; 6 feet in height, or taller; dark, long hair sometimes fair; eyes, always blue and striking; is considered handsome by members of the fair sex. Wanted for Murder and Sedition in Ireland. £1,000 Reward. I was cycling from Drumshanbo down into Roscommon. I had committed a murder; I'd caved in a rozzer's head with my daddy's leg on Beresford Place but they weren't after me for that one or the share of soldiers I'd killed in 1916. As for sedition, it had become my middle name. I was Henry S. Smart. Sedition: words or actions that make people rebel against the authority of the state. That was me. And, as I approached the half-hearted outskirts of Strokestown under cover of the sleet that had kept me company all the way, as I passed the leading scout, a fat boy resting his heaving chest on the handlebars of his sister's bike, a fat girl who loved me and Ireland and was always dying to prove it, as I took a mental note to reprimand and kick him for waving at me as I cycled past him, as I looked forward to the bed and shelter that were waiting for me in old Missis O'Shea's house in Rusg and tried not to worry too much about the soup that was part of the bargain, as I did all this nine men in Tipperary shot dead two policemen.

What a day that was. In Dublin, the foundation of the Irish state and in Soloheadbeg the murder of two poor peelers, the first official killings of the War of Independence. Two huge events and I missed both of them. Although my mark was in both places. In Dublin Jack Dalton wore my suit because he'd left his jacket in the fists of two G-men who'd come very close to arresting him on Infirmary Road the night before and, in Soloheadbeg, most of the men who lay in ambush for five days waiting for the cart of gelignite for the quarry and the two peelers who came with it, they had been trained by me. They sat silently and still for five wet January days as I'd taught them to do, Seamus Robinson and Tim Crowe, Paddy O'Dwyer. I'd made them perch on stones in fast, freezing water for hours of the day and night and told them that their ability to lock themselves stiff and snap out of it while the warning twig was still breaking or the enemy bullet was still travelling to the chamber, this line between stillness and speed and their sureness on it was the thing that would keep them alive or kill

210

them and I told them that they would be living on this line for the years that it would take to beat the British or until they died, whichever came first. They lay in ambush for five days, the men I'd trained and the others with them, including the one who lived long enough to write the book and so became the man who fired the first shot for Irish freedom. They waited, although they went to Dan Breen's mother's house each night, which was never part of their training and stupid, leaving themselves open to the eyes and tongues of the quarry workers on the road. And on the fifth day the peelers arrived with the cart and they shot them, Constables McDonnell and O'Connell, two local men, one of them a widower with four poor brats, and they took the cart and then nearly killed themselves and half of Tipperary by driving the springless cart loaded with a hundredweight of frozen gelignite over a rough road made of loose stones and holes. And they left the detonators on the quarry road beside the dead peelers. They did it without H.Q's knowledge or sanction – bored, young, stupid men itching for their big day – but it became the first real action of the war. I knew nothing about it, and heard nothing for weeks; I was cycling down through Roscommon for a big day of my own.

—Good, good, good, said old Missis O'Shea.

She poured lukewarm water over my fingers and released them from the frozen handlebars.

—Could you not wait till the summer for your manoeuvereens, young fellow? she said.

—Men trained in the winter win their wars in the summer, I said.

—Well, isn't that well put? she said. —Come in out of that weather now. It's a soft day but there's a hard crust on it.

I parked the Arseless in the long barn and in the morning there were men there waiting for me, men and boys, cold, eager and cranky.

—Are you the fella from Dublin?

—I am.

—Ivan says you're going to show us how to kill the English.

—I am.

—I didn't know there was learning in that.

—Ah there, I said. —There's killing and there's killing.

211

—What d'you mean?

—Well, there's killing and getting caught and there's killing and not getting caught. And there's killing the fellas who are paid to catch you.

—The peelers?

—Yep.

—Why would we want to kill them? They're not so bad.

—Go home.

—I was only saying.

—Go home, I said. —You're not ready for the fight.

—I am.

—You're not. Go home.

It was the same everywhere. I'd home in on some poor eejit who was only voicing what all his friends were thinking and I'd have to humiliate him and put all their fears on him until they began to hate him for his weakness and for showing off theirs. There was the Dublin problem to be got out of the way as well: they hated anyone or anything from Dublin. Dublin was too close to England; it was where the orders and cruelty came from. And the homespun bollixes in Sinn Féin and the Gaelic League were to blame too; Ireland was everywhere west of Dublin, the real people were west, west, west, as far west as possible, on the islands, the rocks off the islands, speaking Irish and eating wool; the Leaguers lived in Dublin but they went west for their holliers, to the real people. I was in old Missis O'Shea's long barn with a batch of the half-real people; they spoke English but they knew that they were more Irish than I was; they were nearer to being the pure thing. Yet here I was lording it over them, not like the English or the old landlords but a bit like one of their own, a returned Yank or something, like them but not enough. I dressed like them – my suit was on Jack Dalton – and I looked like them but I was from Dublin. They knew that I had expertise, that I deserved to be their master and they hated me for it. I didn't care. I didn't relish it but it didn't interest me. Besides, there was some sort of inverse relationship between their animosity and my success with their sisters, wives and mothers. I could live with their hostility.

And this now was nothing special. The lads in the barn

wanted to back their friend but they were afraid of exposure. They blamed him for bringing it on, and me for being so genuinely superior. But the resentment and malice weren't crackling. They were just cold and scared, giddy for adventure but afraid of it. I was going to rescue them.

—Is there anyone watching the road?

A bright spark behind the others spoke now for the first time.

—Sure, that's all we do all day.

We had a laugh and I told the chap I'd just sent home to keep watch out at the gate instead. He seemed pleased enough at this and the rest were pleased for him.

—That's the first thing you'd want to get into your heads, I told them, and waited. —As of this morning, you're all wanted men.

I watched that news register. They were delighted; they always were. Wanted men, just like that, for turning up to meet a Dublin man in a long barn. They started to like me.

—What's your name, son? I asked the lad who was going out to the gate.

—Willie, he said.

—Willie what?

—O'Shea.

—Any relation to old Missis beyond?

—No.

—Any teachers in the family?

—No.

—Good man. Off you go.

He went out and I stared at the rest until they grew restless and I let my heartache melt into disappointment. There were ten or eleven of them, ranging in age from twenty-three or so down to fifteen and sixteen. Farm boys in big boots made bigger by the season's muck. They'd be good. They were strong, used to fighting the weather, familiar with their own company. They'd have shot rabbits and stray cats.

—Any spies in the barn? I said.

That shook them. They stiffened and wobbled, tried not to look at each other. Then the bright voice behind them answered for them.

—Not a one, it said.

—How d'you know? I asked them all.

—We're all chums here. We're cousins if we're not brothers.

He'd stood up now and I could get a look at him. It still wasn't easy. He was small and relaxed, like a drunk jockey, strolling behind their shoulders.

—And you are? I said

—I'm Ivan.

My contact. The single name I'd brought with me from Drumshanbo.

—O'Shea?

—No, he said. —And there's no teachers in the family either.

It was my turn to wobble.

—Grand, I said. —That's the next thing to get into your heads. You're all wanted men. And you're spies. Don't get me wrong, I'm accusing no one. I'm including myself. You're wanted men for one reason: you're in the Organisation. I'll swear you in soon, but you're here with me this morning and that alone is an act of sedition. Before you even put on a uniform or handle a gun. You're already breaking the British law. As of now every word you say is important and possibly dangerous. A careless word can get you shot or your pal beside you arrested. The wrong word in the wrong ear makes you a traitor and a spy.

I'd impressed them again. I watched them inflating; they were important, singular men, and I'd told them so.

—So think before you open your gobs.

—It's the way I always go about it, said Ivan.

—Good, I said.

—What's your own name, boss? said Ivan.

—I'm Captain O'Linn, I told them.

—You must know what you're up to if they've made you a captain, he said.

—I do, I said. —Right, men. This is the wrong time of day for our kind of business. You'll be missed and there'll be talk. Where's the big house?

—What d'you mean, like?

—The old landlord's, I said. —Where is it?

—That'll be Fitzgalway's, said Ivan. —Shantallow Manor.

214

—Grand, I said. —Shantallow. We'll meet there tonight at seven. Sharp. All of you?

There were nods and grunts, no dissenters.

—Off you go now, I said. —You're a grand-looking body of men and you'll take some beating when you have the uniforms on you. See you tonight and bring your shovels with you. And go out across the haggard so you're not seen from the gate.

The compliment would get two or three more to turn up; it had cost nothing and it hadn't been much of a lie. That and the prospect of uniforms and the excitement of going home the secret way across the haggard; they'd be good for another couple of boys.

—Good day, Captain.

—See you later, I said.

I wasn't a captain, or any other rank.

—You don't exist, Collins had said. —Do you understand that, Henry?

—I do, I said.

—We'll give you your rank when it's all over.

—I'm not pushed, I said. —It's all me bollix.

But I called myself Captain for these lads. It made me important in their eyes and it was the rank that a lot of old land agents had had back in the days when they'd had the power to evict and destroy. Here was I, one of their own, carrying the agents' old label.

—Ivan, I said as he passed me on his way to the barn door.

—That's me, right enough.

—I want to talk to you.

—And I want to listen to you, Captain.

We went back across the yard to the house. We sat down in the kitchen. Ivan worked the bellows and the new heat poured over us. The fireplace was as big as a room. We sat on stools right inside it. There was a picture of Robert Emmet, darkened by the years and smoke, on the wall beside me. There were old postcards stuck in behind it; there was one of all the 1916 leaders and a Patrick's Day card from America, a man with a pig under his arm.

—Good lads, good. Good.

Old Missis O'Shea was climbing down from the attic.

215

—That's a great blaze you've got going there. Use up all the turf on me. We're surrounded by the blessed stuff.

She looked at Ivan.

—You're very welcome, young fellow, she said. —I won't ask you your name. That way, when they ask me for it, I'll be able to say I don't know and not have the lie hanging over me, especially at my age.

—It would be a lie, said Ivan, —and a whopper. Sure, I'm the only nephew you've got that's called Ivan.

—Lord God, Ivan Reynolds, but you're a terrible spoiler. Your mammy was right, God rest her. You're a desperate wee melt.

—She never said that about me.

—Maybe it was one of your brothers she was talking about, said old Missis O'Shea. —Or your father.

—It was probably him, said Ivan.

They were fond of each other.

—You'll eat me out of house and home, now that you're here, said old Missis O'Shea.

—I will, said Ivan. —And I have the captain here to help me with the work.

—A captain no less, said old Missis O'Shea. —Don't tell me the name now. It's dangerous enough knowing the rank. And you'll have a mouthful of tea with it.

—Not for me, I said. —I hate the stuff.

—Sure, don't I know it, Captain, she said. —I just love the way you keep saying it.

While old Missis O'Shea murdered the food at the fire Ivan and myself shifted our stools to the window and got down to talking. He listed off the useful men to know and the men to stay away from. He filled me in on the geography and the politics of Rusg –

—Rock solid, boy. To a man and cat.

and the four or five parishes around it –

—Go-boys, the lot of them.

while the smell of old Missis O'Shea's cooking joined the heat coming from the fire.

—D'you like the girls, Captain? he said.

—They're better than the boys, I said.

—Now you're talking, he said. —No competition. There's some nice republican young ones around these parts and one or two game ones with no interest in politics at all. I'll point you at them.

—Thanks for the offer, Ivan, I said. —But I've never needed help on that score.

—You're not a captain for nothing, Captain.

—You'll be a captain yourself one of these days.

—Please God, he said.

—Are ye too busy to sit at the table, Captain? said old Missis O'Shea.

—We are, said Ivan.

—It wasn't you I was talking to, but I don't hear the captain disagreeing with you. You'll have it in your hand, so, she said. —Sure, it's hardly a dinner at all.

It was incredible, the nicest stuff I'd ever tasted. Griddle cakes, and a bit of cabbage that was perfect. I wasn't used to fresh vegetables and, judging by the grub that had come my way in friendly houses all over the country, not many other people were either. Stirabout and slidderjacks and cakes of rough bread the size of bike tyres, flitches of cured bacon that had been hanging for centuries from hooks in the kitchen ceiling, spuds, spuds and more of them, good, indifferent and rotten, and strong, rough tea a small-sized rat could dance on. I wasn't complaining. It was grand and it was filling and as good and better than what I'd grown up on. I'd never known freshness and surprise, so I didn't miss it. Until I put old Missis O'Shea's griddle cake into, even before I put it into my mouth, when its steam grabbed my nose hair and fucked it.

—Fuck —Pardon the language.

—That'll be the griddle cakes, she said. —They're not too bad today.

—They're – I don't know what word to use, I said.

—I've tasted worse, said Ivan.

—I've never eaten cabbage before, I told them.

—It's not too bad, said Ivan.

—No, I said.

They hadn't understood, so I spoke again.

217

—This is the first time in my life that I've ever eaten cabbage, I said. —And d'you know what?

They were speechless; I could tell by their faces; stunned. The creature from Dublin; they'd known we were different but this news I'd just thrown at them was the most shocking thing they'd ever heard. Old Missis O'Shea brought her shawl up to her face.

—And d'yis know what? I said.

—What's that? said Ivan.

—This is worth dying for, I said.

I pointed at the food.

—The right of the people of Ireland to eat grub like this.

And I meant it, every word. Old Missis O'Shea hid under her shawl.

—You've a friend for life there, Captain, said Ivan.

—He's a fool of a boy, said old Missis O'Shea, —but he's hit the nail on the head this once.

And she ran out into the yard.

Drilling the new men on the local big shot's demesne was an idea I'd picked up from Ernie O'Malley, that and digging the graves.

—It'll rid them of that fear and respect they have for the planter, he'd said when we'd last crossed paths, in the Glen of Aherlow. We'd slept the night on the ground and woken up white with the frost.

—Are you frightened of anyone? he'd asked me.

—No, I said.

—They are, he said.

He meant everyone else, the people of Ireland. He wasn't a long walk older than I was, Ernie, but he had the stance and talk of a man who'd lived many big lives and learnt well from all of them.

—They're frightened of their betters, he said. —And that means virtually everybody they encounter outside of their own tight circle. It's the result of hundreds of years of colonialism. And that's our task, Smart. We have to convince them that they have no betters.

—You could start that process by calling me Henry.

—Point taken, he said. —Henry. This is a revolution of the mind.

—Fair enough. It's cold, isn't it, Ernie?

—Yes.

They were at the gates, in under a big bush, when I cycled up, nine of them, most of the men I'd met that morning, more than I'd have expected. Ivan was at the front.

—That's a fresh one, Captain.

—Any more to come?

—I wouldn't bank on it.

—Shamey said he's not coming.

—Never mind Shamey, said Ivan. —That fella let his mother die in the workhouse.

—And his father as well.

—The mother's the one that matters.

—Let's go, I said.

—Why are we going in there? said one of the big lads behind Ivan.

—Well, for a start, I told him, —this is the last place the peelers will be looking for us, if they've heard that there's something going on. And they probably have, seeing lots of lads cycling past the barracks on a night when there's no dancing. They'd never think for a minute that you lads would have the nerve to drill in there. And why shouldn't you? It's land that was robbed off you.

—What are the shovels for, Captain?

—D'you have rifles?

—No.

—If the peelers do turn up you can hit them with the shovels. Let's go.

They began taking their bikes from the hedge and ditch.

—Will we need them at all? said one of them. —Sure, aren't we going in over the wall?

—No, we're not, I said. —We're going in through the gate. Look at the wall, sure. It's falling down. It's a fuckin' disgrace. We'll go in the proper way. No lamps.

In we went, ten men on bikes, past the rust-eaten gates of Shantallow, under the big trees that marked the houses of the

219

planters, crunching over the few patches of gravel that were left on the road. I cycled at the pace I'd have taken through Strokestown at noon – this was a confidence-building exercise – and they followed me. It was a noise you never caught in the city, the whirr of bike chains in action together. It was one of the great sounds of the war. I swerved off the road just where it turned from the trees. I didn't bother looking at the big house. I went under the trees, ducked the branches, and cycled across an open field where cows stood stupid waiting to be maimed. The moon was out and shining for us. I growled at the stars. At the far side of the meadow the long shadow of more trees made a wall of the night and that was where I braked and dismounted. The others caught up and stopped. I counted them. There were no deserters.

—Gather around there, I said.

They made a tight line between me and the house.

—Most of this war will be fought under cover of darkness. Get used to it.

—What's there to get used to?

—Shut up and listen to the captain, said Ivan. —There's more to darkness than just the dark.

—In the war against superior numbers, I told them, —the darkness of night is our greatest ally.

—See now? said Ivan. —I told you.

I was reciting passages I'd learnt from a book I took with me everywhere, a book with no cover that I stitched into my coat, *Small Wars: Their Principles and Practice.* This was a bit I'd read in the bed that morning. But I was talking to the wrong audience; I saw that now. These lads hadn't grown up with streetlights and rows of open tenement windows. They already knew how to move and hide in black darkness, better by far than I did and ever would.

—Right, I said. —Divide yourselves into pairs.

In fact, they were all already better guerrillas than I'd ever be.

—Right, I said. —One each of you face the house. Who owns it again?

—We do, said a voice. —You said yourself.

—Yeah. But until we're ready to take it back.

—Fitzgalway. The hoor. He's never there.

—Right. Face the house. Stand apart. Arms out. Put a distance between yis.

—He has a daughter that paints.

—Right, I said. —The men not facing the house. It's your job to creep up on the other lads without them hearing you do it. Then we'll reverse the roles.

It was natural to them. They were poachers and the sons of poachers, creeping around and behind generations of Fitzgalways and their rabbits, cutting the tendons of their cattle, avoiding their agents and bullies, grabbing the arses of their scullery maids. They were people who had had to move furtively through their own place for hundreds of years, who had survived by hiding themselves. And still did, out of habit and necessity, and for entertainment, like Ivan, devoting so much thought to being an eejit, pretending to be one, giving his life to it. They were all masters of disguise and invisibility. I had nothing to teach them. I was the man from outside who would bring importance to their skills simply by stating them. I'd show them that their traits and talents were the stuff that made warriors.

—Right, men. Halt.

The only thing I could add was discipline. Precision, order and bearing – the restraints that would make soldiers out of them.

—In a line.

I picked on one, Willie O'Shea, from the barn that morning.

—What height are you, O'Shea?

—I don't know, Captain. I never measured meself.

—You're about five foot eight, I said. —Stand up straight. Attention!

My shout woke the shadows.

—Now look at you. You're five foot ten at least. You're a bigger man than you were a minute ago. How does that feel?

—Not so bad.

—Attention!

Even the cows moved.

—Shoulders back. Why?

—That's the place for them.

—Sometimes it's good to be small, other times it's good to be bigger. If the enemy has to see you approaching, if that's the only way to approach, if surprise isn't an option, then he should see you approaching big. Make yourselves small when you're ducking the bullets but let him know that when you get right up to him, when you're past his bayonet, you're going to be much bigger than him. Straight line there! That's no line at all, crooked or straight. The average Irishman is three inches taller than the average Englishman. Did you know that?

—I never measured an English —

—Shut up! It's true. You're bigger than them. That's why they enlist Irishmen into their army to do their fuckin' empire building for them. And Welshmen are an inch smaller again. Remember that the next time you're eating your dinner. Attention!

The land around us was alive. The air above was a clatter of wings and scratches.

—Name those birds making the racket.

—That's a lark, the contrary one. And there are robins right on top of us.

—There's an owl at his dinner; I can hear him gulping on the fur.

—Missel thrushes.

—There's a fecker in there I don't know.

—It's a storm-cock; there he goes.

—That's enough, I said. —Do you know why I asked you to tell me those names? When we should be getting the hell out of here?

—Because you didn't know them yourself, maybe.

—You're right but that's not the point. The point is, you know them. You know something that I don't. You have an advantage over me.

—There's not much advantage in knowing the cries of ol' birds.

—You're dead right, I said. —There's not much advantage. But there is an advantage and it might be useful. One time in a million maybe, but it's there. And you'll be waiting for it. Listen to this. There is no such thing as useless information. Listen. You might find yourself on a train beside a soldier, an

222

officer, a peeler on his day off, say, and he might be interested in, Ivan?

—The noise that birds make in the dark.

—Exactly. He might be a bird watcher, one of those fellas. You get talking about birds. You loosen him up. You give him something, he gives something back. Information that's much more useful to us than the noise of birds. It might happen, it might not. But you're there and ready if it does. There is no such thing as useless information. What's the name of the gamekeeper?

—Reynolds.

—More useful information.

—Why's that?

—He's coming across the field.

We lay in the ditch behind the bank of trees with the bikes and shovels all around us.

—See now, I whispered to Ivan as we watched the gamekeeper moving among the cows and turning towards the gate. —You know the fucker's name. Even that's useful to know.

—It wasn't a hard name to find, Captain, said Ivan. —He's my father and he's off for his feed of porter. And ye might as well know this as well, lads, if ye meet that peeler on the train. He's an ornithologist. That's what the bird watchers like to call themselves.

—I hope it's not a long journey, said Willie O'Shea. —I wouldn't want to be stuck beside one of those fellas for too long.

—You could get up off your hole and sit somewhere else.

—He could, said Ivan. —He could sit beside a peeler that has an interest in stupidity. He'll be on the road now, Captain. Have you seen enough of this ditch?

—I have, I said. —Once you've seen one ditch you've seen them all.

—You're the captain, Captain, said Ivan. —But you earned your stripes in the big city. There are ditches and there are ditches. And this one here is hardly a ditch at all. There's more useful information for you.

I told them to cycle as far as the road's bend for the house and to take their shovels off the crossbars. We leaned our bikes against the trees and I walked them across the road to the steps that brought the road down to the lawn, right under the house. I looked at the house now. All turrets and other fuckologies, held up by yard-deep ivy. The windows were lit but none of the men seemed too worried now.

—How many Fitzgalways are there in there? I asked.

—It's hard to tell with them always coming and going, said Ivan.

—If they were all at home how many?

—Five.

—How many men?

—Just the two. The ol' fellow and the young fellow.

—Right, I said. —Dig two graves.

—We're not going to kill them?

—No, I said. —But we can. Any time we want. Any time we need to. We're in control here. Dig.

—They're beyond in England.

—So are we, I said. —Dig.

And they did. It wasn't late in the evening and the ground hadn't yet hardened, so they were soon through the crust and into the wet muck.

—It's a grand bit of soil, all the same.

There was grunting and laughter coming out with the shovel-loads. I watched the house.

—Tell us, Captain, said Ivan after twenty minutes.

He was up to his chin in the grave.

—Is this one here for the ol' fellow or the young fellow?

—I hadn't given it much thought, I said. —You choose.

—The young fellow. He's not as big a man as the ol' fellow, so we're finished. There's room for his horse in here with him.

Ivan climbed out of the grave and all the others followed him.

—Good work, men, I said. —These'll be found in the morning if not before and then they'll know. British rule in these parts is over.

And that was it for the weeks and months after. All over Ireland. Whipping the local boys into shape.

—Eyes right!

Forcing punctuality on them.

—Eyes front!

Making an army out of them.

—Eyes left!

I ran them and biked them and made them crawl through winter bog water. I went to their homes, in windows, over half-doors and dragged them out. I pulled them off bikes and women. I marched them through rivers, over mountains. I made them carry their bikes through the bogs. I taught them semaphore and lamp codes. I taught them how to get across stretches of land with nowhere to hide from the high road except the shadows. I put the years and inches on them. It was tough going. I broke their fuckin' hearts. These boys worked hard all day and had to become soldiers at night. I brought them near fun and death. We went on long bike rides with stones in our pockets and we often ran into the peelers in their black uniforms on moonless nights, cycled right into them, and the men came away blooded, happy and anonymous. And I took the Widowmaker from off my back one evening when there was enough of the day left for them all to witness me shooting the wheel out from under a peeler's bike as he cycled past us on the road to Tulsk. I let them bring me to all the barracks, Scramoge, Roosky, Termonbarry, and I let them tell me what cover to use, which adjoining shop to burrow through, who were our friends along the street and who weren't. I gathered them in guarded barns and lectured them on tactics and military precedent. I blinded them with the wisdom I'd lifted from *Small Wars: Their Principles and Practice*. I gave them flanks and sorties and enfilades and they gave me the geography and we stayed the nights playing our own local chess on the floors of the barns.

I knocked on the door of the local curate and I told him that the Sinn Féin people up in Dublin had told me that he'd be the right man to mind the money for the guns we had to buy. I knew that the inclusion of himself, Dublin and Sinn Féin all in the one sentence would win him over to our dangerous cause, and I was right. He held on to the bits of money that the men gave me every Saturday, minus my 10 per cent, and kept it all in a sock and a ledger under the housekeeper's bed.

I got the men to enrol other men, to go beyond their parish, beyond their fear and hatred, into the villages and on to Strokestown and further. I needed more men and a greater variety of men. I needed blacksmiths and jewellers and men who knew metal and springs, men who could charm engines, who could make bombs from nothing, men who were married to women with sisters married to peelers, who lived beside the barracks, contacts, eyes, ears, postmen and railwaymen. I wanted to leave behind a company of one hundred and twenty men, trained, armed and primed for the assault that was coming.

I cycled to Dublin with the priest's sock in my coat. Ivan and Willie were my scouts. I brought them to Shanahan's and showed them famous men and we cycled back to Rusg with the promise of ten rifles and, while I entertained Cathleen, the big girl in Kinnegad, Ivan got on with her sister and Willie threw the priest's empty sock into the river, and by the time we cycled back through Athlone they were ready to take down the barracks with their teeth. It had all gone to plan: I'd be leaving soon and I wanted Ivan to take over. The men elected their own commander and other officers but it was always tricky; it had been a problem in other places. They'd be ruled by their place in the local pecking order and they'd vote up, for the big farmer, the teacher or the lad in the bank with the brother a priest, big noises in the parish but hopeless soldiers. Ivan was born to it. He had respect, know-how, he never slept. But he was no one; he'd no land, no connections. I wanted to leave him in charge, our own man. The coming war was his big chance and I needed him to see that, to fight for the leadership and what he could do with it. Cathleen's sister and the pints in Shanahan's had done their job. Ivan wanted more.

The rifles arrived, ten brand-new Lee-Enfields in a bed of oil and straw, and I watched as they held and rubbed them and passed them on to their friends. The rifle gave them power, style, military legitimacy; it made men of them, the men who meant business. I showed them how to dismantle and clean them and they queued to do it, like jealous sisters wanting their turn with the baby. They bathed the guns with Rangoon oil and a can of 3-in-1, patted a plug of Vaseline into the muzzle and breech and put them back together again. I gave them each a bullet and let them fall in love with it.

I brought them out on a cloudless night and made them stand out on the road, on a wide, clear patch away from the corners. And, one by one, I made them shout it, and Ivan shouted and loudest and longest.

—Fuck you, God!

Straight up at the stars.

—Fuck you, God!

All of them.

—Right, boys, I said. —You're in.

I never stayed in the same house for more than a few nights. There were peelers hanging around the roads, since the killings in Soloheadbeg and other skirmishes, and Crossleys full of soldiers were becoming a daily sight. I moved on and often I stayed away from houses altogether. I lived in the hill country where the peelers never ventured. I lay in against walls with my thoughts of Victor and women. I ate hare and hedgehog with the tinkers and slept with them too and stayed well clear of their women. The women stared at me and knew I'd never touch them. I stayed in friendly cottages and ate the silent meals and kneeled while they said their rosaries. I lay on the floor and listened to the crickets.

—Put your socks beyond on the dresser, Captain, for the crickets eat the socks of strangers when they're sleeping.

I listened to the crickets and felt very far away. I wondered why I was doing it, far from Jack and Collins and songs written about me. But some memory of belief would calm me, a feeling of belonging that came when I thought of the people I knew and, always, it was parts of them that came to me – Victor's hand, my father's breath, my mother's lap, Connolly at my shoulder opening the words, his finger following mine across the page, Annie and her singing, her dead husband's empty sleeve, even Granny Nash's whispering as she rode deeper into the stories in front of her on the table, Victor's cough, my mother's broken words, Paddy Swanzy's back, him falling on Moore Street, Miss O'Shea running into the bullets on Henry Street, Victor under the tarpaulin and the frost on the gravel path that morning behind Grand Canal Dock, his cheeks, I rubbed them and rubbed them and all I wanted was to hear another cough, and Victor on my shoulders and Victor beside me at the school railings and Victor and me falling from the wall on to our father's stomach and the grunting of the fat rozzers trying to follow us. And I knew why I was there, on the damp floors of those strangers' houses, and I knew that I was right and it gave a point to my loneliness and made a good friend of my anger. I came back to old Missis O'Shea's as often as was safe and prayed as I pedalled that there'd be griddle cakes waiting for me. And they were always there, always, with the cabbage and the chat.

She had bad news when I cycled up to her door.

—You're very welcome, young Captain. But the water's gone astray on me.

Her well had gone dry.

—And in April too, she said. —The water falling out of the sky in buckets but none of it coming out of the ground.

I dropped a stone into the well, and nothing came back except the noise of the stone hitting more stone.

—The diviner's a mysterious man, she said. —God alone knows when he'll come our way again. He was through here last spring.

—I'll find you water, I said.

I took the leg from the holster under my coat.

—I have the power.

—Good man yourself, she said. —That's the powerful leg you have there.

I had the power but I hadn't used it since the day I'd discovered it and escaped from Richmond Barracks, and I'd never controlled it. I held the leg in front of me now in both my hands and I walked slowly from the well, away from the house and the yard. Old Missis O'Shea was behind me; I could feel her walking in my shadow. I waited for it to happen. I remembered the shake and my blood racing, pulling me towards the river under the barracks. I turned to the east. She followed; I heard her feet. I remembered being dragged and every bone I owned bending towards it, quivering, promising to snap if I didn't move. I waited for it. There was no hurry, no

228

urgency yet. I waited for the rush. It would happen; I knew it would.

She spoke.

—Two and two?

I stopped.

—Don't know, I said. —Two and two what?

—Griddle cakes.

Meanwhile, after the killings at Soloheadbeg, parts of the south were now military areas, open prisons that made trade and courting almost impossible; buying and selling sheep had become an act of sedition, and kissing was downright treason.

—Griddle cakes, she said.

—Who made them?

—I did.

—Four.

De Valera decided to go on to America, to raise funds and heckles, much to the dismay of those who were afraid of Collins and the tight hold, getting tighter and meaner all the time, he seemed to have on everything – the money, the weapons, ideas, secrets, the loyalty of the hardest men and women. Collins, Minister for Finance, set up the Republican Loan. *You can restore Ireland's Health, Her Beauty and Her Wealth: Subscribe today to the Irish National Loan.* And he was escorted into the centre of Dublin Castle by Ned Broy and spent hours reading fat files in their treasury of secrets and bad business. He read his own file: *He comes of a brainy Cork family.* He read mine: *He comes of no known family.* At a meeting in Cork, Alfred Gandon, Minister for Commercial Affairs and the Sea, spoke of his days in the G.P.O. with Pearse and Connolly and the dark days after in Dartmoor and Lewes, and of how his faith in the Republic had never once wavered. A body was found in a ditch in the Wicklow Mountains, a placard around the neck. *Spy – killed by I.R.A.* And on the 24th of June, 1919, in Thurles, a peeler called Hunt was shot in the back. The terror was now systematic. The way to the state's heart was through its police force. *Shun all policemen and spies! Three cheers for the I.R.A.*

I turned.

Brown eyes and some slivers of hair that had escaped from a

bun that shone like a lamp behind her head, even on the miserable day we were standing in.

—Four, I said.

—*Maithú*, Henry.

A mass of the finest brown hair, endless hair that was dying for fingers to comb it. Hair that had once washed over me.

—It was the leg that did it, she said.

Her hand reached out and she wiped some of the rain off the mahogany.

—You still have it.

—I do.

And there they were, the little brown buttons, running the length of the same brown dress, like the heads of little animals climbing quietly to her neck, only now, nine or ten years later, they seemed to be crawling down to her boots, her muck-fattened boots, her laces untied and trailing. And those laces were the wildest things I'd ever seen.

—How are you? I said.

—Not so bad.

—It's been a long time.

—Not so long.

—You're getting wet.

—And so are you.

The same brown-black eyes, but already I could see that she was different.

—Well, I said.

—Well.

In little ways. She was different in small parts of herself. The corners of her mouth, her nose, there was something about her shoulders. She was thinner. There was more of her now gathered under her eyes. She'd been sick. She had the face of a woman who'd been sick for a long time, whose mind was still back in the sick time. I looked for the horrible redness that ate the cheeks of men and women who were coughing to their deaths, and children too. But there were no red wounds; they were the cheeks of a woman who was out in the rain.

—You're looking well, I said.

She blushed, and I remembered that too.

—So are you.

—I make the effort, I said.

—You're still a great man for the answers, she said. —Your britches are gone.

—They were beyond saving, I said. —They went out a window. She's your mother, isn't she?

—Yes.

—She told me there were no teachers in the family.

—She wasn't telling a lie. Why didn't you get yourself a new pair?

—The old ones had become too famous, I told her. —I saw you going out the side door.

She knew that I was talking about the G.P.O.

—They made us do it, she said. —They never wanted us there in the first place. All we were good for was cooking stew and sewing haversacks. I'm a better shot than the lot of them.

—A better ride, too.

She blushed.

—You're the same as ever, she said.

—A bit older.

—It comes with the life, I suppose.

—No more teaching, no?

—No, she said. —No more teaching.

—You were a great teacher.

—Thank you, she said. —But I can make only one proud boast about my teaching days.

—What's that?

—I'm the woman who taught Henry Smart to write his name.

—That's right. But I'm not Henry Smart around here.

—I know, she said. —You're different men in different places. You told me to remember that, on the day you left the school. Do you remember that?

—I remember, I said. —I remember every second. Every sum and hymn.

—So do I. Well.

—We're getting wet and I've water to find.

—Right, she said. —I'll leave you to it.

—Right, I said. —I'll be seeing you.

—Yes, she said. —You will.

231

I'd gone only a few yards through the muck when the leg started hopping in my hands, and humming. I watched the raindrops dancing to the tip of the shivering peg – *we'll go home be the water* – and dropping down to more water. I let go of the leg before my blood started to race and it jumped from the remains of my grip and dived straight into the muck. The leather strap was all I could see. I knew where the well would be. I bent down to pull the leg from the ooze and felt, for a fraction, the coarse wool of an old coat on my neck and a man's sweat warmed my cheek, gone before I could stand up straight, before I knew properly what they were. But the smell of old, murdered blood that came with them, the smell that had drenched my father's coat, stayed under my nose until long after the rain had gone and the cousins and nephews were digging through the rock to the groundwater.

We were married on the 12th of September, 1919. A ruined teacher and a gunman on the run. Our wedding present from Collins was my birth certificate and four extra years added to my life; according to the Republic-issued cert, I was born on the 11th of May, 1897. That made me twenty-two, just ten years younger than my bride, an unusual difference, strange, but not a scandal. And from Jack Dalton I got my suit, cleaned and wrapped in brown paper, with a bullet hole where his shoulder would have been if he'd been half the man that I was, picked up in a skirmish on Winetavern Street. Neither Mick nor Jack attended the wedding. They were on their way – Jack was to be my best man – but military activity had held them in Granard. That was what they told me later, the next time I was up in Dublin to shoot a G-man and I saw nothing in the excuse to give out about. Getting any distance by road without coming up against a roadblock had become a lucky day's work. By the day of our wedding, the times were racing.

We were married by our priest, the treasurer, owner of the sock that had gone into the river behind Kinnegad. The church was emptied, except for himself, the happy couple and Ivan, my emergency best man –
—Thanks, Ivan.

—For what?

emptied, just for the vows, so that my true identity would remain unknown. And another secret inside that secret: I put fingers to my ears when the priesteen turned to my fiancée and said: —Do you —

I pushed the fingers in.

And out.

—O'Shea, take this man to be —

We became man and wife without me hearing her Christian name. She was and stayed my Miss O'Shea. I never knew her name.

And there was the hooley in old Missis O'Shea's house, tables out in the yard to make room for the dancing inside. Her own table and more borrowed from family and neighbours, decked high with sandwiches and cakes, crates of porter and minerals, and on one of them only griddle cakes, great piles of them, and children and women around the table burrowing into them like cornered ferrets. The whole day, from dawn to the dawn of the day after, was guarded by the men I'd trained and who were now under Ivan's command. Men on the roof of the church, on the approach roads, hidden back in the hedges, men at the gate of the church, behind stones in the graveyard, in the car parked outside the creamery. And they led the way to the house and more of them followed and ringed us. The procession was a show of force: we controlled the town. We had our supporters, plenty of them, but there were also plenty who hated and feared us, who hated what we were doing. We let them see – they were behind the lace curtains of the town as we marched past – how easily we could take over, how inevitable it was. If we couldn't lead them, we'd force them to follow us. And Ivan's men were on the roof of the long barn, in the fields and bogland surrounding the house, behind the bright stone walls. The car outside the creamery, now empty of men, was a gelignite bomb waiting for any armoured car or foot patrol to pass it. They were armed to the gaps in their teeth now; Lee-Enfields, Winchesters, and some Red Army Mosins, Smith and Wessons and some good-looking R.I.C. carbines, taken from the burning barracks in Muckloon. They had home-made grenades, tins filled with blasting powder, and a few grenades that had been made in Germany before the end of the War. They had a sergeant in an abandoned cottage near Cloonfree Lough and a promise to deliver him safe home if the day passed without interruption.

The peelers stayed away.

We grabbed a few minutes for ourselves, away from the dancing and back-slapping.

I gave her a German pipe, a beautiful thing, my face carved into the black wood of the bowl. She held it carefully by the shank and gazed into the face.

—It's exactly you, she said.

—Put it in the window when it's safe for me to visit, I said.

—A husband visiting his wife, she said. —What sort of a world is it we're marrying into?

—It'll be a better one soon, I said.

And, the day that was in it, I believed what I'd said.

She gave me a pair of britches, and a snake belt to hold them up.

—Not that you'll be needing it, she said as she watched me putting them on.

She took the two steps over to me and started unbuttoning them. She put a hand on my cheek.

—My child bride, she said.

—Fuck off, would yeh.

—Say that again.

—No.

—Do what you're told, Henry Smart.

—Fuck off.

—Again, Henry.

—Fuck off.

—What would happen if they came in now?

—Who? The priest?

—Oh God.

We were in the scullery, in the dark behind the kitchen. Its coolness was welcome after the heat outside.

I grabbed her to me.

—The peelers?

—Oh —

It wasn't the same as the room under the G.P.O. but it did

234

us fine and we did it proud. We fucked without grazing our knees on the flags, without stopping for balance or breath, for the first time since that first time, after months of staring at each other, rubbing against each other, ignoring, torturing each other. We blew up together and held on to each other till our bodies calmed down and we could feel and hear the dancing from the kitchen outside and the end of it, and old Missis reciting *Dangerous Dan McGrew*. We knew that Ivan was leaning against the other side of the scullery door. Ivan had become a big man in the parish, a man who might have killed a peeler, a man who had it in his power to leave any man dead in a ditch with a piece of paper pinned to his lapel: *Killed as a spy by the I.R.A.* Power had gone to Ivan's soul. He had cut the hair off girls who'd been seen giving soldiers the eye, tied them to gates and railings, their hair cut with shears and a singeing machine. And he always kept a lock of the hair, to post to the victim weeks later. He'd gone further than that. He'd punched two pig rings into a young one's ears, because she was a peeler's niece and her boyfriend had refused to stop seeing her. He'd hanged a donkey from a tree for delivering turf to Strokestown barracks. And he'd become a great man for the letter writing. *Unless you withdraw your services from the local peelers within three days of receiving this notice you will undergo the extreme penalty at the hands of the I.R.A. i.e. DEATH.* They had a style that was all his own. *Please yourself now, but failure to carry out the above order will be frowned upon. Yours faithfully. The Firing Party.* We never had many recruits and fewer real ones, devoted men, soldiers who were prepared to give up everything and do anything for the fight. Collins himself said that there were never more than three thousand fighting. So, savages like Ivan did the work of hundreds. We scoured the country looking for Ivans. He was on the other side of the door now, so the scullery was ours for as long as we wanted it.

—Your mother?

—Oh God —

I had a photograph of the day that I managed to hold on to until it was burnt in front of my eyes, in a warehouse in Chicago just before they shot me. We're sitting on a bench in front of whitewash that must have been the side wall of old

Missis's house. You could tell from the wall that it was a hot, glaring day. I'm in the suit from Clery's, before I changed into the britches, my shirt whiter than the wall, and a Thompson sub-machine-gun, a great-looking gun but overrated, draped across my lap. She's in a dress she'd made herself from looking at the pictures in a book of legends of the Fianna, white linen broken with embroidered birds and monsters biting their own tails and a massive Tara brooch holding a cloak to her shoulders. Her hair is loosened; her bun has become a frame for her face: she was perfect that day. The butt of the Thompson is nudging her knee. Ivan is behind us in full uniform, one hand covering his holster, the other unseen. Ivan the Terrible, later to become Ivan Reynolds T.D. He was already getting fat on his future. He's standing behind Miss O'Shea and looking away, keeping an eye on his men on the barn roof, a fringe he'd let grow over the summer curtaining the other eye; he'd met Collins in May and hadn't cut the hair since. And the bridesmaid is beside Ivan, right behind me. She was a Reynolds, too, no great friend of Miss O'Shea's, just a female cousin neither too old nor young to be her bridesmaid, and even in that old photograph, ruined by the sweat, rain and wear of the fugitive life, years of it by the time they'd caught up with me and I was standing against that wall in Chicago, and years since I'd last seen Miss O'Shea and longer still since I'd held her, even then as the photograph burned and curled in front of my face, I could see that the poor girl was blushing and I could see too where Ivan's other hand was going as he looked at his men on the barn. Ivan was feeling his cousin. On the 12th of September, 1919. Dáil Éireann was finally declared illegal by the British Government. They had, said Arthur Griffith, *proclaimed the whole of the Irish nation as an illegal assembly*. Detective Constable Daniel Hoey, who'd been on every rebel's wanted list since 1916, got what was coming to him right under the gates of Dublin Castle. And Henry Smart, gunman and water diviner, got married to Miss O'Shea, gunwoman in waiting. Another big day for Ireland.

I was gone the next day. I dumped the bike in a friendly shed

236

outside Mullingar, a walk to the station and onto the train. Off at Kingsbridge. A ring of soldiers at every door.

I kept walking.

G-men sweating in their trenchcoats watched every face coming towards them as they leaned against pillars and pretended to read newspapers. I stared straight through them, a man in a hurry, and walked right up to the door.

—So who are you?

An English accent. There were no more Irish soldiers. A sergeant. Not unpleasant. Backed up by twitchy youngsters and two Crossley cars behind them on the street.

—Michael Collins, I said.

We laughed.

—Reggie Nash, I said.

—And what are you up to then, Mister Nash?

—I'm on my way home, Sergeant, I said. —The wife's after having a baby.

—Congratulations. What's in the briefcase, or am I being rude?

—I'm a traveller for Kapp and Petersen, I told him as I opened the case and showed him my display of pipes.

—Goodness, he said.

They were beautiful things, four lines of the most elegant pipes, gleaming and expensive, only one empty space, where my own face had been the day before. He was mesmerised. His arm moved slightly, and stopped. He wanted to touch them but was scared of their elegance. He shook slightly, and spoke again.

—Alright, he said. —Off you go, home to your missis. Boy or a girl? Hang on. Excuse me.

He lifted the tail of my trenchcoat and saw the leg sitting in its holster.

They all took small steps back and I heard the neat thump of a breech bolt being pulled. The crowd right behind me stopped shuffling.

—What's this then, Mister Nash?

—A display item, I said.

—Come again?

—A display item, I said. —It's a giant-sized match.

I hoped to Jesus that they were all fresh off the boat, that none of them knew that the pipes were made by Kapp and Petersen and the matches by Maguire and Patterson.

I showed him the strap.

—The idea being that it gets hung above the tobacconist's door.

—It don't look much like a match from here, sir.

He was relaxing now, curious.

—That's probably why no one wanted it, I said. —I have to agree with you. But, like you, Sergeant, I have to obey orders. A boy.

—Come again?

—The baby, I said. —A boy.

—I've got girls myself, he said. —Sorry for delaying you, sir.

—Goodbye, Sergeant, I said. —I hope the rain stays away for you.

Out onto the street. More G-men leaning against the river wall. Away. Past them and gone. Across the bridge and away. Into the streets where the G-men weren't welcome.

—I'm married now, Granny, I told her.

—Does she own both her legs? she asked.

She'd been reading the *Independent*. She put her finger under the last word and looked up at me. She looked at me properly for the first time since I was a child fighting on her daughter's lap.

—She does, yeah, I said.

—Then you'll be very happy, she said.

She was still looking at me.

—Are you not very young to be getting yourself wedded?

—I'm twenty-two, I told her.

She lifted her finger, brought it to the top of the page and dropped it under the date.

—So I've been reading news that's four years old, she said.

—Tell me more about Gandon, I said.

—Gandon in 1919 or Gandon in 1923?

—1919.

—It's hard to remember, she said. —It's such a long, long time ago.

—I'm seventeen, I told her.

—Ah, she said.

She took her finger off the date.

—He's a changed man, she said.

—How is he?

—Have you any books for me?

—No.

—My lips are sealed, so.

—What about a wedding present? I said.

—He's a changed man, she said. —A Shinner and a Minister, no less. Talking about important things beyond in the Mansion House. Changing his name to O'Gandúin.

She turned the page of the paper and whacked it flat on the table.

—I know all that, I said.

—That wasn't your present, she said. —It's this: he isn't changed at all.

—What d'you mean?

—When will you have books for me?

—Tomorrow, I said. —I'll get them tonight.

—By females?

—Yeah.

—He's still up to his old tricks, she said. —The things the wooden fella used to do for him. Except he has other eejits now to do his dirty work for him. He hasn't changed a bit.

—You know Smith?

Collins was sitting on his desk.

—I do, I said.

—He's yours, he said.

This was Collins's latest office, a new one added to the five or six he used every day. The Ministry of Finance, hidden behind a name, Hegarty and Dunne, Insurance, a company that didn't exist, in a room up two flights of stairs in Mary Street. Like all the others, it was clean and bare of virtually everything except paper. He brought his own filing system everywhere with him, nails in rows along all four walls and his papers pinned to them in an order that only he, the inventor, understood.

We were alone. We were almost always alone when we met now. Behind the desk he was Minister for Finance; where he was now, sitting on the desk, in front of me, he was President of the Supreme Council of the I.R.B. He'd give me a name and I'd deliver a dead man.

I was one of the Squad, one of the secret elite. An assassin. There were nine of us, then twelve, and we became the Twelve Apostles and the name stuck even when, with deaths, arrests and executions, there were less and more than twelve of us.

—Do you have any scruples about the taking of life?

Dick McKee had asked the question just before I'd been sworn into the Squad. They were looking for a strange mix of man – dissident and slave, a man who was quick with his brain and an eejit. They knew what they were doing when they chose me; I was quick and ruthless, outspoken and loyal – and such an eejit it took me years to realise what was going on. Collins and Dick Mulcahy, Chief of Staff of the I.R.A., stood behind McKee. I was sitting on a straight-backed chair in another bare room.

—Not usually, I said.

—At all? said McKee.

—Well, I'll tell you, Dick, I said. —I wouldn't want to kill animals or children. But if it's rozzers we're talking about, I'm your man.

I was their man alright.

I was with Collins now. He was sharing himself with me – I was one of the chosen – sharing his time, risking his security, in return for which I was going to kill Detective Sergeant Smith of the G Division.

—He's been warned, said Collins. —He said Thanks and told the lads to feck off. Brave man.

—When?

—Tomorrow.

—Who'll be with me?

We worked in pairs.

—You'll find out when you meet him.

I rested my foot on the kerb, at a corner under a hanging tree on Terenure Road. The city was dead. Two minutes to the midnight curfew and I was far from home. My room on Cranby Row, the one I'd shared with Jack, was still there, but I couldn't go near it; the homes of the wanted men were watched all the time. I was more than two minutes' cycle away from anywhere with a suitcase full of stolen books, all by female authors, strapped to the back of a bike I'd borrowed from Collins. I had nowhere to go. There was the water beneath me but I didn't want to abandon the bike or drench the books. I'd spent the night slithering into big houses around Kenilworth Square, spent hours reading the titles and authors on the spines, selecting the best and the fattest, from off the shelves and the bedside tables of sleeping owners. I listened. Not a sinner out, except me, not a footstep or a bike chain complaining. I heard the Rathmines bells giving out the hour and then I heard the roar of a motor and saw a giant headlight coming from Highfield Road.

I was over a hedge with the bike and the books when the caged lorry raced past and braked about fifty yards past me and reversed, and braked again. I heard boots hit the ground and screams from a woman.

—Halt there! Halt!

I looked over the hedge and saw a couple, a lad and a young one, being hauled from a hedge just like mine, caught in the headlights and soldiers milling around them. There were more shouts as the pair were thrown onto the lorry, and it roared off. I had to drop below the hedge again as a prowler was suddenly there in the centre of the road, a car with no lights and an engine that purred under the silence. It crept past. I listened through the hedge, made sure that it didn't slow or stall, and I heard it turn onto Orwell Road.

I could stay where I was, huddled in against the wall and hedge and hope that no foot patrols came my way. I could knock on the door behind me and hope for the best. I could get on the bike and dash and hope for even better luck, and go – where?

Mister Climanis.

—Mister Smart! How late, how nice!

—I'll go away if you think it's not safe.

—Mister Smart! Please! Come in. Come in. Please.

He stood out of my way and I stepped onto a stairs that started right against the door. He ran out and took my bike. He pointed at the suitcase I was now carrying.

—Bombs, yes?

—No, I said. —Books.

—Books? he said. —Nice but no good. Go, go. Up, up. Please.

He pointed to the doors at the top of the stairs.

—Maria! he roared, and slammed the door. —Maria! Come see who is here!

There was a tall woman waiting when I got to the top of the stairs. Mister Climanis was right behind, shoving my legs with the front wheel.

—Forward and up! Look, Maria. I have here my secret friend. Mister Smart.

—Hello, she said.

—A most important republican man, said Mister Climanis. —With a suitcase that is full of bombs!

She was tall and beautiful.

—Go 'way out of that, she said.

—They're books, I told her.

—Books? said Mister Climanis. —I misheard.

And he laughed.

She got out of my way and he pushed me through the open door into the kitchen. He parked the bike against the wall outside before he followed me in.

—They are dangerous books, I hope.

She followed him. She patted his black hair, as if to calm him.

—They're for my granny, I told him.

—See, Maria? he said. —The Irish. They engage in war but still think of family.

—I know, she said.

—Of course, he said. —Maria is Irish. We will drink to Ireland. My home.

He opened a press and took down a bottle of Jameson and I

noticed that there were two more bottles left in there when he closed it.

—I am without two things, he said. —Glasses and manners. Mister Smart, I apologise. This is Maria, he said. —This is Maria Climanis, he said proudly. —My wife.

He leaned over the kitchen table and spoke quietly for the first time that night.

—It was my hair, Mister Smart. Maria fell in love with my hair. Is that the truth, Maria?

She'd come back, carrying three glasses.

—Yes, she said. —Without your hair you wouldn't be half the man, David.

—Not good enough for you.

—No, she said. —Certainly not.

She clinked the glasses.

—They were in the bedroom, she said. —We're fierce drinkers in this house, Mister Smart. There are glasses everywhere except where they should be.

She dunked them in a bucket of water and wiped them with a corner of her cardigan. She was very young.

—Now, she said as she plonked them on the table. —Off we go.

—The night is young, said Mister Climanis.

—The night is always young when you're around, David, she said.

—Ah, said Mister Climanis. —I love you so much. Maria is the tallest woman in Ireland, Mister Smart. The only woman with a perfect view of my hair and so. She fell in love.

—That's true, she said. —When we have babies they'll nest in your hair.

—Did you hear that, Mister Smart?

—Yes, I said.

He was filling the glasses

—I am in love, Mister Smart, he said. —Every time I see this woman. Every time I hear this woman. Every time I think of this woman, I thank the Russians. We will drink to the Russians.

—I thought we were drinking to Ireland.

243

—Ireland, yes, said Mister Climanis. —Ireland, Russia, Latvia.

—Don't forget the United States of America, she said.

—Each one, he said. —Every one.

He swallowed half his glass.

—Alabama, he said. —The night is young.

Mister Climanis was Latvian. I'd met him in Mooney's on Abbey Street one evening when I'd no meetings or killings and I knew where I was going to sleep and how long it would take me to get there. I was enjoying my own company when a voice and black hair were suddenly sitting beside me.

—You are a strange thing, he said. —An Irishman with no long face.

—The unlucky ones have long faces, I said. —The rest of us are long in other departments.

He laughed, and I liked him. We spoke to each other without getting into a conversation; all strangers were spies and neither of us was lonely. I noticed the shavings on his jacket sleeves.

—You're a carpenter, I said.

—Pipes, he said. —I make pipes. I make the most beautiful pipes.

And, sure enough, the shavings themselves were beautiful, delicate twirls, babies' ringlets in different shades and lengths, and all surrounded by a fine dust like dark salt.

—I'd like that, I said. —I'd like to be able to do that.

—Please, he said. —Hold up your hands.

And I did.

—Very steady, he said. —You can do it.

—I've other things to do, I said.

—Yes, he said. —Every Irishman has other things to do. You will beat the English because your drinks are better. I will now buy two drinks and then you will buy two. I like this custom.

I met him when I could, when I was in town. He was always in Mooney's between six and seven o'clock, on his way from work; he liked to cross the river for his pint, to get the air into his lungs and clothes. I began to miss him if I was near Abbey Street and we were unable to meet. He asked for nothing except my company and I loved to listen to him; he told me everything. And I told him everything. I couldn't understand what was happening to me. It just seemed safe and right. It was in every crease and gesture: he was a good man.

—Mister Smart, he said one night. —I have an Irish wife. And now I have an Irish friend. I thank the Russians for this. For making of me a man with no country.

He lifted his pint.

—The Russians.

—The Reds or the Whites? I said.

—The colour is not significant. You like my new word?

He got me the pipes, one at a time once or twice a week, his idea.

—A man crossing borders must have a job, he said. —You are now a seller of pipes.

—I'm not crossing borders, I said.

—The soldiers and policemen make their own borders, he said. —All my life I have been crossing them.

He held the pipes before me and gave me their names and woods. He handed them over to me, like children he'd never see again. And one night before I got married, I watched him carve my face onto the head of the last, black pipe, the one that would fill the case.

—You are not difficult, he said. —Handsome men have not many features. That is the difference between handsome and beautiful.

—I'm not beautiful, so?

—No, you are not beautiful, Mister Smart.

—Just as well.

—Yes, he said. —We have beautiful women. We do not need beautiful men. There, he said. —Please. Give this pipe to your beautiful wife.

—I will, I said. —Thank you.

—It is not difficult, he said.

And now I was in his flat for the first time, looking at his own beautiful wife.

—Your wife, he said. —Did she like my pipe?

—She loved it, I said. —She leaves it in the window so I'll know when it's safe to visit.

—Ah, said Mister Climanis. —Maria, is what my friend, Mister Smart, said, is it romantic?

245

—God, yes, said Maria. —It's gorgeous.

—Maria teaches me a new word every day, he said.

—And that too is romantic, she said.

—My wife's a teacher, I told them.

—Ah, said Mister Climanis.

He opened the press and took down a new bottle.

—To romance. To teachers!

I was right up against his back when I shot him; his coat killed some of the noise. He was falling when I turned away. It was in his voice, the grunt and half-words that fell out of him, he couldn't understand what was happening. Four gates away from his home, on his own street, long before dark.

Archer passed me, already aiming his Parabellum. I walked on and heard two more bullets going into Smith, felt them in my legs as Smith was nailed to the pavement. It was late afternoon. Not a traditional killing time, but we were out to terrify the police. There were no safe times or sanctuaries. There was no one on the street, although there were kids somewhere near. I heard doors being slammed and windows, as the gunfire echoed and faded very slowly. Archer was beside me.

—Seven kids, he said as we walked past Smith's house. —It's a hard business.

—He was warned to back off, I said.

—I know, said Archer. —I shot the man, didn't I?

Then we heard him.

—You cowards!

Smith was standing up. He was huge there. Legs apart and holding on to nothing. There was blood pouring off his coat to his feet and trousers. And he stood up even straighter.

I ran back towards him and shot twice. Once into the mess on his chest. Once into his face. It came away from bone and seemed to linger in front of me for the time it took him to fall again. I turned and ran back past his house. No children calling now, nothing except the echoes of my shots. I couldn't hear my feet on the ground.

Archer turned left. I turned right. The gun burnt my leg

through three layers of cloth. The Black Man was at the corner of Drumcondra Road and Fitzroy Avenue. A punch-drunk ex-boxer, he wandered the city and slept where he dropped; made huge by coats and their stink, he waddled through cordons and roadblocks. I dropped the gun into his pocket without looking at him or breaking stride and walked on up Dorset Street.

I was free now, no more vulnerable than any other young man in the city. Another murder that would be made heroic by night-time, another verse added to my song. Another act that would bring undeserved punishment down on top of a city already restless and excited. I took off my trenchcoat – I had no gun to hide – and draped it over my shoulder. Crossleys charged past me. The city was being taken over by young, nervous soldiers with steel helmets and fixed bayonets, kids with English accents, and England was getting further away every day. I straightened my tie. Distant police whistles joined nearer ones. I was a young man on his way home from the office. People dashed to get home before the shake-up, and the raids. I put on a bit of a spurt myself; I didn't want to look too innocent. I'd meet Mister Climanis and catch up with the Black Man later on, across the city.

I turned onto Gardiner Street and began to run.

I pedalled, she steered. We rode in from the west, nicely downhill. She sat on the crossbar in front of me.

—How's your arse?

—Not so bad, she said.

She held the handlebars and my arms were around her, clutching the Thompson. She'd invented it herself, a rack that clipped onto the handlebars and held the gun nice and steady; the cyclist could steer with one hand and fire accurately without slowing down or falling off. I was wearing my riding britches – she'd made me wear them. She was wearing the skirt of her Cumann na mBan uniform – I'd made her wear it.

—No more sandwich making for me, she'd said.

We sailed past jaunting cars and a cart carrying milk churns to the creamery on the other side of town. We'd cased the town the day before; we knew the streets we needed. It was the tail-end of market day. We cycled through drying dung. Ballintubber was still packed but, nicely for us, the post office was at the near edge of the commerce.

—Is the door open?

—It's wide open, she said. —Like yesterday.

—Hang on tight, so.

As we came up to the door I lifted my arse off the saddle and hoisted the front wheel of the Arseless, to get us over the low step. We collided with no one but frightened them all.

—Brake! I shouted.

And Miss O'Shea did just that, front and back. We stopped dead. I dropped a leg to hold us up, and let go of a short round into a Wanted poster on the wall in front of us. Bodies and shawls hit the deck and slivers of bullet-hot brick pinged and dug in all around us.

—Good morning! I yelled into the thick silence that was left after the screaming and shots. —No messing and there'll be no one hurt.

—This post office is a relic of the British presence, said Miss O'Shea, —and is now closed.

She hopped from the crossbar as I got off the Arseless on the other side. She held and turned it, front wheel to the door, as I went over to the counter and vaulted it.

She was talking again.

—All you people should subscribe to the National Loan. It's your patriotic duty and a sound investment. There will soon be republican post offices in place throughout the country. In the meantime, keep your money at home. Notify your local Volunteers of this and you'll never be robbed.

I grabbed a sack and handed it to the woman on the working side of the counter. She needed no further instructions. She swept everything in front of her with a meaty arm, banknotes, coins, stamps and rubber stamps, money orders and telegram pads, the crust of the jam sandwich she'd been finishing when we'd cycled through her door.

She held out the sack.

—Thanking you, I said. —You're not the proprietor?

—I am not, she said. —She's above selling her calves.

248

—You will be, I told her. —When the time comes. The country needs handsome post mistresses.

—I'll hold you to that, she said. —You were in yesterday, weren't you?

—That was my brother, I told her. —He said you were a great-looking birdie.

—Tell him I never fly far.

—I will, I said. —He'll be chuffed.

—So will I.

Over the counter again, I landed on an oul' one's back.

—Sorry, missis.

—For what?

And I was back on the Arseless. Miss O'Shea hopped onto the bar. I held up the sack before I shoved it between my gut and her back.

—This money will be spent by the Government of the Republic of Ireland. Every penny will be accounted for. (Minus my 10 per cent.) —Apologies for any inconvenience. A few minutes on a dirty floor is a small price to pay for freedom. Up the Republic!

Inspiration.

I pulled the trigger and the door crumbled in front of us; the world under the roof was falling apart.

And intimidation.

We were gone, out the door, back onto the street. The stuff of more ballads. *The rebel and the rebellette then cycled out of town.* The earlier machine-gun fire had drawn the peelers. *But not before they'd taken on the forces of the Crown.* Four of them were making slow, fidgety progress, coming down from the market square. Peelers on foot or even on bikes had become a rare sight. They were deserting the outlying barracks since the burnings had started; they stayed in the towns behind the barrack walls and travelled in caged lorries or Crossleys. I looked past these four, for sight of reinforcements or machinery.

—What was that I heard about a great-looking birdie? said Miss O'Shea.

—That was called indoctrination, I said. —A bit of flattery makes great rebels. Look at Ivan.

249

—I'd rather not, she said.

They were on their own, the peelers, two on each side of the street. Miss O'Shea steered the Arseless straight at the two on the left. I opened fire and would have decapitated them if they hadn't been so quick off their feet. Then she tilted us to the right and one of the gobshites, who had to hitch his pants before he ducked, took two bullets in the neck and dropped, still holding the knees of his uniform trousers. There'd be no undertaker to scrape him up; anyone touching a dead peeler would soon be needing his own undertaker.

—And, tell me, Henry Smart. Does indoctrination stop at words?

—Usually, I told her. —Don't worry about that one, though. I've seen better tits on a sack.

We cycled through the square and town with nothing more frightening than cattle, dogs and the open mouths of red farmers to meet us.

—And an arse on her the size of the Congo.

I hugged Miss O'Shea. I could feel her heart as we raced past the creamery and onto the road that went north-east to Tulsk. We let everyone see the route we were taking. Outside the town and alone on the road, we turned right onto a narrow road with a beard of rough grass growing down its centre, and right again onto an even narrower road where the grass was most of the road and we were heading south now, back past the town, past small farms and broken stone walls. We rode into the dark until it was too dangerous and, in a wood behind Kilbegnet, we lay down and rode away the night on a bed of stolen stamps.

—Who's the Jew? said Jack.

The first time I'd seen him in over a year.

In a room in Sinn Féin's Harcourt Street headquarters. Sinn Féin had been outlawed but the office was still open and operating. The Castle needed work for its spies.

—And how are you, Jack?

—Who is he? he said.

—Who's who?

—The little Jew you're knocking around with.

—That might be Mister Climanis, I said. —I don't know if he's Jewish. He's Latvian.

Jack snorted.

—He's grand, I said.

—Stay clear of him.

—He's grand, I said.

—Fucking do what I say!

He stood up, took his hat off the desk and walked past me, out the door.

—Come on.

He went up the stairs. I followed him. He kept going until he came to a ladder that brought us into the attic. A hole had been knocked through the connecting wall. We went through it. My head was clear and singing as I went through another hole into another Harcourt Street attic; the dust and darkness couldn't distract me. But, still, I could make nothing of what had just happened. *Stay clear of him.* Had I been warned or advised? Threatened? I didn't know. I'd no idea and nothing that would bring an idea to me. Mister Climanis was sound. I knew that much. But so was Jack. I was better off keeping my mouth shut for the time being, until I knew a bit more and didn't feel so slapped and stupid.

—Here we go, said Jack.

He started thumping our side of the attic door with his foot. We heard someone climbing steps, a key inserted and turned by a nervous hand.

—Did you ever, when we started, said Jack, —think we'd have to go to all this trouble for a bloody pint?

We walked across the city. It was a cold, dry January day – 1920 – and it hit its coldest as we crossed the Liffey at Butt Bridge.

—You'd need more than a hat on a day like this, said Jack. —There'll be snow before the weekend.

—There was snow in Roscommon yesterday, I told him.

—That doesn't count, he said. —It's a blessing there, covering up the bloody kip.

We walked through a patrol of the King's Shropshire Light Infantry, on the Liberty Hall side of the bridge.

251

—That's a hardy one, men, said Jack. —It'd put drips on the ends of your bayonets.

They said nothing but smiled back at the friendly faces.

On, to Phil Shanahan's and we found a corner for ourselves. We nodded to secret men we knew and there were other, younger men who nodded at Jack, lads I'd never seen before. I met some of them again in later days, some I worked with, others I never saw again. All organisation men. Expendable men, and the smarter men who decided who lived and who died.

—That's Dan Breen beyond, said Jack.

—Don't I know it, I said. —The fuckin' head on him.

—It's the contents of the same head that leave me gasping, said Jack. —Sometimes I wonder what the hell we're up to, letting these creatures loose on the country. He has half the population terrified. And I've to have a new ballad written about the bastard by the weekend. He wants to bring it home with him to Tipperary. It's no exercise for a mind like mine. Writing songs about gurriers like him.

—It'll soon be over, I said.

—It will in its hole, said Jack. —You don't honestly think that, do you?

—It had crossed my mind, I said.

—Uncross it then, he said. —We haven't a hope, man. Am I depressing you at all?

—No.

—Good. We cannot win and winning is not our intention. What we have to do, all we can do, is keep at them until it becomes unbearable. To provoke them and make them mad. We need reprisals and innocent victims and outrages and we need them to give them to us. To keep at them until the costs are so heavy, they'll decide they have to go. But we'll never beat them.

—Who are you trying to impress, Jack? I've heard all this before.

—I'm just reminding you. You're too pleased with yourself. Too bloody well fed. It's only starting, man. Those bastards in London are paying more attention to the Mad Mullah in Somaliland than they are to us. We're going to have to go

252

harder at it. A bit of our own Mad Mullahs. Breen beyond. Your pal, Ivan Reynolds. Yourself. The only way. The real killing is going to have to start soon. And I'm not looking forward to it. There were only eighteen R.I.C. men killed last year. Mick told me that this morning and it shocked me because sometimes it felt like a bloodbath. And look it here.

He took a newspaper cutting from his back pocket and handed it to me.

—Sent to me from Liverpool, said Jack.

A recruitment ad.

—They're bringing in mercenaries, said Jack. —They're going to top up the R.I.C. with hard men from Liverpool and Glasgow and Christ knows where else. Their own bloody Breens.

—So what?

—So we're going to see a scrap like nothing we've seen before.

—So what?

—That's the spirit, he said. —It's good to see you again. I've missed you. Are you a father yet?

It was good being with Jack again. Talking, meandering through the day. I was back. I'd been alone too much. I had Miss O'Shea, but every word and pause was sex; every sentence was a minefield and I stomped on every syllable in the easy hope that my leg would be blown off. I lived for it. Even now, away from her, glad of the rest, I wanted her enough to stand up and run all the way to Roscommon.

—Another.

—Sacrifice.

—Awhh —

—Reprisal.

—Awhhhh —*Maithú, maithú* —

There was no one else I could talk to on my travels. I was alone and I had to stay that way and, most often, that suited me fine. But sometimes, usually in the early evening when the urge for drink and tobacco smoke was strongest, I mourned the living as well as the dead and I ached for Dublin.

—I'll tell you, man, Jack said later that night. —The peasants will form the backbone of this nation.

—They will in their holes, I said. —They couldn't form a fuckin' queue.

It was the smart-arsed, giddy remark of a man who hadn't been properly home in a long time. Dublin was a hateful kip but, Jesus, sitting now in its subversive heart, surrounded by the smoke and smell and the noise from outside, I felt the homesickness like a sudden, slow bite into my heart, because I knew that I was going to have to get up and go away again the next day.

—The R.I.C. are all decent men, Jack said now.

—Never liked them, I said.

—Decent men, he said. —It's a job. A career. I've a brother in the R.I.C. Did I ever tell you that?

—No.

—Stationed in Cork. I've another brother a priest, the brother in the R.I.C. and we've our own pump in the yard at home. We're a respectable family, the Daltons. D'you follow me?

—What happened you? I asked.

—I'll be respectable when the time is right, he said. —On my own terms.

—What about your brother?

—I've been telling him to get out. But he's a contrary man. It was a different place when he joined up. He doesn't understand.

He stared at the table as if his brother was on it, looking up at him in his uniform.

—Is Gandon still your landlord? I asked him.

—I've no landlord at the moment, he said. —I live out of a suitcase and it's my own.

—Did you read about him saying he was in the G.P.O.?

—I wrote it, said Jack.

—Why?

He snapped his eyes away from the shine on the table.

—He's too busy to be writing speeches, he said. —That's my department.

I knew I had to be careful.

—I don't remember seeing him in the G.P.O., I said.

—He was there, said Jack.

He looked straight at me.

—Other people remember him.

He took another piece of paper from his back pocket, still staring straight at me.

—Here's something else to remember. A job for you.

He pushed the small square of notepaper over the table to me. I picked it up and read it.

A name.

—Give it back.

I slid it back over to him. He took a match from his box – Maguire and Patterson – lit the paper and dropped it into the ashtray.

—You know what to do.

—Yes.

—I know you do.

Whiskey had joined our pints. I could have stayed there with Jack for the rest of my life. The whiskey sent the world away; the night would never end.

—Listen to this, said Jack. —I picked it up this morning. Listen now.

He looked at the ceiling.

—If our opponent is to be made to comply with our will, we must place him in a situation which is more oppressive to him than the sacrifice which we demand.

—That's what we're up to, I said.

—Exactly, said Jack. —A lad called Count von Clausewitz wrote it. In 1832. I'll make a few adjustments. Take out *opponent*, put in *enemy*, and I'll credit it to Mick in the next *Bulletin* and hope that none of the foreign correspondents have read von Clausewitz recently. That's my job, man.

—You're feeling sorry for yourself.

—D'you know? I am. I should never have let them know I had brains. I'm a civil servant with no state, man. A pen pusher. Another thing I do, come here till I tell you. An invention of my own and I rue the day it came into my head. I bring the foreign journalists, the newly arrived lads, on tours of the city and we meet all these people on the way. Accidentally, like. Out to Sir Horace Plunkett's place and he tells them about all the creameries being burnt down. Then on to the

255

Shelbourne. I go for a wee-wee and three priests up from the country sit beside him, spot his accent and tell him about all the atrocities they've seen in their parishes. Then out we go, and who do we meet? Madame MacBride. Jesus, man, she's a clown. She brings us off for tea with Missis Childers and the pair of them give us more atrocities. What a pair, man. They're frightening. We end up in Vaughan's and Ned the porter, a man of moderate nationalist views, fills him in on the sorry state of the country and what's needed to put things right. It's a good tour, I'll grant you, but that's what I am every time a new hack hits town. A bloody tour guide. But you're the real thing, look at you. You're the one that'll be remembered, not me.

—You'll be alive.

—Is that supposed to comfort me? You smug little shite. I'd die for fuckin' Ireland. D'you hear me? I would. Today. Now. If they'd let me. You remember that name?

—Count von Clausewitz.

—The other one.

—Yes.

—Have you said your prayers?

—Yes, he said.

—Good man.

I put the gun to the back of his head and shot him. And another one for luck. The name on Jack's piece of paper.

Away from streets and walls, the noise wasn't much and it was gone before he settled face-down in the leaves, after first falling sideways. There was no hurry. We were miles from anywhere. Me and Annie's dead husband. In the mountains above Dublin.

I had a note and a nappy pin. *Shot as a traitor and a spy. The I.R.A.* I put the gun on the ground and grabbed hold of his coat with both hands. I made sure that I didn't grab the empty sleeve. I turned him over onto his back. I didn't look at his face. I flicked open the note, opened the pin and fastened the note to his lapel and I didn't let myself remember that I'd once worn his clothes.

I picked up the gun – it was cold again already – and I

walked away, under branches that were trying to grab each other in the wind. I walked for half an hour, to the edge of the woods. I sat against a tree and waited for daylight and the end of the curfew.

10

—Pass us the bucket.

—Say, Please.

—Please.

—There.

—Thank you.

—For what?

Another rocket exploded above us, to the west. It had come from a window below us.

—They'll see that one in Strokestown, I said. —We've half an hour.

—That's plenty.

—Unless they're on their way already.

They were the Black and Tans, the mercenaries Jack had warned me about in January, the last time I'd seen him. The sweepings of England's jails, he'd called them in the *Irish Bulletin*. He got great mileage out of it; they were still being called that years after they'd gone home and most of them were dead. What they actually were was veterans who'd been unable to get work in England and Scotland after the War and who'd now been promised good money, ten shillings a day, to sort out Ireland. They were soldiers of a kind, not the peelers we'd been fighting up to now; they were foreigners and savage, and their presence in the country was proof that we were winning.

I put the bucket down on the flat section of the roof and picked up the sledgehammer. I wanted a few more slates off before I poured the paraffin down the hole, into the barracks. As I lifted the hammer, my stomach turned and screamed.

—Christ!

—What's wrong? she said.

—The fumes have gone to my guts.

It had happened before.

—Oh, God love you, she said. —Here. I'll pour.

I sat on the roof. I looked at the sky and breathed long and deep and ignored the stars. I'd had the headache for hours but the stomach cramps were sudden and fierce. Gelignite head, was what we called the ailment. From inhaling nitro-glycerine fumes as frozen gelignite thawed under a low roof. An occupational hazard.

The Vickers gun inside was off again, cutting holes in the houses across the street. They were wasting their bullets. The lads who'd let the peelers see them at the windows were long gone. The houses were empty. We were after the Vickers – it was a prize and a half, well worth the gelignite head – and there were two Lewis guns in there as well. And up to twenty Lee-Enfields and ammunition to feed us for weeks. We were desperately short of cartridges; we went right through the war, always a few minutes from defeat.

The barracks front was two long lines of steel-shuttered windows, with slits for rifles. There was also a porch, right below myself and Miss O'Shea; it had been built up and reinforced to accommodate two men and the Vickers. Luckily, the barracks had been designed and built in less troubled times and the gable end was windowless and unprotected, just high and thick-walled. Our ladder was against that wall, carried in three parts over fields and nailed together behind a stone wall to the left of the barracks that any sergeant with half a brain would have knocked down after the first shots of the war were fired two years before.

Miss O'Shea was finished with the pouring.

—Lovely job, I said.

I was on my feet again.

—Mind yourself.

—I'm grand, I said.

My head swam in fumes and the gunfire played with my ears as I unwrapped the rope from around my waist, and the sod of turf at the end of the rope. Through the more general racket I could hear little pings, bullets being fired from deep below us that couldn't break through the boards and slates. The sod had been lying in a basin of petrol for days. I held it well away because my coat was petrol-wet now too. Miss O'Shea lit a match and put it to the sod. The flames quickly climbed the sod to the rope and I dropped it into the hole.

We were knocked to our knees. She grabbed me. A slate hit against my head and something cut into my cheek. I saw blood drop into her eyes. And flames sliding towards us. She was up before me. My coat was on fire and the pockets full of tin-can grenades I'd made myself that afternoon. I slid out of the coat without unbuttoning and threw it onto the roof of the porch. I wasn't burnt. I looked at her. She was fine.

—They're flinging the bombs, I told her.

Our own men were lobbing bombs up onto the roof. We took a route that stayed clear of the flames, over the roof to the ladder.

—I thought they were to wait till we came back down, she said.

—So did I, I said. —Heads will roll.

The ladder was waiting for us. Neither of us said anything but we were both relieved when we saw it.

—After you, she said.

—Fair enough.

My feet found a rung and I was down the ladder three steps at a time. She was right after me, sliding so fast she landed on my head.

—Exciting all the same, isn't it? she said.

—Is everything sex with you, woman?

—Just about, she said.

We ran at the stone wall, and over.

—Which one of you cunts threw the bombs?

I grabbed a shape beside me.

—Not me!

—Fuckin' Ivan, I muttered.

There was no sign of him. It had more than likely been an accident, the bomb throwing, bad timing, fear and inexperience, but Ivan was getting dangerous. He was lord of his part of the county. He owned what he wanted and decided who lived and died. The old Fitzgalway house, Shantallow, was a shell now, one of the first of the old Protestant homes to go, and the cattle had been driven away and now carried the Ivan brand, somewhere safe. I was the only thing between Ivan and total power but my visits were sporadic. I was needed elsewhere – everywhere – in the parts of the country where the men had to have the fight kicked into them. We were only active in half the southern counties and a big part of my job was to create activity where there had been none. There was no rest. This now, the attack on Tonrua barracks, was a night out with Miss O'Shea.

The roof of the barracks was blazing now. Slates were cracking and I could hear the eaves joining the roar. I crept along, behind the stone wall, to get closer to the front of the building. I could feel a bump now where the slate had clouted me and my skin felt tight and very raw. I arrived in time to see a white flag coming from an upstairs window. Men around me and further away cheered. There were twenty-one of us in the column.

—No one to be shot, Willie, I said to Willie O'Shea who'd come up beside me. —They've surrendered.

—We'll have to accept it another day, Captain, said Willie. —The Tans are on the road. Four tenders of them. They're already shooting.

I could hear them. Two minutes' drive, less, unless our men had had the time and sense to bring down a loose wall across the road to block the tenders. Or unless they'd dug a trench across the road earlier in the day.

—Anything in their way? I asked.

—No, said Willie. —Only us.

It was my own fault. I should have taken control, instead of just turning up and falling in.

We left the ladder against the wall.

It was a blow. We'd badly needed the guns and bullets. We had none of the war-winning things, armour-piercing bullets or grenade rifles, no bombs worth more than a cough or a puncture. Most of our explosives were hand-made, and burying landmines that had been made by a lad who could hardly tie his laces was the stuff that sorted the men from the boys. And because of the nature of our living, on the run, two

261

steps ahead of the next raid, it was difficult to keep our guns in proper shape; they were falling apart, rusting into the fields and ditches. We'd needed those guns and we'd needed the victory, the sight of the enemy coming out, hands up.

The going was difficult. The ground was wet and unpredictable. It had been cut up by the hoofs of cattle and hardened by the cold. The Tans' headlights caught the corners of our eyes, then sprayed across our shoulders and made black shadows of the way ahead. We heard the boot nails scratch wood as they abandoned the tenders to chase us. I checked that Miss O'Shea was beside me; she was and there was another wall right on top of us, straight out of the darkness. It was a region of walls, low and old; they fell away under us as we tried to get over them. The Tans were right behind us now. We could feel their steady pace in the ground. They were fit, angry men. There was an army of them on our backs. We ran out of the power of their headlights. We could hear the walls behind us, crumbling under their organised weight. A flare zipped above us, and crackled. And there we all were, caught in bright red light, running across a hopeless field, up an uneven bastard of a hill and far from the next stone wall. And the firing started.

The R.I.C. had abandoned the isolated barracks – Tonrua was one of the last – but the country wasn't ours any more. The Black and Tans were always around the corner. They'd even taken back the sky. Aeroplanes flew above the trees, along the rivers. Permits from the military were needed for cars and even bikes were prohibited in areas where ambushing was regular. We were living in bunkers, organised into flying columns and active service units, small armies on the run. Surprises, ambushes and raids. Sniping and disappearing. There was no time for training; we learnt as we ran. The days of amateur rebellion were over. Most of the original peelers had resigned, retired or died – replaced by the nut-hard bastards who were chasing us. Jack had been right; we hadn't a hope of winning. There were too many of them, they were too well armed. They'd been made savage and bitter by the War and what they'd come home to. All we could do was hang on. Their uniforms were a mix of constabulary black and military khaki; they refused to be policemen or soldiers. They were a

262

new thing, a new, desperate animal. They stayed in the towns behind sandbagged walls but they came at us in their Peerless and Rolls-Royce armoured cars, in steel-plated Lancias, in tenders, on motorbikes. Our lads had left their homes and jobs, the ones still in the fight; we'd left everything and we lived on the run and underground. Our numbers had fallen to the hardest few, the expendable boys with nothing to lose. We slowed them down with felled trees, barbed wire and snipers and our little landmines. We made their lives a constant misery. But they kept coming. We blocked the roads, blew up bridges, cut down every telegraph pole. The raids increased and improved; walls were tapped for hollowness, backyards were dug, rooms were measured, length and breadth, records kept of their dimensions. We were running out of places to hide. We had to hang on. We had to keep at them. Because they were our greatest ally.

We couldn't turn to face them yet. We needed that wall ahead but it was still far away. The flare pointed a red finger at each of us. Low bullets made steam of the dew. We could feel them warming the air. I put my hand out and Miss O'Shea was there to grab it. We ran and we knew that we were in their rifle sights. We were fast and we knew that we would die together.

I felt the bullet in Miss O'Shea's arm; it shook mine. We kept running. She didn't slow down. She didn't even moan. The blood slid down between our hands.

They did exactly what we'd expected and wanted them to do. They murdered priests and mayors. They declared war on every man and woman in the country. Fermoy, Balbriggan, Templemore, Cork, Granard – they burnt them all – Mallow, Milltown Malbay, Fermoy again. They dredged up stories of Cromwell and centuries of dormant hatred. They corked their faces and went berserk. They took people from houses and shot them. They shot children. They shot livestock. With the secret blessing of their government. We pulled the trigger and they went off.

Her hand slipped from mine but I had it again. We were still together. I got her sleeve into my grip. The flare above us was dying. Night was creeping back but it was taking the wall from

263

us. We were still in the middle of nowhere. I felt another bullet. They were killing her slowly.

There were no neutrals. They burnt the creameries. They stole wedding rings. They destroyed farm machinery. They sneered at old women and young girls, pointed rifles at them as they raced by in their tenders. They beat up schoolboys. They closed down towns and made them starve. They declared all Irish people Shinners and made terrorists of them all. *We have murder by the throat,* said Lloyd George. And, all the time, we were their puppet masters, the men and woman running across the field and a few hundred other men and women hiding in ditches and under other fields, and our own puppet masters in Dublin, in Shanahan's and their shifting H.Q.s and hideouts. We knew how to make them set fire to the right creamery, in the quiet, law-abiding area, how to draw them to the right house. We controlled them. We just had to hang on.

She was still running, still right beside me. We couldn't surrender. We were armed, in a martial law area; we'd be executed or killed on the spot. And I'd a gun full of split-nosed bullets, dum-dums; they'd use them to kill us slowly if they got us alive. Her hand still gripped mine. Her pain was in her breath, though, and the stiffness of her grip. We were nearing the wall. I could see it clearly now. If enough of us made it over, we could turn on the Tans and worry them. Shoot a few – they'd be the targets for a few minutes – and slow them down. Make them dive long enough for us to get properly away. To where we'd hidden our bikes. Where we were in charge. The wall was right in front of us. Black, solid in the night. Another bullet entered Miss O'Shea; she dashed ahead of me, knocked forward by the shot. She kept her feet. She squeezed my hand and let go. I grabbed it back. I wanted her pain. At least my share. I wanted it all. The wall. No distance now. Five big strides, six, seven. They weren't going to kill her. I'd carry her there, and the rest of the way. I'd plenty of run in me. Still holding her hand, I ran ahead. I turned to lift her as she caught up with me and, as I swerved to catch her and lifted my arm to hoist her to my shoulder, the bullet slid in and I was falling hard and I couldn't see anything, didn't know anything, and when I was able to see again and think, when I looked and saw the ground jumping below me, she was carrying me.

Every time I opened my eyes I was in a different place. I fell in and out of different rooms and dreams. I lay on beds, stone, under sacks. Pigs near, or baking bread. Or nothing at all. Nothing. I rolled away from there, until I knew I was alive. The pain, beyond the skin, a pain becoming bone. The only thing keeping me alive. She wasn't beside me, and sometimes I knew it, she was. Lying beside me, breathing with me. I felt her hand on my face, my cheek. And someone else. The smell of a child in the room. I tried to see but light flung itself at my eyes. He was near me. Victor was there. I tried to call but my throat was locked and solid. And I was in the back of a motor car. I could smell the leather, feel and hear the road under me before I closed my eyes. And once, I knew I was right under old Missis O'Shea's roof. Miss O'Shea was right beside me. I woke again for a second and I was somewhere else. Pitch dark. Alone. I closed my eyes and everything was gone. Sun in my eyes, no light at all; pigs outside the window, petrol; damp from the wall I was lying against, heat from her as she moved in her sleep; hungry, sick, always thirsty, always parched and sore. Noises below or beside me, no noise whatsoever. People under the window, boots on cement. Wheels going, motors. Birds giving out in the trees, a branch scraping the wall. Pain, torn awake by it. In my chest, my side. Pulling apart, tearing. Someone handling me. Pushing. Cutting me. Water. On the roof above me. Different roofs. Slate and thatch, corrugated iron. Under a hot tarpaulin, a smell of liquid grass. I was nine again, searching for Victor. Crying. Awake again under a proper roof. Rain slapping the roof. And water on my skin. Warm water being brought over my arms and chest. On my lips. I felt my lips being softened by the water and I slept. The rattle of a cart going over stones. I was in the cart, the back of the cart. Under straw. I suddenly knew that I had to stay still. I could hear other wheels going over the road and other sounds as well, life going on, and I knew that I was being brought through a town. I knew my name and I knew that I was a wanted man. And I

265

knew that I had other names. I knew exactly who I was. I was injured and in pain. But the pain was fine, poking me awake. I breathed around it; it got no worse. It was a throb, a reliable thing. And it was going to go away. I'd been shot and now I was on the mend. If the straw was swept aside I'd be able to stand and run. I'd been saved by Miss O'Shea. I took a breath, my face to the side, not tickled too badly by the straw. She'd carried me away from the Black and Tans. I took a deep breath and knew that I was Henry Smart and that I was alive and still magnificent.

I must have dozed. The cart went off the good road and I was battered around on the boards. The straw poked at me. I heard humming that took on words and went back into humming. *Oh Paddy dear and did you hear the news that's going around?* A man on his own with the sun away to the side and comfortable. I was tempted to call out to him. *The shamrock is by law forbid to grow on Irish ground.* I could call if I wanted to; I thought I'd be able to. *And if the colour dum-de-dum is England's cruel red.* But I didn't. I was thinking again, gathering up the consequences. Maybe he didn't know I was in his straw; maybe other men had put me there. Maybe he wasn't alone. *Let it remind us of the blood that Irishmen have shed.* Maybe the song was for my entertainment as well as his own, but maybe there was a gun at the other end of the notes, waiting for my head to come up out of the straw. I moved my hands around me. Whoever had put me there, they'd left me without a gun or leg. All I grabbed was straw. I felt my fingernails. They were long; they'd been left alone for weeks. I decided to wait. To be ready. No more dozing. I was Henry Smart. I was shot and recovering. I wanted answers but they'd come if I waited.

—Never ask questions, Victor.

—Why not?

—If you just watch and listen you'll get better answers. I could have told you she wasn't married meself.

—How?

—No rings, son. No rings on her fingers.

—Oh yeah.

—Oh yeah is right. Watch and listen and the answers will come strolling up to you. What do you do?

266

—Watch and listen.

—Good man.

Beside me in the desk. The heads of little brown animals climbing to her neck. Victor's leg leaning into mine. Tarpaulin against my face. The crib, an old zinc basin, nicely stuffed and padded. Straw tickling my nose. A fall into black and the river below. Welcome to the Swan River, boys. The smell of an old coat and the rushing water.

I was awake. The cart had stopped. I was ready and sweating. Dust in my eyes.

The straw was lifted.

There was a man there alone, his hands full of the straw, no gun or menace. It was grand and I was hungry.

—What time is it?

—Spud time, said the man with the straw.

—Thank Jaysis. I'm starving.

—That's often the way.

He put down the straw and helped me off the cart. I stood. My legs felt strange and unowned.

He was fifty or the other side of it; it was harder to tell in the country.

—No hurry, he said.

I took a step.

—Good man.

And another one.

—Oh good man.

And another.

—You'll need no more encouragement from me.

He threw the straw back into the cart and walked into the house. He'd left the donkey between the shafts.

The door was low and open. I stooped carefully so I wouldn't lean too far forward and quickly. I couldn't see the ground or a step. There was no light from a window and I was blocking the door.

—Where am I? I said.

—You're six foot to the right of your dinner, said the man with the straw. —And there's nothing in your path.

I made it. I found a chair with my hand and dropped onto it. And then I felt the steam rising from the plate below me. It cooled the sweat that was running off my face. I was already exhausted. I could see the table and the man sitting opposite me and then I heard and saw a woman walking away to one of the corners. It was still too dim to see her face and nothing in her movement gave her age away.

I found the fork and a knife. They were heavy but I managed to get the skin off my first potato and only needed a short rest before I got a lump of it to my mouth.

—Balls of flour, said the man.

—Where am I? I said.

—Back where you started, said the man. —In a manner of speaking.

He was beginning to annoy me.

—Where am I? I said.

—You're in Tonrua, mister, said the woman.

—He is not now, said the man. —He's in Muckeragh.

—Don't listen to that old cunt, said the woman. —You're right beside Tonrua. You could throw a stone from here at the barracks that's burnt.

—But the stone would fall well short of it.

—You just shut your mouth now, you old cunt, she said. —You'd give the man a headache. Like the one you're always giving me.

—Tonrua is one parish and Muckeragh is another one altogether.

—And you're one old cunt and your father was another one altogether. Just shut up out of that or I'll go over there and smack you. She brought you here on her back, mister.

—Was she alright?

—She was. She had bullets in her but not like the one you had. They were lodged in her arm just, away from the vital things.

—And what happened then?

—We got you into the cart and brought you on to a safer place.

—'Twas me that brought you, said the man.

—'Twas me that told you to, said the woman.

—Just me or the two of us?

—The two of you.

—And then?

—And then a doctor that's a friend of Ireland looked at the bullet hole in your side and he discovered another one in your front. The bullet went clean through you and tidied up as it went along. You're a lucky man, mister.

—He is.

—Shut up, there. The bullet didn't as much as singe a rib when it was trotting through you.

If it had been one of my bullets, one of the dum-dums, I'd have been pulped. I wasn't sure why – there was no such thing as a fair fight and there was no God out there to thank – but I decided never to use them again.

—And her? I asked.

—She recovered fast. They say. He had a night's work taking the bullets out of her arm but he did and she was able to thank him for it.

—She's the holy terror, he said.

—Shut up there, you, and fill your mouth with them spuds that I dug and washed and cooked special for you.

—I will. Because I'm hungry.

—You will because I told you to. Our Lady of the Machine Gun, they're calling her, mister. She's robbing banks and the big houses and killing those new Tan bastards into the bargain. She'll soon have us free of them and that'll be a day worth getting up for.

—It will indeed, said the man with the straw.

—What would you know about it? she said. —You old cunt, you know nothing.

—Maybe so, said the old cunt. —But at least I know that much.

—Shut up now.

Her head was as rough as her language. I couldn't manage any more food – I'd hardly touched the mountain of spuds but I already felt fat and useless – but I used what energy I'd left to turn and look at her properly. She was a hard-looking item, much younger than her husband, but that was often the way in the bog where women would marry dead men to escape from the clutches of spinsterhood. She'd a big round face, and angry red skin like a crust. She must have spent all day staring into the wind. Her feet were bare and her toes were huge, mountainy old things.

—Will you have a cup of buttermilk to wash down the praties? said the man.

—Listen, pal, I said. —I'm a Dublin man. I wouldn't let that muck near my mouth, thanks all the same.

—You're a wise man, mister, she said. —That stuff's only old cow piss that would make you sick to your stomach.

—I never heard you deride the buttermilk before, said the man.

—You'll hear plenty if I have to get up now and go over to you. You don't have to say something to think it.

—That's true enough.

—What would you know about the truth, you old cunt? This man here needs his rest. You go away, now.

The man stood up.

—I will, he said. —It's been a long day.

—Every day is long when you're in it, she said. —Go away to your bed.

—I will.

He walked to the door. The light was screaming through it into the kitchen. He went out.

—Where does he sleep? I asked.

—Where he drops, she said. —For all that I care. You'll sleep down here, beside the fire. There's a bed above but it's as well to be down here if the English bastards or the Scottish ones get it into their heads to call on us. Or the cunts from Wales for that matter. Sleep with your clothes on in case you have to run.

She drew back a checked curtain and there was a small bed, built in against the side of the fire. The bedspread surprised me, a field of bright diamond patterns.

She was standing beside me.

—Now, she said. —Your revolver is under the bed with the wooden leg you were holding when she brought you here that night. There are only two bullets in the cylinder but two's twice as good as one, I suppose. I fell out of a tree once, mister, and my leg broke on me but I managed to crawl back across the yard, in here to Mammy. One leg or the both? she said, wiping her hands in her apron. The one, I said. Be thankful for your blessings, she said. You'll have the good one to concentrate on while the broke one's mending. And I agreed with her, mister, even though the pain was something desperate. But she still went out with the axe and cut the tree to fuck out of it. She didn't leave a root or a leaf. D'you know what she said then? Let that space where the tree used to grow be a reminder always to you that your mammy loved you. She died young on us, mister, and I think she knew it was coming when she went out with the axe. I'll never leave this place. I couldn't bring the hole where the tree was with me and I'd never want to be too far from that hole. Now, if you have to get up in the night, you can piss over the half-door. Only make sure the Tans aren't out there, waiting. They've been doing that, I've heard. It's as well to have your fellow safe away in your trousers when those cunts call. And I'll tell you straight now and not bother with the formalities: I'm available for the ride. What do you think of that, mister?

—What about your husband?

—What husband?

—The man that just left.

—That old cunt? she said. —That's no one's husband these years. That's my father. So, what have you got to say for yourself? D'you want to climb up on me or don't you?

—Can I have a bit of a nap first?

—You can, indeed, she said. —You're not mended yet. I'll not come between you and your recovery. Ireland's freedom comes first in this house. Will I wake you up?

—I'll probably wake, myself.

—I'll be waiting for you, she said. —I'll not be far away.

—Grand, I said. —That'll be something to look forward to. Good-night, so.

—Sure, it's only two in the afternoon. But good-night anyway. I'm a good hold, mister. I've been told that before, and more than once. I'm not much to look at but a travelling man once told me that I go like one of them sewing machines.

Her bottom lip hung over her chin.

—I'll bear that in mind, I said.

—Do, she said. —We've a power of rocks and furze around

271

here but the handsome men are few and far between. It'd be a shame to let the chance go by.

—It probably would, I said.

She went up the steps to her bed. I took her advice and kept my clothes on but it wasn't the Tans I was scared of. I listened to her saying her prayers, then I heard her using the bed to get off her knees. Clothes hit the deck and she lowered herself onto the bed.

—Good-night now, mister.

—Good-night, I said.

—You get your rest.

—I will.

—Do.

I made a very quick decision and, like that, I wasn't frightened any more: I'd ride her. I'd fuck her the once and no harm done. It took the load off my mind and I began to sink into the bed and the sleep that came with it. Just before I fell out of thinking, I realised something: I was wearing my britches, the ones Miss O'Shea had given me on our wedding day. They hadn't been on me on the night we'd run from the Tans. She'd put them on me some time in the last weeks, she'd undressed and dressed me. The britches were her love letter to me and I was reading it when I fell asleep.

She was on me.

Her hand over my mouth.

She'd come down the steps from her bed.

Her weight on top of me, I couldn't see a thing.

I'd changed my mind completely: I was going to stop her. I couldn't put up with this. But my arms were caught under the bedspread and she was digging away at the other end of it.

I bit her thumb. To get it off, and the rest of her big hand. I bit and knew immediately, as sure as the teeth that bit were mine, the thumb I bit didn't belong to the woman up the steps. I knew that thumb; I knew the blood and loved it.

—Miss O'Shea?

—And who else would it be?

—There's a yoke up the stairs dying to rape me.

—Don't I know her? she said. —She'd rape me if she could

272

find a way. Let's go, so. The Tans are out and about. There are no safe houses any more.

I found my boots and carried them to the door. It was well and truly night now but I was able to follow her over the yard and a gate and through a field that wasn't too bad on the feet. She had two leather bandoliers, in an X across her chest, and a revolver sat on each hip. Her hair was tucked into a cap, what I thought was a Glengarry. She'd our Thompson sub-machine-gun on her back and trousers tucked into her boots. I recognised them, even in this dark; they'd once belonged to Annie's dead, dead husband.

We stopped at the far end of the field and I put my boots on. While I was doing that, sitting on the wet grass, she bent down and kissed the top of my head.

—We're both alive, she said.

—And kicking.

She had the Arseless hidden away in a ditch across more fields. This time she cycled and I sat on the crossbar. We rode through the middle of the night and she, a gorgeous bat folding me in her wings, dodged the holes in the road and knew all the corners where I saw none.

She kissed the back of my neck.

—You've been making a name for yourself, I said.

—I'm like you now, Henry, she said. —I've many names.

—Our Lady of the Machine Gun.

—That's my favourite.

—And what about your arm? I asked.

—The best thing that ever happened to me, she said.

—How d'you mean?

—When the first bullet went in I couldn't believe the pain. I didn't think it was possible. I still couldn't believe it when the second one hit me, but it was no worse than the first. And the third one was barely a tickle. I don't know if it was the same man did the firing or if they were all aiming at my arm but if I met him today I'd thank him.

—Before you shot him.

—Yes, she said. —Now's not the time for sentimentality. I knew when the third bullet hit me that I could stand up to anything. I've nothing to fear. There's no stopping me now, Henry.

—Is your arm not sore?

—It's agony, she said.

She braked. She was off the bike and we were lying against a ditch two seconds before headlights ripped the night and a tender roared past, its wheels a few feet from my face. Before it was gone back into the dark, I saw two rows of men, facing each other on either side, rifles across their knees. I couldn't see uniforms but they didn't look like Black and Tans. They were gone.

—Wait, she said.

I wasn't going anywhere.

It was a rumble for a long time before it took a shape – Miss O'Shea slid deeper into the ditch and I followed her example – and an armoured car rolled past. It sent stones and dirt on top of us; we could feel it shredding the ground. And I could feel my wound now, for the first time since Miss O'Shea had come and rescued me. I watched the car continue. It was metal that had no shine, topped by a gun turret that scanned the sides of the road as it followed the tender into the dark.

Its growl was there for a long time after it had gone and the pain was getting worse. It was as if the weight of the passing car had opened up the wound from the entrance hole of the bullet slowly to the exit.

—Who were they? I asked when it seemed safe to whisper.

—They're new, she said. —Too new to have a name. But they're worse than the Tans.

They were the Auxiliary Cadets. The Auxies. All former officers and sergeants, they came from the same bitter world as the Black and Tans, but they were paid more, a quid a day, and their uniforms were more complete and army-like, dark blue, coloured up with their war ribbons and topped by Glengarry caps. The one on Miss OShea's head had come clean out of the mess when she'd lobbed a grenade into the back of a tender; it had landed at her feet. They were middle-class thugs, unemployed gentlemen, soldiers of fortune, men out for adventure or looking after the wife and kids at home in London and Dundee. They'd learnt their killing in Belgium and France, the Punjab and Gallipoli. They'd killed Cossacks, Turks and Zulus. These guys knew their stuff.

—Are you alright? she asked.

—I'm grand.

I stood up out of the ditch.

—But I bet my pain's worse than yours.

—Men, she said. —You always have to win.

—No, listen, I said. —I'm not doing this to best you.

And I fainted.

We crossed the Midlands many times, a crazy route of ambushes and burnings. We hit the quiet places; we put them on the map. We lived at night and hid inside the day. When we were very lucky, we spent a few hours in a bed or got two days' worth of dinner off the one plate, or we spent daylight in a bunker under a field, away from the aeroplane that flew low all day or the eyes inside the armoured car turrets. We stayed out of the stone wall country. We cycled east where the hedges grew fat and high, where two rebels in love and their bicycle could sometimes hide.

We lost the Arseless somewhere in Westmeath, at a bridge that crossed the Yellow River. We were under the bridge, padding the arch with gelignite, when the rumble above dislodged the stuff around us. An armoured car had stopped right on top of us. We grabbed hands and slid into the river. She smothered a gasp but I felt at home in the freezing water. Men got out of the car – a hinge squealed, feet hit the road. I held up the Thompson with my free hand and, together, we floated away from the bridge, under some hanging trees, carried by the river without help from hands or feet. Not a lap or splash, the river did it for us. The river and the night. And the sparks from the Auxies' flare. They found the bike and Miss O'Shea's empty gun rack. Their torch ran the length of the handlebars and, gradually, they knew what they were looking at. The one with the flare, making up for lost time, sent it up to the sky before he'd got properly out from under the arch. The sparks came back at him and landed on the gelignite that had dropped to the thin bank of earth between the wall

275

and the river. It didn't blow the bridge but it kept them occupied until we were well away and on dry land, mauling each other in the weeds to get our blood running again. She roared when her bad arm hit my head and I roared when her knee pressed my chest and we both roared when a mouse ran over my back but the Auxies were doing roaring of their own – they set fire to three farmhouses and shot a publican in Crookedwood – and no one important heard us.

We fucked our way across Slieve Gullion, bared our arses and wounds to the sleet that ran up the mountain after us and we never felt the cold. When we sneaked into Oldcastle just before dawn, a Sinn Féiner who owned a safe shop – he was later nailed to a tree after the Tans had been fired at as they drove through the town – told us that we had to go to Templemore.

So off we went.

A big peeler, the District Inspector, had been shot dead in Templemore and the Tans had shown their displeasure by setting fire to the Town Hall and other parts of the town. They commandeered anything they could find in a bottle and drank the lot before they went on to torch three of the nearest creameries. The locals took to the fields and stayed out there until the Tans were all back behind the walls of their barracks and sleeping. Except for the hardy and stupid, the town was deserted when a wee priest-to-be, a seminarian, home on his holidays, being fattened by his mammy for the winter, ran into a shop to buy his *Independent* and kept running when he heard the skid of a tender turning outside on the street, up over the counter, through the door, and he came to a halt in the shopman's hall when he saw all the statues and the holy pictures bleeding. There was blood on every wall, in every corner, delicate lines of the red stuff running from every saint and son and mother of God.

And that was where we went, after our rest in the councillor's attic, south to Tipperary, to stoke the miracle, on two new bikes, on the orders of Michael Collins. The councillor offered us his own bike.

—I could never get up on a bike that wasn't stolen, I told him. —Thanks for the offer but it's a matter of principle.

So we fecked two good bikes that were sitting against the kerb outside the R.I.C. barracks. They were solid enough to be peelers' but, even if they weren't, if they belonged to a couple of citizens who'd just gone into the cop-shop, we felt grand about taking them because they'd no business going in there at this stage of the national struggle. A nice one each, parked between a couple of armoured cars, both with crossbars.

We cycled the night, south through Fennor and Tevrin, away off the big roads. But the nights were too short for journeys of any length, so we buried the machine-gun in a wood beside Coralstown. We shook the muck off each other's clothes and continued into the day, husband and wife, on our honeymoon, a cycling tour of the Midlands. I wore my suit and tie, my respectable credentials, and my arsenal under my coat. She put her weapons and ammo in a bag and we became a young middle-class couple from Dublin – and Protestant, to explain away Miss O'Shea's trousers.

Rochfortbridge, Tyrrellspass.

—Name?

—Michael Collins.

We saw smoke from a burning farmhouse and got back onto the little roads. We spent a night in a barn outside Timahoe and another under a hedge near Templetouhy. We washed, I shaved and we got to the edge of Templemore with the morning crowds.

I took off the collar and tie. I ripped the right leg of my trousers at the thigh and tore around until the leg dropped to my boot. I threw the cloth into the ditch and Miss O'Shea helped me strap my now trouserless leg up with my tie. She tied a good knot that wouldn't go until I wanted it to. And then, for the first time, I donned my daddy's wooden leg.

It fit. It hummed.

—He must have been a big man, she said.

—I remember him being huge.

She helped me strap the leather harness onto my own leg. My leg was doubled, bent at the knee, two sets of folded bone, flesh and muscle. Yet the harness fit snugly, no adjustments needed.

—Like a glove.

277

—You were born to it, she said.

I buttoned up my coat and we were off again, no longer a honeymooning couple, but two out of the thousands of country people converging on Templemore to see the holy things that bled for us. We left the bikes in a field and walked. I leaned on Miss O'Shea; it added authenticity and the leg took getting used to. I missed not having a heel or sole and my real heel was digging a trench in my arse, but the wooden leg didn't act up. It went where I wanted it to go. It stood up to my weight and stayed put, although I felt frail and wary of the distance between me and the ground, as I went forward on the real one.

—Is it this way to the miracles, mister? said Miss O'Shea.

—'Tis, said a man who was selling bottles from a crate of minerals on the side of the road. —There was a girl cured of her consumption yesterday, they say.

—It's your turn today, Michael, she said to me.

—A new leg'd be harder than consumption, I said.

—It's a question of faith, young fellow, said the man. —Not difficulty. Have you faith?

—I have, I said.

—And are you thirsty?

—I am, I said. —But I've no money.

—On with you, so, he said. —Good luck to you now and walk past this way again if the statues give you a new leg. Or a new wallet.

—I will, I said. —And I'll kick those bottles of lemonade up your arse till the fizz comes out of your fuckin' ears.

—Don't draw attention to yourself, said Miss O'Shea.

—That's exactly what I'm here to do, I said.

—But the right kind of attention, she said. —That man will remember more about you now than's necessary. When he hears about it.

—You're right, I said. —Sorry. We could always kill him on the way back.

—We could, but it seems a bit harsh.

We got in with the crowds descending on the town, a crawl of farm carts, bicycles, charabancs, motor cars and pilgrims like ourselves on foot. The walking wounded and men and women on stretchers, carried by their children, and children

278

coughing blood, men carrying the damage of war, legless, armless, skinless. The slobbering brainless. And the best of Ireland's freaks, they were all on the road to town – pinheads, hunchbacks, dwarfs, a couple of bearded ladies – they were travelling together, in a battered Ford, hanging off it, on the roof or walking along beside it. We got in among them.

—An old soldier got his knee back working.

—I heard that one. And a lady from Thurles got her back straightened.

—There was a girl cured of her consumption yesterday, I said.

—Any news of little men made taller? said a dwarf, and him and his friends laughed and didn't mind a bit when other people joined them.

And deeper into the town the rosaries started and, with the heat and the packing and excitement and news of the miracles, people started fainting and bodies were lifted over heads, to doorways, through upstairs windows. *I'll sing a hymn to Mary.* The impatient sick made their ways along the roofs. A man holding a crutch in his teeth slid over the slates towards the shop with the statues. *Mother of Christ, Star of the Sea.* And the dwarfs sang hymns of their own. *Pray for the midget, pray for me.*

—A bald man went home yesterday with a head of hair.

—If it's curing vanity She is, there's hope for us all.

—Scalped he was, after the Tans set a fire to him.

—Still and all, a good cap would satisfy most men.

The best of the statues and a couple of the pictures had been moved out into a yard behind the shop. They were on a table, on top of a white cloth. When the yard was full, when the shopman's cousin decided that there was room for no more pilgrims, the shopman's wife led a decade of the rosary and the crowd were given two more minutes to have their fill of the statues. There was an untarred telegraph pole on its side across the yard, in front of the table, like an altar rail and the lucky ones at the front could kneel and rest their elbows on it while they waited for something to happen. The yard was emptied after the two minutes, measured out by the cousin on his own watch. There was only the one gate, so it was a push between those coming and going. When the yard was empty, it was filled again. Another decade, another push, screams and admonitions. Curses and last prayers.

—Mind the baby!

—What a place to bring a baby.

—It's a dying baby, bad cess to you.

—Maybe the dying has been reversed.

—Maybe. We'll see, the mite.

—There's colour there in the poor creature's cheeks, look.

—We'll see.

—That's fine colour.

—Please God; we'll see.

This had been going on for five days. Not a peeler or Tan in sight. The town was in the hands of the pilgrims and hawkers. And the North Tipperary Brigade of the I.R.A. They were running guns and bombs through Templemore, under cover of the lame, in the carts and cars of the near-dead. There were crates of mineral bottles full of petrol, brown parcels of gelignite, being passed over the heads of the crowd and wanted men hiding in every second attic. The armoured cars and tenders were in the barracks yard, going nowhere because of the crush in the streets. The town was a free state. The seminarian who'd seen the first blood was at home, exhausted, sliding in and out of consciousness, and a grand layer of straw had been laid on the cobbles under the poor lad's window, to swallow the noise that had been disturbing him and keeping him from his recovery. The street where his mother's house was had been renamed Whispering Street. There'd been no miracles, only the rumours distributed by the men and women of the North Tipp Brigade. The statues had stopped bleeding and the seminarian wasn't there to get them flowing again.

But I was.

We pushed through the silent people leaving.

—What did you see?

—The backs of many heads.

—No blood?

—No blood.

We shoved our way to the middle of the crowd. We stepped over stretchers, got tripped by crutches and little men. The shopman's wife was looking cross and important. She had her daughters near her, in charge of the altar-table. A statue of the Virgin, a crucifix, a Sacred Heart, warped and stained behind the old glass. I saw no blood.

—I see it.

I whispered it, a tiny worm on a hook.

—What d'you see, young fellow?

—Oh God, I said. —I see the blood. It's pouring from her eyes.

—He sees it!

—It's pouring out of her! He sees it!

The shopman's wife yelled hush; we were crowding into her rosary.

—The young fellow sees it!

They were turning and trying to turn, the crowd in front of me and beside. Someone fell, away to the left. There was shoving and counter-shoving, whispers and yells.

—I see it too! Miss O'Shea shouted, as she got her hand under my coat and pulled the tie.

—Something's happening! I yelled. —The pain! Oh, Mother of God!

And it *was* fuckin' painful. My leg had been packed up at my arse for hours. Released, it roared, the blood rushed as my foot dropped to the ground.

I fell.

I clutched my knee and unstrapped the wooden leg. I held it up.

—His leg's after growing!

The new bare leg stuck out from under my coat. I gave it a twitch, and another few. All around me, the people fell to their knees. I hid a sharp stone in my hand. I cut the skin beside the knee and gave them running blood.

There was howling and more fainting. One of the dwarfs looked over the heads of the kneeling throng.

—It's a grand long one, he said. —More power to you, young fellow.

He couldn't hide the sadness on his face but he nodded across at me. Miss O'Shea pinched my thigh.

—Did you feel that, Michael?

—Yes! I felt it. It's flesh, and sore with it.

281

—The Virgin's after giving my brother the leg he lost when the fox bit him. Twenty years ago!

—It's not in Our Lady's power to give anyone a leg, said the shopman's wife. —It is through her intercession —

But no one was listening to her. Even her daughters had abandoned the altar and were climbing over the telegraph pole and the kneeling pilgrims to get a good look at the fine man with the new leg.

—Twenty years he's been without the leg, said Miss O'Shea. —Stand back, stand back!

She slapped two of the shopman's daughters back against the wall of pilgrims that surrounded us.

—Can you stand up, Michael?

—I don't know, I said.

She helped me to my feet. I put weight on the new leg.

—It's just like the other one, I said.

I walked in the small circle left me by the crowd, then trotted, then ran. The pilgrims laughed and applauded, hugged one another, reached out to touch me as I dashed past, and others cried and shook and hit their own ailments. I stopped and lifted the wooden leg to the sky.

—I won't be needing you any more, I yelled.

—Give it here, young fellow, said the dwarf.

I spoke to the leg.

—But I'll keep you with me as a reminder of this day!

—Is the real one not reminder enough for you?

—And look! said an old lad who'd got to the front of the crowd. —Look at his foot. He got a boot with the leg that's a perfect match for the other one!

—That's Our Lady for you, boy. Who else but Herself would have thought of that.

They were stopped by a scream.

It was one of the daughters.

—I see the blood! I see the blood!

They turned and pushed for the next miracle and there was a man standing right against me.

—Dublin, he said, softly.

—I'll need trousers.

—They're all arranged.

—Will they match the jacket?

—They won't. But we've a new jacket for you as well. A suit.

—Will it fit?

—Your measurements came down from Dublin with the order.

—Good Jesus, I said. —We can't lose.

—Are you Jewish, Mister Climanis?

—Mister Smart, he said.

He put his pint back on the counter.

—Mister Smart. I am a Jew. But I am not Jewish.

—Stop messing, I said. —Are you or aren't you?

—Mister Smart, he said. —I am. But I am not.

—Okay, I said. —You win. What are you then?

—It is very hard for me to explain. But I will endeavour. New word, Mister Smart. Two days old. I will endeavour to explain. After this.

He lifted his pint and took a wallop of it.

—I am a Jew from Latvia, he said. —I am a Jew and a Latvian. My father was a Jew. My mother, grandfather and everybody. Jews. But I am not Jewish. The Jews are a people. So I am one of the Jews. Jewish is a religion. I am *not* one of them. Mister Smart, I do not like religions. There are no prophets or gods or the one the Irish people like so much, mothers of gods. My Maria likes that one. I say nothing. I am a very happy man.

—Are you a communist?

—Mister Smart. I am a communist but I am not a communist.

He was enjoying himself but I was still worried. Jack's warning to me – *Stay clear of him* – had been at the back and the front of my mind for months, almost a year, and this was the first chance I'd had to talk to Mister Climanis since I'd heard it. The mere mention of a name, a name on a piece of paper, was often a death sentence. I'd been delighted to see Mister Climanis well and happy and sitting at the counter.

—I was a communist, he said. —But the Bolsheviks, they

entered our *shtetl*. Our village, Mister Smart. They burnt my house and they murdered my wife.

I looked at him. I clung to my glass.

—Yes. I am sorry. They did this because I was a Jew. And my wife, she too was a Jew. She was in the house. I was not. So I am not a communist, Mister Smart. But I believe in communism. But not when it comes with the Russians.

—I'm sorry, he said.

He shrugged, and nodded.

—We will drink to the Bolsheviks, he said. —To their painful deaths. I have told Maria, my wife. She loves me more because I am a widow. But now I am not a widow.

—Did you have children?

—No. No. No more sad stories.

I left him alone for a while. I emptied my glass and lifted a finger to the curate behind the counter; the same again.

—Will you do me a favour, Mister Climanis?

—This is a question I can answer easily. Yes.

—Be careful, I said. —Will you?

For the first time, I saw him worried. He was even scared, and angry. He looked behind him. He looked at the curate delivering the drink. He stared at the glasses on the counter.

—Why are you asking me to do this thing? To *be* this thing? Careful.

—I don't know, I said.

—Mister Smart. Please. I am careful. I am careful always. Please, explain. Or I will hate you.

Every word had been carefully selected.

—Your name was mentioned, I said.

—Yes.

—These days that means you'd want to be careful. There's nothing else I can tell you.

—I understand, he said.

He waited, then spoke again.

—Was the name of Maria mentioned?

—No, I said.

He nodded. He sat there, looking at his glass. I watched him shaking slightly. He didn't touch the glass. The head on his pint shrank and yellowed.

—I will go home, he said, after minutes of nothing.
He stood up.
—Mister Smart, thank you.
—I'll keep you posted, I said. —If I hear anything.
—Mister Smart, he said. —That is not good enough.
He was gone.

Archer – Dynamite Dinny T.D. – kept his Parabellum aimed at the pair in the bed while I opened the wardrobe. Rooney was at the door, keeping an eye on the corridor. The chambermaid who'd brought us to the room had gone back to her bed in the attic; we'd promised her five minutes before we started shooting. There were two more boys outside on the corridor, from the North Dublin Brigade, kids out on their first job. They'd been shaking so much, Rooney had taken their guns and offered to mind them until they needed them. There were more in the foyer, more outside. More in other hotels, other corridors, other rooms and lodgings, houses, scattered throughout the city. Sunday morning, the 21st of November, 1920. Five minutes after nine o'clock.

I found the uniform, among dresses and other jackets. I pulled it off its hanger and threw it on the bed. I'd wanted to be sure that we had the right man, and now we knew.

—Did you serve in France? said Archer.

—Yes, said the man in the bed.

He was sitting up straight. He was still holding the cigarette he'd been smoking when we burst in on him.

—Did you earn yourself any medals?

—Yes.

—Well, here's a few more to add to your collection.

And he fired twice.

Feathers and noise smothered the room. I saw the woman screaming but I couldn't hear her. The man still sat against the headrest but his head was now thrown to the side, onto the woman's shoulder. The pillows behind him were demolished, his pyjamas were suddenly soaking red, he still held the burning cigarette.

Archer pointed the gun at the woman.

—Cover yourself up there; you're a disgrace.

She did.

I fired. One bullet into the chest of the dead man. I was remembering Smith, the way he'd stood up for more after we'd killed him. The woman tried to get away from the dead man's weight but the body followed her as she leaned to the left. She began to whimper, but stopped herself.

The noise of the gunfire had been replaced by the smell. *Get out when you smell the cordite.* Advice to all assassins, given to me by Collins, years before.

—Come on, I said.

In other rooms, in other parts of the city, in houses on Baggot Street, Lower Mount Street, Earlsfort Terrace, Morehampton Road, upstairs in another room of this hotel, the Gresham, there were men lying dead, on beds, landings, in gardens. Thirteen of them. Secret service agents. Members of the Cairo Gang. The pick of the new crop.

We'd been bumping off the Irish-grown G-men for almost three years. Every death brought resignations from the G Division, dashes out of the country, new, unhappy lives in England, America, Argentina. They were replaced by secret service men from England, spies and assassins, clever men who were getting closer and closer to Collins. Mick still cycled around the city and held court in Vaughan's Hotel and Devlin's but he knew that his days and hours were numbered. There were arrests, releases, disappearances – they were getting closer every day. The Cairo Gang, the Castle-based murder gang, were roaming the city, directed by the nods of spies at street corners, at pub counters, outside churches, on trams. They were good. They knew how to spend money and how to rattle the limits of loyalty. They were closing in and Collins decided to get them before they got him and the rest of us.

Who were they? Where were they? Hints were searched for and followed. What front doors were slammed after curfew? Who came and went, kept themselves to themselves? Any trace of an accent in a Hello or Thank you? The city was combed for the hush-hush men, the men who came and went. Collins's men in the Castle, Nelligan and MacNamara, found the names of the men with curfew passes. Waiters, maids, hotel porters were courted and interviewed. Postmen took scenic routes to addresses on Morehampton Road and Earlsfort Terrace, and delivered the letters a little late, when they were sealed again and crispy dry. Names were added to names. They were examined, tested, found spot-on or off the mark. And, the night before this Sunday, they were divided amongst us, Collins's Squad. *My* Black and Tans, he called us. We were the ones who'd do the killing.

—Hang on, said Archer.

He went to the dead man's side of the bed. He picked up the cup that was on the small, doily-covered table, still steaming. He tasted the tea.

—Sugar!

He spat it back into the cup and poured the lot onto the bed, on the eiderdown over the dead man's legs.

—There must have been ten spoons in it, said Archer. — How many sugars did he take?

She didn't answer.

—You!

—I don't know, she said.

—What d'you mean?

—I don't know. I didn't know him. Leave me alone.

Archer looked at me; he was slow and angry. He looked back at the woman in the bed.

—You're supposed to be his wife, he said.

Were we after killing the wrong man?

—Well, I'm not his fuckin' wife, she said. —And I'm no one's fuckin' wife.

She threw back the bedclothes and stood out of the bed. She was naked and gorgeous, bloodstained and furious. Archer looked away.

I pointed at the wardrobe.

—The clothes aren't yours?

—No!

—Where is she?

—He said she'd gone to a funeral in England.

—Come on, I said to Archer. —Let's go.

—What about this piece?

—She saw nothing; come on.

Rooney opened the door. Archer passed me, and out. If the woman had been dressed he'd have shot her.

I caught up with Archer. This might be a no-come-back job, Collins had warned us. And Archer's tea-tasting had delayed us. We ran down the stairs. Across the foyer. Our boys at the door, we walked straight past them. Down the steps, onto Sackville Street. Still showing signs of damage four and a half years after the Rising. Right, towards the Rotunda. Walking. No running until we had to. A quiet Sunday morning. And fresh. A wind from the river on our backs, helping us on our way. Left, onto Findlater Place. The wind spinning rubbish in the corners. No sign of the military, no sounds from behind us. The city still off work and yawning. Left, onto Marlborough Street. Britain Street next. Right, then left onto Hill Street. Two boys ahead of us. More behind. Across the old graveyard. Temple Lane, a gate and a wall, Grenville Place, and across the street. My heart butting my ribcage. Quiet still, bells, the odd voice streets away or behind bricks and glass. Grenville Lane, Bath Lane. Door opened, a safe house. We went in, me and Rooney. The boys kept going, Archer kept going – he dropped his gun into the Black Man's pocket and went to half-nine mass in the Jesuits' church on Gardiner Street. The boys behind us kept going. Home, a few more streets and alleys, to their breakfasts and mammies.

We were left alone in the kitchen, with our rashers, eggs and mugs of tea.

—We should have shot her, said Rooney.

—She won't say anything, I said. —She'll be gone by the time they get there.

—Sleeping with an Englishman, he said. —For money.

—At least she wasn't doing it for nothing. How's your egg?

But I'd decided: my war was over.

I heard her mumbling, following her finger across the page. Two fingers now, right and left hands, whizzing across and down – she was reading two pages at once. I looked around the small room, made smaller by the walls of books that surrounded and dropped their dust on me. The window had gone since the last time I'd visited.

I took a book out of my pocket and put it in front of her. I'd only a few left. Granny Nash owned almost all of the woman-written books in Dublin.

—*The Lamplighter,* she read. —Maria Susanna Cummins. Never heard of her. Leave it with me. I'll give you something if I like it. I'll have it finished by tonight.

I pulled the book from under her hand.

—You caught me out that way before, I said.

—*Castle Rackrent* it was, said Granny Nash. —Stupid oul' nonsense. Go on. Put the book on the table.

I did.

She picked it up and put it to her nose.

—You got this one in Terenure, she said. —O'Gandúin whispers names into the ears of the men that matter. Alfie Gandon says Hello.

She stared at me.

—You're just like your father. And that's no compliment.

289

PART FOUR

11

I couldn't see.

—Name?

I didn't answer.

—Name?

I didn't answer.

And one of them, more of them hit me again.

—Name?

I didn't answer.

Again, and again.

Then nothing. I heard nothing, no one leaving the room – if I was in a room – no one coming back. Not a whisper or shuffle. Nothing. Not a thought. Nothing.

Then a voice.

—Take off the blindfold.

My arms weren't tied. They had been; I was sure of it. I'd felt the ropes tightening, burning. I remembered trying to pull my arms away. I'd seen the chair; I'd seen it before I'd stopped seeing. I remembered being hit with the butt of a rifle. Because I was trying to stop them from tying me to the arms of the chair. They were free now, my arms. I lifted my hands to my face. I wanted to touch where the pain was worst but I did what I'd been told to do: I took off the blindfold. I had no memory, none at all, of it being put on, the cloth over my eyes, the knot. I found the knot and pulled it off from the back, over my head.

I didn't want to see. What was waiting for me. More. Worse. I didn't want to see. I knew things now: I was standing up. I wasn't sitting at all. I knew that I was standing. I could feel it in my legs. There was nothing against my back. I wasn't tied or trapped.

I opened my eyes. I could do it. Nothing for a while. It wasn't darkness. A wall. I was standing in front of a wall. Very close, right up to it. I could think: they are going to shoot me against this wall, they are going to execute me. Now. A word on the wall. *Fuck.* Scratched. Other words. Dates. Names. Too many. I didn't want them.

I hadn't budged. Not since I'd opened my eyes. I was sure of it. Long ago. I'd looked at nothing else, only the wall, only this part of the wall. I moved my eyes. They moved for me. They obeyed me. A corner. I moved my head. Wall. No colour. No door. No uniforms.

No noises. None near. Behind me. But I could hear things from far away. Laughter. Someone screaming. Pipes holding on to running water. But nothing behind me. No breath or metal.

I moved.

I am Henry Smart.

I turned.

No boots or shoes. My feet were bare. I felt the stone and grit. Toes had been broken. I knew that. I could feel the pain, I could see. I remembered. Purple, yellow, mangled. They had stamped on my feet. One of the first things they'd done. I knew what had happened. It made sense.

I turned slowly. More boots, more bayonets, fists, pliers, waiting for me. But I had to turn.

Nothing.

A door. A steel door. The shutter closed. The eye closed. The same grey as the door. A mattress. To my right. I went to it. Just me. My feet were crying, so far to go. The room was empty. I was going to make it. The door stayed shut; nothing outside. I was going to lie down. *I am Henry Smart.* I couldn't move in proper steps. I could only shuffle. *I am Henry Smart.* I was cold. It was good: I knew that I was cold. I needed time. I needed time again, one thing followed by the next. Chunks of time.

I told them nothing.

I lowered myself onto the mattress. I didn't want to fall. I wanted to do it properly.

I told them nothing.

My hands were on the mattress. I lowered my back, my head. The straw pricked my neck. And everywhere. I was naked. The door stayed shut. Pipes, running water. Behind the walls. I pulled my legs onto the mattress. A window, high up. Bars. One, two, three, four. Four. I knew: they were letting me do this. This was no escape. They were letting me rest. Watching, behind the closed door.

I told them nothing.

Granny Nash's room.

—What's your name then, c'nt?

—Michael Collins, I said.

Stupid. I knew when I was saying it – those days were over – too late to stop myself. I saw his arm move, the Auxie's, and there was nothing I could do: the butt of his Webley hit me right across the eyes. And they were all over me, stamping on me, standing away, getting the kicks in. They dragged me off the ground. They pushed me against the wall. The books fell away behind me.

—Fa'king 'ell.

And I fell against more books, through this wall, and my head hit the real wall. For a while, they'd lost me – I'd gone under the books. I could tell by the way they dragged me out – they were going to murder me. They pulled my feet, climbed in at me over the books. One slid past my eyes: *Castle Rackrent*.

—Which one of them did you kill!

—Which one?

—In cold fa'king blood!

—Get his shoes off.

—Get his own fa'king shoes off.

—Get your shoes off, c'nt.

I tried to hide my face with my shoulders as I bent over to untie my laces. I watched my hands. If they shook, I was guilty. If they didn't, I was guilty. I got the shoes off quickly. I was co-operating, still thinking.

—What are you doing here?

—Visiting my granny.

—Your what?

—My grandmother.

—Where is she?

—I don't know.

The boot went straight down. Pain so fast and pure and shocking, I didn't know which foot. I roared. More books dropped to the floor.

I didn't know where she'd gone. She'd been in the room when the door had come down. We'd heard tenders racing past outside – brakes, gunfire, a scream. Army boots hit the road. Rifle butts hit a front door not far from ours.

—You're caught now, she'd said.

I knocked over books and found the window.

—They're cordoning off the street.

—They're very methodical, she'd said as she finished the first page and turned to the second and third. —They start at the top of the street and work their way down. House by house. Like they're collecting the rent. You've five minutes if you —

And that was when her door came down.

The man in front of me now was an officer. His chest was a mess of war ribbons.

—We have you, he said. —Yes?

—I was just visiting my granny.

—At the end of the day, he said. —But what were you doing at the start of the day? We know, don't we?

He was forty, or more than that. He'd trimmed his moustache that morning, probably while we were bumping off the secret service bastards.

—We have you.

He looked straight into my eyes.

—Yes, he said.

And he stamped down on my foot.

—Downstairs and shoot him.

I was pulled through a tunnel of boots, bayonets and rifle butts. Out onto the landing, and thrown down the stairs. There were hands to meet me and I was pulled by the hair to the next steps and pushed. Out to the street. It was lit by searchlights on armoured cars at both ends of the street. I was pushed straight into a beam.

—Now, c'nt.

I felt gun metal on my forehead. I couldn't see anything.

—Close your eyes once, once. Close your eyes and I'll shoot the top of your fa'king Shinner I.R.A. Irish c'nt's head off.

I looked straight into the light.

That was then. I remembered. I'd been caught. Sunday night – how long ago? – after the killings and the other killings, that afternoon in Croke Park. In Granny Nash's room. I'd gone there – stupid, stupid, fuckin' stupid – to try and get more out of the Granny. Away from the safe house, out into the fury of the Tans and Auxiliaries.

The door opened. And I opened my eyes. I knew where I was. The cell. Fours walls and a mattress. A window, four bars, and a door. Now shut again.

There was man on the floor right beside me. Getting up, face down. Coughing and groaning. There was blood coming from his mouth.

—Bastards.

He shook his head. Blood hit my legs and chest.

He was dressed. Trousers, shirt, no collar. Jacket. A cap in the pocket.

He looked and saw me.

—Jesus, he said. —And I was feeling sorry for myself. Look what they did to you.

He was twenty-four or five. His hair was long and wet but I could see a scar running a line across his forehead. It was an old one, part of himself for a long time.

I said nothing. I sat up. I didn't know if I could talk. It was a long time since I'd spoken. I didn't know how long. I'd lost that time. I was starting again.

—Here.

He shook himself out of the jacket and handed it out. Then he came closer and put it around my shoulders, without touching me. He sat back on the floor.

—It's all ahead of me, he said. —Jesus. Hang on, he said. —I know you.

He looked, as if trying to see through lace curtains. He whispered. He looked back at the door first.

—You're Henry Smart. Aren't you?

I looked at the window.

—Aren't you?

I lay back on the mattress. His jacket was under me. I left it there. I closed my eyes.

I opened them.

—I'm Ned Kellet. Don't you recognise me?

I closed my eyes.

—I'm right, amn't I? Henry?

I looked at the window.

—They're after killing Dick McKee and Peadar Clancy. We'll be next.

I closed my eyes.

He sang.

—*Do I want to see my mammy any more? Do I? Yes, I do.* Henry? In your own time.

I am Henry Smart. I am Henry Smart. I am Henry Smart. I am Henry Smart.

I opened my eyes.

He smiled.

I closed my eyes.

I opened them.

He was gone. I'd heard nothing. He'd left his jacket. There were trousers on the floor, at the door. And a shirt. I stood up. I picked up the jacket. It was my own. Made and bought in Templemore. *I was once in Templemore.* I put the clothes on. *I was there.* No shoes, no socks. I walked the cell and read the walls. I forced myself out of the shuffle and pain. I walked properly, over the agony. *She was with me.* I read every name and date. *1864. Murphy.* I read an entire wall. *Ned Kellet 14th of December. 1920. Up the Republic.* It was getting dark. A day was ending. That was what happened; days began and ended. I read while I could. I leaned against the wall. The light was being taken from the cell. There was enough for one last name. *Henry Smart. 23rd of November. 1920.*

I went to the mattress. I lay down. I closed my eyes.

—Dalton.

I opened my eyes.

—Stand up.

298

I did. There were two of them. One in uniform – an Auxiliary – and another one.

I got off the mattress.

—Do we call you Jack or John? Or Seán?

I waited.

—Well?

The one not dressed as an Auxiliary took a paper from inside his jacket. He flapped it open.

—We have your release papers here, Mister Dalton. There's no point in holding you any longer, you've nothing more to tell us. But we need your name in full.

It was time to speak.

—My name's not Dalton.

—But it is.

—No, it's not.

—But you told us —

—No, I didn't. I have only one name and it's Nash. My name is Fergus Nash.

—Jack Dalton, you said.

—No.

—Why would you have said Jack Dalton? You were obviously in some distress.

—No.

—Why Dalton? Of all people.

—No.

—You know him, of course.

—No.

—There's been a misunderstanding, he said. —None of this should ever have happened. Is there anything you'd like?

—No.

—Would you like to know where you are?

—No.

—Why not?

—I'm in a cell. That's as much as I need to know.

—Perhaps you're right. I like you, Fergus. I'll see what I can do.

I stayed standing there long after the door had been shut again and they'd gone.

I was still there when the door opened and a new man came in with a tray. He put it on the floor.

—Mister Fry said you were to have that.

He left me alone again.

It was good food, deliberately good. I left it there. I sat down on the bed, then I lay down.

—Where do you live?

I opened my eyes but I didn't look at anyone.

—Dublin.

—Where?

—I won't tell you.

—Why not?

—Because you'll raid my home and terrify my wife and children. More than they're already terrified.

—But if you've nothing to hide —

—I've nothing to hide, I said. —My name is Fergus Nash.

—Come on.

I looked.

A pair of shoes beside me, on the floor beside the mattress. I sat up. There were no socks. I said nothing. I put on the shoes. They were loose, a fine man's shoes. There were no laces.

The door was open.

The Auxiliary stood aside. I walked to the door. There was a narrow passage, too narrow to run through.

—Left.

I remembered what left was and turned. There was another grey door at the end of a long row of closed doors. No sounds came from any of the cells.

The man behind me spoke.

—I'm in the Welsh Republican Army.

As I neared the door at the end of the passage, I passed an open door and I saw the man who'd called himself Kellet, on the floor. An Auxiliary stood over him and drew his foot back to kick him. The Welsh Republican pushed me forward. I heard a scream as the door before me was opened and I was out in the air and day. The light tore at my eyes. I was pushed to the back of a lorry, parked five yards from the door. I couldn't climb; I was lifted, thrown on. I lost a shoe. I said nothing. There were eight Auxiliaries sitting there, four on

300

each bench, facing each other. Two of them got up. They tied my hands to a steel bar that ran across the top of the lorry. One of them picked up a piece of board from under the bench. There was a piece of string looped to it. He put it around my neck.

—Can you read it, Pat?

Bomb us now.

—Yes, I said.

—You're our insurance, mate, he said. —They won't kill one of their own. Nothing personal.

The engine started and I recognised streets as the lorry cut through them. I'd been in Dublin Castle. I fell out of the lorry and swung from the bar as the lorry ripped around corners. I saw people on Dame Street running for cover, even after the lorry had passed. Five minutes later we were tearing up Thomas Street and I knew that they were taking me to Kilmainham.

The lorry stopped for the first time since starting and I was able to get my feet back onto the lorry floor. I'd lost the other shoe. The lorry moved again, crept this time, into a yard. They untied my hands and let me climb down.

—Know where we are?

—No.

—This is where your Shinner friends were bumped off in 1916.

The Stonebreakers' Yard.

I looked around as they led me to a door. It was just a prison yard, just a wall. But I knew where I was. I knew exactly where I was for the first time in – weeks, months, it could have been years.

The cold came with the dark. Another passage. Another iron door. Another cell. Smaller, tighter than the last cell. Colder, crumbling.

I was alone again.

There was a light this time. A gas jet high up on the wall. It gave a sick, shifting light that made shadows, then killed them. I saw some old blankets in a corner and sat on them. The light made more shapes, snuffed them. I knew where I was. *We'll go home be the water.* I knew exactly where I was. I lay on the floor

301

and covered myself with the blankets. I closed my eyes. *I saw light and the river rushed out into the day, but I knew that I was safe; weeds and overhanging branches hid me from harm. Past the Metropolitan Laundry. Suds and the washed-out shit of the filthy rich tore at my eyes but a hand I knew I could feel lifted my head, then lowered it into clean water and I was under again, in darkness. Light again, behind Kilmainham Gaol, tucked under the wall, and away. Back under the city. Bow Bridge and the Royal Hospital, under St John's Road and I was in a sewer again and I felt fingers under my chin – safe safe safe – holding my mouth over the goo.*

I woke.

There was no water. It was dark. I was hungry. It was years since I'd eaten. A slamming door had woken me – I knew, although I couldn't hear anything now. And I could see nothing. I heard feet, three or four pairs of boots on the damp flags of the passage outside. I heard keys jangling, scraping. It was very dark. I sat up. The door opened and dirty light fell into the room. Followed by a man, who hit the ground hard. The door was closed, the key turned. It was dark again, darker than before. I heard the man breathing through a swollen mouth. I stayed still. The breath rattled. The man groaned.

I knew who it was.

—Help.

I stayed where I was. I heard him crawling. I couldn't see anything but I knew exactly where he was. I covered myself with both blankets, put them quietly across my shoulders.

—Is there anyone there?

A hand touched my foot. I kicked.

He fell back.

—Who's there?

I said nothing. His moving stopped. I waited the hours until the dawn gave enough light.

He looked at me. He sat in the opposite corner.

—Henry, he said.

They'd done more damage to his face. They'd given him another jacket.

—I suppose you know, he said.

I said nothing. I didn't close my eyes this time. I looked across at him.

—They're shooting us this morning.

The time had come for words.

—Fuck off, I said.

He looked horrified, upset, angry, let down, one by one, exactly one second for each emotion.

—What's the point? he said. —Fuck off, yourself. Jack always said you were a snarly gob.

He sighed.

—You think I'm a fuckin' spy, don't you?

I stared at him.

—I don't blame you. I'd be the same. You might be the fuckin' spy, for all I know. Jesus Christ, what have they done to us?

I was hungry.

—I just don't want to die with you thinking that I'm a spy and I'm not exactly sure why it's important.

He started crying.

I'm hungry.

Boot nails outside, keys. The door opened. A voice.

—Nash.

I stood up.

—Good luck, he said. —Nash.

I walked to the door, out to the passage. The guard put the cuffs on me while another one aimed his Webley at me. I was shoved once, then let walk on my own steam. Still barefoot. Still painful. More doors. Noise. Other prisoners. Someone pissing nearby, behind a door. Whistling too. I saw three prisoners. They stared at me. I walked past them. I didn't look at them. Another door. Opened from inside, pushed towards me. I walked through. Another passage. A room.

—Sit.

A chair. One of the guards stayed with me. I could smell last night's drink off him. The outside world. He rested his back against the wall. I could have taken a run at him.

There was another door, at the far end of the room. It opened and Jack Dalton came through, into the room. He looked at me briefly, and away. He was carrying his beatings too. He was followed, pushed by another guard. He walked past me, across the narrow room and out the door I'd come through.

—Your turn, said my guard.

I stood. He nodded and I walked to the new door. There was another guard waiting for me. He held my arm and pulled me into another room. He stopped, and stood me in front of a large iron box. One small square of the box's front wall was covered in black felt. At first I thought I'd been put in front of a camera – I remembered the zip and flash of a camera; another room, other guards. Between hidings? I didn't know – but I now saw two slits in the felt.

I was being looked at from behind the felt.

There was another officer standing beside the box.

I looked at the floor.

—Look up.

I looked straight at the slits in the felt. I saw the felt flutter very, very slightly. I saw the wet shine of a pair of eyes. I did something I'd forgotten could be done: I smiled.

I am Henry Smart. If that's a woman in there she won't betray me. Or a sissy man.

—Turn to the right.

I turned.

I heard whispering.

—Face forward again, said my guard.

—What's forward?

A hand grabbed my hair and pulled my head to face the Judas box again. I stared at the felt slits, and smiled again. I had no idea who was looking at me, deciding who I was. I could think of absolutely no one.

—Okay, said the guard beside the box. —We've seen enough. Get that ugly bastard out of here.

I was led to the door and handed over to the other guards. More doors. Handed over to other Auxiliary guards. Back to the cell, cuffs off. The guard unlocked the door.

—Alone again, he said.

I walked into the cell.

—Want to know what happened to your mate?

—No.

—Took him out and shot him.

304

—Good.

He laughed. He closed the door and locked it. And unlocked it immediately and new men charged, a rush of them, over each other – they caught me on my way to sitting down – and they were around and on top of me. Batons and gun-butts, boots again.

—Smart!

—Smart!

—Henry fa'king Smart.

They were gone again. I heard the lock. I wouldn't be moving for a long time. Back to square one. But, no. I knew where I was. I still knew. I knew who I was. So did they. But they didn't. They didn't, until they heard it from me. They had to be careful. The world was watching now. They'd killed innocent people. They needed me to tell them who I was. I could think. I lay on the floor.

I opened my eyes.

The one without the uniform, the one the guard had called Fry.

—You've let me down.

He was Irish. He was alone.

—Mister Smart. You've disappointed me. You could have cost me my job.

I could speak.

—Nash.

He stood on my hand.

I am Henry Smart.

Other feet and voices.

I closed my eyes.

I opened them. I was hungry. The door was open. I saw boots, heard the door being pulled shut. The feet again. I was hungry.

—I've a message for you.

Something was held in front of my eyes.

—Hurry up, he said.

I could sit up.

I took it. It was warm.

—Thanks.

I'd seen him before. He wiped his hands on his jacket. Then

305

he wiped the jacket. He went to the door and pushed it open. He didn't look back.

I sat against the wall.

And ate the griddle cake.

I was Henry Smart. I was sitting in a cell in Kilmainham Gaol and I was eating a griddle cake that had been cooked very recently by my wife. It was her best yet, the best and only thing I'd ever tasted. But I didn't cry.

I read the cake carefully as I swallowed it. I followed every sound of the retreating guard, and the one sound that had been missing, one very important sound. I stood up. I could stand straight. It hurt but it wasn't difficult. I could move; I could walk. I walked to the door. And pushed. He hadn't locked the door. The key turning in the lock had been missing. The door opened for me.

It was a very short journey from the cell to the Stonebreakers' Yard, a short walk for men who were to be shot at dawn, a few steps and a door away. But I didn't move. I listened. I listened for breaths, scrapes.

Nothing.

I moved. I had no shoes. My feet on the flags, they wanted to run. I could run. I was full of the griddle cake, already free. I could run right through the last locked door. But I went slowly. I listened at the end of every step. I watched for shadows, the glint or click of metal.

I could already hear the water, I knew it through my bones. I was being dragged there. Across the yard, over the high wall – no bother at all – and down into the water, the Camac River, tucked under the wall. Down into the cold, the cleansing, numbing cold. And away. Back under the city, free. I knew exactly where I was going.

I waited at the door. I listened. Distant life, trapped voices, away far behind me. I held the handle. It was heavy and cold, something that hadn't been touched in years. But the handle turned smoothly and I put my other hand against the door and pushed. Very, very slowly. I stopped at every hint of a creak. I listened for discovery, response. But there was nothing. Nothing beyond the door. I pushed, a small bit more. The yard was empty. It was dark outside. I slid out.

306

—I've another message for you.

The griddle-cake guard. I was done for, fucked.

But he was alone.

The moon and the city over the wall let me see him properly. He was holding out his hand and this time it held a sixpence. The hand was shaking.

—Your tram fare, he said.

—I was going to go the opposite way.

—She said the tram.

I took the coin. He slid past me, back into the prison. I moved along the wall, towards the high gate. It annoyed me, her deciding my route of escape, and means. But I fought it. And enjoyed it – ordinary feeling, resentment. I stepped away from the wall and walked to the gate. The owner of the biggest, most exposed back in the world. The gate was open, of course, very slightly ajar. It gave out as I pulled but it came, and I was out.

It was like the back of a dancehall. There were Auxiliaries and their mots up against every wall and tree on the street, kissing and feeling, grunting and sucking. I was the only man on the street without a partner. There were no other sounds.

—Excuse me?

He turned from his woman and wiped his mouth on his sleeve.

—Could you point me to the nearest tram stop?

—Top of the street, to the right.

—Good man; thanks.

—Good-night, mate.

I winked at the woman over his shoulder – he was welcome to her – and went.

I enjoyed the wet ground under my feet, the stones, the puddles. I enjoyed the cold – it was freezing and I hadn't a shirt or anything else under my jacket – and the wind whipping at my trousers. I enjoyed the new dirt in my lungs, the lights of the city, everything about the place. The works. I had to run to catch the tram. And I could run, no bother to me. I knew the driver, Tim Doyle. He stuck his head out his side window.

—How's yourself?

—Not so bad. I'm just after escaping from Kilmainham.

307

—Good man yourself. In you hop.

I went upstairs. I didn't want a roof over my head. It was empty on the top deck. James's Street, Thomas Street, the Cornmarket – I looked down at the world and loved the feel of the seat against my back.

She got on at Lord Edward Street. We said nothing for a while. I wasn't sure if we were still alone. I didn't want to look behind me. I was free as long as I looked ahead.

—It's nice, she said.

—Yep.

—Have you my change for me?

—He hasn't come up for the fare yet. How did you persuade your man to help me escape?

—Flattery, Henry. It makes great rebels, remember?

I looked at her. And gasped; I couldn't help it.

—What happened?

Her hair was gone.

—Ivan's boys cut it off me, she said.

—Why?

But I knew the answer.

—I've been getting in his way.

She ran her hands over her head.

—It's grand, she said. —It's coming back and only a few grey ones. Do I look too old for you?

—No. What about me?

—You'll mend.

—I'll kill him.

—No, she said. —You won't. There are more important things than my hair.

She rubbed her head again.

—You should have seen it just after they cut it and let me go. I was scalped.

There was nothing too drastic about it now; she was a woman with short hair. A beautiful woman with short hair.

—When did it happen?

—Just after we were in Templemore. November, last year.

—Last year?

She looked at me. Then she took an *Independent* from her

pocket. She unfolded it and showed me the date. March the 22nd, 1921.

—Four fuckin' months.

—They flew.

—They fuckin' did.

—I missed you.

She rubbed my hands in hers.

My feet were sore and bleeding. A chunk of my brow was flapping over my left eye. My jaw ached, my teeth were loose, and some gone. There were ribs broken, toes smashed. My back was killing me. My ear was ripped. My balls were kicked huge and screaming. The burns on my chest and neck were being scraped by the cold and the rough threads of my Templemore jacket. I didn't know if I'd ever sleep again. I was very, very old.

We got off at the Pillar.

—Where now? I said.

—Home.

—Where's that?

—Ah, Henry.

12

Kevin Barry had been executed. Terence MacSwiney had died in Brixton Gaol after refusing food for seventy-four days. His story gripped the country; men and women walked miles every morning for news of his decline and resilience. Rory O'Connor had taken the war to England and set fire to warehouses on the Liverpool docks. Catholic refugees were pouring over the new border, getting out of the new Ulster, away from the guns and hammers of the B Specials. *Forget not the boys of Kilmichael, those gallant lads stalwart and true.* Tom Barry and the West Cork Flying Column ambushed and killed seventeen Auxiliary Cadets. Jack Dalton, recently let out of Kilmainham, wrote their song in his Mary Street office and the boys, hard men with years of fight behind them, became instant heroes. Ivan Reynolds was on the rampage, getting fatter on power and all the food and drink that got in his way. He'd broken the knees of a twelve-year-old spy in Ballymacurly and placed the placard around his neck: *Too young to be shot – keep your mouth shut.* He took four men from a village and shot them on the road – *a bloody pile of spies.* In Dublin, the curfew hour was now ten o'clock; patrols prowled all night on rubber soles. The Igoe Gang roamed the city, rozzers brought up from the country, on the lookout for rebels from home, with licence to kill on sight. An I.R.A. Intelligence Squad roamed the city, looking for the Igoe Gang. There were executions and counter-executions, reprisals and counter-reprisals. The British trained their own flying columns and sent them after the I.R.A. columns. The war had become a cross-country race between running gunmen. They took no prisoners. 17th Lancers and Lancashire

Fusiliers, Auxiliaries and Tans disappeared into the bogs and the Lancers and Tans, when they caught their men, invited them to escape and shot them. *Failed to halt, attempted to escape.* The boys kept up the fight by sniping from long distance, and when there were no men to shoot at they searched the sky and shot down British carrier pigeons. They burnt down loyalist shops and houses, they trenched and mined the roads, they pulled up the tracks, chopped down telegraph poles. Aeroplanes were sent after them, but there was nothing to see. They were under the ground. Lloyd George wouldn't talk to de Valera until the I.R.A. had handed in its weapons. Alfred O'Gandúin was arrested in his office on Nassau Street and interned without trial in Mountjoy. He continued his government work from his cell. He elected not to go on hunger strike; his dinner came over the wall at the same time every evening. Collins was running the fight but talking peace: *We started the war with hurleys and, by God, we'll finish it with fountain pens.* And Ireland wasn't the only colony giving lip; badly needed troops were taken from Macroom and Athlone and sent off to other cranky places: India, Egypt, Jamaica. Martial law was extended to Wexford, Waterford, Clare and Kilkenny. And Henry Smart slept.

He slept and ran. Nursed by his short-haired wife who fed him griddle cake soaked in warm milk, his bones knitted, his bruises faded. Nursed by his beautiful, older wife when she wasn't off ambushing troop lorries and robbing banks, he was becoming, once again, a fine figure of a man. Nursed by his beautiful, pregnant wife when she wasn't off winning the war and defying the local warlord's edict that an Irishwoman's place was in the home, when she wasn't under the local warlord. Henry Smart recovered as he ran. He ran, even though his war was over and he'd take no further part in the killing. He slept in the dugouts that hid the men of the columns from the planes and armoured cars. He slept in the safe houses that hadn't been burnt, in the houses that would still take men on their standing. He slept under one roof and heard a voice that sent him running from the house: *I'm still available, mister.* Old Missis O'Shea's house had been torched and she lived now in the long barn. Henry slept in the burnt ruin because the

311

Black and Tans rarely set fire to the same house twice. He slept and often woke up roaring.

—I could have killed you there, Captain.

He was sitting beside the mattress, his mouth three inches from my ear.

—If I'd wanted to.

—And why would you want to?

—No reason, said Ivan.

It had been a long time since I'd seen him. It was getting dark and he was a wide shadow against the wall behind him.

—How come the baddies are always fat? I said.

He smiled.

—You're a brave man, Captain.

—So are you, Ivan. Get your fuckin' face out of my ear.

We were in the old kitchen. It was black-walled after the fire, and empty. The window glass was gone and much of the wall around the door had collapsed. The few attic boards that had survived could take the weight of a tarpaulin, so there was a roof right over us, although the rest of the room was open to the sky and the rain.

It was raining now. I could hear and feel it.

He wasn't alone. I couldn't see anyone else but Ivan wouldn't have ventured anywhere without numbers to look after him.

—So, Ivan, I said. —Why the visit?

—Old times' sake, said Ivan.

—That's nice, I said. —I've been hearing all about you.

—Ah now.

—You're getting ahead in the world. Fair play to you.

—I can recognise sarcasm when I hear it, Captain, he said.

—Good man. How's the hair-cutting business?

—We'll say no more about that. Only, I didn't order that one, Captain. It was done on some other buck's initiative.

—And he's been dealt with?

—I didn't say I didn't approve of it, Captain. Have you any control over your wife at all?

—No, I said proudly.

—I'm inclined to believe you, he said. —But, all the same, I don't believe a word. You're a fine man, Captain. We all think

312

that around here. No doxie could ever take the starch out of your trousers.

—Get to the point, Ivan.

—Right, so. I'm the commander of these parts. I've letters from Dublin to prove it, and a hundred and seven men waiting to hear anyone who says different. Fair dues now, if she wants to join Cumann na mBan and give the boys a hand, fine. No better woman. We'll always have need of the rucksacks and sangwidges. But she's going bananas out there, Captain.

—What's she doing?

—What isn't she feckin' doing? In a nutshell, Captain, she's queering things for the rest of us.

—The young men on the make.

—Ah now, Captain. I'd have sent her on her way long ago only she's my cousin and married to yourself.

—I'll tell you what, Ivan.

I didn't move.

—Touch her again and I'll fuckin' kill you and any other bollocks that gets in my way.

—I know you will, Captain. Or die in the attempt. Which is why I'm here.

—Go on.

I was still lying on the mattress. My gun and leg were with me, under the blankets.

—I'm just back from Dublin, Captain, he said. —I heard things. Not that I listen to much of what that Dublin crowd has to say. But anyway. There are people there that aren't too happy with you. At all. Big people, mind. I don't know why, Captain, but one or two of them would be happy to see the back of you. Does that upset you?

—No.

—I believe you, Captain. Sure, you knew already.

I didn't.

—Didn't you?

—Go on, Ivan.

—If it was anyone else, I'd be happy to oblige them. I'd arrange that they wouldn't have to see you or your back again. But we go back a long way, Captain.

—That we do, Ivan. I fuckin' made you.

313

—You fuckin' did. Spot on. But that, now, is another reason why it would make sense for me to finish you off. I'm king of the Republic around here, boy. And I don't want reminders that I was once a runt that people only noticed to laugh at. All the originals are dead, Captain. All the lads that met beyond in the barn that morning.

—Long ago.

—Long ago. We're the only ones left.

—So, I said. —What's the story?

—It's this. You're still alive. And you needn't be. But you are. Because I say so.

—Because you're scared of me, Ivan.

—You're dead right there, boy. I am scared of you. But I've been scared of other men and they're all fuckin' dead, every fuckin' one of them, so listen to me now.

—I'm listening.

—I know you are. Call your wife off and you'll both stay alive. I'll give you the money to get to America or wherever it is you want to go that's far away.

—I hadn't intended going to America, Ivan.

—Listen, Captain, he said. —Enough playing around. Here's how it is. I'm a businessman. You said it yourself there, a young man on the make. That's me, boy. I discovered this a few months ago only. All these years I thought I was a soldier, a warrior even. A fuckin' nation builder. Fighting for Ireland. And I was. But here's the truth now. All the best soldiers are businessmen. There had to be a reason for the killing and late nights, and it wasn't Ireland. Ireland's an island, Captain, a dollop of muck. It's about control of the island, that's what the soldiering's about, not the harps and martyrs and the freedom to swing a hurley. Am I right, d'you think?

—You might be.

—You might be open to persuasion?

—I might be.

All light had gone by now. I couldn't see his face.

—I was doing my accounts one night there and I suddenly realised that I already controlled the island, my part of it anyway. The war was over. Nothing moves in this county without my go-ahead. I have cattle, land, a cut of the

314

creameries, the pubs. Every bloody thing. I'm even in on the Sunday collections. I'm a strong farmer these days, Captain. Can you credit that? What was I three years ago?

—A little lad.

—That's right. A harmless poor eejit. Not these days, boy. I've freed fuckin' Ireland. Nobody works without the nod from Ivan. A sweet doesn't get sucked without a good coating of the profit ending up on Ivan's tongue. I'm a roaring success, boy. You should be proud of me.

—I am.

—You're not and I don't mind. An Irishman is in charge around here, Captain. We're free.

I heard him breathe deep.

—Congratulations, I said.

—Ah now. I just got to the finish line before the rest of the boys, that's all. But I admit it, Captain. I'm pleased with myself. I'm a shining example to us all. I believe every word of that and – I shouldn't be saying this to you of all people – but it makes me feel bulletproof.

—What's it got to do with my wife, Ivan?

—Right. The purpose of my visit. Listen to this now. Peace is on the way. There are men meeting men in London and Dublin, on the way to London and Dublin, on the boat to Holyhead and back. They're talking about talking and soon they'll be talking and that'll be that. Ireland free in some shape or form. It'll happen before the end of the year. There'll be one almighty row about it, holy war, boy, brother against brother and the rest, but I'm in no hurry. I'm ready for it and I have no brothers, only dead ones. I'll be on the right side. I'll be ready to lead my people into the new Ireland.

—And it'll be very like the old one.

—It might well be, Captain, but it'll be ours.

—Yours.

—Ah now. I've stopped the war here. There hasn't been a Tan or a Volunteer killed around here since Christmas. I've made deals with them. The Tans, the Auxiliaries, the Military, the poor old peelers. All of them. They still charge around in their tenders and armoured cars but they're looking after business. For me. There's no martial law around here, boy. Only the name of it.

—I think I understand now, I said. —My wife keeps killing them.

—Spot on, boy.

—She's making life complicated.

—She's costing me a fortune, Captain. She's interfering with free trade and I can't have that.

—I'm going to sit up now, Ivan, so don't panic.

—Don't worry.

I sat up.

—D'you see my trousers anywhere near, Ivan?

—They're right here, Captain. I went through them before I woke you.

—And you found fuck-all.

—More or less.

—Give them to me here.

I stood up and put on my Templemore trousers.

—So tell us, I said. —What about all the killings, if the war's over? The spies and that. The shops being burnt.

—You have to show the flag, Captain, he said. —Let them know you're there. And when it's over and the guns are rusty, they'll love me and remember who freed them. But they'll also remember that they were once terrified of me, although they'll never say anything about it. It's only my version that'll get talked about. They'll love me and elect me because I'm the man that freed his country.

—And the Tans setting fire to houses and the creameries. They're with your go-ahead too, are they?

—No no, said Ivan. —Not all of them. They have to report back to their people. The forms they have to fill in would do your head in. They have their quotas to meet. Like the rest of us.

—But you could stop them.

—How, like?

—You could stop them from setting fire to a place if you told them not to.

—I could, he said. —Nine times out of the ten. Money

316

would have to change hands. But not necessarily from mine to theirs.

—What about this place?

—What about it?

—The Tans burnt it.

—There now, he said. —I thought it would stop her.

—My wife?

—Who else?

—But it didn't.

—Stop, he said. —She's a holy terror. And there's poor Auntie now, out living in the barn. It's shocking.

I tied my laces. I walked through the hole where the door had once been, out to the yard. The rain had gone.

—Not a bad night now, I said.

—I've stayed out in worse, said Ivan.

—I'll talk to her, I said.

—That doesn't sound very promising, Captain.

—I'll talk to her, I said. —That's all I can do. She's her own woman.

—She's your wife.

—I'm her husband.

—You're a tricky man, Captain.

—And you're a cunt.

—I can see why you'd say that. And I don't mind a bit. But what I can't see is this I'll-talk-to-her business. But, sure.

He took a bottle from his coat pocket.

—We'll drink to it.

—We won't.

—I will.

—Fire away.

I'd smelt it off him earlier. It was going to kill him; I could see his face out here – it was killing him already. But much too slowly. He still had years left in him.

—Is it poteen?

—Fuck off, boy. It's Remy-Martin.

I was grateful to Ivan.

There was no pretending now: I was a complete and utter fool, the biggest in the world. It had been niggling away at me for years but now I knew. Everything I'd done, every bullet and

317

assassination, all the blood and brains, prison, the torture, the last four years and everything in them, everything had been done for Ivan and the other Ivans, the boys whose time had come. That was Irish freedom, since Connolly had been shot – and if the British hadn't shot him one of the Ivans would have; Connolly would have been safely dead long before now, one of the martyrs, dangerous alive, more useful washed and dead.

It was too late. I'd taken men up to the mountains over Dublin and shot them. I'd gone into their homes – because I'd been told to. I'd killed more men than I could account for and I'd trained other men to do the same. I'd been given the names of men on pieces of paper and I'd sought them out and killed them. Just like my father, except he'd been paid for it. I knew: if I'd been given Connolly's name on a piece of paper I'd have done it to him. Because better men than me had ordered me to. It was too late to deny it. I'd have thrown him into the back of a car and brought him up to the Sally Gap. I'd have blindfolded him. I'd have gun-whipped him to shut him up. I'd have dragged him from the car and kicked him away from the road. I'd have pushed him to his knees. I'd have told him to say his prayers and I'd have shot him in the back of the head before he'd finished. I'd have stepped back to avoid brain matter and blood, skull chips. I'd have done it and it was too late to ask why. And I'd have put another bullet into his head, for luck. Because cleverer men than me had told me to.

—I'll talk to her, I said.

I was a slave, the greatest fuckin' eejit ever born. Now I knew and I wasn't going to do anything about it. Because there was nothing I could do. The dead men weren't coming back.

But I'd kill no more, not even Ivan.

—Tell us, I said. —Did you ever meet Gandon?

—O'Gandúin?

—Yeah.

—No, said Ivan. —But I'd love to, and I will. Running the country from a prison cell, he is. There's not much anyone can teach me but he's one man who could teach me a thing or two, or even three.

And why were the heads in Dublin unhappy with me? I

318

didn't know yet but I did know what their unhappiness meant: I was dead.

—Stars tonight, said Ivan. —The sky's full of them.

—Yeah.

—You don't see those boys too often around here.

—No.

But I wasn't looking. I knew that there was one of them up there, spinning and whooping, spitting sparks.

—I'm getting married, Captain, he said.

—Anyone we know?

—No one you know. A good family. There'll be four priests at the top table.

—D'you want me to be best man?

He laughed.

—You're gas.

—I'm going back to bed, I said.

—That's the place I'd like to be, said Ivan.

—But you're a busy man.

—Now you're talking, boy.

—Good-night, Ivan.

—Good-night, Captain.

He walked away, towards the gate to the road. And from around the place, off the roof of the barn, behind the new well, his boys emerged and followed him. I knew none of them and none of them looked at me as they passed. All young lads, some of them younger than me. Leather-gaitered, trench-coated, dripping bandoliers. They were there, and gone. I waited. I heard a car, Ivan's. I saw the lights cut the night down at the road. I waited until the engine wasn't part of the night any more. I listened. They'd gone. There was no one moving out there, and no one not moving, making the night go around him. Ivan wasn't going to kill me tonight.

I went back through the hole to the kitchen.

—Come to Dublin with me.

—No.

—Please.

—No, Henry, she said.

319

It was June, 1921.

—I have to go, I said.

—I know.

—I've people to see.

—I know.

—Come with me.

—No.

It had been two days since Ivan's visit. We were in a dugout somewhere under Roscommon, a good long wooden room made of railway sleepers and the roof off the pavilion of the Ballintubber Cricket Club. The Tans had raided old Missis's the morning after Ivan came and set fire to the long barn. Old Missis was with her sister. I'd taken my father's leg with me when I'd run from the Tans, but I'd left the gun.

I'd just arrived, tumbled down into the dugout, a few minutes before, the latest bike tumbling after me. Bedding and rugs were piled along one side of the room. There were holsters and some rifles hanging from wooden pegs. The air was stale. There were sods carefully laid over the hatch, until night would make it safe to open. There was a lad in a trenchcoat in a far corner, at a desk with sawed-down legs, working away at a typewriter. His fingers on the keys made the only sound in the room, until I spoke again.

—There's no more fighting to do, I said.

Ivan had been right. The truce was on the way.

—Don't cod yourself, Henry.

—Okay, I said. —Try this then. The baby.

—I'll slow down when the time's right. Don't worry.

—You're beginning to show.

—I can still cycle a bike and fire a gun and cycle away again.

—I'm going tomorrow.

—I know.

—I'll be back.

—I know.

—Here, son.

The kid at the typewriter turned.

—What?

—Go for a walk, will yeh?

320

He looked at me, and stood up as high as the roof would let him.

—Right, so, he said. —I'll, eh —

—Come back tomorrow.

—Right.

He went up the steps, waited, lifted the hatch and the sods over them, and climbed out to the rest of the day.

We wrapped ourselves together.

—Do me a big favour, I said.

—I probably will, she said.

—If you're not going to give up the stunts, keep them outside Ivan's area.

She looked at me.

—Alright, she said. —I'll do that.

—Sound woman. I love you, Miss.

—I love you too, Henry.

—I'm doing no more fighting.

—I know.

—You don't mind?

—You've done plenty.

—I wish I'd done none.

—You're saying that now.

We lay on the beaten muck floor. Face to face, an arm each wrapping us tight. I put my hand on her belly. Then I put my arm over her again and rubbed her back between the shoulders. I stopped and just held her.

It would be lifetimes before I held her again.

—Will you do *me* a big favour? said Miss O'Shea.

—No.

—I'm still your teacher, Henry Smart.

—Yes, Miss.

I lifted my head to her ear and whispered.

—The Manchesters.

—Oh.

—The 17th Lancers.

—Oh.

—The Machine Gun Corps.

—Oh God.

—It still works.

321

—It always will.

The door opened slightly. It wasn't one of the faces I'd wanted to see.

—Yes?

She was worried, holding the door more closed than open, ready to slam it if I moved any closer.

—I'm looking for Mister Climanis, I told her.

I was hoping to see the name bring change to her expression. But it didn't. She was looking out past me, into the dark.

—Our name's Phelan, she said.

—Or Maria Climanis, I said.

—Who?

—They used to live here, I said. —David and Maria Climanis.

—Climanis?

—Yes.

I was still hoping: they'd been leaving when she'd arrived, they'd left her a forwarding address, they'd looked happy – anything that could keep me going.

—What sort of a name's that? she asked.

—He's from Latvia, I said.

—Well, we're from Harold's Cross, she said. —Me and Jimmy.

—He has black hair, I said.

—Who has?

—Mister Climanis.

—Oh.

—You'd remember it.

She shrugged, and shook her head.

—He lived here, I said. —With Maria.

—It was empty when we moved in, she said.

She was looking at me properly now.

—Really empty, she said. —Nothing. Not even wallpaper.

—Thanks anyway, I said.

It was coming up to curfew; time to find a hiding place.

—No one had lived here for years, she said. —We could feel it. The cold.

I turned back to her. She was still there, showing half her face at the door.

—How long have you been here? I asked.

—Six months, she said. —I hope you find them.

—Thanks.

I heard the door close as I walked away. A Crossley screamed out of Brighton Square just as I found an alley. I leaned into the darkest corner as the tender tore past, followed sharply by another. They knew where they were going. I could feel water racing near me, the Swan River, my father's favourite. I could feel its pull, but I wasn't ready to disappear.

I sat in Mooney's on Abbey Street three evenings in a row. I walked his route, backwards, from the pub to his work at Kapp and Petersen, in broad, uneasy daylight. I stood on the bridge for hours, the only one there – no one ever loitered. I took his tram home.

I'd been seen. I knew it.

I hadn't contacted anyone.

The Truce was on the way but there were scores to be settled in the last days and hours of the war, final points to be made, victories to be claimed. I was being stupid. Standing in one spot, following the same route more than once, I was being very stupid. But I knew the signs. I'd lived this life long enough to know that I had eyes in the back of my head, and I knew how to read the sweat on my back. I knew the city better than anyone. I knew how to fade into the stone, how to slide free of the tightest corner. I walked Terenure and Rathgar at times when he'd be coming home from work. And, in the mornings, I followed the grocery and bread vans as they crawled at the pace of their customers, looking for Maria. Everywhere watched by men in trenchcoats. Theirs and ours. Igoe's men walked alongside me, on the other side of the street. Squad men and others I didn't know but recognised held up the corners as I passed. I nodded. They nodded back.

On the fourth day I gave up. I was wasting my time. I'd always known it. Abbey Street was empty. It was full of the rush of people going home but there wasn't a trenchcoat in sight. No one across the street on Wynn's steps, no one between me and Sackville Street. No one at the corner, or at the Henry Street corner.

I was expected.

I walked up Henry Street. To No. 22 Mary Street. I went in the open door – nothing to hide; no rebels in here – no one to stop me or ask my business, up two flights to Jack Dalton's open door.

He looked at me.

—The man, he said. —How are you?

—How was jail? I asked him.

—Couldn't take to it, he said.

—Me neither, I said. —What did you do to him?

He sighed.

—Who?

—Do I have to name him?

—Yes.

—For fuck sake.

He waited.

—Climanis.

—Never heard of him.

—Where is he, Jack?

—I told you to stay away from him.

—Where is he?

—Where he is isn't important, he said. —It's not a question that should occupy you. Any more.

I took a chair from against the wall and sat opposite him.

—I'm too late?

—You always were.

—Why?

—Why what?

—Come on; why did you kill him?

—I didn't.

—Why was he killed?

—Why were they all killed? He was a spy.

—He wasn't a spy. He was just a —

—Listen, man. He was a spy. That's all there is to it. Like it or fuckin' lump it.

—He wasn't a spy.

—He patrolled the pubs looking for eejits like you. To pour their hearts out to the poor foreigner who'd been run out of his own country.

—He wasn't a spy.

—Those blackguards have no bloody country.

—Did you get him because he was Jewish?

—He was a fuckin' spy. I told you to stay away. But you fell for him, didn't you?

He was forcing himself to stay in his chair, leaning out of it, dying to charge over the desk at me.

—Is he up the mountains?

He stared at me.

—Is he buried?

He stared.

—Where's his wife?

—He had no wife.

—He did. He was married.

—They weren't married. How could they have been? Who'd have married them? A Jew and herself.

—Where is she?

—I don't know.

—Was she there when they took him?

—I don't know.

—He didn't even believe in religion, I said.

—Worse yet, he said. —He believed in nothing. A wandering bloody Bolshevik.

—They killed his wife.

—My arse they did. More wives. You fuckin' eejit, man. Listen to me one last time. He was a spy. We had evidence. Witnesses. He got what was coming to him. Fair and square. Like the others. The ones you dealt with. I wouldn't have had the bastard bumped off just because he was a Jew. But listen here, while you're sitting there. We've nearly got rid of the English. And we want no more strangers in our house. Those guys, the pedlars and the moneylenders, your poor little friends with no country of their own, they're roaming the country getting the small farmers into hock. Ready to take the land off them when the time comes. They're all set. Just when we're rid of the English we'll have new masters.

—They won't be Jewish, I said. —I've met some of our new masters.

—And they're our own, aren't they? Do you have a problem with that? Or did Climanis convert you?

—What about the Jews in the Organisation? Your man, Briscoe. And Michael Noyk.

—Pandering to our patriotism for the sake of their own interests. They know what side their bread is buttered on. If they're allowed to eat butter. Or bread. For fuck sake, man. Did it never occur to you to ask yourself why they've been run out of every country they've ever landed in? Or is every other country in Europe wrong?

He sat back in his chair.

—Mind you, you always were a bit of a Bolshevik yourself, weren't you, Henry?

—Yes, I said. —I was.

—Until you heard your name in song.

He laughed.

—*A friend to the Yid, was the bold Henry Smart.*

—You wrote it, didn't you, Jack?

—You wrote it yourself, you fuckin' eejit. It was only ever a couple of lines.

He sat up.

—Are you still with us?

I didn't answer him. I didn't move.

He slid a piece of paper across the desk. I turned it and read.

—Know him?

—Yes.

—Can you handle it yourself?

—No, I said. —I don't think so.

—Fine, he said. —I'll get someone else. But I'll leave it twenty-four hours. How's that for fair play?

I looked at the name again. *Smart, Henry.* I slid it back across the desk to him.

—It's not your writing, I said.

—No, he said. —You wouldn't be on my list at all. Even though you've let me down.

I nodded at the paper.

—Why?

—Well, he said. —If you're not with us you're against us. That's the thinking. And there are those who reckon that you're always going to be against us. And they're probably right. You've no stake in the country, man. Never had, never will. We needed trouble-makers and very soon now we'll have to be rid of them. And that, Henry, is all you are and ever were. A trouble-maker. The best in the business, mind. But —

He opened a drawer and knocked the slip of paper into its mouth.

—It'll stay there for a while yet. Now, get out. Before I'm seen being nice to you.

I stood up.

—Is that the only piece of paper? I asked.

—I wouldn't know.

—I'm dead.

—Yes.

—Because I'm a nuisance.

—Because you're a spy.

—Oh, I said. —Fine. Were any of them really spies, Jack?

—You killed plenty of them yourself, he said. —Of course they were.

Archer and Rooney nodded. They stood across the street from Jack's office. I knew they wouldn't be waiting for dark or a quiet spot. They'd be happy to kill me in daylight. I'd done it myself; I knew the score.

So I shocked them and ran. Up Mary Street, across Capel Street. I sprinted between the carts and cars. Into Little Mary Street. I knew I'd have to be a corner ahead of them. Onto Anglesea Row, up to Little Britain Street. I could hear hammering feet. I didn't look back; I didn't have time. No time to think about dodging bullets. Left, a few yards and I had the manhole cover in my hands. It was as weightless as the one I'd thrown in Richmond Barracks. This time I held it over my head, arms straight above me, and I walked, dropped into the hole, and I left skin on the rusting edge of the cover as I dropped into the river. Archer and Rooney ran onto Little Britain Street and found only the remains of a clang in the air.

I swam and walked against the flow of the sludge, up the Bradoge River. Under Bolton Street and the back of Dominick Street, under, under, and up for a while at Grangegorman, and down again, with the stench and ghosts and only one way to go. I came up at Cabra, stinking but alive.

And that was it for months, most of a long year. I crossed Ireland in the groundwater. I crept at night and stayed under during the day. July came, and the Truce. And I could relax a bit because now only the Irish were after me. I stayed off the roads and let a crust of dirt and crawlers hide me from the few eyes that met me when I came out of the ground. The I.R.A. were the police now and, respectable citizens that they'd been waiting to be, they kept the town streets clear of louts and cornerboys and, whenever a tramp or tinker was seen approaching town – some poor clown who'd been wandering the country since he'd been demobbed, looking for somewhere to take him – a gun was pointed and he was invited to turn around. And as I got braver and dirtier I became one of the tramps. I enjoyed being turned away by the boys who were on the lookout for Henry Smart. They were the flag-waggers, the hangers-on who'd joined up after the Truce. But I stayed well clear of the real boys, the lads who'd been through all of the war, who still kept themselves to themselves and roamed the country in Fords now that there was no one to chase them. They were the ones who scared me; they knew me and their war wasn't over yet. I lived on fecked eggs and the odd bit of dinner a Protestant widow would give me at the door, her own little act of rebellion.

Collins and Griffith went to London. De Valera stayed at home and so did Mister O'Ganduin, out of jail and holding down two ministries. And I missed the birth of my daughter. There was no tap tap outside her window as she fell into the world. I stayed out of Roscommon and well clear of my growing family. It would be more months before I'd know that she was alive and female. I went further west, into wild places where republics meant nothing and the English had never really been, to places that had been killed in 1847. I went south to the cow country where the big farmers didn't give a shite for free-states or boundary commissions. I hid there and in other places while the Free State was born and the Civil War trotted after it. Men with vengeance on their minds settled their scores. They put each other against walls and fired. It was brother against brother. But they left the rest of us alone and I walked from North Cork to Roscommon without being looked at and I got to see my lovely daughter on the day Michael Collins was killed.

She was five months old by the time I got to hold her. I held her now and she smiled, a gummy grin that made me weak. She was pink and cream. Every movement of her tiny fists and face seemed a new miracle. I looked for me in her, and for other people too. For Victor and Miss O'Shea, for my mother and father. Excitement rippled along her body. She arched her back and I had to open my arms further, to trap her gently.

—Dying to walk, I said.

—Mischief on her mind.

I had the baby but there was no Miss O'Shea. She was out there somewhere, hanging on for the Republic, fighting Ivan and the new National Army.

—There's no more fight in you, young fellow?

—It's only a word, I said.

—Maybe so, said old Missis. —But words are important sometimes. There was a lot of blood poured for that word, republic.

—We fought the English, I said. —Not the words in a dictionary. The English are gone.

—And what about Ulster?

—Fuck Ulster, I said.

—Ah, now.

—Ulster can be another day's work.

—Maybe you're right, said old Missis. —But there's no talking to her.

—I know.

—Of course you do.

I touched the baby's face, her cheek. Her skin was like the softest water. She grinned again and dribbled and shook herself. Before I'd noticed it, one of her hands had grabbed my beard. I gave her one of my fingers and she held onto it.

—Long fingers, I said. —Who's she like?

329

—She's a new invention altogether, said old Missis. —I've seen babies and babies but none of them like this little angel. She has the best of both of you, maybe.

Then it hit me: something was missing.

—What's her name?

—She's nothing yet, said old Missis. —She was waiting to hear from yourself.

—I've no idea, I said. —Just, not Melody.

—Melody? she said. —That's only an ol' English name. She'd never agree to that.

—Not Melody, I said.

We were in old Missis's sister's kitchen. I sat in a chair and the baby, already straight-backed, sat on my knee.

—An Irish name, said old Missis. —Something like her own.

—Fine, I said and, instinctively, I put my fingers to my ears. The baby, freed of my arms, fell back but I caught her in time and pressed her to me. I laughed. I pressed her to my chest and felt her quick heart. She kicked her legs and gulped. I hadn't washed or shaved for the best part of a year but she wasn't scared of the old tramp holding her. She seemed to know: she'd met her father, and approved. I looked at old Missis, to share my happiness, and saw her looking down at the baby, who had her head turned to me. Her little mouth was wet and open and she moved her head, as much as her new neck would allow, searching the cloth in front of her – she was looking for a nipple on my coat. Her lips met months of dust and harder dirt. I held her out before she could suck at its history, and old Missis took her in her hands. She lowered her, back first, onto the floor and, gently, put her old foot on her tummy. The baby chuckled and drooled, and lifted her arms and feet, coiled herself around the foot.

I stood up and took off the old coat. I took it to the door and threw it into the yard.

—I could do with a wash, I said.

—I couldn't disagree with you, young fellow.

—And a shave.

—It'll take years off you.

—That's asking a lot of a razor.

—You're still a great man for the remarks.

—And then I'll have to go.

—You know best. She'll be glad you saw the little one.

—I've to do some things.

—It won't be too long now and all the things to be done will be done and you'll be able to live a quieter life, the two of you.

She nodded at the baby beneath her foot.

—The three of you.

—I hope so.

—That's enough for now.

I got off the train a new man, again. I was wearing the clothes of another dead man, old Missis O'Shea's brother-in-law. Another brown suit that was tight under the shoulders and gave my ankles a fine view of the passing countryside. But there was room for two of me at the waist.

—He must have been huge, I said.

—He was a nondescript poor man, said old Missis. —But I remember him being fat.

I'd shaved and old Missis had cut my hair. I was fed and rested. The leg was polished and my baby daughter's smell fizzled all around me. I wasn't hiding anymore.

I saw her very quickly. Just half an hour leaning against the quay wall and there she was, coming out of Webb's, her top half hidden inside the tent of her shawl. I could tell by the black wings that her jutting elbows made as I followed her over the river: she was carrying books under her arms.

The Civil War was over in Dublin. Sackville Street was now O'Connell Street and it was rubble all over again. She went into a house on Hardwicke Street and I got there in time to hear a door inside slamming and I ran up the stairs and got to the door while it was still rattling.

She was already sitting at her old table.

—Climanis, Granny.

—The dead arose.

—I'm not dead.

—It's only a matter of time.

—Climanis, Granny.

—Books.

331

She'd brought all the old books with her. Her free space was barely a cupboard. I kicked at a column beside me.

—I gave you nearly every fuckin' book here!

—And I've read them all, so they're no fuckin' good to me.

—Then why do you keep them?

—Because they're mine.

There were nine books, from under her shawl, in two piles on the table. I put one pile on top of the other and grabbed them. I walked to the door.

—Climanis, I said. —Or you'll never read these.

She looked at me.

—Alfie Gandon says Hello.

I put the books back on the table, in their original piles. I walked back to the door.

—And your wife's in Kilmainham.

I sat on the steps and got my heart back. I stayed there for a few minutes. Then I stood up. Dolly Oblong's was no distance away.

I had an accent to match the suit.

—I came up to sell the cattle for the daddy, I told the bouncer. —And I was feeling a bit lonely.

And I was in. The real daddy's leg hidden in the brother-in-law's trousers. Past the bully, a thick-looking gom whose mouth hung loose. I was in. Into the smells and hints that men paid for. The darkness and promises. The hall was empty. There was a piano being murdered in the room on the left. I kept going and there was no one to stop me. It was early in the day. Down a deep hall, away from the rugs and piano. To a stone stairs, an empty kitchen, and a scullery. And a door and a key. I put the key in my pocket and I went back up to the working part of the house.

I followed the piano. There was a scrawny old consumptive pounding at the keys, some song that had once been American, and beyond him a couch and three pale, bored girls squeezed along it. Until they saw me. Even in my second-son-of-a-small-but-respectable-farmer disguise, I was still the best-looking man they'd seen in years and they were up and all around me before I'd seen them properly.

—How much do ye charge?

And they liked me even more when they heard me because they were country girls themselves who'd lost their way and they immediately saw in me a letter from home and the best fuck of their lives.

—A guinea.

—A pound.

—Nineteen and ninepence. What's your name?

There was a hand in mine and I let her lead me out of the room and up the carpeted stairs where my father's leg had carried no tap tap. It shivered in my trousers now; it knew where it was.

Into a dim room.

—Shut the door, darling.

I did and I watched her dropping her shawl to the floor.

—I don't normally take my clothes off, she said. —But today's a hot day. What's your name?

—Ivan, I said. —What's your own?

—Maria, she said.

—What part of the world are you from?

—I'm not telling, she said. —What about you?

—Not far from your place, I said.

I got onto the bed and she pressed herself to me.

—Just so's you'll know, I said, and this was the real me talking. —I never paid for a ride before in my life.

—You'll have to pay for this one, she said. —They'd kill me if I didn't cough up.

—Grand, so, I said.

And I flicked my tongue across her nipple.

—And we're all called Maria, she said. —My real name's Eileen.

I was in the right place.

Dark.

It had been a long time since I'd walked in streetlight. I walked out to Clontarf and watched the tide coming in. And back into town. No curfew to beat, no rushing tenders. I found the back alley without having to search for it. Over the wall, the broken glass was no problem. The half-hearted garden, the girls' only freedom. I unlocked the door; the scullery was empty. The kitchen, the stairs. Piano. The carpet. I hugged the dark red wall. Up the stairs up, three at a time. Grunts, beds protesting. A dark red corridor. A mean laugh, a giggle. Eileen's door, others.

And the right door. A good thick door. My knock was a small thing on it.

I walked into the dark and closed the door behind me. Its canvas cover settled back into place. I could see nothing but I knew she was in front of me. Her powder was all over me.

—You are in the wrong room.

—I don't think so.

The bed groaned and now I could see her. A head made huge by hair that was plenty for six or seven women. The bed groaned again as she leaned to my left and turned on a lamp.

Fair play to my father, she was gorgeous. Twenty years after he'd first laid eyes on her. She moved slowly back to the centre of the bed. She was hair and lips and eyes that were black, just beyond the power of the lamp. She was wearing a red gown that showed off white shoulders and all of her was massive. Her softness was firm and she still shone like a young one.

—You're Missis Oblong, I said.

—Am I?

—Yeah.

—Good.

—The queen bee herself, I said. —I'm looking for Gandon.

—O'Gandúin.

—Gandon.

She sighed.

—You have business with Mister O'Gandúin?

—Yeah.

—And the nature of the business?

—I'm going to kill him.

—I see.

She didn't move.

—You are a very handsome man, she said.

—So I've been told, I said. —But flattery isn't going to get you far.

—And money?

—No.

—You are stupid, she said.

—Probably, I said. —Where will I find him?

—Here, she said. —But not right now.

—I'll wait.

—I am not a prostitute – I don't yet know your name.

—That's right.

—Little boys, little boys. I am not a prostitute, mysterious man in a suit that is not his. I am not a prostitute. Nevertheless, this is a brothel. So I must charge you for the time that you spend in this room while you are waiting for Mister O'Gandúin. Perhaps you would prefer to wait outside.

—No, I said. —I'm grand here.

—Yes, she said.

We stared at each other. She was a killer, a brasser, her hair was a wig. The lips, though, were real, red, huge and open. She drank from a glass that was under the lamp and peppermint joined her powder in the air as she refilled the glass.

—Will he be long?

She sighed.

—Ah, she said. —He will be here immediately after he has escorted his wife home from the theatre.

—I didn't know he was married.

—Yes indeed, she said. —Mister O'Gandúin decided that a wife of the right type would advance his political career. I am sure that he loves her. Why will you kill him?

—He killed some people.

—I will pay you if you succeed.

Her tongue. It lay just behind her lips. I felt it on my neck; I was so sure of it, I put my hand up to feel her spit. But my neck was still dry.

—Why? I said.

—You think, I think, that I am a woman scorned.

—Probably.

—Yes, she said. —That is reasonable. That is a good story. But not true. I am disappointed, yes. I am speaking to you of

335

these matters because I believe that you will kill him. Or that he will kill you. I have always been disappointed. I was thirteen when Mister O'Gandúin fucked me the first time. Does that shock you?

—No.

—No. It hurt then. It hurts now. And he has not fucked me in many years. I am frightened.

People died, people lived while she pulled strings from her bed. My father had been sure of it.

—Will I tell you why I am frightened?

—You might as well.

—He is going to kill me. Mister O'Gandúin is a national politician, of a new nation eager to prove itself to the world. The world is watching Mister O'Gandúin and he loves this. More than the girls here in his house. More than anything. But he has been slow to give up his old life. He is still Alfie Gandon. He was worried that the new nation would not live. And so, he kept his old business interests. This house. His other interests. But he was wrong. The nation will live and he must kill Alfie Gandon. He must kill the past. I am his past and he will kill me. One night, like tonight perhaps, he will decide that the time has come and he will kill me. Tonight.

She sat up; she grew.

—He comes, she said.

I could hear nothing.

—Kill him, she whispered.

And the door opened. I got behind it and the leg out and over his head as he came into the room and looked at Dolly Oblong. Through the gap at the door hinges I could see that the hall was empty. I looked at her, and her eyes gave nothing away. I pushed the door back with my foot and brought the leg down hard on the side of his head. He dropped. I stood over him, one leg each side of his neat, small man's body. There was no blood yet; I hadn't cracked anything. I bent down and pulled him up by his hair.

—David Climanis says Hello.

His body stiffened; he was thinking. I pulled at his collar. I lifted his head as he choked. His hands grabbed furiously at the front of his shirt. He pulled away the collar pin and fell forward. His face smacked the carpet and made very little noise. I pulled off the collar and threw it away. I searched under his shirt and found a blue ribbon. I pulled again and two pieces of leather, two little bootstraps came out with the ribbon.

—Jesus, I said. —It's true.

He was looking at the leg. I'd been leaning on it, like a walking stick. He lay quietly, cheek to the carpet.

—Henry Smart, he said. —Do you remember Henry Smart, Dolly?

—Yes.

—Meet his son and heir.

—Good evening, Mister Smart, she said.

—Your father would be proud of you, said Gandon.

—Why did you have Climanis killed?

—Your father would never have asked that question. He was a loyal and obedient servant. Although, admittedly, we never met.

I put the tip of the leg down on his open hand.

—Why did you have him killed?

—He stole something that belonged to me.

—And what about Maria?

—Exactly.

—What?

—She belonged to me.

I hit him again. I whacked his neck but the carpet took the zip out of the swing.

He groaned and quickly laughed.

—I need a bodyguard, Henry. The job's yours.

—No, thanks.

—Why not? You've been working for me for years. Just like your father.

I hit him harder, cleaner.

—All those spies. And you were all so eager to rid me of them.

I hit him.

—Detective Sergeant Smith. You must remember him. Smith of the G Division. You risked your life despatching that

337

greedy tyke. And I never had the opportunity to thank you. Or pay you, for that matter. Let me. Please.

I hit him again.

—You could look after my business interests, Henry. While I steer the ship of state. It would work. It would work very well.

I hit him again.

He wouldn't give up.

—Kill her, Henry. I'll reward you handsomely. Dear Dolly.

—What about Annie's husband?

—Never heard of him.

I hit him again.

—David Climanis says Hello!

I wasn't angry any more. I was just murdering him. I could have stopped.

—Henry Smart says Hello.

He laughed.

—Maria Climanis says Hello.

He laughed.

I hit him again. I'd broken his head, the carpet was drenched and so was I before he stopped laughing. But still, he wasn't dead. I could see it in his back, life, intelligence waiting for the chance. There was bone and brains on my trousers and hands before I was certain that it was over and I dropped the leg and stood up straight. My back was killing me.

She was sitting exactly where I'd left her.

—There are two things that I will tell you, she said.

I went to the window and wiped my hands on the curtains. It was busy outside on the street.

—He killed your father.

—Why?

—He knew too much and he was trapped.

—And the other?

—He killed Maria.

—Why?

—An example to the other girls. She came back for a day, her face black and blue, and then she was gone.

—What was her real name?

—Maria. He named her himself.

—I don't get you.

338

—Maria Gandon says Hello.

—His daughter?

—In a way. He named them all Maria. It was good for business.

I stood at the bed.

—What'll you do now? I asked her.

—What I always do, she said. —I am a businesswoman. I must be ready. They will soon close us down and throw us onto the street.

—Who?

—Your friends. The new people.

She pointed to the end of the bed, where Gandon's body was leaking.

—He would have done it, she said. —You will dispose of him?

—I'll drag him outside and leave him there, so they'll find him on the steps of a hoor-house.

—He will be moved.

—Who by?

—By your friends. Or by me. A dead minister on the step would be bad for business. And the morale of the new nation.

—I'll do it anyway. Did you see the body?

—Which body?

—My father's.

—No.

—Maybe he got away.

She picked up her glass.

—It's not impossible, I said.

—No, she said. —It is not impossible.

I nodded at the body.

—It was a waste of time, wasn't it?

—No, Mister Smart. It was not. I will not charge you for the time.

—Thanks.

—You are welcome.

I came out of the water behind Kilmainham. Washed, cleaned. A beautiful morning, I felt myself drying even as I hauled myself onto the bank. I'd left the leg in the water, before I'd climbed into the Camac stream from the Liffey. It was well away by now, out in the bay. And I'd be following it soon.

It was still very early but the batch of women holding vigil at the main gate were already buzzing, reciting the rosary. Madame MacBride, Missis Despard, Mary and Annie MacSwiney and some others. Kilmainham was jail now for the diehard women and girls; there were three hundred of them in there, locked up by the Free State government. And my wife was one of them.

The women stopped praying when they saw the good-looking wet man standing in front of them.

—I'm looking for Missis Smart, I said.

—Who are you?

—Her husband.

One of the women jumped up.

—This way, she said.

I followed her.

—They love the visits, she said. —It gives them a lift for days. All of them.

She brought me around a corner, under the high wall of the jail, and across the road. She turned and pointed up, across the street and the occasional traffic, over the wall, to one of a row of top-floor windows.

—See that one?

—Yeah.

—Wait now.

She shouted.

—May! May!

I could see now, a head had appeared at the window. I couldn't see a face; it was too high up the wall.

A shout came back.

—Good morning!

—Get Missis Smart! Her husband's here to see her.

The head disappeared.

—I'll leave you alone.

—Thanks.

—For what?

340

I didn't have to wait long. I saw hair at the window and I recognised it.

—Hello!

—Hello! I yelled. —Can you see me?

—No!

—I'm grand!

—So am I!

—I'm going away!

—Yes!

—I have to!

—I know!

—Look for me!

—Yes!

—She's beautiful!

—Yes! They let me have a photograph!

—Just beautiful!

—Yes!

—Like you!

—Ah now!

—What's her name!?

—Saoirse!

—Oh!

—D'you like it!?

—Yes!

—I have to go! They're coming to drag me away!

—Look for me!

—I will!

—Look for me!

She was gone.

And so was I. I'd killed my last man.

When I went past them, the gate women were huddled around a paper.

—The boys are after getting O'Gandúin, said Mary MacSwiney.

She wasn't upset.

—Last night, the woman who'd shown me the window told me. —Coming home from his sodality. He must have been in a state of grace, all the same. Or near enough to it.

Another martyr for old Ireland.

I was going. I couldn't stay here. Every breath of its stale air, every square inch of the place mocked me, grabbed at my ankles. It needed blood to survive and it wasn't getting mine. I'd supplied it with plenty.

I'd start again. A new man. I had money to get me to Liverpool and a suit that didn't fit. I had a wife I loved in jail and a daughter called Freedom I'd held only once. I didn't know where I was going. I didn't know if I'd get there.

But I was still alive. I was twenty. I was Henry Smart.

I could not have written *A Star Called Henry* without the information, ideas, images, phrases, maps, photographs and song lyrics I found in the following books. To their authors, thank you.

Kevin C. Kearns, *Dublin Tenement Life: An Oral History*; Ernie O'Malley, *On Another Man's Wound*; Robert Kee, *Ourselves Alone*; Robert Brennan, *Allegiance*; Peter Hart, *The I. R. A. and its Enemies: Violence and Community in Cork, 1916–1923*; W. J. Brennan Whitmore, *Dublin Burning*; Peter deRosa, *Rebels*; eds. Adrian and Sally Warwick-Haller, *Letters from Dublin, Easter 1916: Alfred Fanin's Diary of the Rising*; Max Caulfield, *The Easter Rebellion*; Piaras F. MacLochlainn, *Last Words: Letters and Statements of the Leaders Executed after the Rising at Easter 1916*; Padraic O'Farrell, *Who's Who in the Irish War of Independence and Civil War 1916–1923*; Sinead McCoole, *Guns and Chiffon*; Margaret Ward, *Unmanageable Revolutionaries: Women and Irish Nationalism*; Erica Bauermeister, Jesse Larsen & Holly Smith, *500 Great Books by Women: A Reader's Guide*; Richard English, *Ernie O'Malley: I. R. A. Intellectual*; Dermot Keogh, *Jews in Twentieth-Century Ireland*; Tim Pat Coogan, *Michael Collins*; Clair L. Sweeney, *The Rivers of Dublin*; J. W. de Courcy, *The Liffey in Dublin*; James Plunkett, *Strumpet City*; James Joyce, *Dubliners* and *Ulysses*; Francis Stuart, *Black List, Section H*; Dan Breen, *My Fight For Irish Freedom*; Richard Bennett, *The Black and Tans*; John Finegan, *Honor Bright and Nighttown*; J. J. Lee, *Ireland 1912–1985: Politics and Society*; Luc Sante, *Low Life*; Peter Somerville-Large, *Dublin: The Fair City*;

eds. F. H. A. Aalen & Kevin Whelan, *Dublin: From Prehistory to Present*; Jacinta Prunty, *Dublin Slums 1800–1925: A Study in Urban Geography*.